WRAPPED UP IN YOU

REAL AMERICAN COUNTRY
BOOK 2

JENNIFER CARR

Edited by
ASHLEY ANDREWS

Published by JCarr Writes (jcarrwrites.com)

ISBN-13: 9798987063835 (paperback)

ASIN: B0CW9MRCWV (digital)

WRAPPED UP IN YOU - PLAYLIST

If you like to listen to music while you read, there's a Spotify playlist curated specifically with a song for each chapter of *Wrapped Up in You.*

Scan the QR Code below to coordinate your reading and the song.

PROLOGUE - NASH

There are a number of ways to potentially lose a college baseball scholarship. You could cause a minor explosion in the school's Chem Lab (that was technically not my fault). You could release pigs into the school overnight as part of a senior prank just to have said pigs wreak havoc and practically destroy the school (that was partly my fault). Or you could get drunk at an off-campus party your first semester of college and do who-knows-what into the early hours of the morning just to have blurry images pop up in the college newspaper (OK, that's all on me).

And here's the thing-I'm grateful for baseball and for my scholarship. No, really, I am. I'd be an idiot to turn down a full ride, even if it was for baseball. Not that there's anything wrong with baseball.

Baseball has been part of my life since I could hold a bat and throw a ball. The first time I put on that catcher's mask and squatted behind home plate, I had unlocked something inside me that felt supercharged. For the longest time, baseball became my identity. It didn't hurt that I was good at it. Through Little League and high school, I became the All-Star catcher. When college scouts started coming around, it was all my dad could talk about—his son was going to make it to the big leagues one day, no doubt about it.

Growing up on my family's peanut farm in a small town in southern Georgia, my future was pretty much determined the day I was born. It was the same farm my grandfather's grandfather had started. Since my grandfather died a few years ago, that left me and my dad. Even though no one ever expected her to do it, my sister Cody has always loved the manual labor far more than I ever have. But I'm the oldest and the son, so that left the weight of my dad's expectations on me—to always work the farm, to stay in the same small town, doing the same small-town things.

And unless something really big came along, it'd be the same farm my grandkids would grow up on. And there would be nothing wrong with that if it was what I wanted. I probably sound like a selfish jerk. While I can be, that's not what this is.

The problem was, I wasn't sure exactly what I wanted. There were a few things I thought about wanting, but more than anything, I wanted to make my dad proud. It was the least I could do if I was determined to leave the farm. And the one thing I knew I was good at that definitely had Dad's stamp of approval was baseball. Getting a scholarship to a small four-year college was the break I needed to start down the path that would make my dad proud and take me away from the small-town farm life.

Funny enough, even if you do play college baseball and are good enough to potentially go pro, it doesn't mean fate has made it part of the plan. I mentioned the potential ways to lose a scholarship. There are also some pretty sure guarantees. For instance, you could be in a car accident that crushes your kneecap, making it impossible to be a catcher.

Truthfully, I wasn't thrilled with the hand I'd been dealt at the time. But the old adage is true. "When one door closes, another door opens." And to say another door opened would be an understatement. But I should probably back up and fill in some blanks before getting too far ahead of myself.

It all started with four borrowed pigs.

PROLOGUE - CASSIDY

There was not a lot about my childhood that would be considered traditional. My dad was a professor of Anthropology at a large state university while my mom devoted her life to my education at home and the career she hoped I would pursue in music. After being homeschooled and graduating high school at sixteen, my mom pretty much had total control over me, which meant I spent most weekends either playing or singing at weddings or performing on stages at fairs across the state.

I was nine when my mom entered me into my first singing competition. I'd taken third place and from then on she'd made it her mission to make sure I had every opportunity to do better. At first it was fun getting to travel and sing. My curiosity always piqued as I came into contact with new people and places. Eventually, the pressure was more with every new stage or arena. For me, the experience was enough. My mother, however, insisted that I was working toward a future of success and there was always room for improvement.

By the time I was fifteen, I'd performed on so many stages in multiple states that trying to recall any specific one was like trying to pick out a single design in a kaleidoscope. Each performance blended into the next, a blur of faces, lights, and applause. Despite my mother's unrelenting drive for perfection, my passion for music was slowly overshadowed by a growing sense of burnout and the pressure to seek my "big break".

It was around then that I realized I wanted something different for my future. The constant travel, the never-ending competitions, the relentless pursuit of what felt more and more like an ever-elusive dream—it was all too much. I wanted to go to college, to explore other interests, and to find out who I was beyond the stage. Telling my mom was one of the hardest things I've ever done, but it was also the most liberating.

Little did I know that decision would lead me to an even bigger stage that gave me more than any "big break" could ever give. But I'm getting ahead of myself.

1

NASH

As the last week of high school approached, my group of friends and I decided we needed to leave our mark on the school to be remembered for years to come. So, we hatched a plan for the ultimate senior prank - one that would go down in history.

My best friends, Jake and Alex, were hanging out in my room one evening, the three of us sitting in a circle on the floor. We had been brainstorming ideas for weeks, but nothing had quite felt right until now.

"I've got it," Jake exclaimed, his eyes wide with excitement. "Pigs."

Alex and I exchanged glances.

"Care to elaborate?" I asked, extremely curious about Jake's sudden inspiration.

"My Uncle Harvey raises pigs. I say we borrow a few of them for the night, release them in the school, and number them 1, 3, 4, and 5. We'll leave out number 2, so it looks like one's missing. It'll drive everyone crazy!"

The idea was absurd, but the more we talked, the more it seemed like the perfect prank. We knew it would be a lot of work, and there were risks involved, but the thrill of it all was too tempting to resist.

After agreeing on the plan, we wasted no time hashing out details. The plan was to drive out to the farm late Sunday night, load the four pigs into the back of a truck, and head to the school in the early hours of Monday morning. For reasons that will not be confessed, we were aware of a broken lock on a window in the softball coach's office that allowed us to unload the pigs into the school.

Around 3:00 A.M. Monday morning, after we'd painted numbers 1, 3, 4, and 5 on the pigs and finagled them into the back of Jake's pickup truck, I started having doubts about the next part of the plan. The excitement I'd had mixed with anxiety and gave me some hesitant feelings about what we had planned to do.

As we sat in the truck that had been backed to the window we would use as an entrance, I asked, "Are we sure about this?"

"It's going to be hilarious," Jake said, as he popped open his door, slid out, and walked to the tailgate. He'd been my best friend since he moved to town to live with his uncle in third grade, but that didn't mean his ideas were foolproof.

I considered backing out, but only for a second before opening my own door. Alex followed, then quietly clicked the door closed. Alex's agreement to go along with the plan surprised me, especially considering that his dad was the principal of our high school. But he did, and now he seemed just as wary as I was starting to feel.

With adrenaline pumping through my veins, I jiggled the window of Coach Harbor's office until it slid up and open. I stepped inside and waited for Jake and Alex to set up the makeshift corral on either side of the truck bed to ensure the pigs only went one direction—into the building. Jake prevented the pigs from retreating and urged them forward until Alex could reach one of them and physically convince it to exit the truck. We let the pigs out one by one, releasing them into the school.

Before I opened the door of the office and shepherded the animals out and into the hallway, I turned to my buddies and asked, "Are we sure the pigs will be OK? They're not going to get hurt or anything, right?"

"Nah, they'll be fine. They'll just run around and stuff. Come on, let them out and let's get out of here," Jake said, sticking his head through the window.

Once the pigs were out of the coach's office and in the main hallway, I pulled the door closed, exited through the open window, then made sure it was closed securely. Jake, who hadn't stopped smiling or talking about how hysterical he thought it was going to be to see people looking for a missing pig in the building, dropped me off at my house. I was exhausted, but having practically wrestled pigs for the last several hours, I smelled like a barnyard on a hot day. So I peeled off my sweaty stinking clothes, took a shower, then collapsed into the bed where I started playing all the worst-case scenarios as I fell into a restless few hours of sleep.

Though I couldn't pinpoint it exactly, at some point in my life I became known as the funny guy with an adventurous streak. It was not a title I set out to earn. The truth was, I felt more unlucky than funny as most of the stories I told were born from moments of, "if it could go wrong, it did". But rather than have anyone sympathize when I'd share one of my misadventures, I always got laughs. On the one hand, it was always nice to bring a smile to someone's face. On the other, my reputation became "the fun guy always up for an adventure".

At first, I will admit, it was kind of fun. Even if it was at my own expense most of the time. Over the years, however, there was almost this sense of expectation from others that mingled with an internal need for validation that had become almost like an addiction I had to feed regularly. Together, they created a combination almost as strong as the explosion I accidentally created in the chemistry lab junior year. I accidentally caused the explosion in the chemistry lab junior year, but we didn't discover that the natural gas connection was faulty until a week later. So, ironically, the one time I wasn't trying to show off or be funny, my actions resulted in the school closing for multiple days and me having to show up with the professional cleaning crew to clean up the mess.

Honestly, the older I got, the more aware I became of the effect my actions could have, while the words "consequences of your actions" echoed through my head in my dad's voice on a regular basis. It never failed, though, that even when I was trying to avoid consequences, they tended to find me.

When my alarm went off, my head felt like it weighed a ton. Between the lack of sleep and the adrenaline hangover, it was going to be a long day. And I had to work in the afternoon, which meant the day was going to whip me hard. I could only hope that the stunt we pulled was as simple and funny as Jake had promised.

I pulled into the Stop 'N' Go gas station on my way to school to grab an energy drink. As I was lifting the drink from the cooler, the side of the conversation I could hear from behind the counter froze me in place.

"Pigs? Are you serious?" Mrs. Marge asked the person on the other end of her call. After a few beats, she said, "Oh, Harvey is gonna be pissed."

I wasn't exactly sure how her call ended as my brain had kicked into overdrive. The fact that pigs belonging to Harvey Winstead were being discussed at this time on this day could be no coincidence. I stood there with the cooler door open, debating my next course of action. Jake and Alex needed a heads up just in case. Could we all stay home and take a sick day or would that look too suspicious? Mrs. Marge's voice snapped me back to reality.

"You alright there, Nash? You look a little pale and wobbly."

I blinked a few times before pulling the canned drink from its row and closed the door. Mrs. Marge always had the latest gossip. The store was like the town's unofficial meeting place, where news spread faster than a flash of lightning on a humid summer night. The aisles were stocked with local produce and the bulletin board by the door was a patchwork of local events, farm equipment for sale, and the occasional lost pet notice.

With a forced smile and a nod, I said, "I'm good, Mrs. Marge. Just a little out of it today. It's Monday and all." It was the best I could come up with on the spot. Fortunately, she bought it.

"I bet that Senioritis is getting really hard to fight these days. Just one more week, right?" she asked, as I slid the canned drink across her counter.

"Yes ma'am. One more week."

My thoughts were all jumbled together as I was still trying to process what I'd done and what I'd heard.

"I hear you got yourself a baseball scholarship. I know your mama's real proud of you. We all are."

My cheeks heated at the praise. With the mention of graduation and my scholarship, I couldn't help but think how much trouble I might be in by the end of the day, and I hoped it wasn't enough to jeopardize either of those things. And seeing as how we lived in a small town, news was already traveling fast.

"Thanks, Mrs. Marge. I better get to school. Gotta study for those finals."

"You have a good day, sweetie. And stay outta trouble."

"I'll try," was all I said as I backed the door open, then spun on my heel and headed for the school.

When I pulled into my parking space, I knew things were not good. I could sense it. Jake and Alex had clearly been waiting for me as they were practically at my door as it was opening.

Jake seemed giddy while Alex looked almost as uncomfortable as I felt.

Jake was smiling like an idiot as he said, "Dude, I think this is going to be the best day ever. Dr. Stephens has apparently been heard yelling profanities through the school. They're not even letting students in and several teachers have gone in and come right back out. It's awesome."

Students who had arrived early for school formed groups outside the front of the building, staring in disbelief and whispering amongst themselves. Occasionally, an adult would run past the doors in what looked like a panic. It was clear no one had any idea how to corral four rogue pigs running wild in the school. It was pure pandemonium. I wondered how many they'd managed to catch. That's when I remembered Mrs. Marge's phone call.

"Jake, when I was at the Stop 'N' Go, Mrs. Marge was on the

phone with someone and she was talking about pigs and Harvey being pissed. Do you think someone has made a connection already?"

His smile fell slightly. "No way," he paused. "Do you think we should go offer to help or something?"

We all stared in the direction of the school before I said, "It can't hurt."

Making our way through the parking lot, Alex, who had been completely silent, mumbled, "I have a bad feeling about this."

It was pretty obvious we were all having second thoughts, but it was far too late for that now. A minute later, we were standing in front of the main entrance, where we watched Mr. Johnson, the freshman history teacher, walk through the foyer. His shirt was halfway untucked, his typically neat hair was a mess, and he was muttering to himself as he carried a trash bag he was holding at arm's length. A knot formed in my gut. This would not be good.

With one last look at one another, Alex pulled the door open and followed Jake and I entered. Apparently, the chaos that ensued once we left the pigs with free reign over the school was beyond anything we could have imagined. Papers lined the floors, some of which were colored with dark-colored streaks that made my insides flip. The smell in the building was rancid.

The school's security had apparently been alerted and had begun a desperate attempt to restore order. But the pigs proved to be quite resourceful, finding hiding spots in classrooms and corners of the building that no one would have expected. Their squeals and grunts echoed through the hallways, along with voices hollering instructions. As the madness raged around us, we stood frozen in place and no one even questioned our appearance. Guilt began forming like a dark cloud hovering on all sides, just knowing that we were the masterminds behind this mess. But there was no turning back now. The best we could do was step up and offer to help make it right - without admitting any involvement.

"Where do we even start?" I muttered.

"Divide and conquer?" Jake suggested.

Without another word, we each headed a different direction and started what would be an hour of gross misery. There was pig poop everywhere. Desks and chairs in classrooms had been turned over, trash cans were upturned and if there had been trash in them, it was no longer. I was so overwhelmed the only thing I could think to do was to pick up the trash, then start righting the desks and chairs in the classroom.

When the last chair was in place, I heard a voice over the P.A. system say, "We have pigs 1, 3, 4, and 5. It looks like we're missing pig 2. Keep your eyes open."

Resting my hands on the back of the chair I had just straightened, my chin fell to my chest. I knew they would never find pig 2 because there was no pig 2. I needed to find Jake and Alex because the only way this mess was going to wrap up faster is if the truth came out about how many pigs they were looking for. But to share that information meant revealing complicity.

My knuckles turned white as I gripped the back of the chair. This prank should have been funny, but it had taken a turn and had definitely been way more destructive than I think any of us thought possible. As I headed for the doorway, the P.A. system kicked on again.

The principal, Dr. Stephens, announced, "Alright, y'all. It appears that we've got all the pigs. Thank you all for working through this. I think we're gonna go ahead and cancel school for today so we can get some professionals in here to clean. I'll let the rest of the teachers know but if you need to reset your classroom, get that done and we'll see y'all tomorrow." There was a long pause before he added, "And Nash Montgomery and Alex Stephens, get to my office, now."

My heart sank as my head began pounding and I suddenly felt clammy because of nerves. Every step had me feeling like my feet were cased in concrete.

With his head down and his hands stuffed into his pockets, Alex leaned against the wall outside his dad's office. When he heard me coming, his head raised. Seeing me, he shrugged his shoulders as though defeated.

"What's going on?" I asked in a whisper.

"Apparently, Jake tried and take the fall after confessing that there wasn't another pig on the loose. Dad didn't buy that he could do it by himself."

My cheeks puffed on my exhale as I ran a hand through my hair. "Geez, we're idiots," I said to the empty room.

About that time, Dr. Stephens' door opened, and he motioned for us to come in.

We walked into the office, heads down and steps shuffling. My heart was pounding with anxiety. Jake slouched in one of the chairs across from the principal's chair. He took his seat behind his desk, a stern look on his face, and wasted no time in getting to the point.

"Boys," he said, his gaze fixed on Alex, who glanced up, then back to the floor.

The three of us exchanged nervous glances before forcing ourselves to meet his eyes.

"I have to say, I've seen my fair share of senior pranks over the years, but this...this is on a whole different level." Principal Stephens sighed heavily and leaned back in his chair. "Do you have any idea how much damage those pigs caused?"

We hung our heads, knowing full well that we were in deep trouble. The principal continued, "Not to mention the disruption they caused to classes and the emotional distress to some of the teachers and even students. This is unacceptable."

I swallowed hard and managed to speak. "Dr. Stephens, we didn't intend for it to get this out of hand. We thought it would be a harmless prank, but we understand it went too far."

His expression was one I'd seen a few times on my dad's face when he was trying to be understanding, but was still mad as a hornet. "I don't doubt that you didn't intend for this to happen, but the consequences are real, and we need to address them. We've already spoken with your uncle, Jake. Harvey is quite upset about all of this. If he so chooses, we're going to have a serious discussion with the local authorities about this matter and we'll definitely be contacting your parents," he said, pointing at me.

The mention of my parents sent shivers down my spine. My dad's voice echoed in my head, constantly reminding me about the "consequences of my actions." I wondered how I would explain this to my parents, especially with a college scholarship hanging in the balance. I felt like such an idiot for potentially screwing up the one thing I was most proud of and excited about.

Jake spoke up, "We're willing to help clean up the mess and cover any damages."

Dr. Stephens nodded. "That's a good start, but this will also reflect on your records. Scholarships and college acceptances could be affected by this incident." He looked at each of us, his stern glare remaining on Alex.

His words confirmed the very fear that had just been running through my head, causing the knot in my gut to tighten. Was I that desperate to go to college? Not really. School was fine, but I could take it or leave it. Did I love baseball so much that I couldn't wait to practice and play for months out of the year? Nope.

But I needed that scholarship.

Sitting in the principal's office felt bad enough after admitting to the prank, but the heavy silence made everything worse. We were in deep trouble, and we all knew it. I couldn't believe we thought this would end any other way. Glancing at my friends, I could tell they were thinking the same thing. We were stuck, waiting for whatever punishment was coming our way, and the tension was like a thick wall we couldn't break through.

The chairs we sat in might as well have been hot coals, making us squirm and wish we were anywhere but here. The clock ticked too loudly, reminding us that every second brought us closer to facing the consequences. We had confessed, yeah, but actually dealing with the fallout? That was a whole different ballgame.

Just when I thought it couldn't get any worse, the door swung open. My stomach dropped. My dad walked in, and the look on his face told me I was in for it. Jake's uncle was right there with him, and his frown was just as deep. Seeing them together, disappointment written all over their faces, made the whole thing feel even more real. There was no escaping it now.

Before I could offer up any kind of defense, Dad held up a hand and said, "We'll talk about it at home." He then proceeded to talk in hushed tones with Dr. Stephens and Harvey as Jake, Alex, and I waited outside the principal's office.

A few minutes later, we were once again face-to-face with Dr. Stephens as my dad and Harvey headed out to load up the pigs and return them to the farm.

"Alright, boys, here's the deal. You're going to spend the next however many hours it takes to get this school back into shape. You'll help cover the cleaning fees of the professionals. You will serve one hundred community service hours each this summer at The Youth Club in some capacity. And because none of you have ever done anything to land yourselves in this kind of hot water, I won't be holding your diplomas hostage. You will all three still graduate and it won't go on your permanent record. And your guardians have all been made aware of your required service hours and they will be signing off on them every week. Any questions?"

We all three mumbled, "No, sir."

"Then get to work."

Stepping out of the principal's office, we could finally breathe, as if we'd been underwater and had just surfaced. We shared a look, a mix of relief and the dawning realization of the work ahead. The lecture was over, the consequences laid out, and now it was time to face the music. Not just at school, but at home, too.

We changed into our gym clothes in silence, the tension from the office slowly unwinding. Once we were ready, we huddled briefly, nodding at each other. "Divide and conquer," I said, trying to inject some enthusiasm into my voice. It was going to be a long day, but at least we were facing it together.

The day flew by in a blur of activity. We split up, tackling the cleanup in shifts. Pig feces, overturned desks, shattered glass—it was everywhere. The mess was bad, but the stench was worse, hanging in the air like a cloud of guilt. As I scrubbed and swept, I couldn't help but think this was a pretty accurate metaphor for the mess I was in personally.

At some point, sweaty and tired, we regrouped, sharing water and a moment of quiet. "Look, guys," Jake started, breaking the silence, "I know I dragged you into this mess. I'm sorry. This was on me."

"No, man," I said, shaking his head. "We all went in together. It was stupid, but we did it as a team."

"Yeah," added Alex, "and we're fixing it as a team. Let's just get this mess cleaned up and maybe make this the last prank we pull."

We nodded, the weight of the day settling on us.

"Alright, let's finish this up. Then we can figure out how to apologize to everyone else we dragged into our mess," I said, feeling a bit more hopeful.

2

NASH

As I entered the house, the sight of my dad's face was all it took to shatter what little composure I had left. His expression, a mix of disappointment and concern, cut through me. I couldn't even muster the strength to meet his gaze, my posture defeated, shoulders sagging as if bearing the weight of my choices.

"Have a seat," Dad instructed, his voice steady and imposing. It carried the same authority he used in his business dealings, a tone that brooked no argument and definitely promised consequences.

Reluctantly, I complied, choosing the chair farthest from him, my eyes locked on the table's worn surface, not daring to look up. The knot of anxiety in my stomach twisted tighter, a sensation all too familiar in moments like this.

"You stink," he remarked, the blunt observation void of judgment.

Under different circumstances, I might have laughed it off, but the severity of the moment anchored me in place. I could only nod, a silent acknowledgment of my current state.

"Listen, Nash. You know what you boys did was stupid," he continued, his voice never escalating but carrying a weight that demanded attention. "You know better than to take risks like that with everything you have at stake. I won't even bother asking what you were thinking. You boys have a way of getting yourselves into some tight situations, but you've always gotten out fairly unscathed."

For a moment, his serious expression broke as he chuckled. "Well, except maybe that time you lost both your eyebrows to that can of hairspray and the lighter."

A faint smile tugged at my lips despite the rollercoaster of feelings inside.

"But this was foolish and irresponsible on so many levels, Nash. Those pigs were technically stolen. Do you know how much you would have been on the line for if one of them had been injured or worse? And the destruction they caused - you're lucky there weren't charges pressed."

His words hit me like a physical blow. I could feel the disappointment radiating from him, and it only deepened my regret. My elbows resting on my knees, I dropped my head to my hands and tugged at my hair in frustration.

My voice was barely above a whisper when I finally spoke.

"I'm really sorry, Dad. I know when I was having doubts I should have shut it down or at least backed out. I never thought it would be this bad."

He studied me intently, his eyes searching mine for something– maybe understanding, maybe a glimpse of the son he'd hoped I would be. Whatever punishment he planned to dole out on his own would be well deserved. And when it came, there was zero shock factor.

"I know you. And I know you didn't mean for everything that happened to happen. But it did. And I know Principal Stephens gave you boys a lot of service hours, and that's good. Since I already worked out a deal to pay for a lot of the damages, you're gonna have to work to pay me back. That means when you aren't doing community service, you're working for me. Unless you're dead or dying, you're up with me and the chickens. Got it?"

"Yes, sir." It was all I could muster. There was already a list of chores I did every day and twice as many on the weekends. That meant whatever he had in store for me was going to be a whole lot worse. And it probably still wasn't enough to make up for what it cost him.

~

EVEN THOUGH IT WAS LATE, everything that had happened still left me feeling wound up. I took a shower, but rather than head to bed, I sat down at my desk. Logging in to OurSpace, I scrolled through several posts from the last few days. There were a few comments on the last video I'd uploaded of me singing *Wrapped Up in You* by Garth Brooks. They were all positive, but only one had my full attention.

@Wildfire: As always, so good. Mind if I join you? <Click to Open Attachment>

Smiling and insanely curious, I immediately clicked on the link which opened the file. At first I only heard the sound of me singing with my guitar.

After the first few lines, the girl I only knew as *Wildfire* slid a bow over the strings of a fiddle and played along as I sang.

I leaned forward, thinking I'd be able to discern anything about her from the recording, unable to wipe the smile from my face. *Wildfire* and I had randomly met through a post about country music a few months back and had engaged mostly through comments on each other's stuff. We'd never had a full conversation, but I felt like I knew her. I listened to the new recording several times and every time my heart pinged with this weird sensation that made it feel out of sync with the rest of me.

After what was probably the seventh time through, I clicked open a direct message box.

@GuyWithGuitar: That was amazing. I can't stop listening to it. I needed that after today. PS You can join me anytime

It was late. I knew from her profile that she was from West Virginia, so that meant it was late there, too. I didn't expect one, but to my surprise, a reply appeared almost instantly in the chat box below my message.

@Wildfire: I might just do that. How are you?

My heart started racing, and I felt a little lightheaded for a minute. This was teetering on real conversation, and the idea excited me and terrified me. I'd never been one to talk to strangers on the Internet, but for whatever reason, this girl didn't feel like a stranger. Before I could think too hard about it, I wrote back.

@GuyWithGuitar: I made some bad choices that led to pretty crappy consequences and I let a lot of people down.

@Wildfire: That is probably my biggest fear. Want to talk about it?

@GuyWithGuitar: About your biggest fear? Absolutely.

@Wildfire: Ha! No, about how you're feeling.

@GuyWithGuitar: We could trade stories.

Several minutes passed by and I was sure that I had pried too deeply and scared her off.

Disappointed, I started to click Sign Out when a message came through.

@Wildfire: OK, but we keep it basic. No identifying things like names or locations.

My excitement was back.

@GuyWithGuitar: Deal. This might take a while for me to type.

@Wildfire: Same.

A few minutes later, I'd typed and read everything more than once, hashing out the story about the pigs in the school and having to set things straight. I told her about the punishments, but that I would rather serve the time than lose my baseball scholarship. Right as I hit Send, her message showed up.

@Wildfire: I say that my biggest fear is letting people down, but there's a lot more to it than that. More specifically, I don't want to let my mom down but I also don't want to be trapped in the plans she's made for me. At some point she's gotten into her head that I need to pursue performing, singing, getting famous but that just isn't my style. Unfortunately, the only time I've ever tried to bring it up, she reminded me that she's my mother and she knew what was best for me. Anyway, she has all these aspirations for my future and it feels like I have no freedom to choose my own path. But if she's got some kind of insight I don't have, going against her wishes would disappoint her which would weigh heavy on me. And oh my gosh I've never said any of this to anyone before...

I read her words so many times I could almost quote it. This was a glimpse into a stranger's life that had me wanting to reach through the screen, wrap her in a hug, then lead the charge to letting her make her own choices. Like I had any idea what that charge would look like. I didn't care. I was invested and ready to swoop in and save the day. My track record may be filled with unfortunate choices that led to unfortunate results, but they were always my choices. I don't know what I would do if that was taken away from me.

She probably thought I'd signed off as long as I'd sat here without responding, but I wanted to decide how to tell her that I was here to cheer her on without sounding like a weirdo.

@GuyWithGuitar: I don't even know what to say to that other than I'm sorry you are dealing with that kind of stress. But I want to tell you that as talented as you clearly are, if it's not what you can see yourself doing forever, then you shouldn't feel pressured into doing it. Do what you have to right now, but decide what it is you want to do and make a plan that will let it happen. And if you need some extra encouragement, you can count on me.

I waited again for what seemed like a short eternity for her message to pop up. When it finally did, I grinned as I read the entire thing.

@Wildfire: It took me so long to respond because I had to stop laughing so I'd stop crying. The pigs... I'm not saying it was a good idea but that is the funniest thing I've ever heard. I'm sorry it went sideways and you're

having to deal with the fallout. I guess every choice has its price. Yours could have been higher, so maybe consider that the bright side. And who knows, maybe you'll learn something about yourself this summer you didn't know before.

And thanks for your encouragement. I know I'm in this situation for another year and a half at least probably until I'm nineteen but I like the idea of making a plan. I just have no idea what I want to do since I've never really been given an option. But it's something to think about. I'm glad we finally did this - I've been fiddlin' with the idea of sending you a message (pun intended) but wasn't sure what to say. I'm gonna call it a night. Maybe we can do this again sometime.

@G*UY*W*ITH*G*UITAR*: *I'm glad, too. We can definitely do this again sometime. Night Wildfire.*

@W*ILDFIRE*: *Night Guy.*

There was no reason for me to feel this way, like I was liable to float away on a light breeze, but I couldn't convince myself otherwise. I stared at our messages for a few minutes, letting my vision blur in and out of focus as I thought about who I might have been talking to. She was a musician—a really good musician—and she had a lot of pressure being put on her. Aside from knowing she's sixteen and from West Virginia, there were a lot of blanks left to be filled in. I wondered if she'd ever fill them in for me or if we were bound to this anonymity in an impersonal space.

A sudden rush of fatigue hit and a huge yawn forced itself from my lungs. I leaned forward and logged out of the OurSpace site and shut down my computer before falling back into bed. My last thought was the sound of the mysterious fiddle playing girl from West Virginia as I drifted off to sleep.

3

NASH

I would have thrown the alarm across the room if I'd been able to move, but after a week of loading and unloading bales of hay, mucking stalls, and pulling fence all before 8:00 A.M. I wasn't sure I'd ever be able to move faster than my Grandma Edna, and she'd passed away when I was twelve. God rest her soul. Instead, I groaned as I slowly rolled and reached for the clock and forced it to be silent.

It was still dark outside, which was not convenient, but it meant that it hadn't reached scorching hot temperatures. With a heavy sigh, I pushed up and turned to put my feet on the floor. My eyes were heavy and were determined to close again.

I heard movement downstairs—Dad, likely pouring his second coffee of the morning. I forced myself out of bed and shuffled to the bathroom. Moving slowly, I pulled on old jeans and a worn-out T-shirt, knowing today's tasks would not differ from the last week's.

Once I was downstairs in the kitchen, my dad's chipper voice greeted me with, "Mornin', son."

I tried to reply, but it came back more of a mumble, which made him chuckle.

As had been the routine for the last week, I grabbed a bagel and shoved it in the toaster before fishing out the orange juice and filling a Mason jar. The kitchen, with its eclectic mix of old and new, always felt comforting in its familiarity.

Bagel toasting, my thoughts slowly started to gather. I thought about Dad, how hard he worked. His hands were always rough and stained from working in the field or fixing things, but his spirit never wavered. The kitchen often bore witness to his hardworking nature, from the early-morning coffee stains on the counter to the evidence of his late night tinkering at the kitchen table. There were usually makeshift projects spread out, pointing to his never-ending to-do list.

I admired him, always had. He had a resilience I hoped I'd inherited. The truth was, I wanted to make him proud, not just to impress him, but to show I'd learned from him. He had this quiet strength, a way of carrying burdens without letting them weigh down his smile. As he rinsed his coffee cup, his smile remained locked in place. I wondered if he saw that same strength in me or if my recent mistakes had clouded it.

I took a drink of orange juice, letting it bring me back to the present. But the thought lingered. I wasn't just working off a punishment; I was proving something to him and myself. That I could handle responsibility, that I could face consequences head-on, just like he would. Maybe, through the hard work, I could get closer to the unspoken standard he set, the one I aspired to reach.

"I've got to ride over to Harvey's and look at his tractor this morning. Will you be alright on your own? I know you start at The Youth Club today, so just do what you can get done," Dad said as he washed his coffee cup and set it on the rack to dry.

"Yeah, I'll be fine," I answered, my voice finding a bit more strength.

The toaster popped up my bagel. I quickly grabbed it, tossing it onto the plate on the counter. The smell of toasted bread mingled with the lingering scent of coffee filled the kitchen.

"Alright. I'm gonna head out then so I can beat the heat. It's supposed to be a scorcher so don't overdo it," he advised, his concern evident even as he prepped for his day.

With a nod, I said, "Yes, sir." I watched as he walked out the door, his confident stride and calm demeanor a reminder of the man I hoped to become.

Between my overused muscles and the early hour, lifting the bagel seemed to take four times the effort it should have. It became one more reminder of my stupid, impulsive mistake that had landed me here in the first place. With the last bite of the bagel shoved in my mouth, I stood and washed my plate in the sink before grabbing a bottle of water and heading for the barn.

I started with feeding the goats and cleaning out their stalls before heading to the cow barn. We didn't have a lot of animals as dad's family had always run a peanut farm. My grandfather added chickens and cows before I was born and Dad brought in goats when my sister Cody joined 4-H two years ago. While they were technically her responsibility, cleaning out their barn fell to me in the mornings as part of my arrangement with Dad.

The peacefulness of the morning caused my mind to race rather than clear and I started thinking about the day that I'd be spending at The Youth Club. I'd read through the information packet more than once after the orientation I'd attended last week. It sounded like a really great program for kids. They chose different tracks for the summer and learned a new skill like art or learned the ropes of hiking and survival. My anxiety came into play when I thought about the fact I would be leading the track they called "Jam Sessions".

Jake and Alex had been sitting at the table with me when the director, Chad Muñoz, announced to the room that the music teacher from the elementary school who had been slated to run the Jam Sessions had gone on bed rest and would be out for the summer. He then asked if anyone would be capable or willing to lead the track on short notice. Jake shoved his elbow into my side, causing Alex to snicker when I jumped. The movement got Mr. Muñoz's attention. He was staring directly at me when I turned away from giving Jake a scowl.

I was only thinking about how angry I'd be if Jake got us in trouble before we even started serving this part of the punishment.

Then Mr. Muñoz saw Jake still trying to nudge my arm with his elbow. Now I was thinking about how much more trouble I'd be in if I pummeled him.

"Is there something I need to know, guys?" he asked, a hint of annoyance in his tone.

"No, sir," I said immediately, keeping my eyes straight ahead.

I could practically hear Jake roll his eyes when he said, "Nash is a music guy. He plays the guitar and sings."

As I considered how much trouble I might get in for punching the guy in the nose, my back teeth ground together. However, Mr. Muñoz quickly interrupted those thoughts when his eyes lit up and he said, "Really?"

The hopefulness in his voice dissolved the rising frustration I'd been feeling and turned it into what felt more like a lead weight. I picked up a guitar in ninth grade to try and impress Kortney Martin, and discovered I was actually pretty good at it. Turned out, a lot of girls liked guys who could play the guitar, but it never translated into anything more than flirting, followed by the dreaded friend zone for me. By Junior year, music had become more of a private escape. I'd tried my hand at lyrics and had some buddies online that had given me some positive feedback every now and then. But music had never been something I shared with anyone.

Jake had known I played guitar from the day I bought the thing. He only knew that I could do more than play the guitar because he'd been a snoop and found some recordings I'd uploaded to OurSpace when he was using my computer for a homework assignment. I set my account to private, and only added contacts I didn't actually know because I didn't want people I knew personally to have an opinion on something that was so personal to me. I didn't even have Jake on my contacts list.

I shifted uncomfortably and cleared my throat. "I guess, but I know nothing about teaching music," I said.

"You don't have to. Mrs. Barnett sent her lesson plans and they're pretty basic. If you're up for it, it sure would help us out," Mr. Muñoz said, though it sounded a lot like pleading.

Clearing my throat again, I lifted my chin. "Yeah, ok, I'll, um, I'll look at it and let you know if I can make it work."

Shoulders sagging in relief, Mr. Muñoz nodded and said, "Come to my office when we're done here."

And that was how I found myself spending the next few days after that meeting adapting a set of lesson plans involving classroom instruments to use rhythm sticks, doing a lot of searches about teaching kids how to write song lyrics, and sending a lot of prayers into the universe hoping these new plans didn't blow up in my face.

I was tossing the last fork of straw into the wheelbarrow when my sister's voice, as lively as ever, interrupted my mental spiral. "Hey, loser!" her voice was teasing, laced with the familiarity that only siblings share, as she approached. When she noticed that her animals' stalls were completely reset, she punched my arm lightly. "Thanks for doing that. You could have started with the cows and I would've done this."

Lifting the wheelbarrow with ease, I began walking it toward the barn doors, a smile breaking across my face. "I know." As I pushed the cart toward the compost pile, Cody walked with me, her steps light and quick to keep pace. There was no denying she was my sister, especially when she smiled. That smile, wide and genuine, lit up her face and mirrored my own. We shared the same walnut brown hair, hers falling in gentle waves that caught the sunlight, and dark brown eyes that seemed to sparkle with mischief and warmth. Those eyes, a rich, deep brown like polished chestnuts, were a gift from our mother, conveying emotions words sometimes couldn't.

Cody, two years my junior, had an energy about her that made her feel larger than life despite being a good five inches shorter than my six-foot frame. As we stood there with the wheelbarrow between us, it was easy to see that we were related, but we also had plenty of differences. Where my hair was short, hers cascaded in a lively dance around her shoulders. And while I had the broad shoulders of someone who worked on a farm, she moved with a grace that belied her strength.

She was one of my favorite people, not just because she was my sister, but because of who she was at her core. Her goodness and sweet nature were as much an integral part of her as her physical features, making it impossible not to immediately love her.

"So, you ready to teach little kids how to clap or whatever?"

Even though it sounded like she was trying to check on me without checking on me, which immediately had me feeling defensive, I had to remind myself that she was the only person who'd ever been honest with me to a fault one hundred percent of the time, but also seemed to actually get me. She was two years younger than me, but we had very similar personalities. Cody was naturally the star of any show and took center stage without even meaning to and embraced it. She was also far less impulsive than I was, which kept her out of trouble but also made her aware of the trouble I regularly landed myself in. And every time, she was always there to remind me I wasn't a bad person, and that she was in my corner, no matter what. Long story short, she was my favorite person and I would do anything for her any time. The way she picked up on my anxiety, though, was annoying. Because that meant I had to talk about it.

Staying silent as I dumped the straw into the compost and shook the wheelbarrow a few times to empty it, I decided to be honest with both her and myself.

Using the end of my shirt to wipe the sweat off my face, I sighed heavily then faced Cody. "I'm as ready as I'm gonna be, I think. If I said I wasn't scared to death I'd be lying. It's one thing to tell 'em how to find the rhythm in a song or to put words together, but Mr. Muñoz thinks I'm capable of corralling a bunch of kids while teaching them. I wish I had his confidence but I'm terrified and stressing out about it."

She was smiling like I had said something hilarious and she was trying not to laugh.

"What is that look for?" I asked, grabbing the wheelbarrow and pushing it back toward the barn.

"Nash, you have nothing to worry about. You're practically a little kid at heart just with a lot more experience under his belt. If anyone will know how to wrangle a room full of barn cats, it will be you. I bet you could probably predict their next moves before they even know their own next moves."

I stopped in my tracks and stared at her. On the one hand, I wanted to be offended because I was nineteen years old. She was pushing it by comparing me to a little kid, considering I was legally an adult. On the other hand, however, she was unfortunately right. All I had to do was look at what I was doing and why. And it wasn't the first time I'd found myself paying for my rash behavior.

Dropping the handles of the cart, I took my hat off and ran a hand through my hair. Blowing out a hard breath, I stared across the massive fields of green leafy peanut plants.

"Think about it, Nash. You're probably better qualified to teach those kids than some older adults. And they're going to love you. I know I always have the most fun when you're in charge," she said with a wink.

She wasn't wrong. We had our fair share of inside jokes and memories from a lot of the times our parents left us home and me in charge. The massive pillow and blanket fort had become a sort of epic memory, and that had just been a year ago. We spent an entire weekend building and living in a fort constructed of every pillow, blanket, and sheet in the house. It took up the living room that we had rearranged. And as the rules Cody had created for our fortress stated, we couldn't bring furniture inside.

Our parents had been a little annoyed and very confused when they walked in after their quick trip and right into a wall made of blanket. We all laughed, of course until mom informed us we'd be washing everything we'd used, which had taken a while. But the memories were worth it. It was inside the walls of that fort Cody and I had bonded over our feelings about the pressures we felt to look or act a certain way, even though it didn't always feel genuine. The fact she was never shy about being real with me was why I knew I could trust her to tell me the truth about handling the kids.

Letting my gaze slide to her, I held out an arm and tipped my head. "Come here."

She took a step, then thought better of it. "You're gross, so no."

But it was too late. She was close enough for me to grab her arm, so I did and pulled her in for a hug. "Thanks, Cody. You're the best little sister I've ever had."

She laughed and hugged me back. "I'm the only little sister you've ever had. And you are the worst smelling brother I've ever had."

4

CASSIDY

Staring at the overstuffed suitcase in the middle of the bed, surrounded by the clutter of packing—discarded clothes, more accessories than I'd wear in a single weekend, and my favorite boots—all ready for another series of performances.

"Cassidy, make sure you pack the denim skirt and your boots," Mom called out.

Her voice was getting louder, which meant she was heading for my room. The room that was practically a shrine to my musical achievements, showing off all the trophies and ribbons I'd won over the years-a constant reminder of my mom's dedication to my success.

"They're already in the bag," I said with a sigh as I picked up a shirt and folded it before shoving it into the bag.

Mom entered, her eyes briefly scanning the room before settling on the shelf lined with trophies and awards. She ran a finger over one of the glass trophies on the shelf with a satisfied gleam in her eyes.

"Good," she said, a hint of relief in her voice. "You can't go on stage without them."

I nodded, feeling a familiar mix of emotions. Excitement for the upcoming performances, yes, but also a twinge of resentment. There were times it felt like I was living my mom's dreams instead of my own.

"Do you have everything else?" she asked, her tone brisk now as she scanned the items on my bed.

"Yeah, I've got it all," I replied, forcing a smile. "I double-checked."

"Alright," she said, turning her attention back to the trophies. "You know how important these shows are, Cassidy. They could be your big break."

"I know, Mom." I tried to sound enthusiastic, but my voice came out flat.

She looked at me then, her eyes softening. "I'm just proud of you, you know? You've worked so hard to get here."

"I know," I said again, this time more sincerely. "Thanks, Mom."

With one last satisfied look around my room, she left, closing the door behind her. I let out a long breath and sat on the edge of the bed, staring at the suitcase. It was almost like staring at my future, packed neatly and ready to go, yet so heavy with expectations.

As I zipped the suitcase, a spark of rebellion zing through me. I imagined telling her I didn't want to go, that I wanted a weekend free of stages and songs. I imagined standing there, defiant, insisting on a couple of days to just be a normal teenager, hanging out with friends or binge-watching my favorite shows. The idea felt so freeing, like finally getting a breath of fresh air after feeling trapped for so long. But the reality was different—I needed to perform, to meet that unseen executive who might or might not be in the audience because Mom worked hard to make these things happen.

With my suitcase packed, I went over to my desk where my computer was open to the OurSpace website. It was a site where most users uploaded their favorite music or shared original work. I did that sometimes, but for the most part, I used it as an audio journal. This was my escape, my little corner of the internet where I could share stories and songs, unscripted and real.

I clicked the red Record button and started talking.

"Hey, y'all," I began, trying to inject some enthusiasm into my voice. "Looks like I'm headed to the fair this weekend. Might channel my inner SHeDAISY, or maybe Gretchen Wilson—feeling a bit 'jacked up' lately!" I chuckled, hoping my attempt at humor would mask my underlying reluctance.

My mood immediately improved when I started talking about a recent wedding I'd played at, diving into the story of a couple who'd met at a theme park, playing roles they never imagined would lead them to the altar. "She was a princess, he was a knight, and somehow, despite all odds, they found their fairytale ending," I narrated, my voice softening as I lost myself in their story. It was moments like these—people with their stories I only met because of music—that kept my love for music alive, despite the grind of constant performances.

I ended and uploaded the recording and almost immediately, a comment pinged in response.

@GuyWithGuitar: Hey Wildfire. Keep your chin up. Your prince is out there just waiting to find you. He'll be a lucky guy when he does. And maybe don't channel anyone. Just be you - I think that would be the best.

His words brought a smile to my face, a genuine one this time. *@GuyWithGuitar* had become a staple of my online life, a friend who knew the persona I presented to the world but encouraged the person I was behind the scenes even though he didn't actually know me.

@Wildfire: Thanks, Guy. That's really sweet. Have a good weekend.

As I typed my response, there was a brief flicker of excitement in the otherwise mundane routine of my life just before shutting down the computer.

I stood and glanced around my room at the life packed in a suitcase and the accomplishments displayed on my shelves in the form of trophies.

Mom's voice called from downstairs, breaking my reverie. "Cassidy, we need to go!"

Grabbing my bag, I took a deep breath and glanced at my reflection in the mirror. The girl staring back at me was no longer the wide-eyed child excited for every new stage. She was someone who had grown accustomed to the routine, yet still harbored a flicker of hope for something more. She just didn't have a clue what that something more was.

"Coming!" I replied, dragging my suitcase towards the door. The apprehension that filled me as I headed for the stairs was heavy. Maybe this weekend wouldn't be just another performance. Maybe, just maybe, it would be the start of something real.

5

NASH

I knew the air conditioner wasn't broken because I was standing directly under the vent and feeling the cold air. That cold air was having no effect on the amount of sweat forming on my forehead and under my arms. I may as well have been running laps around the field in the mid-afternoon sun for all the good it was doing.

I'd wrapped up the chores, jumped in the shower, grabbed my backpack and guitar and headed for The Youth Club. Mr. Muñoz wasted no time in welcoming me and guiding me to the room I'd be using for the summer. He reminded me I'd have three different groups of kids that had been sorted by age and gave me a clipboard with the names of kids in each group.

Just looking at the list of names gave me anxiety. I was only nineteen, barely out of high school myself, and now I was supposed to lead and teach these kids? What if they didn't listen, or they thought I was boring?

"Any questions for me?" Mr. Muñoz asked.

"Uh, yeah. Are you sure I'm qualified to do this?" I asked, certain the nerves were evident in my voice.

He chuckled and slapped me on the shoulder before we were interrupted by a flurry of activity. The first group had arrived. A whirlwind of motion and excitement, they burst into the room like a tornado. Laughter, shouts, and chaos filled the air as the group of first, second, and third graders funneled in through the door.

"Hey, hey, hey, settle down, everyone!" Mr. Muñoz called out, trying to be heard over the ruckus.

The room quieted mostly, and he said, "This is Mr. Nash. He's going to be leading the Jam Sessions this summer because Mrs. Barnett is getting ready to have her baby." This elicited squealing sounds from some of the girls. "I need all of you to be on your best behavior and treat Mr. Nash just like you would any of your teachers. And most of all, have a great time."

The room erupted again in noise and cheers as Mr. Muñoz opened the door without a backwards glance. I'd hoped his influence would have inspired a longer-lasting silence, but clearly, that was not to be the case. Silently, I walked to the front of the room and picked up my guitar.

I strummed a few chords, but it had about as much impact as a whisper in a hurricane. So I did what had always worked to get my attention when my dad did it. I licked my lips, placed my finger and thumb just inside my mouth, and created an ear-piercing whistle that could likely be heard through the door.

Just as I'd suspected, the room went quiet, and rather than give them a chance to start up again, I said, "OK, like he said, I'm Nash. And here's what we're gonna do. We're gonna start with a game. It's called 'Musical Freeze.' When I start playing, you dance, jump, twirl, whatever you want. But as soon as I stop, you freeze like statues. If you move before the music restarts, you're out. Got it?"

The kids' eyes lit up, and they nodded eagerly. I began strumming my guitar, and the room erupted into a wild dance party. After several seconds, I stopped the strings from vibrating and once there was no sound, the movement in the room slowed. All nine pairs of eyes were on me.

Trying to suppress a grin, I started playing again, and the dancing started again. We kept playing the game until I felt we were all a little more settled.

"Alright, great job. Now, let's circle up here on the floor and talk about music."

I rested my guitar back on the stand and sat down in a circle with a group of kids who looked excited to be there and who looked surprisingly attentive.

Wanting to test one of the games I'd found in my research, I said, "Everything can be music or rhythm if you listen. Let's each take a turn saying our names and counting how many claps or beats our names have. I'll start."

We went around the circle and by the time the last girl in the circle, Dominique, had clapped out her name, I was starting to think I might just survive this experience. Then I checked my watch and realized I still had forty minutes left to fill. I started pulling from every bag of tricks I'd brought with me. We reached the final ten minutes, and I questioned how I would manage to repeat it two more times.

"Can you actually play real songs on that?" one of the boys asked, pointing to my guitar.

Leaning over to grab it, I chuckled. "Sure. Y'all want to end with a song?"

The room erupted into voices shouting out different song suggestions, but quickly silenced when I whistled once again.

I pointed at a boy named Dixon and said, "Pick a song."

"Gold Digger!" he yelled back.

I pointed at a girl named Lilah and said, "Pick a song."

"Since You Been Gone," she practically whispered.

"Alright, if your vote is for Gold Digger, stand behind Dixon. If your vote is Since You Been Gone, stand behind Lilah."

The kids shuffled, and I was more than a little thankful to see more than half the kids standing behind Lilah.

"Looks like we're taking on some Kelly Clarkson. Lilah, if I give you a cue, you want to start us?"

Her cheeks turned bright pink.

I made a different suggestion. "OK, how about I give a nod and your group starts us and if you know the song, you sing with? If you don't, keep the beat or dance or even play your best air guitar."

When I was met with very enthusiastic cheers, I started strumming. A few minutes later, the last chords were humming to a close with almost a whisper of the last line "since you been gone" from around the room.

After a beat of silence, the kids were all begging for another song.

"Listen, y'all gotta move on to the next track but we'll do it all again tomorrow if you think we can get along as well as we did today. What do y'all think?"

Everyone was immediately in agreement.

"Alright, go line up and wait for the signal to go," I instructed.

I had to be a little more creative the older the kids in the class were, but overall I think it had been a successful plan. The seventh and eighth-grade boys had little to no interest in what I had to say until I told them that girls really liked guys who knew music. It probably wasn't the most mature route I could have taken, but it got their attention, nonetheless.

By the time I got home, my brain felt like a fried egg on a hot skillet and I wasn't sure my shoulders were strong enough to hold my head up for long. I walked into my house and was greeted by my mom and sister, who were working side by side in the kitchen. They were clearly baking something based on the mouthwatering smells I was experiencing.

They both turned and greeted me when they heard the door close behind me.

"You survived!" Cody exclaimed as she rolled out the pastry in front of her.

"Barely," I said, but couldn't keep from smiling back at her.

"You do look a little worse for the wear," my mom suggested.

"Thanks," I said, rolling my eyes and trying not to laugh. "Whatever y'all are working on smells amazing. But I'm too tired to even investigate for myself."

"There's a strawberry pie in the fridge and a peach pie in the works," Cody waved her rolling pin.

"Mmm," was all I could get out after a deep inhale.

"Why don't you go lie down for a few minutes. I don't want you to overdo it," Mom suggested.

"Thanks, mom. I think I will. Let dad know I'll head out there soon, if he asks, OK?"

My guitar suddenly felt like it weighed a hundred pounds as I carried it up the stairs. Dropping it just inside my bedroom door, I laid down across my bed and didn't move again for two hours. When I finally mustered the energy to get back on my feet, I was met with the aroma of freshly baked pies lingering in the house. My stomach growled, which had me hustling to get downstairs. I found Mom and Cody still in the kitchen, both looking up with warm smiles as I entered.

"Feeling better?" Mom asked.

"Much," I replied with a genuine smile as I walked over to her and kissed the top of her head. "Dad still in the field?" I asked, swiping a biscuit from the pan on the stove.

"He is, but he'll be in for supper, soon. How about you help me get the table set and you can be on evening chore duty?"

"You sure? I think he's got in his mind that if I'm home, I should be working." The thought of doing any kind of manual labor sent a tension through my shoulders.

Mom, ever the master of the situation, playfully slapped a stack of napkins into my chest. "What do you call this? You're here, you're working. I think that's more than enough," she said with a soft chuckle, her eyes sparkling.

Wrapping her in a gentle hug, I took the napkins, my heart feeling lighter. "Love you, Mama."

"I know you do. Now, let's get this table ready," she replied, her words laced with affection and a hint of her usual playful tease.

When we were all around the table, we started passing dishes and catching up on one another's days. There was a level of confidence I felt building that I hadn't had that morning as I talked about my day at The Youth Club. I knew better than to assume the next day was going to be perfect, but I was surprised at how excited I was to see how it panned out.

Instead, as soon as my head hit the pillow, I was out faster than a dead lightbulb - until 4:00 A.M. rolled back around.

6

CASSIDY

The weekend started with a flat tire halfway between home and our destination. We waited an hour for the roadside assistance technician to arrive. I pulled out my headphones and MP3 player and tried to think about anything that might distract me from the thoughts that had been building in my mind all morning.

We hadn't been on the road again for long when a giant drop of water splattered on the windshield slowly, followed by a few more. The pace increased until it was full-on raining.

Mom slowed her speed and said, "It should all be gone by morning. I checked the weather and this was just a tiny chance in the forecast. And we're almost there, so it shouldn't be too bad."

I gave a nod and turned my head toward the window and focused on the music playing in my ears as I watched the raindrops race each other across the glass. The song was winding down and the idea I might get myself under control felt hopeless until the next song started. Immediately, my mind felt lighter and my heart started daydreaming. I started humming along until the chorus when I joined in singing, *Cowboy, take me away; Fly this girl as high as you can into the wild blue...* It was a daydream. One I wouldn't mind having come true.

I wondered what it would be like to have a cowboy whisk me away, giving me the freedom to be whoever or whatever I wanted. Having a strong, handsome cowboy to swoop in and make my dreams come true sounded like a great plan.

But then I'd have to ask myself what those dreams actually were. I'd lived every day of my life on someone else's schedule. At sixteen, with seventeen just around the corner, I had no idea how to make my life my own. And how would my mom even react to the thought of me doing anything other than singing on stage after stage or playing the violin for groups of people at weddings who couldn't care less if the music was live or recorded in the first place?

"Ugh!"

I froze, not having meant to make that sound aloud.

"Cassidy?"

I pulled my headphones down around my neck and tried to school my face to neutral.

"You alright?" Mom asked.

"Yeah, just thinking through what I wanted to sing tomorrow," I lied. It was a dumb lie, but she bought it and that's what mattered. Sometimes it felt like that's all that mattered to her.

"Want to talk through it?"

"Nah, I think I just need to stop thinking, if that makes sense." And that wasn't a lie. I needed to stop thinking because all I had were questions with no answers, and that wasn't helpful.

Fortunately, by the time we got to the hotel, it had stopped raining hard and was only drizzling. After checking in and getting to our room, we ordered room service. Whether it was the bacon cheeseburger, the hot half baked chocolate chip cookie, or the comfortable bed, I felt more relaxed than I had during the car ride. It gave me hope that everything else was only going to be smooth sailing.

∾

I DIDN'T REMEMBER FALLING asleep, but the booming thunder at 3:00 A.M. was a memorable wake up call. I shot up in the bed, momentarily forgetting where I was. The room was dark, and the rain was pelting the window. Then I remembered that Mom and I were in a hotel room, and I was in town for a performance. Hadn't she said the forecast was clear?

Flopping back down onto the pillow, I sighed. It didn't happen often, but the weather would typically be a factor in whether a fairground would be open. I had mixed feelings about the possibilities. Just because today might get canceled didn't mean tomorrow would. So we were here regardless of what today looked like.

Another rumble of thunder underscored my thoughts. There was little chance I'd be going back to sleep anytime soon, at this rate. I rolled to the edge of the bed and felt around until I found my backpack and dragged it onto the bed. Rummaging around, I found my iPod and headphones and got comfortable again. Scrolling through the songs, I went back to my daydream song and got lost in the picture perfect story that played in my head. It's where my thoughts lingered even after the song changed.

One day I would find my happily ever after with the cowboy of my dreams. He'd be kind, thoughtful, and understanding. We'd go on adventures together, picnics on sunny days, talking about everything, simply enjoying each other's company.

My thoughts grew hazy as I began to doze back off, but I never strayed far from my cowboy. And as we were about to ride off into the sunset, I was pulled back to reality by a gentle shaking and a voice saying my name.

"Cassidy, it's time to wake up, sweetheart," my mom's voice called me to wakefulness.

Groggy, I blinked several times before realizing the room was brighter, which meant the storm must have stopped. When my vision finally focused, I remembered where I was.

"What time is it?" I mumbled, as I felt around in the covers for my iPod that had invariably disconnected from the headphones.

Mom started flitting around the room, straightening and organizing things that didn't need it. I tossed the covers back and found my iPod tangled between the comforter and sheet.

"Looks like the sun's going to be out long enough to keep things from being a muddy mess at the fairgrounds. We're set to be there in two hours for a sound check then you go on at 5:30." Mom was running through the schedule as though it mattered. I rarely had to keep up with it. She always made sure I was exactly where I was supposed to be because she knew if it were up to me, I'd likely be tucked away behind the scenes, dragging a story out of someone.

Mornings were not usually this hard for me, but I was struggling to find the motivation to get out of the bed. I blamed the weather.

"Cassidy, are you listening?" mom asked, her tone more serious than it had been.

I winced. "Sound check in two hours?"

Rolling her eyes, mom let out a sigh. "We're meeting with a record label executive for lunch. So we need to get ourselves put together and get a move on."

By "we" I knew she meant me. She had already put herself together impeccably, with a flawless outfit and makeup, and she likely hadn't been awake much longer than I had. My mother was always at the top of her game, especially when orchestrating every moment of my life.

Reluctantly, I began getting ready, my mind drifting back to my dream and the sense of freedom I'd felt while in it. Sure, the idea of falling in love someday appealed to me. But more than that, I relished the thought of making and keeping my schedule and chasing after my own dreams, whatever those might be.

After we were both ready, we left the hotel and headed to the fairgrounds for the sound check. The venue was surprisingly busy already, which would normally excite me. The anticipation of the day's commitments, however, hung heavy in the air - a lot like the humidity, causing me to break out into a glistening sweat.

We'd acquired our passes and made our way to the stage area. It wasn't the largest stage I'd ever been on, but it was big enough.

"If you'll stay right here, I'll track down one of the crew to find out what we need to do to get things moving," Mom said as we walked through the metal barricades that were marked with a sign that read "Performers".

With nothing more than a nod from me, she set off on her mission. I looked around and watched a group of young teenage girls all wearing matching uniforms stretch as though warming up for some kind of active routine performance of some kind. My guess was they were a dance troupe. Mingled into the group were women who were likely their moms since they were all wearing matching t-shirts with bedazzled words that I couldn't read from where I was standing.

I'd taken Dance for a year and it had been clear early on I would not hack it. It was also clear whose moms were insistent their daughters would. They had this look about them that seemed to threaten anyone who might outshine their dancing princess. These women had those looks. I knew my own mom was proud and protective of me, but dance moms were on a different level. I continued scanning the area when I heard the sound of a banjo coming from behind me.

Turning to find where the sound was coming from, I noticed a woman standing to the side plucking the strings, then turning the pegs. Once she was satisfied, her fingers began to fly across the strings and the sounds of bluegrass filled the air. I felt myself smiling immediately as I watched. My hand began tapping against my thigh. She was lost in the music, a feeling I was very familiar with, especially when I picked up my violin.

The last of her notes reverberated a few seconds before she rested a hand on the strings to silence them. When she noticed me watching, she smiled.

"Do you play?" she asked.

"Just the violin," I answered, returning her smile.

Looking around where I was standing, she asked, "Have it with you?"

"Not this time. I also sing, which is what I'm doing here later," I said before asking, "How long have you been playing?"

The woman unwrapped herself from the strap and laid the instrument in the case open at her feet. "About sixty years," she answered. "Started playing when I was seven and haven't really stopped."

That sounded all too familiar. "Did you ever get bored with it?" I asked, as my curiosity began to build.

With an amused huff, she stuffed her hands into her pockets and studied me for a moment. "Music never gets boring. But I did get bored with stages and lights and smiling all the time."

Her words struck a chord deep inside me.

"Did you do it anyway?" I asked.

"I took a few breaks and focused on myself. I went to school, raised a family, then one day I felt the call of the siren and decided I still had some life in me. With an empty nest and all, I picked it back up and this is where it's taken me for now."

Nodding, I considered my next question. Before I could ask it, the woman said, "Sweetheart, life is a journey, and it's not always about the destination. It's the people you meet along the way, the stories you collect, and the experiences that shape you. Sometimes, the detours and unexpected turns lead to the most beautiful places. You just have to be brave enough to start the journey."

Her words captivated me, making me ask, "But what about your dreams? Did you achieve what you set out to do?"

She smiled, her eyes twinkling with a sense of contentment. "Oh, my dreams evolved over time. I learned that it's okay to let go of some dreams and discover new ones. Life isn't a straight path; it's like a river. Embrace the flow, and you'll find treasures you never imagined."

"Hm," was all I could say.

"Looks like I'm up. Good luck tonight," she said, as she repositioned the strap of the banjo around her.

"Good luck to you, too," I replied. "And thanks."

With a smile and a nod, the woman turned and walked toward the steps leading up to the stage. About the same time, I heard my mom's voice call out my name. I spun around and found her walking in my direction with a stage tech two steps behind her.

"Cassidy, this is Nolan. He's going to get you squared away with your in-ears, and you'll sound check after the bluegrass lady."

Nolan chuckled.

"What?" I asked, wondering why that had made him laugh.

"That bluegrass lady is Sarah Belle Reed. She and her brother Alan Turner started what was probably the most popular bluegrass band twenty something years ago and has written some of the songs being sung by the most famous country stars today," he answered, still sounding amused.

"Holy mothballs," I whispered. Based on our conversation, I knew she had life experience under her belt. What on earth was she doing at a county fair practicing on the same stage I would be?

Nolan seemed to have read my mind and said, "Rumor has it she still likes to do these smaller shows from time to time just to scratch an itch but doesn't do much in public anymore."

"Well, whoever she is, you're on after her, Cassidy. And let's try to make it perfect relatively quickly because we are meeting Mr. Wilder across town and I don't want to be late," my mother interjected curtly.

God-forbid we were late for something she wanted to do, I thought. Immediately, I felt guilty for thinking it. I knew she was trying to do something she thought was good for me. But, like Sarah Belle Reed, I was losing interest in the spotlight and probably had been for a while.

"Looks like you're all set," Nolan suggested as he flipped a switch on an electronic pack that he'd given my mom to attach to the back waistband of my shorts. "Head on up."

Sarah Belle had exited the stage on the opposite end but had remained on the stage, hands resting on her banjo as she watched me approach the microphone. It occurred to me I hadn't asked Mom what song she had delivered to the sound team. Mom and I had curated a list of songs that were my go-to songs, so I wasn't worried. I just had no idea what to expect.

A voice came over my in-ears and said, "Sing something a cappella for us and then we'll set the music."

Lifting the mic from the stand, I shifted into performer mode.

With a smile plastered on my face and microphone in hand, I began belting the same song that had been haunting my dreams.

After a couple of verses and the chorus, the voice was speaking into my ears again. "Give a thumbs up if Trick Pony, *On a Mission*, is the right song."

Trying not to laugh, I gave a thumbs up. As far as I knew, Mom hated the song, but she knew that it was a crowd favorite. The voice gave instructions for signaling adjustments by hand and after another thumbs up, the music started.

Though I didn't put on a show, I sang like I was planning to later. It was too hot, and I was already sweating, so the actual performance would have to wait. When the song ended, the tech asked for my feedback. One more take through the chorus and I felt pretty good about it. There was only so much that could be done beforehand because when crowds, outside noise, anything changed, everything could change.

After setting the mic back into the stand, I headed for the stage exit and noticed Sarah Belle was nowhere to be seen. I reminded myself to check the schedule in hopes of getting to see her perform at some point.

"That was good," mom said as I met her at the bottom of the steps, removing the monitors and receiver as I walked. "You'll move around more this evening, I'm sure," she added. It was a statement and not a question.

"It's so hot and I didn't want to get overheated," I responded, handing the tech to a different sound guy.

Handing me a bottle of water, mom led us out of the grounds and toward the car.

"What's the deal with this man we're meeting? Who is he?" I asked, navigating the parking lot.

"Mr. Wilder is an executive at a recording studio. He's friends with Debbie's husband," she said, as though I knew who Debbie was. "Anyway, Debbie got his number from her husband and gave it to me and suggested I give him a call. So I did and now we're meeting him for lunch in twenty minutes," she finished, before pressing a button on her keyring to unlock the car.

As I climbed inside, my legs met the scorching heat of the leather, causing me to exhale sharply. If it was already this hot at the beginning of summer, I couldn't imagine how hot it would be in four weeks when the fair season was in full swing. I cranked the air conditioning to full blast before my mom pulled out of the parking space.

She reached behind the seat and tugged a garment bag forward and dropped it into my lap. "When we get there, you need to change and clean up as fast as you can. I'd suggest the back seat on the way but it's too hot and you'll just wind up sweating through this," she said, patting the bag.

A sense of dread settled over me. "Mom, why are we doing this?" I surprised myself by asking the question aloud.

She reached for my hand, giving it a squeeze, casting a quick glance my way before returning her gaze to the road. "Because it's what you want. You've always loved music and singing. This meeting is an opportunity to explore a different path, a way to open doors that could lead to a successful music career. You've worked so hard, and I just want to see you achieve the success you deserve. Sometimes, we need to take these chances when they come our way. You're my favorite star, and I'm here to support your dreams."

My stomach flipped and the heat still working its way from the car had me feeling queasy. How could I tell her that this was not my dream, and that it was starting to feel more and more like it had been her dream all along? It didn't matter and now was probably not the time as we were pulling into a small parking lot behind a set of small adjoined buildings. My mom checked what looked like an address on a piece of paper, then looked up at the buildings.

"We're meeting him there," she pointed to the small blue structure on the end of the complex. "Let's run into that little shop and see if you can use their restroom to change," she said, gesturing toward a white wall with a sign that said *Boutique*.

Staring at the painted wooden wall, I sighed. "Mom, we can't just go in and use their store. You'd probably have to buy something anyway, let's just go in and buy something, and I'll wear it out of the store."

She thought about it for several moments before turning the key in the ignition to cut off the car. "OK, let's go. Put your boots on so you can match whatever you find in there."

I dug my custom leather Beck boots from the garment bag before laying the bag across the back seat, then exchanged my sandals for socks and boots. My feet were suddenly suffocating, which was very similar to how I was starting to feel the closer this meeting got.

Bells tinkled over the door when we walked in. The wall of cold air was a welcome blast to the face. A voice called out from what appeared to be the front of the store, welcoming us in and letting us know we'd be assisted in a moment.

The minute I began looking around, I instantly fell in love with everything in the store. The racks were full of clothes I could picture in my closet and I was very particular about what I wore. My eyes were immediately drawn to an adorable ensemble with a washed out teal denim shirt with pearl snaps that was paired with a beige high-low tulle skirt with several layers of fabric. There was a wide brown braided leather belt at the waist.

As I was looking over one shoulder, a voice startled me from my other side. "Hi, I'm Becca. And this would look amazing on you," she said, as we both turned to stare at the outfit.

Smiling, I said, "It's amazing on the rack. Can I try it on? I'm Cassidy, by the way."

"Sure! You head to the fitting room," she gestured to the opposite side of the store with her head. "And I'll grab everything you need."

Thinking she forgot something, I asked, "Do you need my size?"

Beaming, Becca replied, "Nope, I think I've got it."

In the dressing room, I stripped out of my still sweat-dampened clothes and tried to fan myself as dry as I could before putting anything new on. I even sniffed my armpits to see how badly my deodorant needed refreshing. It was holding on, but barely.

A minute later, I heard Becca's friendly voice gushing about something before my mom's voice said, "Which is why we need to hurry. So thank you."

Rolling my eyes while holding back a groan, I poked my head out between the two long curtains and forced a smile. "Boo," I teased.

Becca handed me a hanger with all the pieces hanging on it. "So, you could wear the belt, but I think it would look so great if you tied the shirt in the front. But you can try it either way."

"Thanks," I said, reaching for the clothes. "I love that idea. Be out in a jiffy."

As I was snapping the pearl snaps on the shirt, I asked, "Becca, is this your store?"

You would have thought I had given her the greatest birthday gift she'd ever received by the excitement in her voice when she answered.

"It's all mine. And it's been such a great experience. I get to meet amazing people and learn so much about different styles and trends. I always thought I wanted to go to New York for fashion, but it just wasn't in the cards for me. One day I stumbled across this place with a For Sale sign in the window. It needed a lot of renovation, and I poured my heart and soul into making it the space it is now. It's been a crazy journey, but seeing my dream come to life has been worth every moment of struggle."

She was choked up in the end as though there was more to her story. I didn't ask, even though it was killing me not to.

"And now," she said as I stepped out from behind the curtains, "I've got a future country legend wearing my clothes."

My cheeks heated. "I don't know about that, but I love all of this," I said, gesturing to the clothes on my person.

Becca gasped in appreciation and clapped her hands. "Me, too! This is beyond perfect."

"OK, we'll take it and she'll wear it out," Mom said, sounding impatient. "We're going to be late and you still need to freshen up your face and hair."

"Oh! Use the powder room back there and I'll ring everything up," Becca offered as she pulled the last tag from the shirt's sleeve.

Mom slid my backpack from her shoulder that I hadn't seen her bring in - maybe she'd gone back out to get it.

"I'll go pay," she said, following Becca to the register while I found the powder room.

Three minutes later, I was hugging my new friend and thanking her for sharing part of her world with us.

"It was my pleasure, really. Now, you go kick butt and get famous and when you do, don't forget about the best little boutique in West Virginia."

With genuine reassurance, mom and I delivered the bags to the car then quickly found our way to the small cafe on the corner. We walked inside and tension stretched across my shoulders when I scanned the room and found a man staring with a crooked grin on his face. I'd never met this Mr. Wilder before, but I already had a bad feeling about him.

7

CASSIDY

As a hostess escorted us to the table, Mr. Wilder stood. He exuded an air of smug confidence that made my skin crawl. His overly white teeth gleamed as he extended a hand to my mom, his eyes never quite meeting hers and darting toward and lingering on me more than once. Mom clearly picked up on it, because her smile went from relaxed to forced.

There was one thing I could say for my mom and that was even if she pushed me to do more and be more, she protected me. This wouldn't be our first encounter with a smarmy professional and I was well aware if I stayed this path, it wouldn't be the last. I was extremely grateful that between her intuition and our experiences, I'd never had one of those experiences that you read about in a child celebrity's memoir years after it left them scarred for life.

Smiles plastered on, mom returned his handshake and said, "Mr. Wilder, Genevieve Stanton. It's a pleasure to meet you. This is my daughter Cassidy," she released his hand and gestured to me.

My show smile in place, I shook his hand and gave a small nod. Though there hadn't been many, I had learned in meetings like these it was best to look meek and ignorant. Those who were actually interested in me would draw me out, whereas those who had visions of dollar signs prancing around in their head would vaunt about themselves and drop names left and right. Mr. Wilder was the latter.

When he spoke, his voice oozed with self-importance. "Ah, Mrs. Stanton, the pleasure is all mine. I've been eager to meet you both. Please have a seat."

My unease grew as we exchanged pleasantries and ordered lunch. Mr. Wilder's gaze often strayed in my direction, and not in a way that made me feel comfortable. At one point I found myself discreetly snapping the next to the top snap on my shirt in hopes of diverting his attention away from the mild amount of skin that was visible. His comments became increasingly insincere and self-serving. He spoke about connections he had in the industry, dropping names with a smirk that suggested he believed his mere association was a golden ticket to success. I exchanged a quick, uncomfortable glance with my mom, who, to her credit, was trying to keep up appearances. She attempted more than once to steer the conversation.

During a lull in the conversation, Mr. Wilder leaned in a little too close, his tone turning more insistent. "Cassidy, I have a feeling you could be the next big thing. You have that star quality, that 'it' factor. I can make you a household name. All you need to do is trust me."

A shiver of discomfort crawled up my spine at his proximity. The way he said 'trust me' echoed ominously in my mind, making my stomach churn with unease. I instinctively inched back, trying to put some space between us, my hand balled into a fist around the napkin in my lap.

My discomfort deepened, and from the corner of my eye, I could see a similar unease in my mom's eyes. She had always pushed me to follow my dreams, but this, this encroachment of personal space and the underlying implication in his words, felt different, wrong somehow.

Internally, a battle raged. I wanted to get up and leave, to create some space between me and this guy who saw me as just a tool for his own benefit, or worse. Another part, the part molded by years of my mom's coaching, urged me to stay seated, to smile and nod, to be the compliant, mild-mannered daughter.

But every instinct screamed that this wasn't the path I wanted to tread. I realized, with a start, how far I had drifted from my own desires, caught in the current of my mother's aspirations for me. Mr. Wilder's words weren't just a proposition; they were a stark reminder of a life path laid out by others, a path I wasn't sure I wanted to walk.

Finally, my mom put her fork down and cleared her throat. "Mr. Wilder, I appreciate the opportunity to meet with you, but I think we may have different visions for Cassidy's future."

A look of annoyance replaced his cool demeanor. "You'd be making a big mistake by walking away, Mrs. Stanton."

I watched as my mom gathered her things, her determination unwavering. "Perhaps, but it's a mistake we're willing to make. Good day, Mr. Wilder."

Wadding my napkin and tossing it on the table, I followed my mom out the exit and to the corner of the sidewalk. We stopped only long enough for her to dig her keys from her purse and we wordlessly made our way around the building to the parking lot. Mom was rarely flustered visibly, so I knew if that's how I could see her, what was happening inside was probably worse.

I let out a relieved sigh, as if someone had lifted a heavy weight off of me. I knew my mom wanted nothing more than to see me succeed, but I knew it was a world filled with people like Mr. Wilder. And she wasn't always going to be there to mediate. It was this thought that sent a roil through my gut stronger than the one I'd felt in the café. I'd never navigated these situations before without her.

Finally, after we were situated inside the car, my mom broke the silence. Her voice was soft, and she sounded sad and apologetic. "Cassidy, I'm so sorry for putting you in a situation that made you uncomfortable."

I turned to look at her, my heart heavy with uncertainty. There were a lot of things I wanted to say to her, but I was afraid of hurting her or adding extra stress to the situation. But we'd never find the right time to talk about this. I knew that. Because it had the potential to change a lot of things. Digging my teeth into my lower lip, I felt the words bubbling to the surface.

Before I could make sure my internal filter was on, I said, "Mom, I know you want what's best for me, but I'm not sure if I want to pursue a professional music career. It's just not my dream."

She sighed as I watched her grip on the steering wheel tighten. "I understand that, Cassidy. I really do. But I want you to have something that's yours, something you love and can fall back on. I worry about you. I want you to have financial security, success, and happiness in the future and I think we need to start working toward that now. And you're so talented. It would be a shame for you to not use those talents to go far."

I nodded, my doubts weighing on me. "I get it, Mom. But I need to figure out what I truly want in life, what makes me happy. I don't want to compromise who I am for the sake of a career I'm not passionate about. Music is your dream for me. I want to chase dreams of my own. And right now, I don't even know what those are but I'd like to figure it out."

As I spoke those words, my heart ached with the intensity of a truth I had been hesitant to share. It wasn't easy to admit to my mom that the path she had set for me wasn't the one I envisioned for myself. I had always been a go with the flow kind of girl because there weren't many other options. While the thought of disappointing her filled me with dread, the idea of never being able to find my own path was worse.

I PERFORMED two sets that night, the first to a modest crowd and the second to a larger, more enthusiastic audience. Despite my initial reluctance, once I was on stage, the familiar rush of performing took over. The crowd's energy was infectious, and for a while, I forgot about the pressures and expectations. I was just a girl with a guitar, singing her heart out.

After the show, I met a few fans, signed some autographs, and posed for pictures. Mom was nearby, watching with pride. We headed back to our hotel room late that night, both exhausted but satisfied with the day's success.

The next morning, I woke early, the anticipation of the day's events pulling me out of bed. I had another performance in the afternoon, but the morning was free. I spent it by the pool with my headphones and a notebook, where I started writing out a potential plan for the future. It wasn't long before I discovered writing it down was the easy part.

8

CASSIDY

"The worst they could do was say no, right?" I murmured to myself, gathering my courage. It was evening, and the familiar routine was in full swing. I knew my mom would be sitting in her favorite chair by the window, reading the newspaper, a cup of tea beside her. My dad would be in his favorite chair, engrossed in an article about an ancient civilization or grading papers. This had been their evening ritual for as long as I could remember.

I had spent the last hour in my room practicing what I wanted to say. But the closer I got to the den, the more my confidence wavered. Hesitating at the entrance, I paused for a moment, scanning the room. The familiar sight of family photos on the walls, the soft ticking of the grandfather clock, and the comforting scent of my mom's tea somehow made it harder. I felt a knot in my throat as I stepped in.

"Mom? Dad?" My voice wavered slightly as I stepped into the den. Both heads turned in unison, and I saw the warmth in their eyes as they greeted me.

"Hey, sweetheart," my mom said, putting down her newspaper.

"How was rehearsal?" She asked, referring to the two-hour private violin lesson that took up most of my afternoons.

"It was fine," I replied, though my mind was far from my performance. "Can I talk to you both about something?"

My dad set aside his article, giving me his full attention. "Of course, Cassidy. What's on your mind?"

I took a deep breath, feeling my heart pound against my ribs. "I've been thinking a lot about what I want for my future. I love music, but I'm not sure if a professional career in it is what I truly want."

My mom's face softened, but I could see the worry lines deepening. "Cassidy, you don't have to decide everything right now. You're so young."

"I know," I said, my voice gaining strength. "But I've realized that I need to explore other interests and passions. I want to find out what makes me happy and see where that leads."

My dad leaned forward, his eyes filled with understanding. "It's good that you're thinking about this. It's important to follow your own path."

I felt a surge of gratitude for his support, but I knew I needed to be clear about my intentions. "I've decided to take some classes at the university. I haven't decided on anything specific yet, but I want to explore different subjects and see what piques my interest."

A moment of silence stretched between us as my parents absorbed my words. My mom was the first to speak. "But you're only sixteen, Cassidy. You'll be seventeen in a few months, but that's still so young. I just think you have so much talent in music. You don't need to go to college to do what you're already doing."

My dad nodded in agreement with me. "Cassidy has always been ahead of her peers, and more education can only benefit her. It's good for her to explore her options."

My mom frowned slightly, her worry lines deepening. "But what about your music career? I was actually thinking about booking you for the Harmony Heights Music Festival next summer. It's a huge event with a lot of industry professionals. It could be a big break for you."

I took a deep breath, trying to gather my thoughts. "Mom, I appreciate everything you've done for my music career, but I need to figure out what I want for myself. I don't want to commit to something that doesn't feel right to me, even if it's a big opportunity."

Her expression softened, but the concern in her eyes remained. "I just don't want you to miss out on something amazing. You have a gift, Cassidy. People dream of opportunities like this."

"I know, and I'm not saying I'll give up music entirely," I said, trying to reassure her. "I just want to explore other interests too. I want to see if there's more out there for me. Taking classes at the university can help me figure that out."

My dad chimed in, his voice calm and steady. "It's important for Cassidy to have the freedom to explore different paths. We should support her in finding what truly makes her happy."

My mom sighed, her grip on the edge of the table tightening. "I just worry about you. You're so young, and the world can be tough. I want to make sure you're safe and secure."

"I understand, Mom," I said softly. "But I need to do this. I need to find my own way, even if it's a little hazy right now."

She looked at me for a long moment, then finally nodded. "Alright, Cassidy. Just promise me you'll keep an open mind about your music career."

"I promise," I said, feeling a weight lift off my shoulders.

9

NASH

The two weeks I'd been leading the track at The Youth Club had felt more like a year. The kids were full of energy and excitement from the moment they arrived until the moment they left. The first time I mentioned it to my mom, she laughed and said, "Welcome to my last eighteen years."

While every day was a new experience and I learned something new either about the kids or myself, the feeling of uncertainty never quite went away. I felt like an imposter because I was definitely not qualified to be doing what I was doing. All I could do each and every day was cross my fingers and hope the plan I put together worked.

So far, I was pretty sure Mondays might kill me. The kids would come in after a weekend of summer fun and having probably eaten more junk food in two days than the entire week. You would think that they would come in exhausted and slow, but you would be very wrong. I learned after the second Monday to build in extra active games and activities for my younger groups to try and burn off some of the extra energy.

The first two groups were easy. I had them playing musical relays, which I had modified from years of baseball practices. I had as much fun watching as they had playing - maybe more. My third group was older and I'd struggled to connect with them, probably for that reason. It had only been a few years since I was trying to figure out life in the same ways they were.

Thankfully, Cody had come through more than once with suggestions that seemed to hit home for most of the group. Their favorite activity so far had been her idea to create playlists based on themes - emotions, musical style, rhythm styles, anything that connected multiple songs from different artists.

I was no music expert and hadn't kept up with a lot of popular music. I was content to keep my truck's radio tuned to 95.7 WSJK, All Country, All the Time. But these projects had pushed me outside of my wheelhouse and expanded my musical knowledge bank. It had also motivated me to try my hand at playing some newer and older songs on the guitar. I'd never admit it to Cody, but her help was making me better at a lot of things.

The last group was in a circle on the floor, deep in conversation about their most recent playlists after I'd issued the challenge to create a master song list and then turn it into a set list for a party. Their theme was "emotional rollercoaster" and from what I could keep up with, they were taking this fake assignment very seriously. Well, most of them were. One of the guys, Jet, had stayed on the outskirts of the group from the beginning.

Jet had a surliness about him, always the observer rather than a participant. He rarely spoke during discussions and seemed content to let the others take charge. His eyes were sharp, though, and you could tell he was always thinking about something, even when the group was discussing the latest pop song. I'd tried talking to him on more than one occasion, but he was usually out of the room pretty quickly when the track ended. I wasn't going to let that happen today.

When the track ended, signified by an old school bell ringing outside of the classrooms, I yelled instructions for wrapping up and putting everything away before leaving. Standing at the door, I was waiting for Jet when he approached.

"Hey, man. How's the playlist coming along?" I asked, nodding toward the group still milling about in the room.

Jet looked up, his sharp eyes meeting mine. Something like pain or defiance, perhaps danced briefly across his face before he masked it. "Fine," he said, an edge of wariness in his voice.

"You're a man of few words," I joked. "Is there anything you'd like to see us do that would make the track more interesting?"

His eyes darted to my guitar but just as quickly snapped them back to the floor in front of us. "Nah."

It was fast, but the way he looked at my guitar was definitely with curiosity, almost longing.

Jutting my chin toward the instrument, I asked, "You play?"

Jet's head twitched to the side, which I took to mean no.

"Wanna learn?" I asked.

This got his attention. His gaze locked with mine. He was clearly having a silent debate with himself.

Before he could decline I said, "We could hang out a few days a week after your last track, if it's alright with your mom and Mr. Muñoz and I'll teach you what I can."

For a moment, a spark of excitement appeared in his eyes, only to fade away.

"It doesn't matter. I don't have a guitar."

Whispering conspiratorially, I leaned forward and said, "What if I could find another guitar you could use?"

While hearing the hesitancy in his voice, I could feel the energy radiating from him. "I dunno. My mom probably won't let me. She's got a pretty tight schedule and all."

I had no idea who his mama was or what she did, but I respected a working mom's schedule. Even though my mom worked in the home, she ran a tight ship and she didn't put up with much that would throw it off kilter.

"Tell you what - I'll talk to Mr. Muñoz. With his approval, I'll talk to your mom. If we can work out a plan, we will. If we can't, I'll get creative. Sound like a deal?" I held out a hand for him to shake.

Jet studied my hand for several seconds before accepting it. "Deal."

"Alright," I said, giving him a clap on the shoulder. "Get going." Then to the room I said, "See y'all tomorrow. Now, get!"

When the last kid had left the room, I proceeded to pack up my own stuff. As I did, I thought through the offer I'd made Jet. If teaching him to play guitar would bring him out of his shell or help him feel like he was part of the group, or even boost his confidence a single ounce, I was all for it.

With my guitar case slung over my back and my backpack hooked on my shoulder, I turned off the light and pulled the door closed behind me. Looking around the large main room, I spotted Mr. Muñoz talking to one of the younger elementary kids. Watching the animated storytelling from a distance was entertaining. It had only been two weeks, but it had been eye opening for me. The kids that showed up every day each had stories that ranged from a healthy middle class two-parent home to a single parent home with questionable circumstances and every variety in-between. The thing I noticed, however, was that when the kids were here, none of that stuff mattered. They were all equals and felt comfortable within the walls of The Youth Club.

This was the part of the punishment Principal Johnson had doled out that day I'd been dreading. At the time, I would have chosen twelve hours of hard manual labor a day over this. Now, however, I was glad to have this consequence. Don't get me wrong, I'd go back and undo the stupid prank in a heartbeat. But this experience made up for it in spades. I couldn't remember a time I'd ever felt as competent and useful as I had in the last two weeks.

When the little girl skipped away from her conversation with Mr. Muñoz, I caught his attention and headed in his direction. He held a hand up and I slapped it. With a squeeze, we leaned in and bumped shoulders before taking a step back.

"Nash, my man, you're hangin' in there," his words were part statement, part question.

With a chuckle, I shook my head once and said, "So far, so good. I do have a question for you."

"Shoot," he said, his attention fully on me, though something told me he also had a pulse on every kid in the room.

"Jet Vargas," I said.

Mr. Muñoz's brows furrowed. "Is he giving you trouble?"

I hurried to say, "No. He seems like a good kid. But he's kind of a loner - always hanging back and not really participating."

Looking like he wanted to say something, Mr. Muñoz scratched the side of his face, then took a quick breath. "Jet's a cool kid if you can get to know him. But he comes from a pretty rough background. I'll just say that his mom does the best she can on her own since his dad's been out of the picture since the kid was born. She used to be a regular volunteer here until she started picking up more hours at work. Jet's never seemed to want to find a place here but he's also never been a problem. We've had those from time to time and Jet's not one of 'em." His eyes softened the more he talked about Jet.

I nodded as I listened. Jet didn't seem like the kind of kid that would cause trouble intentionally. I'd known those kids and done my best to steer clear of them. I brought enough of my own trouble with me most of the time. It sounded like Jet needed a place and a way to belong, and I had a gut feeling that my idea would work.

"Well, I talked to him today and it seems like he would be very interested in learning to play the guitar. I told him I'd talk to you and if you gave it the okay I'd talk to his mom or if you needed to then I'd ask you to do it. But I've got some free time in the afternoons that I could spend with him."

The man studied me, nodding slowly. "You trying to work off those service hours faster?" he asked.

"No, sir. And I don't want to charge, either. I just think he needs some kind of outlet and I could help him find it."

Still nodding, Mr. Muñoz narrowed his eyes and studied me a moment longer before his face broke into a smile. "I don't care what anyone says about you, Nash Montgomery, you're a good guy."

My face automatically mirrored his smile. "I don't know about that. I just know how it feels to have the need for validation and constantly thinking it needs to be chased and satisfied just for it to end in trouble. If I can help Jet then that's what I want to do."

"Alright, tell ya what - I'll talk to Jet's mom and see what she thinks. I don't have a problem with it. If we can work it out, I'll let you know," he said.

"Thanks, Mr. Muñoz," I said before extending my hand.

Returning the gesture, he said, "My pleasure, Nash. And for what it's worth, you're doing a great job. I've heard nothing but good things, even from the older crew. And they're pretty hard to impress."

Unable to hide the satisfaction his words brought, I said, "That means a lot, actually. Thanks. I'll see you tomorrow."

With a nod, I turned and moved toward the exit. The events of the day were playing on a loop in my head while I was also making a plan for how to approach the Jet situation. My experience with teaching was limited to teaching my sister, so I opted to use that as a solid starting point. But first, I was going to have to convince Cody to let me use her guitar, which might be harder than teaching a kid how to play it.

MY MIND WAS RACING with so many thoughts for the week ahead that I was surprised when I pulled up at the house. I needed to switch gears and go check with dad to see what he needed me to do, but first, I went straight for Cody's room.

The muffled sound of Faith Hill singing came through the closed door. I knocked a few times and waited. A few seconds later, the music quieted, and I heard Cody yell, "Come in!"

She looked up from the middle of her bed with a book in her lap.

"Hey, Creep," she said, tossing me an amused sisterly look.

"Hey, Nerd," I shot back with the same affection as I stood in her doorway. "I need a favor."

Her eyebrows raised. "Uh oh, that sounds ominous."

I chuckled. "Nah, nothing like that. I need to borrow your guitar,"

I said flatly, not wanting to give her any reason to say no. If she thought for a minute I was trying to get away with something or do anything that would risk her precious guitar, she'd shut me down immediately.

Cody studied me as she closed her book and swung her legs over the side of her bed. She stood and walked to the corner where the vintage acoustic sat propped against the wall in its case. She picked it up and walked it to me and held it out for me to take.

This felt too easy, which made me want to question her. But I reached out and placed my hands on the case to take possession of it, anyway.

"Why?" she asked, not releasing the instrument. Her eyes bore into mine.

Without looking away, I answered, "I offered to give a kid lessons."

Her hard gaze softened. If I had to guess, she was remembering when she'd begged me to give her lessons and it had been the best worst experience. I'd barely had any idea what I was doing, but I couldn't say no to the pitiful doe eyes that had blinked up at me. We'd worked together for months, constantly going back and forth between getting along and me wanting to pummel her with the guitar because she cried every time I'd correct her. I'd get so frustrated that I'd walk away before we'd finished what we'd started.

After several months, I heard this perfect melody being strummed and a familiar voice singing along coming from Cody's bedroom. Come to find out, my beautiful darling sister had been teaching herself to play well before she ever asked me to teach her and had been stringing me along in an effort to spend time with, as well as torture, her big brother. Needless to say, our next lesson became a very big lesson in messing with the bull and winding up with its horns. I corrected and over-corrected every little thing she did, even if she was already doing it right until she finally blew up at me. Once the truth had made its way into the open, we each stubbornly went our separate and silent ways.

It took a couple of days, but the first time I teased her about doing something just to spend time with me, everything had gone back to normal. The first time she asked to sit and play together, our entire relationship had changed. She became as much my friend as my sister. That's why I was pretty sure she'd let me borrow the guitar our grandfather had gifted her that had once been his own. But because it was so special, I may have also had a small sliver of doubt.

"If you promise to bring her home everyday, she's yours - to borrow."

She didn't need to add that last part for me, but I got it. I leaned forward and kissed her on top of her head before taking the case from her grip. "Thanks, Nerd. I think the kid just needs something to make him feel like he has a purpose, you know? And if learning to play the guitar helps, I can at least offer him that."

She took a step back into her room. Her eyes looked a little shiny, even though she was smiling at me. "You're something else, Nash. I think this Youth Club thing has been good for you." She paused, still looking at me like I could have possibly hung the moon. "Have you decided what your major is gonna be in the fall?"

It wasn't the first time the subject had come up, but in the past I would always dismiss it and mention that I could declare General Studies since I was going to college to play baseball. This time, however, her question gave me pause, and I wasn't sure why.

Before I could ask her a reason for bringing it up, she said, "Because honestly, even if you are kind of a jerk sometimes, you're a really good teacher."

With a quick spin on her heel, she headed back to her bed, where her book was lying in wait. I stood frozen in my spot at her door, my gaze becoming unfocused as her words bounced around inside my head.

"Huh," was the only response I made.

Cody's voice cut through my thoughts. "You good?"

Snapped back to the moment, I said, "Uh, yeah. Thanks for letting me borrow this."

I slapped a hand on the hard case and Cody's tone sounded more like our mom's when she was serious. "Hey, be nice to Belle. And close the door on your way out."

With a mock salute, I backed out of her room, pulling the door closed as I went.

I left Cody's room to drop the guitar off in my room and change into work clothes, her words still heavy on my mind. Her comment about me teaching had struck a chord with me. I'd never really thought of myself as a teacher, but maybe The Youth Club was benefitting more than just the kids who attended.

Shaking off my introspection, I headed outside to find my dad. He was in the garage, surrounded by tools and spare car parts. The old Chevy he'd been restoring for years stood there, a labor of love that had consumed much of his free time. It was a project he'd started with my grandpa, and he worked on it occasionally as a way to keep their bond alive even after he'd passed away.

"Hey, Dad," I said, as I walked into the garage.

Dad looked up from under the hood, a grease-covered wrench in his hand. "Hey there, Nash. What can I do for you?"

"Just checkin' in to see what you need me to do this afternoon," I said, leaning down and retrieving what appeared to be a runaway socket.

The sound of metal colliding with metal as he fiddled with an unseen part, coupled with the rhythmic oscillation of the whirring fan in the corner of the room, had an almost hypnotic effect. Combined with the heat, I was immediately overcome with a rush of memories from the summers I spent watching Dad and Granddad work on this same old car. It never occurred to me until after we lost Granddad and I was old enough to help work on the car that this car was mostly symbolic. There was probably enough knowledge about cars in the family to do minimal work, but never actually fix it without professional intervention.

When he finished turning whatever bolt he'd been working on, he stood and wiped his hands on an old grease rag that he'd pulled from his pocket. "It's too hot to do much right now. I thought I'd take a look at this old thing and maybe take a drive into town to look at some new feed Stan got in last week. I guess that means you're off the hook until evenin' chores."

I nodded and stuffed my hands into my pockets, looking around the old building, wondering just how many memories the walls held. The ones I knew about alone were too many to name.

"Somethin' on your mind, son?" Dad asked as he let the hood slam close and proceeded to collect his tools to store them until his next venture out here.

Still gazing around the room, I asked, "Do you think I'm ready to be an adult?"

"Well now," he continued to mill about, putting wrenches and sockets into their cases. "I'm not sure anyone is ever ready to be an adult. Why do you ask?"

I scuffed my boot on the garage floor, my thoughts jumbled. "It's just that college is right around the corner, and it feels like everything's changing so fast and there's so much I don't know."

Dad looked at me with a reassuring smile. "You know, the best way to learn is by doing. Kind of like how we've done with this car. Granddad and I had no idea what we were doin' when we first started tinkerin' with it. We replaced the starter like crazy at first. Then we realized it wasn't even a starter issue to begin with. Just like that, you're gonna make mistakes, but that's part of growing up. And it's okay not to have all the answers right now."

Hearing his perspective filled me with relief. "Thanks, Dad."

He finished storing the tools before walking over and putting a hand on my shoulder. "Anytime, son. Now, let's go wash up and see if there's any pie left before I head into town."

Two slices of pie later, I was headed for a sugar-induced stupor which I was well and happy to be falling into until the familiar sound of a received message echoed from my computer. Instantly I was awake and automatically smiling. Only one person ever sent me messages on OurSpace and she was the reason I rarely logged out anymore. Though, that had been how Jake had stumbled across my music and in turn I'd wound up volunteered for the role as an inexperienced music teacher.

@Wildfire: I did it. I told my mom that music was not my dream.

I couldn't believe what I was reading. It had been a few weeks since she'd confessed her greatest fear was disappointing her mom, and I hadn't brought it up again because I wasn't sure if it would have been appropriate. Now that she had, I was here for it.

@GuyWithGuitar: Oh wow! How did that go over?

@WILDFIRE: About like ice skating on JellO. But it could have gone worse. And we've talked about it a few more times. I think we're making progress.

@GUYWITHGUITAR: That's great. Have you made any plans?

@WILDFIRE: As a matter of fact, I have. AND my parents think it's a good plan for right now. I'm so excited I can hardly stand it.

@GUYWITHGUITAR: Are you gonna leave me hangin?

@WILDFIRE: Well........ I'm going to enroll at the local college and start taking some classes. My dad is a big fan of education and I think it will help me figure out what I want to do with the future.

@GUYWITHGUITAR: Aren't you 16? Don't tell me you're one of those super smart kids with perfect grades that graduated high school early AND you have the musical talent of some kind of prodigy.

· · ·

@WILDFIRE: *OK, I won't tell you either of those things.*

WHAT THE HECK? Was she saying that she was a super smart kid and a musical prodigy? I laughed out loud.

@GuyWithGuitar: *So you are smart and talented. Do you also rescue puppies from burning buildings?*

@WILDFIRE: *I haven't yet but I would.*

@GuyWithGuitar: *Of course you would. So college classes. That sounds like a really good plan. I actually head out for school in a couple months. I haven't decided if I'm excited, terrified, or both.*

I had never actually said it to anyone before. The idea of going to college scared me to death. At home, I had boundaries and parameters and accountability, and I still screwed things up regularly. Could I trust myself to move hours away from home, be on my own, and stay out of trouble? And what was I going to do other than play baseball and hope I got drafted sooner than later? I knew the chances of that happening at all were small, but what else was there?

It was starting to occur to me that while *Wildfire* had been living in restrictive confines, I'd been the opposite. I was like a ship bouncing from wave to wave and there was no captain aboard, but I was always tethered to the dock and never able to get too far from my bearings.

@Wildfire: *What scares you most about it?*

Was I actually going to tell her? I hesitated, staring at the blinking cursor on my screen, unsure if I was ready to open up about my fears. I reasoned that she'd already been open with me about what she was afraid of. There was little to lose if I did the same.

@GuyWithGuitar: Honestly, I don't trust myself to be on my own and outside of baseball, I don't know what I'm supposed to do with my life.

My palms were sweating just from typing the words. This nice, really smart, and talented girl was going to think I was a complete loser.

@Wildfire: What is it about yourself you don't trust?

That question felt like a double-edged sword.

@GuyWithGuitar: It's not that I think I'll intentionally mess things up, but I've grown up with people around who made it their mission to keep me in line. If you take away baseball, which has been my anchor, I'm not sure how well I'd navigate life without those familiar boundaries. The fear is more about the unknown and whether I have what it takes to handle it.

And that was the long and the short of it. Reading it back to myself, I dragged a hand down my face. My pulse was pounding inside my head. Why I cared what a person hundreds of miles away thought about me seemed illogical, but for some reason, her opinion mattered. And I'd just admitted that I was incapable of growing up. I groaned.

@Wildfire: I think it's pretty normal to feel that way. The idea of the future not being planned is scary for most people. But the fact you can put words to it is a pretty good indication that you're braver than you think. Now you'll be aware that you want boundaries and you can surround yourself with people who will hold you to them.

Holy smokes, she was something else.

@GuyWithGuitar: Wow. Thanks. I guess you're right. And dang girl, you really are smart.

@Wildfire: Nah. I just have faith that a guy with no experience who took on teaching music to a bunch of kids and has survived this long will be able to survive anything. In the words of the great Sarah Belle Reed, You just have to be brave enough to start the journey.

@GuyWithGuitar: It's terrifying every single day.

. . .

@Wildfire: Yet, here you are.

@GuyWithGuitar: Here I am.

Warmth filled me as I thought about her words. I was thinking about her words hours after we'd signed off, wondering when I'd get to talk to her again.

10

NASH

Six more weeks passed, and I finally felt like I might have the hang of the job. The kids were learning new things about music. I was learning new things about myself.

I'd also been giving guitar lessons to Jet for four weeks, and his progress was starting to show - both on the guitar and with the group. During those weeks, I had come to understand that Jet's family dynamic was far from typical. He was a sixteen-year-old with a father who had been in prison since before the day Jet was born. I didn't know all the details, but Jet's mom had been a single parent for as long as he could remember. What I did know was that I'd enjoyed watching Jet's journey of coming out of his shell. Even still, I was hesitant to put him on the spot because on the few occasions I had, he'd clammed up or shut down. But I had an announcement today that I hoped he would be excited about.

Mr. Munoz had suggested we host a summer showcase for the performance tracks. The younger groups had been ecstatic and ready to start planning their performances down to their outfits on the spot. I had to reel them in a little and suggest we focus on the performance piece first.

When I told the older group about the showcase, there was a hum of excitement underscored by uncertainty in the room. Jet, in particular, seemed conflicted. His fingers fiddled with the strings of his hoodie, and he avoided eye contact.

After I finished explaining the options for the showcase, I looked at Jet and asked, "So, what do you think? Are you up for it?"

He hesitated for a moment, and I could see the internal struggle in his eyes. Finally, he spoke, his voice soft and unsure. "I don't know. Performing in front of people seems like a bigger step than I can take. I literally just started learning how to play the thing," he threw an arm in the direction of my guitar.

Understanding, I nodded. "I get it. It can be nerve-wracking, especially when you're not used to it. But you've got talent, and I believe in you. You don't have to do it alone." I stopped and thought about it for a moment, then asked, "How about we do it together? You and me, a guitar duo. What do you say?"

Jet's eyes widened, and he looked at me with an expression of surprise and hope. "You'd do that? Play with me?"

I smiled and clapped a hand on his shoulder. "Of course, I would. We'll practice together, and I'll be right there beside you on that stage. We'll support each other."

The whole group jumped in with their voices of encouragement and reassurance, telling Jet it would be great if he'd play for the group.

I watched his cheeks tinge pink at the attention before his hesitant smile made an appearance. "Alright, I'll do it," he agreed right before the entire group huddled around and cheered, some offering him high fives and slaps on the shoulder.

After several seconds of the noise level rising, I broke through it with an ear-piercing whistle. The room silenced, as it usually did. The group knew it meant something new was about to happen.

"OK, we're ready to start making a plan. Let's first decide what we want to work on as a group so Jet and I can work on the accompaniment. Once we have that nailed down, y'all can start deciding how you want to perform for the remainder. The catch is, if you perform solo, you can't perform in a group other than the full group because we don't have the stage for that long. So keep that in mind going forward. Now, what song do you think we could take for a ride together?"

The kids spent the next twenty minutes creating a list of potential songs. I'd loved watching them learn to work as a group and problem solve on their own. I only offered up suggestions or intervened when discussions took a nosedive, which had decreased significantly in the last several weeks.

Once they had a master list, one of the girls, Kiera, spoke up. "We need to narrow this list down so we can take a vote. I think we should come up with a theme for all of our performances so that we have kind of a streamlined thing."

It had been a brilliant idea, and the group seemed to agree, so they set off on making yet another decision. I stood back and watched, amazed how seamlessly this whole summer had been. I mean, there had been times where the kids were off their rockers or we'd had to pivot here and there or when the plans I thought were good went horribly wrong. But overall, in every track, I felt like I had been privy to watching a seed planted, watered, and bloom. These kids impressed me and it had excited me to no end to have been part of it.

Kent suggested, "How about we go with a 'Timeless Classics' theme? We choose songs that have stood the test of time, and we put our own twist on them. It's a theme that can give us more choices, and each of us can bring our unique styles to the table."

Kiera countered, "We don't need more choices, we need fewer choices. So, maybe let's pick a decade and then we can choose songs from any genre that fits the timeless classic theme?"

Kent was satisfied, as were the other members of the group. By the end of the hour, the decade chosen had been the 1980s and the group would be singing *Don't You (Forget About Me)* by Simple Minds. Honestly, I was impressed and relieved. I was impressed that the song had even made the list, but it had more to do with a lot of them having parents familiar with the song. I was relieved because it was an easy enough song that Jet and I should have no problem making it work.

When the bell outside the room trilled, there were actual groans of disappointment that the hour was over. It made me feel good that they enjoyed being here, especially given that many of them didn't have a choice.

"Y'all did great today. We'll figure out the rest tomorrow and start working on where to find music so if you have ideas for that, bring 'em with you. Now clean up and clear out!" I teased.

Once the room had emptied, Jet headed for the chairs we sat in every afternoon and picked up the guitar. I retrieved my borrowed guitar from the storage closet in the back of the room and joined Jet at the music stand.

"I'm glad you're going to be part of the group performance," I said, while arranging the pages on the music stand.

"You really think I'm up for it?" he asked. "I mean, I just started and I don't even know the song they voted on."

His tone was full of self-doubt, and I could feel him wanting to retreat.

"Dude, I've heard the song maybe three times. I don't really know it either but we'll figure it out together. But let's not worry about that right now. Let's work on what we do know and make sure we have these basics in place, yeah?"

His smile, though small, along with a nod of agreement, was like winning first place in any championship. He'd come a long way in such a short amount of time, and he was good. He was really good. I just hadn't been able to convince him of that yet. First things first, we needed to work on his confidence. And I was certain we were on the right path for doing just that.

After the hour was up, I nudged Jet and said, "Tell me you can feel the difference from when you first started?"

He stared at his hands on the guitar and huffed. "I can feel the difference." He almost said something more, but stopped himself. I let the silence hang between us until he spoke again. "And I like the way I feel when I play."

My throat burned with emotion. This kid was super cool, and he didn't even know how great he was. "I'm so proud of you, Jet. You're doing great. At this rate, you'll be better than me by next year. You'll have to start giving me lessons."

Jet rolled his eyes. He thought I was kidding. I was completely serious, but he didn't have to believe me right now. One day he'd see it for the truth it was. In the meantime, I'd keep pouring into him and hoping he'd keep receiving it. If nothing else, he'd end this summer knowing someone was proud of him and believed in him and hopefully believing in himself.

11

NASH

The kids had poured their hearts and souls into planning and rehearsing over the last four weeks. I was pretty sure the entire town was planning to be at the showcase. I'd never seen that many chairs packed into the auditorium. Mr. Muñoz kept saying the crowd was going to be unprecedented. His excitement was contagious.

On the last two days of the camp, after all the kids had gone home, the track leaders stayed and transformed the building from a basic community education space into an art gallery, a photo gallery, a museum, and a performance theater. They used photographs or even art pieces to represent every track. In every single one, there was evidence of growth and change. I had a feeling that if a mirror could see inside me, there would be proof that I'd changed, too. This summer had stretched me in unexpected ways, pushing the boundaries of what I thought I was capable of.

If life was a bike with training wheels, I'd say I was probably ready to take the training wheels off, but with the knowledge that I'd likely crash the first time or two I got on the bike. That's some pretty good progress, considering the beginning of summer felt more like riding a tricycle than a bike.

I walked down the hallway to the room that had become my home away from home this summer. My mind drifted to Jet, who had come so far during this program. At first, he was hesitant and on the fringes of the group. His guitar skills and confidence, however, had skyrocketed. He went from a shy introvert to confidently strumming alongside us on stage.

Jet had told me earlier in the week that his mom and even his grandmother, who rarely left the house, were coming to see him play. When I think about how I ended up here, I can't help but appreciate the irony. The chaos of the last week of school was not something I want to relive. But witnessing transformations like Jet's? It made those missteps worth it.

I was tuning my guitar when Mr. Muñoz appeared at the door and knocked on its frame. I looked up and gave him a friendly nod.

"Hey, Nash. You got a minute?" he asked, walking into the room.

I pulled my guitar strap over my head, placing the instrument on its stand before meeting him halfway. "Sure, what's up?"

"I just wanted to tell you how proud and impressed I am with what you did this summer. I know you weren't here voluntarily, but you stepped up and took on a role that was never intended for you, and you did it so well. You need to know you surpassed all expectations. I'd love for you to consider coming back next summer."

I had to clear some wayward emotions from my throat before I could speak. "Thank you, Mr. Muñoz," I managed to say. "I never thought I'd end up here, but it turned out to be an experience I needed, even if I didn't know it at the time."

He clapped a hand on my shoulder. "Life has a funny way of taking us to unexpected places. Your impact on these kids, especially Jet, has been remarkable. You have a gift, Nash, and I hope you continue to share it."

His words lingered as he left the room, leaving me standing there, absorbing the magnitude of it all. As I finished tuning my guitar, I couldn't shake the feeling that this wasn't just the end of a summer program.

The stage was set, literally and metaphorically. The kids were trickling in as the showcase was about to begin. I pulled myself together and greeted them as they arrived, feeling a renewed sense of purpose.

EACH GROUP DID an amazing job as they danced, sang, acted their hearts out, putting on show after show for what had to be 99% of the entire town. My older track was filling the stage for their final number. I had Cody's guitar strapped over my shoulder and was looking for Jet. I had handed him my guitar ten minutes earlier, and he seemed nervous but ready to go. Now he was nowhere to be seen in the gymnasium.

I whispered to Mr. Muñoz to keep an eye out as I went to search for Jet. It wasn't a long search as I heard the sound of strings being strummed rhythmically from down the hall. Making my way to the classroom, I found Jet with his back to the door, guitar in his lap, and his entire body moving to the beat of the song.

"You know," I said, causing Jet to jump at the sound of my voice. "That would sound great with a small choir of your peers singing along. Don't get me wrong, it sounds great, now. But think how awesome it would be to have backup singers."

Jet didn't move from his seat or turn to face me. Instead, his head fell, and he mumbled, "I don't think I can do this."

I walked into the room, pulled out, and sat in one of the chairs that had clearly been made for a six-year-old. "What's holding you back, Jet?" I asked.

"What if I get out there and forget the entire song?" he asked.

Shrugging, I said, "I'll keep playing. What if I get out there and forget the entire song?"

"You won't," his voice was quiet.

"You won't either," I encouraged.

"How do you know?" he asked.

"Because you're smart, you've practiced, you have worked really hard, and all of that hard work is going to pay off. You've trusted me to teach you this far. Can you trust me one more time?" I asked.

Jet huffed, lifting his head to meet my gaze. There was hope being overshadowed by doubt in his eyes as he scanned my face, probably looking for some kind of certainty. After the briefest of moments, he let out a resigned breath.

"I guess." His voice was low, almost a whisper, echoing the tangle of nerves and bravery he was trying to muster.

I gave his shoulder a quick shake. "Good. Now, what if I get out there and forget the entire song?" I asked.

One side of his mouth quirked up. "I'll keep playing."

With a nod, I said, "Good answer. Let's go."

Lined up in two rows, the group was smiling and looked excited to be on the stage. Jet and I took our seats to one side. I arranged the chord sheets on the stand before tapping my foot six times. At the cue, Jet and I started strumming our respective guitars. After a few bars, Kiera began singing the first verse. The group quickly joined in soon after, and halfway through the song, people throughout the gym started clapping, sometimes on the beat and sometimes off.

I hazarded a glance at Jet, hoping it hadn't thrown him off. He wasn't even looking at the music stand. Instead, he was watching the strings and bouncing along to the music.

As the last notes echoed through the gym, applause erupted, echoed around the space. The kids beamed with accomplishment, and I saw a shy smile on Jet's face. It was a victory. Not just because he made it through the performance, but because he had tackled something he probably never dreamed of doing.

Jet was handing my guitar back when a voice called out his name. A woman rushed toward us, her radiant smile suggesting she was Jet's mom. Beside her, an elderly lady, one I assumed was his grandmother, brimming with pride.

"You were amazing!" his mom beamed, pulling him into a tight embrace.

Jet, both stunned and pleased, murmured into her shoulder, "Thanks, Mom."

His grandmother, eyes brimming with joy and admiration, shuffled forward. "I'm so proud of you," she rasped, extending a shaky arm. Jet responded with a gentle hug.

"Thank you, Grandma," he said, his voice rough with emotion.

Turning to me, Jet's mom asked, "Are you Nash?"

"Yes ma'am. Nash Montgomery," I replied, offering a handshake.

Instead, she enveloped me in a hug, whispering, "Thank you," her gratitude radiating from within.

I patted her back, understanding her emotions. Watching Jet transform into a more mature, skilled, and confident individual had been remarkable.

"It was my pleasure, Ms. Vargas," I said as she stepped back, wiping away a tear.

"Jet's an incredible kid. I'd like to think we had a great summer together," I turned to Jet, who now looked shy under the attention. "We made a pretty good team, right?"

Jet's cheeks flushed pink. "Yeah. Thanks, Nash."

"You bet," I said with a wink. Turning, I added, "It was really nice meeting you, ladies. If you'll excuse me, I'm gonna go put these guitars away. I'm really glad y'all got to be here for this."

I'D STAYED at the club building well after the last family had gone home to help the other workers clean up, break down the stage, and return the chairs to their storage closets. The last song the kids had sung was stuck in my head, and I drummed my fingers on the steering wheel to the beat.

As I pulled into the driveway, the porch light welcomed me home. Stepping through the front door, I was greeted by the scent of warm, sweet peaches and cinnamon. With a deep inhale, I closed my eyes and smiled. It was just one of the familiar things about home that I loved and would miss in a few weeks.

Mom was always baking and playing it off like she wasn't specifically thinking of one of us while doing it. But it was clear what she was up to, especially when she went out of her way to keep other members of the family away until the intended recipient showed up. Which was the scene I stumbled upon as I entered the kitchen and saw her swatting my father's hand, holding a fork over what looked like a pan of peach cobbler.

The sound of the door caught their attention, causing my dad to drop his fork into the pan. Cody was sitting at the table and laughed as my mom huffed and rolled her eyes before wiping her hands on a kitchen towel. She batted Dad's hand again as he reached for the fork.

"Harold, leave it," she scolded.

With a roll of his eyes, he stepped away from the counter and followed Mom in my direction.

Mom's arms opened, and I stepped into her embrace and wrapped my arms around her shoulders.

"What's all this about?" I asked, taking in the scene.

Pulling my face to hers, she kissed me on the cheek, then said, "We are so proud of you."

When Mom stepped to the side, my dad stepped forward and wrapped an arm around me and slapped my back and held on for several seconds before clearing his throat and releasing me.

Cody had popped up from her seat and swooped in when Dad moved and threw her arms around my middle. "Oh my gosh, Nash, those kids were so cute. I can't believe you taught them all of that," she gushed.

Choking out a laugh, a full gamut of emotions rolled through me. "I didn't teach them all of that. They were all pretty smart and talented on their own. I just organized the chaos. That's all."

Mom had retreated to the counter and was fishing the rogue fork from the pan where Dad had dropped it as she said, "Don't discount yourself, Nash. Every parent that knew who you were stopped and told us how much their child had learned and that you'd been at the center of it. So, stop downplaying the work you did and hear us when we tell you that we love you, we are proud of you."

This wasn't the first time they'd told me they were proud of me. I'd heard it my whole life for my academics and sports. It had always meant something to me because I knew they were not just saying it for the sake of saying it. But this time, it hit differently. Maybe it was because the actions I'd taken that had landed me at The Youth Club in the first place had been reason enough for them to be disappointed in me. I'd let that idea eat me up every time I'd been awake at 4:00 A.M. and was stressing about earning my way back into their good graces. And somehow they were still proud of me.

The kitchen felt warm, not just from the heat of the oven, but from the love surrounding me. I sank into a chair at the table, surrounded by the familiar faces that had witnessed all my ups and downs. Cody perched on the edge of her seat, her eyes reflecting genuine admiration. Dad leaned against the counter, a small but proud smile etched across his face, and Mom, with her hands occupied by washing the rogue fork, beamed with maternal love and pride.

"Thanks, y'all," I managed to get out, my voice cracking a bit. Cody laughed, and even Dad tried to hide a smile.

"You did something great this summer, Nash. Don't forget that," Dad said, his tone sincere.

Mom approached with a slice of peach cobbler on a plate, pushing it toward me. "Now, have a seat and enjoy this. You've earned it."

As I savored the sweetness of the peaches, the room filled with casual conversation, mostly about the kids and their performances. Any doubts about the future I'd had dimmed just a little in the light of my family's encouragement.

I'd offered to help Mom wash the dishes and though she refused my help, I grabbed a towel to help dry them. She watched me dry the last plate and said, "You know, no matter where you go or what you do, we'll always be here for you - to support you, encourage you, whatever you need."

It was like she knew exactly what I'd needed to hear. The words settled within me, grounding me in the present while giving me hope for the future. I nodded appreciatively, feeling a deep sense of gratitude for everything that had transpired over the summer and for the people I called family and for this place I called home.

12

CASSIDY

It took me exactly two weeks to confirm that my idea to go to school was simultaneously the best and worst idea I'd ever had. Who knew there were so many classes and majors to choose from?

Sitting in the middle of my bed, I flipped through the massive course catalog, my head spinning with the endless possibilities. I wanted to study something related to music, but not just music. Digital Media Production had caught my eye, but even within that field, the options seemed limitless.

"Introduction to Sound Design," "History of Music Production," "Advanced Mixing Techniques"—these were all exciting, but there were so many others that I couldn't help but laugh. Some classes were so obscure and oddly specific that I wondered who came up with them.

"Underwater Acoustics: The Sound of the Ocean"—I mean, really? Is that even a thing? Then there was "The Art of Foley: Creating Sound Effects from Scratch," which actually sounded fun but also a bit like playing pretend for grown-ups.

Every time I thought I had it figured out, another class would catch my eye. I sighed, scrolling through yet another page of options.

"Okay, Cassidy," I muttered to myself, "you need a plan. Let's narrow this down."

Deciding to start with the basics, I signed up for "Introduction to Digital Media Production." That seemed like a solid foundation. But I couldn't resist adding one more class that intrigued me called "A Historical Perspective on Music and Technology". It promised a fascinating look at how technology had shaped music over the decades, and it felt like the perfect blend of my interests.

I stared at the registration form in front of me; the lines blurred slightly from both excitement and nervousness. Taking a deep breath, I picked up my pen and started filling in my details.

First course: "Introduction to Digital Media Production." I carefully printed the course code next to the name, feeling a rush of determination.

Second course: "Historical Perspectives on Music and Technology." Just writing the title gave me a thrill.

I double-checked my entries, making sure everything was correct. Satisfied, I slipped the form into my bag, ready to take it to the administration office first thing in the morning.

The excitement bubbling inside me needed an outlet, and I knew just where to go. Logging on to OurSpace, I found *GuyWithGuitar* online. He was always good for a conversation.

@Wildfire: Tell me something good about your day.

@GuyWithGuitar: I saw a squirrel steal an entire sandwich on my way across the greens today. Hi, by the way.

@Wildfire: How much you want to bet it was peanut butter and jelly? Hello to you.

@GuyWithGuitar: I'd bet the farm. Now you tell me something good.

I smiled, my fingers flying over the keyboard.

· · ·

@Wildfire: I just filled out my registration form for college!

@GuyWithGuitar: That sounds awesome! I'm really happy for you.

My tummy did a funny little flip reading his message. I didn't have close friends because I hadn't attended school anywhere and my weekends were always filled with shows or wedding performances. But it never failed that when I got to talk to *Guy*, I felt like I was hanging out with my best friend.

@Wildfire: Thanks! Do you need to go or do you want to hang out?

@GuyWithGuitar: I have a few minutes before I need to leave for practice.

A grin worked its way on my lips. We chatted right up until time for him to head out, talking about adjusting to new schedules and routines. He confessed he was tired and feeling some pressure from his coaches to focus more on baseball and less on academics. It appeared we both had found ourselves facing some steep hills recently. Before we signed off, he sent a message that had me both feeling surprised and excited.

@GuyWithGuitar: I've got to run. Do you think we could do this again?

My heart raced involuntarily and my head felt a little swimmy from the rush it gave me, but nothing was going to stop me from responding.

. . .

@WILDFIRE: Absolutely. I'll stay logged in and you can message me later with your schedule.

WITH THAT, he said his goodbye and logged off.

A sigh escaped as the thought of talking to *Guy* again made me giddy. Despite not knowing his real name, I felt comfortable with him in a way I hadn't with anyone else. It was ironic that I considered him a real friend even though we were total strangers. But I didn't care. Our connection was something new, something that felt truly mine, and that made it special.

13

NASH

"Let's go!" Coach Edwards yelled as he clapped wildly and motioned for my teammate, who also happened to be my roommate, to head to home plate. I was waiting, poised to catch the throw coming in from the second baseman. The ball smacked the web of my glove right before I swung my arm down and tagged the runner sliding into the plate.

"Nice snag!" Coach grunted, slapping me on the shoulder. "Better run faster next time, Cubby," he teased before offering a hand and yanking my teammate up from the dirt.

"Alright, bring it in, guys!" Coach Edwards hollered, signaling the end of another scorching baseball practice. It had been a brutally hot practice, and I was feeling every degree of it. To say I was glad to see practice come to an end was an understatement. My mind and body were both drained as I'd spent the last three and a half hours trying to keep my attention on baseball and not the distraction of thoughts about a stranger from the other side of a computer screen.

I'd struggled to engage with the end of practice talk because my mind constantly wandered to the conversation I'd had with *Wildfire* before heading to the field.

The conversation was still occupying my thoughts as we headed for the dugout to grab our gear even though I should have been thinking about the Biology test I needed to study for before tomorrow. A slap on the back from our second baseman, Jason, a stocky guy with a perpetual grin, pulled me from all my thoughts.

"You heard about the party tonight, right?" he asked, eyes gleaming with anticipation.

I nodded, feigning a casual demeanor, though my curiosity gnawed at me. From what I'd heard, a party off campus could mean anything from a bonfire in someone's backyard to an underground gig in a rundown warehouse.

"Gonna be poppin'. You coming?" Chance, the first baseman, who showed up on my other side, tossed the question my way, his enthusiasm contagious.

The idea of letting loose after a grueling practice had its appeal. There was a brief moment of hesitation as I looked over towards the dugout. The thought of talking to *Wildfire* again tempted me to decline. Then, with a nod, I replied, "Yeah, count me in."

The guys exchanged approving looks, and Jason filled me in on the details — some house off campus, music, girls, everything needed to relax after the long day. A knot of warning that I recognized well formed in my stomach and lingered throughout the day.

NAVIGATING THE CROWD, I pushed my way through the mass of partygoers, the music's deep bass thumping in sync with my heartbeat. Wrapped in the noise and the heat of so many bodies, I felt out of place. "Should I even be here?" I wondered, scanning the crowd for any face I might recognize. Back in high school, parties were never my thing. I had friends who lived for nights like this, but I usually stayed clear. The only reason I was here tonight was that it seemed like the thing to do for the team.

Jason emerged from the crowd with a wide grin. "Nash, my man, you made it!" he exclaimed, slapping my back with a force that almost knocked the wind out of me.

"Yeah," I replied, forcing a smile. The place was crackling with energy, but I felt completely out of place. I never really got the whole party scene, preferring the straightforward adrenaline rush of the baseball field or a quiet evening at home with my guitar.

Oblivious to my discomfort, Jason nudged me forward. "Come on, let's get into it. This is gonna be epic!" he said, his excitement clear in his wide eyes and eager stance.

I followed him, trying to look as if I was at ease. Deep down, though, I felt like a stranger in a foreign land. The loud music, the laughter, the casual way everyone seemed to mingle–it was all so different from what I was used to. I found myself thinking about quieter nights, simpler times, and wondered if I even wanted to find my place in this new, louder world.

Handing me a red plastic cup, he said, "Come on, Nash, loosen up a bit. We're playing a game I think you'll be really good at."

Trying not to let my hesitation show, I reluctantly said, "Uh, sure," and accepted the cup. The liquid inside sloshed as Jason led me to the circle of participants.

The rules of the game were explained amidst cheers and laughter. My heart pounded with the thrill. The plastic cup felt heavy in my hand, initially causing me to wish for the familiar weight of a baseball.

As the game unfolded, I got caught up in the competitive spirit alongside a combination of laughter, shouts, and high fives. The uncertainty that had gripped me earlier faded and was replaced with new feelings of familiarity and unity, as well as a slight euphoria.

Ah, crap.

I was tipsy and on the verge of drunk. Even with that thought, I picked up the ping-pong ball and bounced it across the table. Sinking the shot even with the edges of my vision going a little blurry, the room erupted in cheers.

Amidst the applause and laughter, my eyes caught a flash of red hair just outside the crowd. She stood there, a sly grin playing on her lips. I held her gaze as I leaned over to Jason, whispering dramatically, "I retire a champion," and handed him my empty cup like it was a ceremonial sword.

Her eyes twinkled with amusement as I sauntered over to where she was standing.

"Hi," she practically purred, twirling a strand of her hair around her finger. "I'm Riley." Her voice was alluring as a summer breeze.

"Nash," I replied, taking her hand. Her touch lingered, sending a spark of electricity down my spine.

Riley leaned in, her breath tickling my ear. "You seem like you know how to have a good time."

I chuckled, my eyes flicking back to the chaotic ping-pong table. "I'm just a humble Beer-Pong padawan hoping not to make a fool of myself."

She laughed, a sound that was part melody, part mischief. Her fingers brushed my arm as she leaned closer. "Well, Nash, if you're looking for a real good time, I know a few places we could head after this."

The suggestion hung between us, tempting and dangerous. The knot in my stomach tightened, but the thrill of uncertainty was intoxicating.

At that moment, a fleeting thought crossed my mind—*Wildfire*. The thought of her briefly surfaced, momentarily giving me pause, but the allure of Riley and the haze of the night pushed it to the background.

As the night went on around us, Riley and I found ourselves in a quieter spot, away from the crowd. The music pulsed, casting a mysterious glow on her features. She handed me a drink, her gaze lingering on mine.

"To new friends and unforgettable nights," she toasted, a sly grin creeping onto her lips.

We clinked our cups, and I took a sip, the burn of alcohol mingling with the lingering euphoria from the game. As the fiery liquid trickled down my throat, the burn of alcohol intensified, igniting a warm sensation that spread through my body. The bitter taste mingled with the lingering exhilaration of the game. It was as if the electrifying energy from the crowd had seeped into my veins, heightening my senses and amplifying every sensation.

With each sip, a pleasant warmth coursed through my veins, enveloping me in a comforting embrace. The alcohol acted as a conduit, intensifying the rush of emotions that surged within me. My heart pounded in sync with the cheers that still echoed in my ears, and a tingling sensation danced across my skin, leaving a trail of goosebumps in its wake.

As the night wore on, the buzz of the alcohol mixed with the adrenaline from the experience, pushing me further into a state of reckless abandon. The once distant, blurry feeling turned into a full-fledged haze, and my inhibitions melted away.

The party grew wilder, and I found myself at the center of it, participating in increasingly ridiculous antics. At one point, I was convinced that trying to balance on a wobbly stack of chairs was a fantastic idea. Another moment had me attempting an exaggerated impression of Coach Edwards, complete with wildly gesticulating arms and a booming voice that had everyone in stitches.

At some point, I'm pretty sure Jason and I posed with a lampshade on our heads as I serenaded a group of equally inebriated partygoers with my less-than-stellar rendition of "Wonderwall" on an out-of-tune guitar. Laughter echoed around me, blending with the pulsating music.

Somewhere amidst the chaos, Riley was there with an addictive flirtatious energy. Her laughter and sly comments fueled my antics further, pushing me to do more, be more ridiculous. The line between fun and stupid blurred until it vanished entirely.

14

NASH

Sunlight pierced through my eyelids, dragging me into consciousness with a groan. Pressing my palm against my forehead, I felt the dull throb of a hangover and the dryness in my mouth. The scent of stale regret lingered. Slowly, I squinted my eyes open.

I took in the unfamiliar room—walls adorned with posters, a half-open closet door, and an empty pizza box on the floor. Panic set in as I struggled to piece together last night. Where was I?

As I looked down, I noticed that I was still fully clothed, which provided a small comfort. My phone buzzed somewhere on the floor. I groped around until I found it, the screen glaringly bright. A message from an unknown number caught my eye.

> Hey Nash, last night was a blast. Here's my number. Call me sometime, and let's do it again. ;-) Riley

RILEY. I had a faint recollection of the name, but I couldn't remember the specifics. Before I could decide what to do, more photos came through from the same number.

The images showed snippets of the party—laughter, indulgence, and a blurry shot of me clinking glasses with Riley. Reality hit me— I'd partied hard, and Riley had the evidence.

I dragged myself to the bathroom. The mirror reflected a disheveled version of myself, a far cry from the usually composed Nash Montgomery. My phone buzzed again, this time with a text from Cubby.

> Crazy night, Nash! You disappeared with that
> Riley girl. Spill the details when you wake up.

Grimacing, I tossed the phone onto the bed. The memories were a foggy mess, and my conscience screamed at me. The choices of a supposedly carefree night now hung over me like a storm cloud.

My phone buzzed with messages from different teammates, all asking about last night. I ignored them, focusing on how to get back to my dorm. A quick check of my location revealed I was on the opposite side of campus, with only thirty minutes until my Biology test.

Panic surged. I scrambled to gather my things, my head pounding with every step. Outside, the fresh air did nothing to ease my hangover. I needed to move fast, but my body felt like lead.

The campus, usually familiar, now felt like a labyrinth. I finally reached my dorm, sprinted up the stairs, and grabbed my backpack. With just ten minutes left, I raced to the Biology building and slipped into a seat at the back just as they handed out the tests.

An hour later, I emerged, feeling defeated. The test had been a disaster, and all I wanted was to get a shower and pretend last night never happened. I trudged into my room, the scent of day-old microwave popcorn greeting me. Dropping my backpack, I headed for the shower, hoping for some clarity.

Under the hot water, my thoughts wandered to my parents' sacrifices and my coaches' efforts. Each memory reminded me of the expectations I carried, and the weight felt overwhelming. Was I throwing it all away because I couldn't responsibly handle a night out?

Drying off, I stared at my reflection. The face looking back was tired and defeated.

Another message caused my phone to vibrate. This one had my insides tying themselves in thousands of tiny knots.

My office, immediately.

It was from Coach. I knew I was in for it.

Sitting in Coach's office, I felt like a deer caught in headlights. The newspaper page spread out on his desk told a story in photos I barely remembered—one of wild, foolish behavior and complete disregard for consequences.

Coach sighed, running a hand through his graying hair. "Nash, you're one of the best players on this team, but last night... last night was unacceptable."

I opened my mouth to speak, but he held up a hand to stop me. "I don't want to hear excuses. You have a responsibility, not just to yourself, but to this team. Your actions reflect on all of us. You could have been arrested if the police had been called because you're underage. Do you understand how lucky you are?"

The weight of his words settled heavily on my shoulders. I nodded, feeling the sting of regret. "I know, Coach. I'm sorry. I just—"

"I get it," he interrupted, his tone softening slightly. "You're young, and you want to have fun. But there's a line, Nash. And you crossed it."

He leaned back, his eyes searching mine. "I need to know that you understand the gravity of this situation. This cannot happen again, or I will be forced to take major actions. You're lucky these photos are blurry enough that most people will only be able to speculate about who they're of."

Swallowing hard, I nodded again. "I do, Coach. I'll do better."

Coach's stern expression softened further. "Good. Because if you don't, there will be serious consequences."

Leaving his office, the weight of my actions and their repercussions felt heavier than ever. I knew I had a lot of work ahead of me to regain the trust of my teammates and Coach Edwards. And somewhere in the back of my mind, amidst the chaos and regret, I wondered what *Wildfire* would think if she knew.

~

MY PHONE BUZZED nonstop with messages I had no intention of acknowledging any time soon. Tossing it on the bed, my eyes snagged on my computer. Apprehension settled in my gut. *Wildfire.* I'd told her we'd meet back up and then I completely forgot. She'll probably think I'm an idiot if I tell her why I never logged on again. I probably needed to apologize for skipping out on her.

Logging on, I noticed immediately she was at least logged in like she said she'd be. I wasn't sure if I should message her or not. Even though we hadn't made specific plans, I definitely didn't get back to her like I'd suggested I would. The cursor blinked on the screen, waiting for me to make a move. With a deep breath, I started typing.

@GUYWITHGUITAR: Sorry I never got back to you. Crazy stuff happened. How's your day going?

THE CHAT WINDOW BLINKED, indicating that *Wildfire* was typing. I waited, my heart pounding a bit faster than usual. Her response appeared on the screen.

@WILDFIRE: I hope everything is OK. My day's been pretty much business as usual. How about yours?

. . .

HER CASUAL REPLY eased some of the tension within me. There was no reason I should be feeling guilty, but my conscience was threatening to eat me alive.

@GuyWithGuitar: Yeah, just some unexpected chaos. May have bombed a biology test. Managed to survive the aftermath though. So, business as usual for you, huh? Which usual are we talking?

@WILDFIRE: That's a good point. I'm on kind of a break from performing so I guess school is the usual. Sorry about biology. I'm actually about to head to class but we can hang out later if you're free.

I WAS DISAPPOINTED to find out that my distraction wouldn't come from talking to *Wildfire.*

@GUYWITHGUITAR: Sure. Sounds good. Want to say 9:00?

@WILDFIRE: It's a date!

I FOUND myself smiling like an idiot at her last message. Maybe it was because I hadn't been on an actual date in months, or maybe it was because the idea of a zero-pressure date with a girl that fascinated me was exciting. Whatever the case, I was thoroughly distracted by my future plans calculating the hours until I got to talk to *Wildfire* again and didn't hear my roommate enter the room.

Cubby stood in the doorway, a grin plastered across his face that was too knowing for my comfort.

"Look at you, the man of the hour!" he exclaimed, tossing his baseball cap onto his bed with a flourish. "Heard you were quite the charmer last night. Riley's got half the campus swooning and laughing over your escapades."

The door's loud thud as it closed echoed inside my head. I grimaced, feeling the force of last night's choices pressing in around me. "Cubby, man, can you just not?" I rubbed my temples, the throbbing in my head a relentless reminder of my own stupidity.

Cubby laughed, unrepentant. "Come on, Nash, you've got to admit it's kind of epic. You go from Mr. Goody-Two-Shoes to campus Casanova in one night!"

Sighing, I flopped back onto my bed. I wasn't in the mood to relive the previous night's blunders, especially not through Cubby's exaggerated retellings.

"Not feeling so epic right now," I muttered, staring at the ceiling as if it held the answers to my self-inflicted predicament.

Cubby's expression softened as he sat on the edge of his bed, facing me. "Rough morning, huh? How'd the test go?"

I turned my head to look at him, his concern genuine. "Let's just say I won't be winning any academic awards. And somehow I've got to survive two more classes, a workout, and practice."

"You'll pull through, you always do," Cubby said, clapping a hand on my shoulder. "You're Nash Montgomery. You've got more talent in your pinky finger than most of us have in our whole bodies."

His words were meant to be encouraging, but they felt like a weight I was going to have to carry. I closed my eyes, wishing I could escape to a place where my choices didn't have ripple effects that threatened to capsize me.

I didn't have the heart to tell Cubby that his version of me was a myth. That I wasn't the star he or anyone else imagined. That beneath the surface, doubts gnawed at me with sharp teeth, and right now, I felt like a fraud. Because last night's Nash was nothing like the real one. At least, I hoped not.

I laid there for a moment, letting the silence of the room wash over me. Cubby, sensing my need for solitude, grabbed his headphones and turned to his computer, giving me space to think. I turned my head, letting my gaze drift across the room to the guitar that leaned against the wall. Its wood gleamed in the fading light, the strings calling to me.

Pushing myself off the bed, I crossed the room and picked up the guitar. As I held it in my hand, it felt like a natural extension of myself, the smooth curves and edges fitting snugly against my body. I let my fingers drift over the strings, the soft sounds barely audible over the hum of the clicking of Cubby's keyboard and mouse.

I strummed a chord, and the sound filled the room. Immediately, I felt a release of the negative emotions that had been tearing me up all morning. I felt like myself.

I played quietly, letting the melody I'd been working on for the past few weeks flow through my fingers. Each note carried a sense of longing and searching.

I wish I could say I had a moment of revelation or that the heavens parted to shine a light on a clear, straight path ahead of me. Instead, in the cadence and the rhythm, I simply found peace. Music didn't demand the answers; it just offered a refuge where I felt most like myself. That was good enough for now.

Cubby looked up from his game, a question in his eyes. He listened as I played, and slowly, his usual smirk softened into something like respect. "Dude, that's... wow. Is that an original?"

"Yeah," I said, the acknowledgment full of pride mixed with vulnerability. "Still a work in progress."

Cubby nodded, turning back to his screen. "Huh. Cool, man."

I leaned the guitar against my desk and glanced at the clock. Reality hit me like the aftertaste of last night's cheap beer—classes, a workout, and practice were still on my to-do list. With a sigh, I grabbed my backpack and headed back out the door.

15

CASSIDY

The last class of the day had ended in a rush of notes and lectures, leaving me in a post-academic daze that always seemed to settle over the campus as the afternoon waned. Students spilled out of buildings like ants from a hill, each following their own invisible trails. My own path felt aimless except it wasn't. I had a destination—the music building. While I had settled on general classes, I'd also auditioned for one of the chamber ensembles and made it.

The ensemble was a small group, but each member was fiercely talented. Today was the first rehearsal, and the butterflies in my stomach were more like a flock of sparrows fluttering wildly. I wasn't new to performing, but this was different—this was for me. It wasn't a show or a competition. It was just pure, unadulterated music.

As I approached the music building, a wave of doubt washed over me. Had I chosen the chamber ensemble because it was what I truly wanted, or because I felt obligated? My mom's insistence on a future in classical music had always loomed over me, and I couldn't shake the feeling that this decision wasn't entirely my own.

I entered the room, filled with expectancy, the sounds of tuning instruments easing my tension. I was by far the youngest person there, but I knew my skills matched or exceeded those of anyone present. All the years of practice and private lessons guaranteed that.

I unclasped the case of my violin, an instrument that had become an extension of myself, and prepared to play. It wasn't long before the conductor raised his baton, and with a deep cleansing breath, we began.

Even through the warmups, the music we made together was intricate and challenging, a composite of sounds that wove together seamlessly. It was classical, yet it felt fresh and alive. When we hit the final note, perfect and resonant, I knew I was exactly where I needed to be. It had been a long time since I felt this in tune with myself.

Heading for the exit, I stopped in my tracks when heard the distinctive pluck of a banjo. The sound immediately transported me back to the fairground encounter with Sarah Belle Reed, a memory that played in my mind regularly. Her words were never far from my memory: *It's OK to let go of some dreams and discover new ones.* I wasn't sure that playing chamber music in an ensemble was a dream I had, but I did know that playing for myself and no one else was absolutely something I wanted.

Curious, I followed the music, my steps echoing softly in the empty hallway. The melody grew louder, and I found myself drawn towards an open door. Inside, there were three musicians I assumed were students, their expressions alive with the music.

I hesitated at the threshold, watching the scene unfold. The banjo's cheerful twang, the smiles, the obvious familiarity—it was reminiscent of the folk festival I'd performed at a few years prior.

The song came to a close and, as if sensing my presence, the banjo player looked up and beckoned me in.

"Hey, you play?" he asked, nodding towards the violin case in my hand.

I nodded, suddenly feeling a rush of excitement. This was my chance to dive into a different kind of music, the kind that was played for the sheer pleasure of it.

"Yeah, I play."

The group made room for me, and I took my place among them. As I lifted the violin to my shoulder, I felt a different energy coursing through me. This wasn't the structured environment of the ensemble; this was raw and real.

"We're just jamming. Jump in whenever you feel like it," the percussionist said, and that was all the invitation I needed.

The violin transformed into a fiddle in my hands, its voice melding perfectly with the banjo's rhythm. We played, and I got lost in a world of folk melodies and bluegrass tunes, each song feeling like a new adventure. I found myself experimenting, letting go and allowing the music to guide my movements.

Here, in this makeshift band, I was just Cassidy, the girl who loved to play, not Cassidy Raye Stanton, the one whose mother insisted her future was to be on a stage performing.

When the session eventually wound down, I was greeted with smiles and nods of approval.

"You're pretty good with that fiddle," the banjo player said, and I beamed at the compliment.

"Thanks," I said, feeling a warmth in my chest that hadn't been there in a while. It was nothing like the applause from a big audience; it felt like more.

The banjo player, a guy with tousled hair and a friendly smile, extended his hand. "I'm Chase, by the way. We do this every Thursday around the same time. You should join us again if you're free."

"I'm Cassidy," I replied, shaking his hand. The idea of having a regular jam session to look forward to sparked a new kind of excitement in me. "I'd love to. Thanks for letting me play."

As I packed up my violin, the others introduced themselves. There was Mia on guitar and Liam on the cajón. They were all music majors, but like me, they found joy in playing outside the rigidity of their courses. We exchanged numbers and made plans for the next session.

Leaving the music building, I noted the sky had turned to a canvas of deep blues and purples, the campus lights starting to flicker on. I felt invigorated, as if the music had recharged something inside me. And a quick glance at my phone told me I only had a little while to grab dinner before I needed to be at my computer to talk to *Guy.*

THE DRIVE HOME WAS QUICK, my mind already racing ahead to the conversation with *GuyWithGuitar.* Stepping inside the house, I kicked off my shoes and headed straight to my room, my movements feeling slow as the day caught up with me. I shed my day clothes for comfortable sweats and pulled my hair into a haphazard bun. As I flipped on a small desk lamp, its soft glow cast a cozy ambiance around the room. I hit play on my playlist, letting the low hum of indie folk music fill the space.

I opened my laptop and navigated to OurSpace, my fingers tapping a steady rhythm on the desk in sync with the music. The familiarity of the chat interface was comforting. I was thinking about what to talk about, hoping he'd share his 'crazy stuff' or wondering how he'd react to my afternoon's experience after rehearsal. There was a warmth in this ritual, a sense of reaching out across the digital void to someone who felt both familiar and distant.

The icon blinked. *GuyWithGuitar* was online. My heart did a little flip. I typed out a quick greeting, not caring if I seemed eager. I was.

@Wildfire: Hey! How's your evening going?

His reply came quickly, the words appearing on the screen bringing an immediate smile to my face.

@GuyWithGuitar: Hey back! It's been a long day, but I'm good. How about you?

My fingers flew across the keyboard, describing to him the ensemble and the impromptu music session. It felt good to share, to have someone who seemed interested in these little details of my life.

As our conversation continued, we danced around various topics.

I'd had a question that had been lingering in my mind, and I wasn't trying to be nosy but, I liked knowing stuff about his life. It seemed so normal in a lot of ways.

@Wildfire: You mentioned some crazy stuff happening the other day. Was it just the Biology test?

There was a long pause before he replied.

@GuyWithGuitar: Yeah, just doing what I do best and acting without thinking. But I'm dealing with it. And I definitely bombed the biology test. Not my finest hour.

I laughed softly, sympathizing with him. His response was vague, but I respected his privacy, knowing that everyone had their boundaries. Besides, we had agreed not to get too personal.

@Wildfire: We've all been there. Don't be too hard on yourself. Life's more than just tests, right?

We seamlessly shifted between serious and lighthearted topics during our conversation. I found myself opening up more and could not stop talking about the joy I'd found in playing music I love just for myself.

Every message from him was a window into his world, and I wanted more of it. It was more than a shared love for music; it felt like finding a friend who understood *me.*

A message popped up on the screen, drawing me back from my thoughts.

@GuyWithGuitar: I've been working on a song. It's not fully polished yet, but I'd love to get your take on it.

The thought of hearing music he created himself sent a thrill through me. It felt personal.

@Wildfire: Yes, please! I can't wait to hear it.

A moment later, a notification appeared, indicating that *GuyWith-Guitar* had sent an audio file. My heart fluttered with anticipation as I clicked to open it.

As he sang about searching for direction and having doubts about his choices, the melody that poured out was infused with a longing. I couldn't help but feel every chord and every lyric he sang. And his voice–it was like a warm embrace that enveloped me and reverberated through me. A shiver went down my spine.

I sat back, a hand unconsciously landing over my heart that was racing. The room around me felt strangely still. My fingers trembled slightly as I typed.

@Wildfire: That was amazing!

I waited, watching the screen intently as his reply bubble popped up.

@GuyWithGuitar: Thanks. It's just something I've been feeling, you know?

His vulnerability made the digital space between us feel smaller. I contemplated whether it would be okay to ask about the meaning behind his song before sending my next message.

@Wildfire: It's a beautiful song. It feels like it's coming from a place of introspection. Is songwriting a way for you to figure things out?

Another pause. When his response came, it was thoughtful.

@GuyWithGuitar: Yeah. Music helps me process things, put feelings into words and the melody just kind of happens.

I nodded to myself, understanding completely. Music had always been my refuge, a way to express what words alone couldn't.

The conversation drifted back to lighter topics, but the impact of his song lingered in my thoughts. It was a glimpse into his world, his struggles. I felt special to have been a part of that moment.

I knew I needed to log off and get to bed, but I found myself reluctant to say goodbye. These conversations had become something I looked forward to, a highlight of my day when we had them. But I had a full day of class and rehearsal ahead of me in addition to my regular private lessons.

@Wildfire: Thanks for sharing your song with me, and for the chat. I looked forward to it all day.

. . .

@G*uy*W*ith*G*uitar: Same here, Wildfire. We should do it again soon.*

I reclined in my seat, feeling content.

That night I dreamed about a guitar playing cowboy sweeping me off my feet and whisking me away to a place we played music together as he sang to me.

16

NASH

Dragging my cleats through the dirt, I replayed the last practice in my head—the missed signals, the dropped catches, moments that weren't like me. Coach had been on me lately, and not just for the slip-ups on the field. My grades had been slipping, a fact that hadn't gone unnoticed. And it's what landed me back in Coach's office.

Knocking felt like tapping on the lid of my own coffin. When I entered, Coach was sitting behind his desk, the usual lineup of player stats and game strategies replaced by my latest academic report. The air was thick with the scent of leather and old coffee, but it was the look of serious concern on Coach's face that lingered heaviest in the room.

"Take a seat, Montgomery," he said, gesturing to the chair across from him. His fingers were steepled, eyes not leaving the paper that might as well have been a rap sheet. "This isn't just about your performance behind the plate. Your academics are part of the deal here. You know that."

As if it were quicksand, I sank into the chair and nodded. "I know, Coach. I've just been... It's been a rough few weeks."

"Rough for you means rough for the team," he shot back. "You're the backbone out there, Nash. The catcher sees the whole game. If your head's not in it, the team's not in it. And these grades..." He tapped the report as if it were a warning bell. "This isn't why you're here on scholarship, but it matters."

His words were a jolt. I was the catcher—the guy who called the shots on the field, who kept the pitchers in check, who held the team together. But lately, I'd been the one unraveling.

"We've got people keeping an eye on the team, Nash. They might not be drafting freshmen, but they're always looking out for emerging talent. What do you think they'll see if this keeps up? You've got potential, but you need to show you can handle the pressure, on and off the field."

I left his office feeling heavier than I ever have wearing full catcher gear.

Since that night at the party with Riley, I'd literally stepped into a role without even auditioning for it. We never had a conversation about becoming a couple; it just happened. One week, I was some guy from a party, and the next, I found myself holding her hand, meeting her for lunch, and walking her to classes—it had all happened so easily. Falling into a relationship with her felt like slipping into a stream and letting the current take me. It was the natural next step, right? That's what I had told myself, anyway.

Lately, though, I was overwhelmed and exhausted, trying to balance my commitments to Riley and my academic responsibilities. I spent every spare moment either at social events with her or catching up on assignments. The pressure to maintain our "perfect campus couple" image was stressful. My own plans and ideas took a back seat to Riley's plans for our future, and our once carefree relationship was starting to feel like an obligation.

But it wasn't all bad. Riley's infectious laugh made her the life of every party, and her laughter at my jokes always lifted my spirits. She was a great kisser, adding a spark to our connection. We always turned heads and received compliments wherever we went, and Riley's invitations to the best parties kept our social calendar exciting. I just needed to find a better balance.

Then there was baseball, the one constant in my life, the thing I used to love more than anything. It was becoming just another box to tick. The field, once a sanctuary, had turned into another stage where I performed. Between Riley's relentless social schedule and the grueling baseball practices, I was spread too thin, clearly losing my grip on the parts of my life that I used to feel in control of.

Every practice, every missed catch and fumbled play, was a reminder of how off-balance my life had become. Coach's words about focus and potential only echoed what I already knew—I was losing sight of who I was.

IN MY ROOM, I tossed my gear onto the floor and slumped onto the bed. My muscles ached from practice, and my mind was a tangled mess of thoughts. When I looked up, my eyes landed on my computer. Without thinking, I reached for it, my fingers itching to message *Wildfire*. With her, I could just be Nash—not the athlete, not Riley's boyfriend, just... me.

I opened the browser, and my heart gave a little leap when I saw she was online. Taking a deep breath, I began to type, my fingers somehow able to confess things to her that I hadn't even admitted to myself.

@GuyWithGuitar: I don't think I love baseball like I used to but I'm doing it because it makes my dad happy.

I hit send and waited, my heart pounding in my chest. The seconds stretched into what felt like hours until her reply popped up.

@Wildfire: So you're on a path that you didn't choose, and you desperately want to find a way to carve out your own?

My jaw dropped, and I stared at the screen. She had this uncanny ability to articulate exactly what I was struggling with. Relief and uncertainty swirled in my chest as I considered her words. They were a mirror to my own thoughts, a reflection of the very ones that had been taking root inside me.

@GuyWithGuitar: That's exactly it. Coach called me out after practice.

Says I'm not focused. Maybe he's right. I love the game, but there's this pressure because of my dad and because of my scholarship... it's like I'm scared to want anything else. But I feel like I want something else.

I hit send and waited for her reply. My fingers hovered over the keys after sending that last message. It was a confession, one I hadn't even planned on making, but with *Wildfire*, it felt safe to be honest. She had this way of understanding, of seeing through the chaos to the heart of what I was feeling, even though she had no idea who I was.

@Wildfire: It's OK to have off days. What's important is that you don't lose sight of what you love. If I've learned anything in the last six months it's that you're allowed to question things. It's OK to explore what you really want. The scholarship might determine your play, but it doesn't have to dictate your passion.

I leaned back, feeling the tightness in my shoulders relaxing. She was right–somehow she was always right. It was as if she could see through the screen, through my mess, and find the truth hiding underneath.

@GuyWithGuitar: It's just hard, you know? Baseball used to be my escape. Now it feels like a trap. Because of the scholarship, and because it was always supposed to be my ticket out. But what if it's not what I want anymore?

I was waiting for her reply, feeling completely exposed, but also strangely free. I was sharing parts of myself that I had kept locked away, parts that I was only now beginning to acknowledge.

Her reply didn't take long.

@Wildfire: Then you find a new dream, a new escape. You're more than just a baseball player, Guy. You're a person with a world of possibilities ahead of you.

Her words were like a ray of light pushing through the darkness and in that moment, I felt a glimmer of something I thought I'd lost —hope.

⁓

THE DAYS that followed were a whirlwind of reflection and subtle shifts. Coach's words, Riley's constant demands, and *Wildfire's* encouraging messages echoed in my mind. The field still felt like an obligation, but the conversations with *Wildfire* were slowly rekindling a sense of purpose I thought I'd lost.

One evening, after another grueling practice, I sat in my room staring at my cleats. The once comforting dirt stains now seemed to mock my indecision. Taking a deep breath, I grabbed my laptop and logged in. *Wildfire* was online.

@GuyWithGuitar: I think I need to make a change. I can't keep doing this, pretending like everything's fine.

Her response was almost immediate.

@Wildfire: Change is hard, but it's the only way to find what truly makes you happy. What do you want to do?

I hesitated, the question hanging in the air. What did I want to do? The answer was simple, yet terrifying.

@GuyWithGuitar: I want to focus on my music. It's the one thing that still feels like mine.

@WILDFIRE: Then go for it. Life is too short to be anything but happy. You have to follow your heart, even if it means stepping away from something familiar.

Her words stayed with me every day after that. I just wasn't sure what to do with them yet.

17

CASSIDY

The fall air had turned crisp, leaves painting the campus in a mosaic of reds and oranges. As I walked toward my car, the rustling of leaves caught my attention. I looked up just in time to see a couple walking hand in hand, lost in their own world. For some reason, I instantly thought of *Guy*.

Despite never meeting in person, he had become a genuine friend and an unexpected confidant. Our conversations were a refuge, allowing me to be myself without the added pressure of anyone else's expectations. I wished for that kind of connection on this side of a computer screen.

Once I got home, I dropped my bag on my bed and plopped down at my desk, ready to tackle the mountain of homework that awaited me. Hours passed in a blur of equations and essays, and just as I was about to shut down my computer, a notification popped up. It was *GuyWithGuitar*. My heart did its typical flutter as I opened up a new message.

@GuyWithGuitar: Hey Wildfire, how's it going?

Seeing his message brought an immediate smile to my face.

@Wildfire: Hey Guy, just drowning in homework. You?

· · ·

@GuyWithGuitar: Same here. You'd think baseball practice would be enough, but nope, professors have other ideas.

I laughed.

@Wildfire: Rude of them.

@GuyWithGuitar: Seriously. How was your day otherwise?

@Wildfire: Not too bad. Campus looks like a dreamy postcard with all the fall colors. I saw this couple walking together, totally absorbed in each other. He had a guitar on his back and I wondered if they were talking about music. Made me think of you, actually.

@GuyWithGuitar: Wow, I'm flattered. Do I get to be the dreamy guy in your thoughts now?

@Wildfire: Let's not get ahead of ourselves, Mr. Guitar. He had a guitar, that's all.

@GuyWithGuitar: Fair enough. So, what else is new? Any deep thoughts or existential crises today?

@Wildfire: Not today, thankfully. Just the usual grind. I guess there was also that moment where I wished I had someone to walk with while talking about music, you know? Someone real.

@GuyWithGuitar: I get that. It's weird how we can feel so close to someone we've never met but nowhere near as close to the people we're surrounded with all the time.

· · ·

@WILDFIRE: Yeah, it is weird. But in a good way, I think. It's nice having someone who just gets it. Gets me.

@GUYWITHGUITAR: Agreed. One day, maybe we'll get that real-life connection. Or maybe you'll meet someone who makes you feel as special as you deserve and they'll take my place as the dreamy guy in your thoughts.

@WILDFIRE: Oh, ha ha. But really, that was sweet.

@GUYWITHGUITAR: I can be. Now, go finish your homework and stop distracting me.

@WILDFIRE: Will do. Night, Guy.

@GUYWITHGUITAR: Night.

TURNING OFF MY COMPUTER, I wondered if I'd ever have a connection with another person like the one I had with *Guy,* but in the real world. I never felt like I had to censor myself or be anyone other than me when we talked. Well, except for the fact we didn't exchange real names. But if I were being honest, I'd bet *GuyWithGuitar* tells me more about him than any name he'd give me.

18

NASH

Leaning back in my desk chair, I absentmindedly tossed a baseball up and down as Riley sat cross-legged on my bed, flipping through a fashion magazine.

"Nash, don't forget, you're taking me to the winter ball," she said, her tone more demanding than inviting. "It's going to be epic, and everyone will be there."

I glanced over at Riley, nodding absentmindedly, turning the ball over in my hands. She'd been planning this for weeks, talking about outfits, themes, and photos she wanted for her blog. I didn't share her enthusiasm, but I knew showing up with her would make her happy. Plus, these events weren't all bad—good music, food, and Riley did have a knack for making things entertaining.

"A winter ball, huh? Do I get to be the king or am I just the court jester this time?"

She threw her head back, laughing. "King, of course. Who else would I trust to rule the dance floor with me?" As she spoke, she hopped off the bed and came over to plop down on my lap.

Cubby, my roommate, sat at his desk, his eyes glued to his textbook. But I knew better. He was listening, probably storing information for his usual post-Riley analysis.

"You've got your tux squared away and everything?" Riley nudged me gently, her tone light but serious.

Turning fully towards her, I set the ball down. "I wouldn't miss it for the world," I assured her with a more genuine smile this time. "Especially since it sounds like you've got the evening planned down to the last dance."

Riley's expression softened. "It's going to be so much fun. Plus, I've already picked out the perfect dress, and we're going to look amazing together."

I had to smile at how excited she was. Since we started dating, Riley had taken to planning most of our social life. It was easier that way; she enjoyed it, and I didn't have to worry about the details. Sometimes, though, it still felt like I was just a prop in her perfectly curated social agenda, merely there to fill a spot in her expertly planned scenes.

"Promise me there's no crown involved," I joked, playing along with her enthusiasm.

"No crown, just a killer bow tie," she winked, squeezing my hand excitedly. "We're going to have so much fun, Nash. It'll be a night to remember."

I laughed, feeling her infectious energy. "As long as you're my dance partner, it's a guaranteed success."

Riley stood up, her eyes dancing with delight. She leaned down and planted a quick kiss on my cheek before wiping away the lipstick she left behind. "You're the best, Nash. This is why you're my favorite person."

After she left the room with a spring in her step, Cubby finally dropped his pretense of studying, turning to me with an amused smirk. "Getting your dance moves ready, Your Majesty?"

"Looks like I have to," I grinned, picking up the baseball again. "Can't let my queen down, can I?"

Cubby rolled his eyes, chuckling. "Sure, sure. But you gotta admit, Riley's got you wrapped around her little finger."

I shrugged, not entirely sure how to respond. Riley did most of the planning, and I went along with it. It was simple, uncomplicated.

At least I thought so.

"Just saying, man. Seems like Riley's always the one calling the shots." Cubby's tone turning serious.

I shrugged, a bit uneasy with the implication. "It's not like that. We just... work well together."

"Sure, bro," Cubby replied, his smirk saying more than his words. "Just make sure you're not losing yourself in her plans."

I considered his comment as the baseball made its way back into my hand. Riley did tend to dominate our plans, but it was just easier that way. Wasn't it?

I liked being with her; she was fun, and life was easier with someone else making the plans. But Cubby's question lingered in the air, unsettling.

"Nah, man," I finally said, though a seed of doubt had been planted. "Riley and I are good. She just likes things a certain way, that's all."

Cubby shrugged, turning back to his book. "As long as you're happy, bro.

His words played on repeat in my head as I laid there contemplating Riley's plans—the upcoming formal, my place in all of it–it was comfortable and I liked comfortable.

Later that night, as I stared at the ceiling from my bed, Cubby's words from earlier crept back into my mind. Lying there, I realized I hadn't actually made many decisions for myself lately. It was always about going with the flow, Riley's mostly. The thought unsettled me more than I wanted to admit. Maybe Cubby was right; maybe I did need to think about what I wanted.

Not that it would matter—because the only thing I found myself coming back to time after time would likely always be just outside my reach.

I could see myself hanging out with *Wildfire*. Our conversations were so different from the expectations I navigated daily. With her, I could always be real, unfiltered.

The idea of meeting *Wildfire*, of seeing her outside the digital confines we had, felt more real to me than most of my everyday interactions.

With a deep sigh, I pushed these thoughts aside. The reality was, *Wildfire* was a world away, and I needed to focus on my actual life. Maybe one day, our paths would cross beyond the screen. Until then, I'd hold on to the joy she gave me through our brief online interactions.

19

CASSIDY

The world outside was a canvas of frost and twinkling lights as Christmas approached. I loved everything about Christmas, from the music to the decorations, and even the dreaded white elephant party at my aunt's house that I was currently packing for.

It was a yearly tradition that brought together our large extended family, with cousins, aunts, and uncles traveling from all corners to reunite. Although we didn't see each other often, these gatherings were usually enough to satisfy that need for me until the next year.

The centerpiece of the evening was always the infamous white elephant gift exchange.

Among the oddball gifts was the legendary stained glass painting of a teddy bear holding a balloon. This wasn't just any teddy bear; it looked like it had survived a traumatic event, its wide eyes filled with a peculiar mix of sadness and confusion. The bear had become a family legend, reappearing each year to haunt its next unsuspecting recipient. The rule was simple: the painting couldn't visit the same household twice until every household had had it.

I remembered vividly when my dad had been the unfortunate recipient ten years ago. The bear's unsettling gaze had haunted my dreams for months until we managed to pass it on at the next white elephant party. Now, it was a hilarious tradition, a mix of dread and anticipation, to see who would end up with the bear this year.

A message alert on my computer cut through the silence, jolting me out of my memories.

@GuyWithGuitar: Let Christmas break begin!

Laughing, I sent a reply.

@Wildfire: Yes! Time to eat, sleep, and repeat until we forget what day it is!

@GUYWITHGUITAR: Speaking of Christmas, any special plans?

I debated telling him about the party, but it felt a little personal to talk about my family.

@Wildfire: Just the usual family stuff. What about you? Any plans?

His reply came after a brief pause.

@GuyWithGuitar: Going to the winter formal with my girlfriend. Should be fun, I guess. Then I'll head home to see my folks.

A pit formed in my stomach at the mention of his girlfriend. How did it never occur to me that he might have a girlfriend? Of course, he had a girlfriend. He's kind and thoughtful and talented. He probably has a ton of friends along with his girlfriend. Gah! How did I never consider that? Why would it even matter to me? I didn't even know his real name. I had to get control of the spiral I was headed into before I said something unnecessary.

@Wildfire: That sounds great! Hope you two have a wonderful time. And be safe going home.

I meant it, mostly.

@GuyWithGuitar: Thanks. I'm looking forward to it. She's amazing.

His words stung way more than they should have. My heart twisted with a sharp pang of jealousy, which I knew was completely irrational. I breathed slowly, trying to remind myself that he was just a friend, a faceless guy behind a screen far away from here. But no matter how many times I repeated it, it didn't change how I felt.

He was practically a stranger, just a username, yet somehow, he had gotten under my skin and made a connection way deeper than I wanted to admit. I was caught in a tug-of-war between my logical side and my feelings.

@Wildfire: That's sweet. She's really lucky.

Our conversation was shorter than they usually were, and that was my fault. As I closed the laptop, I had the sudden urge to cry. My room felt too small, the walls echoing with the words and feelings I had only ever admitted to them.

20

NASH

The excitement level was high as the limo cruised through the chilly winter night, weaving through the festive lights on campus on our way to the off-campus event center. Riley, looking stunning in her deep blue dress, was animatedly discussing the evening's plans with her sorority sisters.

She turned and adjusted my tie. The tie had assuredly matched the exact shade of her dress. That kind of attention to detail was classic Riley. I happily sat beside her, content to just be part of her well-organized world.

Smoothing my lapels, she said quietly, as though we were conspiring a covert operation, "Remember, we need to take lots of photos before we go in." Her gaze wandered over me, ensuring that every aspect of my appearance met her standards while also appreciating the view. Her eyes, reflecting the same shade of blue as her dress, sparkled with anticipation and a hint of command. "And we need to make sure we get some good shots of us at the entrance. It'll be perfect for my blog."

I nodded, a smile playing on my lips. This was typical Riley–always thinking ahead, always a step in front of everyone else. Her energy was infectious. Even if, once again, it appeared as though I was just along for the ride.

As the limo pulled up to the grandly decorated hall, we all stepped out into the chilly night air. I could feel the excitement in the air, a tangible buzz that seemed to elevate the moment. We grouped together for photos, the camera flashing as we tried to capture the evening.

Entering the hall was like stepping into a winter wonderland, with elegant decorations and soft, glowing lights creating an enchanting backdrop. I caught sight of some of my teammates, including Cubby, who raised his glass in a silent toast from across the room.

Riley's hand found mine, pulling me gently towards a group of girls I didn't recognize. As she introduced me, Riley's voice carried a tinge of pride. "This is Nash, my boyfriend," she said, her tone possessive yet filled with affection. I couldn't help but feel a slight swell of smug satisfaction when she wrapped her hand around my arm, as if staking her claim on me in front of these strangers.

The evening unfolded like a well-rehearsed play, with Riley effortlessly navigating the social landscape. She was in her element, an ever-present smile plastered to her face, her presence commanding attention. I found myself watching and admiring her—her confidence, her charisma, her ability to make every moment feel significant.

As the evening progressed, we found ourselves chatting with a group of people I had only seen once before. The conversation was foreign to me, and I struggled to keep up. Suddenly, I noticed Cubby and some other teammates motioning for me to come over. Grateful for a chance to relax and check in with my friends, I politely excused us and guided Riley towards them.

"Hey Nash! Come on over and join the real party!" Cubby's voice rang out happily.

Riley's grip on my arm tightened for a moment, her smile faltering slightly. "Excuse me for a moment, I'll just go freshen up," Riley said casually.

Placing a kiss to her temple, I released her and watched her practically float away. Then, turning to join my friends, I felt a welcome sense of ease wash over me. Cubby clapped me on the back, his laughter infectious.

"We were beginning to think Riley had you on a short leash there, Nash," he joked, though I knew how he felt about Riley's inclination to plan things down to every detail.

I chuckled, shaking my head. "Riley's just passionate about the details, you know? She likes things a certain way, and I respect that."

Cubby raised an eyebrow. "Sure, but don't you ever feel like you're just following her lead?"

I paused for a moment, considering his question. "Sometimes, yeah, but that's part of being in a relationship, right? Compromise. Besides, Riley's got this drive that I admire. She knows what she wants and goes for it. I could learn a lot from her."

Cubby nodded, seemingly satisfied with my response. "Happiness is what counts, bro. As long as you've got that, you're good."

I grinned, appreciating his concern. "I'm good, Cubby. Thanks, man."

We laughed and chatted about the upcoming season, the first game, and the formal. It felt good to be with the guys. Not that I didn't enjoy being with Riley and her friends. Riley's friends, much like her, were all about appearances and networking. They were nice enough, but every interaction seemed carefully measured, every conversation a step in a dance I hadn't quite learned all the steps to. But I was learning.

After a while, I excused myself to find Riley. I found her surrounded by a group of her sorority sisters, once again the center of attention. Her face lit up with a huge smile as I made my way towards her, filling me with a sense of accomplishment. It was clear that she wanted me by her side, and I felt honored to be the one she chose.

As the night continued, I found myself drifting between these two worlds–Riley's meticulously planned social sphere and the laid-back, easy-going atmosphere with my friends. The rest of the night was a blur of music and dancing. Before I knew it, the evening was wrapping up, and we walked out of the hall hand in hand, heading to the limo that was waiting to take us back.

Inside the car, the lively conversation from earlier turned into a gentle hum of shared reflections. Riley leaned into me, her head resting on my shoulder, my arm wrapped around her.

"Did you have a good time?" she asked softly, her fingers tracing patterns on my arm.

"Yeah, it was great. You really know how to make the most of an event like that," I replied, kissing the top of her head.

She smiled, a contented sigh escaping her lips. "I'm glad you think so. It means a lot to me that you're here with me, supporting everything I do."

"I wouldn't be anywhere else," I admitted, even though I felt the pressure of the night's events, the expectations, and the role I had to play.

As the sleek limousine came to a stop in front of our building, I couldn't help but reflect on the complexity of my relationship with Riley. Despite the nuances I was still trying to figure out, I knew that this journey with her was one I was going to see through. Her determination and drive were just some of the qualities that made her who she was, and maybe, by joining her on this path, I would find my own way as well.

The world was quiet around us as I walked Riley to the entrance of her building, the soft glow from the lobby lights casting a warm hue on her face. She turned to me, her eyes reflecting a mix of exhaustion and contentment.

"Thanks for a wonderful evening, Nash," she murmured, her voice sleepy.

"Anytime, Riley. I had a great time too," I replied, giving her hand a gentle squeeze.

Her gaze searched mine as if trying to read the thoughts behind my words. "Goodnight, Nash."

"Goodnight, Riley," I said, leaning in. I tilted her chin up slightly and pressed my lips to hers. The kiss was soft, carrying all the emotions of the night.

When we finally pulled apart, her eyes were slightly misty, and her breath came in soft puffs in the cold air. She smiled. "That was nice," she whispered.

"Yeah, it was," I agreed, my voice equally soft. "Goodnight, Riley."

"Goodnight, Nash," she repeated, this time with a dreamy look in her eyes.

As she turned and walked inside, I stood there for a moment, watching until she disappeared into the building.

21

NASH

The morning after the formal was one of those Saturdays where the campus seemed to hibernate. I, however, was wide awake and trying to tune out Cubby's snores as I replayed the night before in my mind. I'd spent the night bouncing back and forth between Riley's friends and mine. It wasn't anything new, but I wondered when it had become normal and expected.

Feeling the need to move, I swung my legs off the bed and stretched as I looked around the space. The room was a mess, clear evidence of our hectic schedules. Baseball gear lay piled in one corner, textbooks in another. I smiled to myself, thinking how this room was a reflection of my life at the moment–sports, school, and everything in between. And baseball season hadn't even started.

Grabbing my phone, I saw I had a text from Riley.

> Last night was magical. Let's grab lunch later?

I texted back a quick confirmation and got out of bed, feeling a surge of motivation. This was my day to catch up on everything from sleep to homework, and I might get a workout in at some point.

Showered, I slipped into my comfortably worn jeans and a faded baseball tee, then headed to the cafeteria, where I grabbed a coffee and a bagel and found a quiet spot in the corner of the room. I pulled out my phone and scrolled through the pictures Riley had sent from the formal. We looked good. And she definitely looked happy.

I knew that Riley prioritized planning and precision, and that she carefully curated her life, while I tended to live in the moment. Being with Riley had brought a semblance of order to my world, which I appreciated. And I was pretty sure I showed her what it was to be spontaneous now and then. Our differences worked.

After finishing breakfast, I decided to spend some time at the gym. The familiar rhythm of weights and the focus on each rep helped clear my mind. It felt good to lose myself in something so physical, so straightforward. As I finished my workout and cooled down, I realized it was almost time to meet Riley for lunch.

I grabbed a shower, then headed to the café where we were supposed to meet. Riley was already there, sitting at our favorite table by the window. She waved as I walked in; her smile lit up the room.

"Hey, you," I greeted her, sliding into the seat opposite.

"Hey yourself," she replied, her eyes twinkling. "I grabbed your usual, I hope that's OK."

"Perfect," I said, grinning. "Thank you. You always seem to know exactly what I need."

"Well, someone has to keep an eye on you," she teased.

"True, true," I laughed, taking a sip of the soda Riley had waiting for me. "Last night was amazing, by the way. Thanks again for being my date."

"It really was," she agreed, her expression softening. "I had a great time. You looked pretty dashing in your suit."

"And you were stunning, as always," I replied.

We chatted easily about the formal, reminiscing about the highlights and laughing over the funnier moments. It felt so natural, so right, being there with her. But as soon as I started talking about a party my teammates were planning, something in Riley's expression shifted.

"So, there's this party my teammates are throwing after the first game," I began, excitement in my voice. "I was thinking we could go together. It'll be fun."

Riley's smile faltered slightly. "Oh, that sounds... interesting."

I hesitated, noting the lack of enthusiasm. "You don't have to come if you don't want to. I just thought it could be fun to hang out with everyone outside of the usual settings."

Riley forced a smile. "No, no, it's not that. I'm sure it will be fun. It's just... you know how your friends can be sometimes. They're a bit too rowdy for my liking."

I tried to mask my disappointment. "Yeah, I get it. They can be a a lot. But they're good guys once you get to know them."

"I'm sure they are," she replied, though not entirely convincing. "I'll check my planner, okay?"

"Sure," I said, trying to keep my tone light. "No pressure."

Riley animatedly discussed her plans for the upcoming sorority events and the latest gossip, while I nodded along. I couldn't shake the feeling of imbalance that I'd just experienced. I didn't like that Riley's commitment to things I cared about was often lukewarm at best.

After lunch, I walked Riley back to her dorm, but I didn't hang around. Instead, I shifted gears and made my way to the library by way of my dorm room to grab my books.

I found a spot in my usual corner, a secluded area that had become my favorite place for studying. As I settled in, I was feeling optimistic.

I pulled out my textbooks and my mind wandered back to the conversation with Riley about hanging out with the team. I knew it wasn't her usual scene, but I figured she would get more comfortable in it if we made the effort together.

Thinking about the team turned into thinking about baseball and all the things I loved about the game–the thrill of it, the relationships I'd forged with my teammates, the feel of the catcher's mitt snug against my hand, the high that came with playing hard and winning. Baseball was more than just a game to me; it had been part of who I was for a long time. I remember my first T-ball game like it was last week. At some point, I even think I became addicted to the smell of red clay.

The sound of a book hitting a table across the room jolted me back to the present. I forced myself to focus on studying for the next few hours, flipping through textbooks and scribbling down notes. It was hard work, balancing athletics and academics, but it was a challenge I had grown to appreciate. It made me feel good, like I was making progress towards something. I just wish I knew what that something was.

There hadn't been any pressure to declare a major when I enrolled, so I was working my way through basic courses like math and science. Everything I'd done since the first day centered on being eligible to play baseball. Now that I wasn't sure that baseball was much more than a hobby and a free ride to college these days, I felt the need to make an actual plan for my life.

As the sun began to set, casting long shadows across the library walls, I packed up my things, feeling a little off kilter. On the one hand, I'd managed to catch up on quite a bit of work, which I'd desperately needed to do. But I'd also somehow convinced myself that I was completely unprepared to do anything with my life that wasn't baseball.

As the season opener approached, Coach pushed us harder and harder, adding to the pressure of finals. He constantly reminded us that every play, every catch, was a crucial step towards our ultimate goal—winning. Each day brought the same question to the surface: what did I truly want out of this journey? Where was I even headed? Winning was great, but even winning a college World Series was only good for a year's worth of bragging rights.

Reaching my dorm, I tossed my books in one corner and grabbed my guitar from the other. My brain felt like a live wire. Strumming the strings mindlessly, I let the music slowly replace every thought. Their vibrations under my fingers felt like a direct flow of energy from my soul onto the strings.

The spell was broken when the sound of a message notification chimed from my computer.

Wildfire.

I clicked on the message, a smile already forming on my face in anticipation.

~

@WILDFIRE: *If you could choose any song to be the soundtrack of your life right now, what would it be and why?*

Her question made me laugh at the abruptness of it.

@GuyWithGuitar: *That feels like a loaded question. Ever heard of Collective Soul? I feel like I could have written their song Heavy. *link to song**

A few minutes went by. I assumed she was listening to the song.

@Wildfire: *Wow. OK. You could have at least picked a depressing song with a catchier tune. Why not Welcome to My Life (Simple Plan) or Under Pressure (Queen or even My Chemical Romance's version would be acceptable). I'm kidding! Anything you want to talk about?*

Her message made me laugh and filled me with a warmth that creeped though my entire body. Suddenly, everyone's expectations, the stress of the upcoming season, and the uncertainty about my future seemed to fade away.

I quickly typed a reply, my fingers moving with a newfound energy, telling her about some of the revelations I'd been having about baseball and the future. Every word I typed was like hitting a pressure release valve slowly, letting go of the things that had been building inside me. This feeling of confiding in someone who truly cared and wouldn't judge me for not having all the answers? There wasn't another feeling like it.

@Wildfire: *You know it's OK not to have everything figured out, right? Life isn't a race, and sometimes the detours turn out to be the most meaningful parts of our journey.*

One time, my mom and I were headed to a show a few counties over. The drive was supposed to be straightforward, but we hit a detour that took us off the main highway. We had to follow these winding, unfamiliar back roads. I could tell mom was stressed, worried about being late. But as we drove, the scenery changed. We found ourselves on this old road lined with ancient oak trees, their branches creating a canopy overhead. It was like something out of a storybook.

We had to slow down because the road was narrow and curvy, and that's when we noticed this little diner right there in the middle of nowhere. On a whim, we decided to stop for a quick bite. Inside, the diner had this warm, welcoming vibe, and the people were incredibly friendly. We ended up having the best homemade apple pie we'd ever tasted.

That unplanned stop became one of our most cherished memories. We laughed and mom actually relaxed a little. It was this moment of unexpected joy, a reminder that sometimes, getting off the beaten path can lead to the best surprises. We made it to the show eventually, a bit later than planned, but it didn't matter. We still talk about it and now I have a hankering for apple pie.

Sorry, I know that's really long, but sometimes you might just need to take a detour to find the best things in life.

I stared at her message, my heart racing as though I'd just run sprints for an hour.

Her words did something inside me, made me want things, to know things. I wanted to know things—about myself, about life, about the unexpected turns that could lead to moments as memorable as finding a random diner on a back road.

For the first time in a long time, I felt a genuine curiosity about all the 'what if' and 'could be' scenarios in my life. With her simple story, *Wildfire* had unknowingly pushed me to want to look beyond the familiar track I was on. And that realization alone was both thrilling and terrifying.

@GuyWithGuitar: How do you do that?

@Wildfire: Do what?

@GuyWithGuitar: Say exactly what I need to hear every single time we talk?

.   .   .

@Wildfire: Oh. I don't know. Maybe because we're not that different.

Her words hit me like a ton of bricks. Maybe she was right. Maybe we weren't that different after all. Both of us, in our own ways, trying to find our paths.

@GuyWithGuitar: You might be right. It's like you're always a step ahead, seeing things in a way I haven't yet. It's kind of amazing.

@Wildfire: I'm just sharing my thoughts. But I'm glad if they help. Sometimes, I guess, it takes someone else's perspective to see our own situation more clearly.

That's exactly what it was. Her perspective was like a mirror, reflecting my own thoughts and feelings, but from an angle I hadn't seen before.

@GuyWithGuitar: You have this way of making me see things differently, of making me question and reflect. Thanks for being that person for me, even if you don't realize you're doing it.

The moment I hit send, I had this crazy desire to hug her just to say thank you, but that would never happen. She always knew exactly what to say and when to say it, making me want to step out of my comfort zone and try new things. Our conversations were more than just words; they were a lifeline, a connection I valued so much. But more and more I wished we could share these moments in person, not just through a screen.

22

CASSIDY

The new year meant a new semester of classes. Six weeks in and the campus was coming to life with the occasional blooming flower and students spending more time outdoors trying to absorb the sun's warmth to make up for the cold gray winter we'd had. This particular afternoon, I found myself in a state of contemplation about the changes unfolding around me and in my own life.

The chamber ensemble allowed me to lose myself in the structured beauty of classical pieces. But it was the bluegrass ensemble that unexpectedly captured my heart. What had started as a whim had grown into something meaningful. The energy, the spontaneity of the music, it was refreshingly different from the disciplined world of classical music and performance.

And then there was Chase, the banjo player with the captivating smile. The music sessions we shared had turned our friendship into something fun and sweet. I'd agreed to go to a New Year's Eve party with him, and by midnight, even though he didn't kiss me, I found myself completely caught up in his charm.

The band started playing at small gigs on and around campus, each show bringing with it a new kind of excitement. For me, there's always been something about bluegrass that just gets under my skin, in the best way. But spending the extra time rehearsing and hanging out with Chase felt even better.

Sitting with him on a blanket under the canopy of a clear blue sky on one of the grassy areas on campus, I gazed upwards, lost in the ever-shifting shapes of the clouds, while he reclined with his head comfortably resting in my lap. The gentle hum of campus life surrounded us—distant laughter, the rustle of leaves in the breeze. These simple unscripted moments were my favorite.

"Hey," he said, looking up at me with those eyes that always seemed to sparkle with mischief, "how about we go out with the band this Friday? Just hang out, maybe hit that new place downtown?"

I smiled at the idea. Hanging out with the band was always a blast. There was a long history of lively debates, impromptu jam sessions, and endless laughter. "That sounds perfect," I replied. "A night out with everyone will be fun. Things have been so hectic lately with classes and rehearsals."

"Yeah," Chase agreed, sitting up to face me. "Let's take some time off and have fun together. No music talk, no stressing over classes or performances. Just us."

Just us. The words lingered in the air, sending a ripple of something sweet but foreign through me. For a moment, I found myself taken by the simplicity and sincerity of his suggestion. I really liked the prospect of spending time together without the usual backdrop of music and performance.

We hadn't talked about it, much less put a label on anything, and most of the time we spent together was alongside other musicians. When we were alone, it was in times like this—not really alone, but focused on each other. Which was fine, but it would be nice to get him to myself one of these days.

"And hey," Chase added with a grin, "it'll be nice to hang out without having to worry about who plays the better solo for once."

I laughed, playfully tousling his hair. "Oh, come on, you know you love the competition."

"Guilty as charged," he admitted with a chuckle. "But seriously, it'll be great to just be us for a night. No expectations."

I leaned back, letting the sun warm my face. "Just us," I echoed, the words feeling like a promise of something easy and uncomplicated.

His alarm went off, a reminder for his next class. Groaning, he rolled to his stomach then popped up with ease before extending a hand, offering to help me stand.

"I think I'm going to hang out a while longer. I'll see you at rehearsal?"

Slinging his banjo case over one shoulder and a backpack over the other, he said, "And Friday night." He had an adorable grin on his face, his eyes crinkling at the corners in that way that always made my heart race.

"Then, too," I said.

"Good. See you soon," Chase said with a wink, leaving me with a flutter of unidentifiable emotions.

As he disappeared into the bustling campus, I lay back on the blanket, staring at the sky. Our conversation replayed in my mind, and the words 'just us' hung in the air, both exciting and daunting. Chase and I had this easy chemistry, an unspoken understanding that felt both exhilarating and confusing.

Were we just friends who enjoyed each other's company? I mean, I wouldn't mind if there was something more beneath the surface to be explored. The thought made my heart race. Usually, we were surrounded by music and friends, a safety net that made our interactions feel less risky. But the idea of spending time together, just the two of us, without distractions, was new and exciting.

I smiled at the thought. Chase had a way of making everything fun and light, yet there seemed to be a hidden depth waiting to be explored. Did I want something more with him? I wasn't sure. But the idea of finding out, of taking that leap, was both scary and thrilling. For now, I decided to let things unfold naturally. After all, the best melodies were often the ones that took you by surprise and swept you away.

Realizing it was time for me to go, I grabbed my stuff, feeling excited for Friday night and whatever might happen.

As I walked toward my next class, there was a lightness in my step that hadn't been there before, a curiosity about what lay ahead. I was at peace, ready to take on whatever came next. Most of all, I finally felt like my life was my own and I never imagined it would feel like this.

23

NASH

It was perfect weather for opening day. The team had just nailed a first game victory, and the high of that win was still buzzing through me. We'd been talking about blowing off steam from the build up all week, and now that moment was finally here.

After showering and changing in the locker room, I was still in my zone when I saw Riley waiting for me. She was dolled up, but her excitement seemed a little too forced. Her smile was a bit too wide. It was an expression I'd seen on numerous occasions when she was selling me on an idea.

Rather than acknowledge it, I casually wrapped an arm around her shoulders and pulled her close to place a kiss on her forehead.

"Hey, babe," I said, unable to hide the lingering energy buzzing through me.

"Hey, yourself." There was a playful tilt to her smile, one that hinted at mischief. "Is that all I get?" she teased, her voice laced with a flirtatious undertone that sent a thrill down my spine.

With a grin, I swept an arm around her waist in a playful, exaggerated gesture. Simultaneously, my other hand found its way to the nape of her neck, guiding her into a spontaneous and theatrical dip.

Riley squealed before I placed a long, hard kiss on her lips. Hauling her upright, she was giggling and attempting to catch her breath.

"Better?" I asked.

Still smiling, she replied, "Much. Great game by the way. How about we hit up the mixer at my sorority house to celebrate the win?"

The buzz of giddiness began to fade as I paused, caught off guard. This was the first I was hearing of a sorority mixer.

"Riley, we've been planning to hang out with the team for weeks," I reminded her.

She ran her hand up my chest, her voice taking on a tone I'd heard plenty of times. "I know, but we can celebrate with your team any time. Sarah Grace said she heard from Paul Johnson that his sister might come visit this weekend."

Grabbing her hand and holding it in place, I stared at her, completely unaware of why I should care that Paul Johnson's sister was coming to visit him.

She must have recognized my confusion because she explained, "Paul Johnson's sister is Heather Johnson."

My expression remained unchanged because even the emphasis she put on Heather Johnson's name did nothing to bring me up to speed.

Rolling her eyes and letting out a huff of annoyance, Riley said, "Heather Johnson? The video blogger who got famous overnight?"

At that, it all started to make sense. She had an angle and Heather Johnson's presence at the sorority mixer would be a big deal for her. I could see the wheels turning in her head, always thinking one step ahead.

"Riley, I get why you want to go," I started, trying to find the right words. "But this team party isn't just another hangout. We've all been looking forward to it, especially after today's game. It's important to us—to me."

Her grip on my shirt tightened slightly, her smile fading. "But think about the opportunity, Nash. Meeting Heather could be huge. And you know I always want you there with me."

There was a pleading look in her eyes, the kind that usually had me bending over backward to make her happy. But tonight, it was different. My team, my friends—we had earned this celebration.

"Riley," I said, holding her gaze, "tonight's about the team. I've got to be there with them. Maybe we can catch up with Heather tomorrow."

The tension between us grew thick. For a moment, Riley looked like she might argue further, but then her shoulders dropped ever so slightly in resignation.

"Fine," she snapped, her voice a mix of frustration and resignation. "Go to your party. I'll just go to the mixer alone, I guess."

We stared at each other as though willing or maybe daring the other to cave. When neither of us would after several quiet seconds, she spun on her heel and walked away. As she did, I felt a twinge of guilt, but deep down, I knew I had made the right call. Cubby, who had been watching from a few feet away, came over, clapping me on the back.

"Man, that was rough, but good on you for sticking to your guns," he said, with no trace of mocking.

He wasn't a fan of Riley and always said Riley was controlling me. I had never seen it that way before, but now I was questioning my judgment.

"Yeah," I replied, watching Riley disappear into the crowd. "Just hope she understands."

The party with the team was everything we had hoped for—a night of celebrating our hard work and victory. Still, I occasionally thought about Riley, feeling a little guilty and hoping she was having a good time, too.

As the night wore on, the laughter and cheers of my teammates around me, I realized it wasn't about the party; it was about loyalty, friendship, and being there for each other. And in making my choice, I had stayed true to that spirit. I could only hope Riley saw it that way.

24

NASH

I reached over to my nightstand and grabbed my phone, a sense of unease creeping in. Although checking my phone first thing had become a habit, today I regretted ever starting it. My stomach twisted as I imagined the messages waiting for me.

The screen illuminated the dim room. Missed calls and texts from Riley lit up the display, each one adding to my guilt and frustration. She was upset. I got that. But I'd needed to stand my ground. Doubt crept in, making me question if I'd done the right thing.

With a sigh, I dropped the phone back on the bedside table.

Sitting up, I felt a stiffness in my shoulders. The room, littered with clothes and empty water bottles, felt smaller than usual. Getting dressed was a step towards normal, but my thoughts were all over the place.

I had no plan when I exited the room but found myself at the cafeteria, which was nearly empty. That was no surprise considering how early it was on a Saturday. The quiet gave me room to think loudly. And my thoughts took full advantage.

Riley, baseball, my dad, the math exam I had coming up on Monday, *Wildfire*.

I pushed my tray away, my appetite gone. My mind was a swirl of

Dad's push for excellence, Riley's plans, and my love for the game. They were puzzle pieces I couldn't fit together. But *Wildfire* was different—a wildcard that made everything feel more vivid. Thinking of her immediately made the noise in my head go quiet. She had nothing to do with the chaos, and she was all I wanted to think about. Her passion for music and our candid conversations were a world away from the surrounding pressures. Next to her, the other pieces didn't seem to matter as much.

Leaning back in my chair, I let my thoughts drift. *Wildfire* cut through the noise, making me question what I really wanted. She was out there, living her truth, making me wonder if I was living mine.

Maybe I needed to have a chat with Coach. He was a straight shooter and wouldn't hesitate to tell me what I needed to hear. Right now, though, I needed to get my head on straight. We had a game this afternoon and my focus needed to be on point.

Cubby was nowhere to be seen when I got back to the room so I reached for my guitar. I had a sudden urge to record the song that I'd been rolling around in my mind for the last several days. It would probably be rough, but something told me I needed to do it.

I hit record and just played. The music flowed, raw and unfiltered, a picture forming of the turmoil and the clarity I was beginning to feel.

After finishing the recording, I sat for a moment in the quiet aftermath, the last notes still echoing in the room. It was like I finally let go of something heavy I hadn't known I was holding onto.

I stopped recording and put my guitar away and hoped to catch up on some studying before I had to be at the field house. A knock at the door interrupted those plans.

Seeing Riley standing there when I opened it caught me off guard. Her expression was stormy.

"Hey, we need to talk," Riley said, stepping inside without waiting for an invitation.

I closed the door behind her, bracing myself. "OK, what's up?" I asked, trying to keep my tone neutral.

"It's about last night," she began, pacing the room. "You made me go to the mixer alone, Nash. You didn't even call or text to check in."

I sighed, running a hand through my hair. "Riley, we talked about this. The team had been planning the party before you told me about the mixer. It was important to the team and it was important to me."

"But what about what's important to me?" Her voice rose slightly, a hint of hurt underlining her words.

Before I could respond, a ping from my computer cut through the escalating tension. I glanced at the screen to see a new message from *Wildfire*. Riley's eyes followed mine, narrowing slightly.

"What's that?" she asked, nodding towards the screen.

I quickly hit the power button on the monitor, a nervous chuckle escaping me. "Oh, it's just some music stuff, nothing important."

"Music stuff?" Riley echoed, her eyebrows raised in surprise. I hadn't meant to say it, but I panicked.

"Yeah, just messing around with some songs. It's really nothing," I said, trying to brush it off. I wasn't ready to dive into this part of my life with her just yet, not when I still hadn't figured it all out myself.

Riley uncrossed her arms, her expression shifting from suspicion to curiosity. "I didn't know you were into that. Why haven't you mentioned it before?"

I shrugged, feeling a bit cornered. "I don't know, it's just a hobby, I guess. Nothing serious." I was eager to change the subject, to steer away from the topic that suddenly felt too personal, too exposed.

She studied me for a long moment, as if trying to read between the lines. Then, seemingly deciding to let it go for now, she sighed. "OK, well, about last night..."

I seized the opportunity to shift back to our original argument. "Right, about that. Look, I didn't mean to upset you, but you know how important the team is to me."

As we talked about the previous night, I was relieved to move away from music and *Wildfire,* yet I felt an unexpected guilt, like I was hiding something. *Wildfire* was just an online friend, someone I knew only through conversations. I had no idea why I felt guilty. I didn't even know *Wildfire's* real name.

We both had a passion for music and there was definitely something about our connection that felt deeper and more real than it probably should, something that went beyond just shared interests. But still, practically a stranger. At least that's what I kept telling myself.

As Riley talked, part of me was listening, but another part was wrestling with these new thoughts and feelings I was having about *Wildfire*. Nobody knew about her and I kind of liked it that way. But, no matter how much I tried to justify it, I still felt guilty. It wasn't about what *Wildfire* and I were actually doing or saying. It was about the part of me she reached, a part that I hadn't shared with Riley, a part that I was only just starting to understand myself.

I found myself giving half-hearted responses to Riley, my mind still tangled in a web of thoughts. I knew I should be more focused on this conversation so I could address the issues Riley was bringing up, but my mind was lost in a maze of questions.

Riley, sensing my distraction, paused mid-sentence. "Nash, you seem miles away," her tone laced with mild irritation.

I shook my head, attempting to clear my mind and bring my attention back to her. "Sorry, Riles. Just a lot on my mind."

She studied me for a moment, her expression shifting. "Is this about us, Nash? Because I feel like you're pulling away. And after last night, I just need to know where we stand."

This conversation was clearly heading for deeper waters than I'd originally thought. "Riley, I'm here with you. It's just... there's a lot I'm trying to figure out."

She leaned in, her eyes searching mine. "But we're OK, right? Because I need us to be OK, Nash. I can't deal with the uncertainty."

Even though I had reservations, I still managed to nod in agreement. "Yeah, we're OK. I'm not going anywhere. I just need some time to sort through some things."

Riley's expression softened, and she reached out to touch my arm. "As long as we're OK. That's what matters. Just don't leave me out of the loop, OK? And I want to be there for you, Nash, through whatever it is you're dealing with."

I forced a smile, feeling the familiar intensity of her demands and expectations. "I won't leave you out, Riley."

As she stood, Riley's gaze lingered on me. "We're in this together," she said softly.

I nodded, recognizing her need for reassurance. Standing up, I closed the gap between us, enveloping her in a gentle hug. Her arms wrapped around me in response, a silent affirmation of our connection. In that moment, despite the turmoil inside, I felt the comfort of her familiar presence.

She pulled back slightly, looking up at me. Her eyes, usually so full of determination, held a vulnerability that tugged at something inside me. Leaning down, I pressed a kiss to her forehead. Riley smiled, a small, contented curve of her lips.

The conversation had helped a bit with the tension, but now I was wondering how long I could balance Riley's demands with my growing need for something more.

25

CASSIDY

S prawled across my bed, I mentally replayed the night out with Chase and the band on a constant loop. It had been the perfect break from the stress of the week, with lots of laughter and music. But amidst the fun, there had been a moment with Chase that had quietly but firmly taken root in my thoughts.

Everyone else had stepped out onto the dance floor as we remained planted in our seats across from one another in a booth. He smiled and immediately my neck and face grew warm and my mind started spinning up with questions.

"If you could relive any moment of your life, which would it be and why?" I asked.

He paused, his smile lingering but his eyes turning reflective. "This one," he finally said, his gaze meeting mine. "Not to change anything, just to experience it again. There's something about right now, this conversation with you, that feels significant. Like it's one of those moments I'll look back on and realize it was more important than I knew at the time."

His answer took me by surprise and it made my heart flutter in a way I couldn't quite name. Chase's gaze didn't waver; it held a depth that I hadn't noticed before.

"What about you, Cassidy?" he asked, turning the question back to me. "Is there a moment you would revisit?"

I found myself lost in thought, considering his question. There were so many moments, each with its own significance, but finding one that stood out amongst the rest was unexpectedly challenging. My mind drifted to family dinners, music recitals, and late-night conversations. Each memory was a piece of the puzzle that made up my life, but none felt as immediate and vital as the moment I was currently living.

"I don't know if I'd relive any moment for fear of messing it up. I think I'm starting to understand that the most important moments might be the ones happening right now," I said, my voice weighted with wonder and realization. "This conversation, this evening, they feel like turning points, even if I can't quite see where they're leading."

Chase nodded, a look of understanding in his eyes. "Sometimes the best moments are the ones we don't see coming. They catch us off guard and end up meaning more than we ever imagined."

We let the conversation settle in the silence between us until the music's tempo changed. A grin spread across his face as the two-step beat filled the room.

"Will you dance?" he asked, standing and offering his hand. My heart skipped a beat, then raced wildly. I had never felt like this before. A rush of nerves and anticipation flooded me, making my hands tremble slightly. My breath hitched as I hesitated, the butterflies in my stomach fluttering madly. Dancing with Chase felt like stepping into a whole new world, one I had only imagined in my daydreams.

But then I looked at him, really studied him. The way he gazed at me, with a gentle sincerity, made my stomach flutter. His eyes held a promise of something new, something thrilling. It was impossible to say no.

As we moved to the rhythm of the music, I found myself getting lost in the moment. Chase was a surprisingly good dancer, leading with an easygoing confidence. The world around us, the sounds of conversations and music, it all faded into the background. There was just us, moving in sync, as if we were the only ones in the room.

The song ended all too soon, leaving us slightly breathless and smiling. "Thanks for the dance, Cassidy," Chase said as we walked back to our booth. His words were simple, but there was an underlying warmth that made me feel seen and appreciated.

As the evening came to a close and we said our goodbyes, I sensed a change in the dynamic between Chase and me. And I really hoped he felt it, too.

I WAS PULLED from the memory by a notification that *GuyWithGuitar* had posted a new upload. Instantly, I was moving from my bed to my desk, my cursor hovering over the notification. Excitement rushed through me as I clicked the link.

As he began to sing, his voice, raw and filled with emotion, enveloped me. This wasn't a song I knew; it sounded like an original, and it sounded deeply personal. The lyrics spoke of longing, of moments lost and found, and of not knowing which direction was meant for him. His voice, combined with the gentle strumming of his guitar, created a melody that was both haunting and beautiful.

As the final chord faded, I sat there for a moment, lost in thought, tears burning my eyes. The song had touched something deep inside me. I always felt a connection to *Guy* and to his music, that went beyond just the notes and the lyrics. It was as if he was singing directly to me, sharing a part of his soul through his art.

Compelled by this feeling, I quickly typed out a message to him.

@Wildfire: That was incredible. It's like you've put into words the things that I've been feeling for so long. How did you do that?

Waiting for a reply, I found myself comparing the two guys and my experiences with them. Chase was tangible. I'd physically been in his presence. His warm hand had held mine. There had been shared glances that had evoked feelings that were new and exhilarating. I'd liken it to walking a wooded trail and stepping into a sunlit clearing.

On the other hand, the connection with *Guy* was an emotional journey, akin to walking along a serene, moonlit beach. His music was like the gentle, persistent waves that touched the shore. Each lyric and melody reaching out and softly caressing the deeper, often hidden parts of my soul. Just as the ocean can stir a sense of awe and introspection, *Guy's* song echoed in the quiet spaces of my heart, revealing emotions and thoughts I had scarcely admitted to myself.

I sat there, battling internally with the emotions both guys evoked. Could it be possible to feel so deeply connected to someone I'd never met? To be so moved by his music that it felt like he was crucial to my very existence? And what about Chase, with his serene smile and the comfortable familiarity that came with spending time together?

Watching as 'online' flashed next to his name, but not receiving a reply, a small wave of disappointment washed over me as it was unusual for him not to respond, especially when he was active.

Shaking off the feeling, I headed downstairs. The familiar sounds of home filled the air. I could hear the clink of dishes, the murmur of the television, the soft hum of the refrigerator. Mom and Dad were in the kitchen, their presence comforting.

"Hey, sweetheart. Dinner's almost ready. Can you set the table?" Mom asked, her voice light and inviting, a pronounced difference from just a few months ago.

"Sure, Mom," I replied, grabbing plates from the cupboard. As I laid them out, I ventured, "So, I have a performance with the blue-grass band next Friday. You both should come. It's at The Local. I know it's not your scene but I think you'd enjoy the music and, well, I'll be playing."

"We wouldn't miss it," Dad said, a smile in his voice.

After dinner, I retreated once again to the sanctuary of my room. Settling into the quiet, I opened my journal, the blank pages inviting me to unravel the web of emotions that had entangled me throughout the evening. With pen in hand, I began to write, each word a step towards understanding the swirling pool of feelings that Chase's presence and *Guy's* music had stirred within me.

It was late when the sound of a message arriving distracted me and had me setting my journal to the side.

@GuyWithGuitar: I don't know that I do it on purpose but you have no

idea how much I appreciate being on the same wavelength with someone like you.

Someone like me? A chill washed over me as I rolled those words over a few times before responding.

@Wildfire: I couldn't agree more. It's not every day you find someone who understands you so deeply. It's like finding an unexpected friend in a crowded room, someone who really hears you over all the noise even though you haven't said anything out loud. I feel understood on a level that's new to me.

His response came quickly, and I eagerly read his words.

@GuyWithGuitar: It's the same for me. Talking to you is like having a place where I can be myself without any filters. You've made me think about my music and my life, in ways I never have before.

His words resonated with me, reinforcing the sense that we were on a similar journey, even though our paths had been so different.

We fell into a conversation that wandered through various topics, each one carving out a deeper connection between us.

As the chat ended, I was left with mixed feelings. Opening up to *Guy* felt natural, but it always left me with questions. I wondered about the real person behind the screen, about the life he led outside of our conversations.

I only hoped he knew how much he meant to me.

26

NASH

Packing my bags to head home for the summer, I was excited to see my family and catch up with Cody and Jet, but surprisingly, I was most excited to start back at the youth center. Thinking about the kids and the showcase last summer had me trying to come up with ways to top what we'd already done.

The fact that I was this excited for a kids' music track at a summer camp pretty much confirmed I'd made the right decision when I declared my major to be Music Education at the beginning of the new semester. If that wasn't confirmation enough, Dr. Simmons had returned our final assignments in Music Theory, and when I looked over mine—A Comprehensive Analysis on the Application of Music Theory in Country Music—he hadn't held back his praise.

"Exceptional understanding," he'd remarked. That was pretty good validation, if you asked me.

A text from Riley interrupted my packing.

> Are you sure you don't want to stay on campus? I'll miss you being so far away.

I rolled my eyes and tossed the phone on my bed. We'd decided to try a long-distance relationship over the summer. I could sense her reluctance; she complained about the whole situation multiple times. She'd wanted me to stay on campus over the summer. Not only had I made the commitment to work the summer program, I just didn't want to. I tried to be understanding, reassuring her with promises of regular calls and maybe a visit if we could squeeze one in.

Deep down, however, I was relieved. The distance would give me some much needed breathing room. Guilt ate away at me when I thought too hard about my feelings for Riley. I cared about her, but the spark was fading. I didn't want to let go or give up before knowing if it might reignite.

When I'd told her that I'd decided to major in Music Education, I don't think she'd actually believed me at first. She couldn't understand why I'd want to teach music and not do something more-like play baseball professionally.

At first I'd taken her words to heart and almost second guessed myself. Then Coach's words from the conversation I finally had with him came rushing back.

He'd said, "Montgomery, there's more to life than baseball. And you can't let fear of the unknown hold you back. You've got to be willing to step out of that safe zone, to find out who you really are, not just what you think everyone expects you to be."

When he dropped that bomb on me, everything became crystal clear. I'd sent an e-mail to my advisor and started the ball rolling in a direction I never pictured myself going in, and it felt exactly right. The only thing that had me worried was telling my dad that baseball was only going to be for now and wasn't going to be my future. But that was a discussion for another day.

For now, I needed to finish packing and get home and hug my mama.

$$27$$

CASSIDY

When I was younger, my mother launched a small business providing piano accompaniment for wedding ceremonies. By the time I turned twelve, I had joined her, playing the violin at weddings. As the years passed, I grew to love singing at the receptions even more than accompanying her. It actually became my favorite part of the job. And every summer, couples hired us every weekend, even into the fall.

My mom, however, had hinted more than once before this last Christmas that she was considering hanging up her "wedding shoes" as she called them. I had kind of gotten the feeling more than once she was trying to tell me something without actually telling me. I'd gotten worried a few times that she was planning some kind of crazy performance tour or something, but when nothing ever came of my suspicions, I let it go.

So, I ignored my thoughts and when the first call came in from a bride looking for a violinist, I told Mom to accept the job, saying I'd take on a few weddings here and there just because I liked the money.

But it wasn't just about the money. There was something magical about weddings, about being part of someone's special day, even if just in the background. That's when an idea struck me. I approached the bluegrass band, suggesting that since we were all trained in classical music as well as bluegrass, we could offer something unique to these events. Surprisingly, they were all in.

It turned out to be the most fun I'd had in a long time. Even with the extra hours of rehearsal and the attempts we made to blend our styles, I was in heaven. Of course, it didn't hurt that Chase, with his laid-back nature and loads of talent, was there smiling and laughing to make the hours fly by.

Before we knew it, we were in the middle of a wedding season that started two weeks before finals had even arrived. I wasn't sure which part I was most excited about—the music, the celebrations, the time spent with the band, Chase. Every time I thought about him, I felt a flutter in my stomach.

He had this way of being flirty and sweet, always finding a reason to sit next to me, and he never failed to make me laugh. But that was it. He'd never indicated he wanted anything more than friendship. I found myself watching him sometimes, and I would wonder if he felt something for me. But how would I know?

It was confusing, this growing crush I had on him. I'd never felt this way about anyone before, and I didn't quite know what to do with these feelings. I wanted to believe that there could be something between us, more than just shared talents and music. But another part, the cautious, logical part, reminded me that a crush could just be a crush, nothing more.

It was times like these I wish I had more girlfriends to talk to. I could talk to my mom, I guess. But that felt like a weird boundary, since we'd never crossed it before. I couldn't talk to Mia because I was pretty sure it would get back to Chase pretty quickly, which would defeat the whole purpose of talking about it.

Rehearsals became this constant barrage of emotions. I'd catch myself glancing at Chase, then scolding myself for reading too much into his friendly banter. There was this one song we played that was a slow, romantic bluegrass number that featured our instruments, and it sounded like they were in a dance of melodies. Every time we played it, my heart raced, and I wondered if he felt the same spark I did.

But as quickly as those thoughts came, I'd push them away. I wasn't willing to risk what we had, the ease and joy of a happy friendship. The last thing I needed was to make things awkward, especially with a whole summer of performances ahead of us.

Then came our first wedding as a band. The setting was a picturesque garden, glowing with the colors of sunset. As we played, everything turned ethereal–the guests, the decorations, even my uncertainties. It was just the music and us, creating magic in the golden hour.

Between sets, while the guests mingled, I found myself near the back of the garden, taking in the view. That's when Chase joined me, his hands tucked in his pockets, a soft smile on his face.

"You were amazing up there, Cassidy." His voice was gentle.

"Thanks," I replied, feeling my face flush. "You were pretty great yourself."

There was a pause, a moment where our eyes met, and I felt that familiar flutter. How was I supposed to survive the entire summer like this?

The evening went by in a blur of music and smiles. As the band packed up, I couldn't shake the disappointment, feeling as though I had held back when I should have put myself out there.

The weeks rolled on, each wedding blending into the next. Chase was always there, he was always charming, his laughter infectious, and his flirting never seemed to wane. But that was it. There was never anything more, never a hint that he saw me as anything more than a friend and a fellow musician.

I found myself writing more and more. Not music for the band, but personal songs, ones that I tucked away in my notebook. They were songs of longing, of confusion, songs that spoke of a heart quietly desperate for something it couldn't have. Writing them felt like a release, a way to pour out all the feelings I didn't dare voice out loud.

One evening, after a particularly beautiful wedding set under a canopy of twinkling lights, I found myself alone in my room with my violin, the strings singing a melancholic melody, the words flowing almost effortlessly:

> *In the dance of our glances,*
> *In the laughs, in the chances,*
> *There's a 'more' that's unspoken,*
> *A heart gently broken.*

I had this constant anxiety that I was misreading everything and was afraid of taking a step that might shatter the beautiful friendship we had. Chase was like a tune that was beautiful, but the lyrics were just out of reach.

As the summer went on, I began to accept that my feelings probably wouldn't be returned. I focused on the music, the performances, and every note I played. It was easier and safer to get lost in the rhythm and the strings than to think about my own heart.

And every time I thought there might be a chance, a flicker of hope, the moment would pass, and we'd be back to our easy friendship, our laughter, our music. I'd always tell myself it was enough. It had to be.

28

NASH

Before I knew it, we were several weeks into the summer. I had settled into a comfortable rhythm that started early with chores, followed by a few hours at The Youth Club, and wrapped up with evening chores. It was like night and day compared to last year when I had to do these activities as a punishment. But now, things were different—I was different. This wasn't punishment, it was a choice—my choice.

One evening, after a long day on the farm, the tiredness in my muscles was a satisfying reminder of the day's work. I found myself in a reflective mood as I joined Dad on the porch. The night had settled around us, the sky a vast, crystal-clear canvas dotted with countless stars.

"Beautiful night, isn't it?" Dad remarked, breaking the comfortable silence.

I nodded, my gaze still fixed on the heavens. "Yeah, it really is."

He took a sip of his coffee, then glanced at me. "Something on your mind, son?"

I hesitated for a moment, taking a deep breath. "Yeah, actually, there is."

So I told him about my change of plans and that baseball and then asked, "Do you think I'm making the right choice?"

Dad turned to me, a slight smile on his lips. "That's the beauty of being young," he said. "You don't need to have everything figured out yet. Life's about exploring, making mistakes, and learning. Whether it's baseball or something else entirely, the choice is yours."

His words were a shock to me. I'd always thought Dad wanted me to follow a specific path, especially with baseball. I shifted uncomfortably, feeling the need to voice a thought that had been gnawing at me.

"So, you're okay if I choose a path that doesn't include baseball?" I ventured, my words hesitant. I had always assumed Dad was hoping I'd go pro, especially with how he always watched my games so intently, cheering me on from the stands, making the occasional comment about my future in the "big leagues".

Dad's hand rested on my shoulder, a firm, reassuring weight. "Nash, all I've ever wanted is for you to be happy and to follow your heart. You've got a good head on your shoulders. Trust it."

I stared at him, a swirl of confusion and relief mixing in my chest. Had I been wrong all this time? I wondered. Had I misunderstood his expectations, projecting my own fears and ambitions onto him?

"But... you always seemed so invested in my games and in my performance. I thought you wanted me to make it big in baseball," I admitted, needing to understand his perspective.

Dad chuckled softly, a warm, comforting sound. "I love watching you play because you love playing. It was never about you making it big, Nash. Did I always expect you to do your best? Yes. But more than that, it was about you finding joy in what you do. If baseball is that for you, great. If not, that's perfectly fine too."

His words sank in, slowly dissolving the weight I'd carried for so long. I'd made a huge assumption and had put unnecessary pressure on myself based on a misunderstanding and chasing a dream that I thought others expected of me, not one that I truly wanted.

"Thanks, Dad," I said, my voice steadier now, my heart lighter.

We sat in silence again, but this time the quiet was peaceful and uninterrupted by my silent questions about the future.

When we did talk again, our conversation turned to the youth center's summer program. I told him about a conversation I'd had with Mr. Muñoz about Jet Vargas. We'd restarted our lessons, and the kid was showing great promise, but a few weeks into the summer, I noticed him more withdrawn than usual.

It took a little prodding, but he eventually opened up about his home situation. His grandma's sickness had hit the family hard, causing his mom to be stretched thin as she juggled work and care-giving. Jet, with his good heart, was clearly worried, but he said his mom just brushed off his concerns, telling him not to worry.

When I talked to Mr. Muñoz about it, he agreed to speak with Jet's mom about the possibility of Jet working on the farm. It was a win-win situation–Jet could earn some money to help out at home, and we could use the help during the busy summer season.

"Jet's going through a tough time. His grandma's sick, and his mom is stretched thin."

Dad's expression grew thoughtful and before I could tell him what I'd mentioned to Mr. Muñoz, he said, "Why don't we see if Jet can help out on the farm? Might do him good, and we could use the extra hands."

I had a sudden rush of gratitude. "That's a really great idea. Thanks, Dad. I'll talk to Mr. Muñoz about it tomorrow."

"You've got a big heart Nash." Dad's voice was so sincere when he said, "You'll be fine as long as you do what it tells you to do."

I smiled, feeling a deep sense of appreciation. "Thanks, Dad."

Dad slapped a hand on his leg before standing with a groan and nodded, a look of approval in his eyes. "Well, you let me know what Mr. Muñoz says. We'll figure out a way to get Jet involved around here."

Following his lead, I stood. Dad gave me a pat on the back. "Get some rest, Nash. Tomorrow's another day."

Excited and wide awake after talking with Dad, I logged on to OurSpace, where I hoped to find *Wildfire*. We had been leaving messages for one another for weeks, effectively playing an online version of tag. It appeared tonight was my lucky night because her status was set to Online.

@GuyWithGuitar: Is this a dream or are you really here?

Several seconds passed, but when her message appeared, a jolt of excitement moved through me.

@Wildfire: I think it's a dream come true! How are you?!?!

Between her week of finals followed by what she called the "wedding season of the century" and my return to the youth program, we hadn't had a real time conversation in far too long.

I caught her up on everything that had happened and told her about the music project I had the kids working on for the summer. She filled me in on her family and the crazy schedule she had in place for the summer. Apparently, she'd practically doubled the number of weddings from the previous summer by bringing in some musicians she'd met at school.

Before I knew it, it was well after midnight and morning chores were just a few hours away. It never failed. My time with *Wildfire* seemed to fly by and was never long enough. There were times when I thought about asking to move our conversations from the computer to the phone, but I was afraid of coming across as a creepy stalker or something.

Instead, I savored the connection we had, even if it was just through typed words on a screen. I knew I had to call it a night, but I hesitated, not wanting to end our conversation.

@GuyWithGuitar: I can't believe how late it is. I've got early morning chores waiting for me.

@Wildfire: I understand. Time always flies when we're talking. I wish we had more of it.

Her response made me smile.

@GuyWithGuitar: Same here. Let's try to catch up again soon, OK?

. . .

@WILDFIRE: Definitely! And hey, don't let those goats outsmart you in the morning!

I chuckled at her playful comment that referred to a conversation we'd had about one of my sister's goats hiding after it had been caught chewing through a bag of feed. These were the moments that made me long to have a real-life connection with *Wildfire*.

@GuyWithGuitar: I'll do my best. Goodnight, Wildfire.

@WILDFIRE: Goodnight, Guy. Sweet dreams!

Signing off, I had an ache in my chest that I didn't want to try to explain. I was grateful for all the meaningful connections in my life, both online and offline. But if I was being honest, my heart desperately hoped there would be a day *Wildfire* and I would meet face-to-face.

29

CASSIDY

The summer days grew shorter, and after each wedding performance, I immersed myself deeper in my own music, trying to drown out my feelings for Chase. He remained charming and friendly, blissfully unaware of the unrest he was constantly causing me. That was on me, though, because I was too cowardly to tell him how I felt.

As the last wedding of the season ended, I felt sentimental. We had all grown, not just musically, but also as a group. Watching him across the room during our final break as he laughed at something Liam had said, I realized I couldn't let the summer end without revealing my feelings.

The night had been perfect, but the unspoken question lingered in the back of my mind like the last note of a song. It was now or never. If I didn't speak up, the 'what if' would haunt me.

When the reception ended and transitioned into a digital playlist dance party, the band packed up our instruments. The physical exertion of the evening gave a sense of finality to the summer's last performance.

Chase and I said goodnight to Mia and Liam, our voices floating on the sounds of the night. As we walked towards the parking area, there was a comfortable silence between us, the kind that had always made our friendship feel easy and genuine.

He walked me to my car, his hands casually tucked into his pockets. The fluorescent glow of the parking lot lights cast a gentle shadow over his face.

"Once again, you were amazing tonight, Cassidy," Chase said as we stopped beside my car, his voice sincere.

"Thanks," I said, my heart racing as I attempted to maintain my composure.

As I opened my mouth to speak, Chase looked at me with a curious tilt of his head, sensing the change in my demeanor.

"Chase, I..." I started, my heart pounding. "I need to tell you something."

His expression softened. "What is it?"

I took another deep breath, my heart racing. "I've had feelings for you for a while now—as more than just a friend. I was scared to open up and put our relationship at risk, but it felt unfair to keep it to myself, just in case." My words trailed off.

Chase's eyes widened slightly, and for a moment, there was silence, a heavy stillness that felt like an eternity. Then he let out a slow breath. Chase's eyes searched mine, a gentle understanding in his gaze. A silence fell over us, not uncomfortable, but heavy with unspoken thoughts.

"Oh," he finally said, his voice calm and kind. "Cassidy, I had no idea. You're amazing, and I value our friendship."

I held my breath, bracing for the words that would follow.

"I'm really flattered, but I can only think of you as a close friend. I hope this doesn't change things between us," he continued, his honesty clear in his eyes.

The words were gentle, yet they echoed with a finality that closed the door on every possibility I had imagined. Disappointment swept over me, but it was quickly followed by a sense of relief from voicing what I'd been feeling.

I forced a small smile, my grip tightening on the car door. "No, it doesn't change things. I just needed to be honest."

As I drove away, the night seemed to envelop me in its quiet. My confession left a hollow feeling in my chest. Tears blurred the edges of my vision, not just from the sting of rejection, but from the release of emotions that had been building up for so long.

The drive home seemed to take forever. My heart was heavy with thoughts of what might have been. He had always been so warm, so flirty, his signals mixed enough to keep my hopes quietly kindled. I had read so much into every smile, every shared glance, but in the end, they were just fragments of a story I had been writing in my head.

I sat in the driveway for a while, allowing myself to feel everything-the disappointment, the confusion, the ache. I focused on my breathing, each inhale and exhale an effort to steady my swirling thoughts. My hand lingered on the ignition key, but I was reluctant to move, to accept the finality of the night's events. The car acted likely cocoon of solitude and it felt like as good a place as any to allow myself to unravel.

After several minutes, I attempted to give myself a pep talk.

"OK, Cassidy, you can do this," I whispered to myself. "You faced the music, you can walk a few more steps."

Pulling myself together, I opened the car door, the night air cool against my flushed cheeks. The familiar path to the front door seemed longer than usual.

The house was quiet, mirroring my mood. I leaned my forehead against the door, feeling its solidity. It was in the quiet that I recognized my desire for someone real to talk to. Being younger than most students on campus, living at home, and being an only child intensified the sense of isolation I was currently feeling.

I wandered upstairs to my room and ended up at the window, gazing into the night. The stars twinkled brightly. I thought about Chase. My heart ached with confusion and embarrassment. I had woven a story around us so compelling I'd believed it myself. The rejection from Chase felt raw. But it wasn't just the rejection that stung — it was realizing how much I had gotten wrong.

The room felt stifling and my fingers itched to pull out my violin, but it was too late to do that. I moved to my desk and absently tidied up, rearranging sheet music and notebooks. The mundane task was almost enough to recenter me.

My mind drifted to *GuyWithGuitar*. He had become an unexpected confidant, someone who understood my thoughts without us ever having actually met.

What would he say about tonight? Would his words offer the comfort I needed?

I settled into the chair at my desk, the need to connect overwhelming. As I powered up the computer, the screen lit up the dim room.

Logging into OurSpace, I checked for *GuyWithGuitar*. My heart leaped in my chest as I noticed his status was online. Hesitation gripped me for a moment as I contemplated what to say.

"Uh, yeah, hi. There was this guy I really liked and he rejected me. Am I an idiot?" Nope. That was not how any conversation with *Guy* was going to start. I settled on basic.

@Wildfire: It's been a while.

As I waited for his response, I felt a small sense of relief. Maybe tonight I wouldn't have to face my thoughts alone.

@GuyWithGuitar: Hey, yeah it has. How are you?

Now what? I'd started this, but did I really want to talk about this with him? I was second guessing myself. I settled for vague.

@Wildfire: Ever had a moment when you realize what you wanted isn't really what you need?

His reply was quick.

@GuyWithGuitar: More than you know. Sometimes I feel like I'm chasing shadows, not really sure what I'm after.

His words mirrored my confusion, making me feel less alone.

@Wildfire: I've always been sure about my music, but lately, everything else seems like a puzzle. Like, how do you choose between what's safe and what might be right for you?

With the amount of time it took him to, I had started to wonder if he was debating with himself whether to even respond to the bombshell of a message I'd just sent.

@GuyWithGuitar: That's the million-dollar question, isn't it? I've been thinking about my future, too. Music, teaching, something that feels right. But making that choice, it's like stepping into the unknown.

His honesty struck a chord with me.

@Wildfire: It's scary, stepping out of what you know. I thought I knew what I wanted, but now... I'm not so sure.

It was crazy how badly I wanted to cross the line and get into personal details. There was something exciting about the anonymity at first, but every conversation had me wanting to know the man behind *GuyWithGuitar*.

@GuyWithGuitar: It's strange, isn't it? How we can share so much and yet know so little about each other.

@Wildfire: It is. Sometimes, I think you understand parts of me better than people who see me every day.

As the conversation wound down, I felt closer to *Guy* than ever. Despite the miles and screens between us, he seemed more real and more present than anyone else in my life at that moment. I wanted desperately to ask him to share everything about himself, hoping he would want to know the same things about me.

Yet, the fear of rejection held me back, silencing the questions that lingered on the tip of my tongue. The possibility of being turned away again was too daunting to face, so I kept my thoughts to myself, wishing for a courage I couldn't quite grasp.

Lying in my bed, the night pressing in, I pondered the night's conversation. The words, though from a stranger, offered a sense of understanding that I craved. In the quiet, I found a comfort that had eluded me with Chase.

"Goodnight, Guy," I murmured to the darkness. "Thanks for being you, even if I don't really know you are."

And with that, I drifted into sleep, the edges of my thoughts softened by just knowing I had a friend somewhere out there.

30

NASH

The morning sun rose over the Montgomery farm, signaling the start of another day. As I went about my morning chores, my thoughts kept drifting back to the summer showcase last night. The kids were amazing. Their energy and talent filled the stage which had them outdoing last year's performance by leaps and bounds.

As I hauled a bale of hay from a trailer and started toward the barn, I caught a glimpse of a figure walking toward me. The faded jeans and backwards hat belonged to one of my favorite kids and today marked one of Jet's last days working on the farm for the season. As the summer went on, I realized he's grown to be more of the younger brother I never had. I was truly grateful Jet had ended up working for us.

The day we offered Jet the job, I saw a weight lift off his shoulders. He was eager to help, to contribute in any way he could. It went beyond having a job for the summer; it was a way to ease his family's burden, even if just a little.

As we worked on the fence later that morning, I was glad to see how much Jet had grown over the summer. It had been amazing to watch him come into his own.

"Can you believe summer's almost over?" I asked Jet as we repaired a section of the fence. The mid-August heat was already beginning to make its presence known.

Jet wiped the sweat from his brow, nodding. "Yeah, it flew by. Kinda looking forward to getting back to school though," he said, a hint of uncertainty in his voice.

I hammered a fencing nail into the wooden post and glanced at him. "You did great here, you know. Not everyone takes to farm work this quickly."

He shrugged, a small smile tugged at his lips. "Thanks, man. It's been... different. But it's a good different."

As we worked, I caught Jet sneaking glances towards the house, where Cody was likely doing her own set of chores. I'd noticed these little looks all summer but never mentioned them. It was amusing, yet also touching, to see him so taken with my sister, yet so cautious about it.

Part of me wanted to give Jet a little brotherly advice, maybe nudge him in the right direction, or at least let him know that it's okay to take a chance sometimes. But another part of me thought it best to let things play out naturally. After all, Cody had a good head on her shoulders. And Jet, well, he seemed like the kind of guy who would treat her right.

I chuckled to myself, realizing how strange it was to be on this side of the equation. I'd been the nervous guy with a crush more times than I could count, and here I was, contemplating the potential budding romance of my little sister. She'd probably kill me if she knew I'd had any of these thoughts, even for a second.

My mind wandered as I worked alongside Jet, the sound of our tools providing the soundtrack of the day.

"So, any exciting plans for your senior year?" I asked.

Jet leaned against the fence, looking out over the fields. "Actually, I was thinking of joining the orchestra at school."

Surprised, I said, "Oh yeah? What got you interested in that?"

"Well," he started, a bit hesitantly, "I saw this guitar player at a school assembly last year. He talked about starting out in a group and learning faster that way. Made me think maybe I could get better if I played with others. And orchestra seems like a good place to start."

"That's a great idea," I said, encouragingly. "Playing with others can definitely help you improve. I know someone who plays the violin in an orchestra. She's pretty amazing."

Jet looked curious, but I didn't elaborate. Mentioning *Wildfire*, even indirectly, stirred up something inside me. It had been a while since we last talked. I made a mental note to check in and see if I could catch her online later.

We continued working on the fence in a comfortable silence. After a few minutes, I decided to break the lull in our conversation.

"You know, I'll be back at the youth center next summer," I said, hammering another nail into the fence post. "Mr. Muñoz already asked me to lead the Jam Session track again."

Jet's face lit up. "Really? That's awesome! It'll be great to have you there again. It made a huge difference this summer, especially for the kids who are really into music."

I smiled, feeling a sense of pride. "Thanks. It means a lot to hear that. I love helping you guys out. It's been more rewarding than I expected."

The conversation shifted to plans for next summer, and we tossed around some ideas for the youth center. It was moments like these that made all the hard work worth it, knowing that I was making a difference.

As the day ended and weariness set in, I lay on an old barn blanket in the pasture, contemplating the future. The thought of returning to school loomed like a cloud in front of the sun. But not because I was dreading classes. That was actually something I was looking forward to. It was everything and everyone else I'd be going back to.

Baseball was now just a means to keep my scholarship. I loved the team, and I really did love the game. Keeping up with the schedule and my workload was a lot, but it was also easier now that the pressure to excel beyond simply winning games was lessened. But it was still a lot of work.

Then there was Riley, who had texted me at least twice a day all summer. Mostly her texts had been about plans for social events to kick off the year. The thought of those events filled me with more dread than excitement. We'd be having a conversation about her plans sooner than later when I got back to campus.

Overall, I knew it was going to be a good year. I wasn't the same guy I was even three months ago. Knowing that, I smiled up at the stars starting to take over the sky. It was definitely going to be a good year.

31

CASSIDY

The first semester flew by faster than the snowflakes landing on my eyelashes as I walked to my next class. It seemed like just yesterday I was nervously stepping into my first college class, and now my second year was beginning.

Fall had quickly given way to snow and ice, mirroring the shift in my life. The bluegrass band, once my musical sanctuary, now left me feeling uneasy and out of place. I thought everything was normal, but I had misjudged it all once again.

Everything changed the day I overheard Chase talking to Liam. His words, meant to be private, echoed in my mind. Chase, with his easy charm and warm smiles, said, "Cassidy's hot, but she's only seventeen. I'm not about to go to jail for her." That single sentence shattered my naïve perception of our friendship. Even if I was only seventeen, I deserved more respect than Chase clearly deemed me worthy.

Leaving the band wasn't an easy decision. With each rehearsal, my resentment and the unspoken tension with Chase grew. He didn't know I had overheard his conversation with Liam, and I wasn't about to tell him. Watching him act like nothing had changed and still trying to flirt with me, I knew stepping away was the best choice.

As I was dealing with my own issues, I discovered something new that really sparked my interest. It was during a digital media class that I discovered a world I had never considered exploring — the realm of digital audio and visual production.

Our professor introduced us to EchoStream, a new social media platform that was gaining popularity for its focus on creative content, especially music and videos.

When I mentioned wanting to consider taking a deeper dive into the digital media studies, my parents were extremely clueless about most of what I was talking about. But more importantly, they were also extremely supportive. They brought me a decent microphone, a high-quality camera, and some basic editing software.

Seeing their genuine interest in my projects, their eyes lighting up as I showed them my first few clumsy attempts at videos, was both encouraging and heartwarming. It seemed they were genuinely happy to see me this passionate about something since leaving the band.

My first few videos were modest — covers of songs I loved set to visuals of campus life, the changing seasons, and snippets of my daily routine. To my surprise, they garnered some attention on Echo-Stream. Comments trickled in, encouraging, critiquing, engaging. With each new upload, I grew even more excited. I was not just creating music; I was telling stories, sharing pieces of my world.

Things took an even more exciting turn after I submitted one of my videos for a class assignment. It was a simple piece, a cover of a folk song set against a time-lapse video of the campus transitioning from empty to full and back to deserted over the course of a day. But to me, it encapsulated everything I was learning and feeling.

After class, my professor pulled me aside. His words took me by surprise. "Cassidy, your video was exceptional. There's a natural talent in the way you blend audio and visuals that shouldn't be confined to just class assignments. Have you considered pursuing this more seriously? Perhaps an internship or a specialized program could give you the experience and exposure you need."

The idea was both thrilling and overwhelming. Until now, Echo-

Stream and my makeshift studio had been my playground, a place to experiment and express myself without the pressure of real expectations outside my own.

But the idea grew on me the longer I thought about it. It could be a chance to dive into digital media, refine my skills, and maybe even turn this into something more than a hobby. And it would definitely open up new horizons for me.

That night, I found myself researching internships and programs in digital media production. Each listing, each program description, felt like a doorway that might lead to a new adventure. I was on the cusp of something big, something that could shape my future. I'd never felt so alive.

32

NASH

My teammates' cheers and high fives kept playing in my head as I sat at my desk, staring at the game ball I received for the winning play at home plate. The thrill of the win still coursing through my veins, I tried to fully absorb the satisfaction of my hard work paying off. This year felt different, bigger.

Baseball, which had once been the center of my universe, now carried a different weight in my life. It felt good.

Things with Riley had gone belly up after a sorority event Riley was insistent we attend. It had already been a long day. We'd had a double-header, and I had told her that I would go, but wanted to keep everything low-key. She'd agreed, but we clearly had different definitions of the phrase.

The event was supposed to be a celebration, a way to blow off steam after a grueling finals week, but for Riley, it was another opportunity for social media content than genuine enjoyment.

She'd dragged me all over the room begging for "just one more picture" because it would "look great on the blog". I finally snapped when I was over it and she accused me of trying to sabotage her career goals and pulling the wool over her eyes by "quitting baseball".

I'd explained so many times that I hadn't quit baseball and that I just wasn't interested in pursuing it professionally, but clearly my words fell on her selectively deaf ears. In her opinion, I was throwing away my future and in her words, "everything we'd planned". When I scoffed and walked away, I knew that was the beginning of the end.

Four days later, Riley had me blocked in her phone and online. I had never felt lighter.

A notification from OurSpace that I hadn't seen caught my attention. She'd clearly sent it during the game.

@Wildfire: Hey! So, there's this cover you did of "Heartland" that's been stuck in my head for days. I'm working on my final project in my music technology class and your version just nails the vibe I'm looking for! It's both fresh and nostalgic, you know? I was kinda hoping (OK, majorly hoping) you'd be cool with me using it for my presentation. It'd be the highlight, for sure!

Her message had me smiling instantly.

@GuyWithGuitar: Hey back at you! Wow, I'm really flattered you think my "Heartland" cover would fit your project so well. Absolutely, use it! Honestly, knowing you enjoy my music enough to share it in your class is pretty awesome. Can't wait to hear all about how it goes. And hey, if your project is as good as your taste in music, I'm sure you're gonna ace it!

Sending the message, I leaned back, a contented sigh escaping me. Our interactions, these small exchanges, they were the best parts of my days.

I could tell she was smart and funny from her messages, which I really liked. We shared a love for music and often sent each other song recommendations. It felt like our own little secret world. I imagined meeting her in person. Would our conversations flow as easily in real life? Would her presence be as warm as our digital exchanges? I longed to discover her unique personality and quirks. All the unknowns between us only fueled my curiosity, making me eager to unravel the mysteries of the girl behind the screen.

Maybe one day. In the meantime, I had a lot of studying to catch up on and recently I'd found a lot of extra free time to do it.

33

CASSIDY

The last class of the semester before finals wrapped up, and Professor Martin caught my eye and motioned for me to hang back. Instantly, my stomach did that weird flip thing it does when I'm nervous. I pretended to fuss with my stuff, waiting for the room to clear out, wondering why she wanted to talk to me.

Once we were alone, Professor Martin leaned against her desk and smiled in a way that didn't completely erase my nerves. "Cassidy, you've got a knack for this digital media stuff. Your projects stand out —they're creative, they're technically solid. Honestly, you're doing work that's a cut above the rest."

Her words floored me. I mean, I liked what I was doing, but to hear that from her? That felt huge.

She continued, "There's this opportunity, and I immediately thought of you. EchoStream is offering a summer internship in Los Angeles. It's pretty last-minute, but I genuinely think you'd thrive there."

I'd done some research on other programs and internships, but none of the ones I'd found resonated with me, so I'd let go of the idea. And I definitely hadn't considered anything as far away as Los Angeles. That felt a million miles away. I've been on stages and in spot-lights, but L.A. felt way bigger than any of them.

"The internship would be hands-on with digital creation and production. It's a real chance to dive deep, to really see what you're capable of," she continued, laying out what sounded like a massive adventure. "You'd need to apply quickly, but I'm here to help. I can write you a recommendation, help prep you for what they might ask, the whole nine yards."

I had to keep myself from immediately saying, "Sign me up!" I knew I was eighteen, but this felt like something I needed to talk to my parents about.

"Thank you, seriously. This sounds amazing. I just... I need to talk it over with my parents," I said, trying to sound more grown-up and sure of myself than I felt.

"Understandable," Professor Martin nodded. "It's a big step. Let me know how it goes. I really see something in you, Cassidy. This could be just the beginning."

Walking into the house later that afternoon, I was buzzing with restless energy. Los Angeles. EchoStream. Actual professional work. The feeling was surreal. But the truth was, I knew I still had to over-come the obstacle of getting my parents on board. They were supportive, but this—asking to go across the country for a summer—was new territory.

I'd rehearsed what I wanted to say to them a million times in my head. My parents knew how much I enjoyed doing what I'd been learning. But this was asking for more than just moral support. I needed them to trust me and likely financially support me. This was a lot bigger than anything I'd done before or even asked to do. This was me stepping up and saying I was ready to go after something huge for myself. And even though I was hoping they would say yes, and I wanted them to say yes, I was terrified they might actually do it.

34

CASSIDY

Before heading downstairs for dinner, I stood in front of my bedroom mirror, rehearsing my lines for what felt like the hundredth time. Trying to balance my enthusiasm with the nerves that twisted in my stomach, I went over the details again.

With one final deep breath, I headed downstairs, my heart pounding in my chest. As I joined my parents at the dinner table, I could feel my resolve wavering slightly, but I knew I had to do this. Clearing my throat, I broke the silence. "Mom, Dad, there's something I need to discuss with you," I began, trying to mask my nervousness.

"I've been offered what I think is an incredible opportunity—Professor Martin thinks I'd be a great fit for an internship with Echo-Stream in Los Angeles this summer." I paused, gauging their reactions. They exchanged a glance, surprise and curiosity lighting their eyes.

"It's a chance for me to really dive into digital media production, to learn and grow in an environment that's at the forefront of the industry," I continued, my enthusiasm battling my nerves. I explained the scope of the internship, what I hoped to gain from it, and how it aligned with my love for music and digital creation.

As I shared my thoughts, I watched my parents closely, ready for the barrage of questions I knew would come. My mom, always the worrier, leaned forward, her expression one of concern and curiosity. "By yourself?" she asked, her voice laced with maternal caution.

A small smile breaking through my nervousness, I said, "Maybe. I mean, Jamie from my class—she's thinking about applying too. We've talked about it, and if we both get in, we'll have each other. But it's not a guarantee that if I got it I wouldn't be alone."

My dad, ever the pragmatist, joined in. "And you're sure this is what you want? Have you applied yet?"

"I wanted to get your thoughts first," I admitted. "And maybe some guidance. This is all new to me, and while I'm excited, I'm also... well, I'm scared," I confessed.

Ever the voice of reason, he continued with practical questions about living arrangements, finances, and how I planned to navigate the sprawling cityscape of Los Angeles. I answered as best as I could, emphasizing my desire for their trust and support.

As the discussion unfolded, their initial hesitance gave way to a more open dialogue about the possibilities and challenges ahead. Surprisingly, the conversation felt less like a plea for permission and more like a collaboration for my future.

By the time we cleared the dinner plates, the almost frenetic energy fueling the conversation had lessened. We moved into the living room, where I expected them to continue to ask questions or dole out advice. The room was silent for a moment, the kind of silence that feels like the even the house was holding its breath. Then, to my astonishment, they both expressed their full support and encouraged me to submit my application when I was ready. It was almost too easy, their agreement too quick. Suspicion swiftly replaced my initial relief.

As if reading my thoughts, Dad broke the next long silence.

"Cassidy, your mom and I wanted to talk to you about something, too. And this feels like a good time to do it."

I stared at them, feeling a little off kilter.

Dad continued, "I've been granted a two year sabbatical to study foreign cultures on site for the anthropology department. We'd been concerned that you might not want to stay here by yourself for that long so we hadn't brought it up. But if you're going to be in L.A., it might be a good opportunity for us to go."

Mom nodded, her eyes soft with understanding. "We wanted to make sure you'd be okay with it. This internship seems like the perfect timing for all of us."

I blinked, trying to process his words. The news felt like a jolt, unexpected but exciting. "Wait, really?" was all I managed at first. It was weird but cool thinking of my parents stepping out of their usual routine, kind of like me heading to Los Angeles.

The room suddenly felt lighter, more open, as if Dad's announcement had lifted some invisible barrier between my dreams and their acceptance. We started chatting about what this meant for all of us, throwing around ideas of where they might go and what I'd be doing in L.A.. It was a lot to take in, and I was still trying to come to grips with the fact that we were all talking about going in completely different directions. The idea of my parents, usually so rooted, handing over this level of freedom was exhilarating, but also disorienting.

After we said goodnight, I retreated to my room, the meeting with my parents replaying in my mind. My apprehension about the internship hadn't vanished, but it had shifted, leaving me feeling like I was on the brink of something big. I just wasn't sure what it would look like in the end.

I powered on my computer, the internship application called to me. Feeling determined and a little scared, I hesitated before each click, not knowing what the future held. The whir of the hard drive spinning filled the quiet of my room as I hovered over the "Submit" button on the internship application. With a deep breath and a heavy dose of nerves, I clicked it. The deed was done; my future, or at least the immediate future, was now in the hands of fate and a selection committee in Los Angeles.

Needing to tell someone, I instinctively navigated to OurSpace. There was only one person I could think of.

But as I clicked Refresh and the page attempted to load, my anticipation turned to confusion, then to a sinking feeling. "Website Not Found." The words on the screen seemed to mock me. Panic rose in my chest. OurSpace, the platform that hosted so much of my music, my thoughts, and my friendship with Guy, was suddenly, inexplicably gone.

The realization hit me hard. Without OurSpace, I had no way to reach out to Guy, no way to share my news or to seek his always helpful advice. We had shared so much, yet I was suddenly struck by how little I actually knew about him. There was no phone number, no email address—nothing that could bridge the gap between our real worlds. The person I had come to rely on, who had become my closest confidant, was slipping away, and I was powerless to stop it. It felt like losing a piece of me and it was leaving a gaping hole in my heart.

I stared at the screen, a hurricane of emotions churning within me. The digital platform had been a constant in my life, a space where I had grown, not just as an artist, but as a person. The thought of it being permanently gone, taking with it my connection to Guy, was devastating—it was like losing a loved one. I tried refreshing the page multiple times over the next few hours with the same result - "Website Not Found".

The quiet of the night offered no consolation, no insight into whether OurSpace's disappearance was a temporary glitch or a permanent blackout.

Before falling asleep, I made a silent promise to myself and to *GuyWithGuitar*, wherever he was. No matter what the future held, I would hold on to the gifts our friendship had provided me, and I would use them as a guide for new adventures. Maybe fate would cross our paths in the real world, just as it had online.

With that thought, a calm washed over me. The journey ahead was a little dimmer, uncertain, but full of potential. And I was ready to embrace it.

35

NASH

As the semester finally wrapped up, the whole campus vibe changed. It was like everyone exhaled simultaneously, leaving behind the stress of finals for the excitement of summer. I was right there with them, feeling this mix of relief that exams were done and this weird excitement about what was next.

I was packing my last box of books when I had a sudden urge to reach out to *Wildfire* to see how her semester had ended. I logged onto OurSpace, craving the connection I found there, only to be met with a jarring message: "Website Not Found." My heart plummeted to my gut. The thought of losing that connection with *Wildfire*, of not being able to share or talk with her again, left me feeling unexpectedly lost. I clicked Refresh a dozen times only to get the same result a dozen times.

Staring at the screen, I started mentally searching for our last conversation. Without it in front of me, I struggled to remember anything about it except how I felt when we logged off. I always felt hopeful and content after we talked and sometimes a little wistful, wishing for more moments like we shared only in person.

With a sigh, I shut down the machine and began unplugging all the cords. I couldn't think of any reason to leave it plugged in any longer. Maybe it had been a sign. Everything had a beginning and an end, and every ending meant a new beginning. If this was the end of one of the best parts of my life, it meant there was a new beginning waiting to start.

THE NEXT MORNING, as I loaded my truck with my bags and headed for home, I thought about the summer ahead. The youth center and the farm awaited. There were plenty of question marks dotting the future, but for once I was okay with that.

36

NASH

Ten Months Later

Kicking off the day with the sun barely up, I found myself deep in the peanut fields, guiding the tractor like I was catching up with an old friend. It was the start of summer in Georgia, that time of year when you can feel the heat getting ready to dial up to "oven" mode. Working the farm like this, getting everything set for the season, used to be my summer norm before college and baseball took the driver's seat.

It had been ages since I last drove the tractor during planting season, not since my high school days. It always happened while I was at school. Yet, here I was, back at it. Every bump and rumble of the tractor sent a reminder through my knee, a not-so-gentle nudge about why I wasn't on a baseball diamond or in a lecture hall right now.

These last ten months had been like stumbling through fog after a bad storm. The spring break accident that took Jason—my teammate, my friend—had turned everything upside down. That night left a hole in my heart and my knee a wreck, every twinge a flashback to what I lost. Baseball, my future, my scholarship... all of it seemed to slip right through my fingers.

While making another turn at the end of the row, I couldn't help but appreciate the irony. The farm, once my escape, now felt like its own kind of prison, marking out the borders of a future I hadn't planned on. But weirdly enough, out here among the endless green, there was a peace I couldn't quite explain. It's like the land, with all its demands, grounded me in a way nothing else could.

As I made another turn, my mind drifted back to that night, as it often did. That night changed everything. We were heading back to campus after a night out; the roads were slick with a light rain that made everything shimmer under the streetlights. Jason was driving, laughter still echoing from his last joke, when a deer darted across the road. Jason swerved, the car skidding, and in those heart-stopping moments, everything went silent. I remember the crunch of metal, the world spinning, and then blackness.

When I woke up in the hospital, the sterile smell of antiseptic was the first thing that hit me, followed by the pain—a deep, unrelenting throb in my knee. My parents were there, their faces etched with worry, but it was the empty hospital bed beside me that hit the hardest.

Jason didn't make it.

The words felt surreal, like they belonged to someone else's story, not mine. I kept expecting him to walk through the door, to crack a joke, to tell me it was all some big mistake. But he didn't, and he never would.

Finishing up the row, I let my mind wander, drifting over the last year's chaos. Out here, it didn't matter who I was supposed to be. I was just Nash, the farmer's son, finding some kind of comfort in the dirt and the grind. My knee might keep reminding me of what I'd lost, but as the sun got higher, warming the earth, I started to think maybe—just maybe—this was where I needed to be. I didn't know why, but the peace I had about it was unexplainable. That thought stuck with me as I killed the engine, stepping off the tractor.

The week I came home from the hospital, still trying to shake the smell of the hospital and the incessant beeping of machines from my brain, my thoughts were anything but reflective. In fact, I was angry. It was the kind of anger that sits heavy in your chest, a constant companion whispering bitter truths about the unfairness of it all. I was mad at the world, at the accident, at baseball for being out of reach, and at myself for not being able to dodge fate's curveball.

That heavy feeling of despair and isolation didn't just pack up and leave when I had to give up my dorm and return home to the farm. It clung to me, thick as Georgia mud on a rainy afternoon, pulling me into an endless loop of what-ifs about the accident. Without the distraction of classes or the adrenaline of baseball, my mind was a playground for regret, endlessly replaying that night, wondering if there was a moment I missed, something I could have changed.

Stuck on the sidelines, watching the farm life go on without being able to dive into the usual chores because of my knee, I felt useless. For eight long weeks, I was more a spectator than a participant, my world shrinking to the confines of our porch and the endless stretches of fields I couldn't tread. But in that forced stillness, music became an unexpected refuge.

My sister, tired of seeing me lost in my storm cloud, started coaxing me back to life with chords and lyrics. Without the physical outlet of work or the escape I found in baseball, our evenings were filled with the sound of her guitar and our voices mingling in harmony.

We'd lose ourselves in old country classics, the stories in those songs echoing some of our own. Sometimes we'd tentatively sketch out tunes of our own making. It turned out to be the lifeline I didn't know I was looking for, a way to navigate through the haze of recovery and loss, one note at a time.

One evening, as the last rays of sunlight stretched across the porch, Cody brought up the summer plans for the youth center, her guitar momentarily forgotten by her side.

"You know, Jet's been talking a lot about the youth center lately," she mentioned, a thoughtful look crossing her face. "He's really hoping you'll ask him to help out with the Jam Session track if you're still leading this summer. He thinks it'd be a great experience. Honestly, I think he just wants to hang out with you but he'd never admit that. And don't tell him I told you that, either." Her eyes sparkled with laughter.

I laughed for what felt like the first time in a very long time. It felt foreign, but had been a much needed reboot to my soul.

We continued talking about the summer program, and how she would be leading a new track called *Trailblazers*. She'd be teaching kids all about agriculture, animals, and outdoor skills. She was clearly excited, and I had no doubt she'd be great at it.

The thought of Jet wanting to be involved in the music track with me was another boon to my spirit.

"Tell Jet he's got it," I'd finally said, the decision feeling right. "I could use the help, and it'll be good to have him on board."

She'd smiled and teased, "Right. And I'll tell him that you really just want to hang out with him, too."

Our back and forth was a reminder of how much light Cody always brings wherever she goes. As the laughter faded and Cody and I returned to our separate thoughts, the warmth of the summer evening wrapped around us like a comforting blanket. Leaned back in my chair, I watched the last sliver of sun dip below the horizon, anticipation stirring inside me.

37

CASSIDY

Time has this tendency to play tricks on you - stretching moments into eternities when you're waiting for something with bated breath. Yet when you become consumed by the chaotic frenzy of life, weeks compress into mere seconds and the changing seasons go unnoticed. Eventually, years roll by and you're left wondering where the time has gone.

That's what I found myself feeling when I thought back over the last year. It was hard to believe how much my life changed after that dinner conversation with my parents.

The internship opened my eyes. Being in LA, right in the middle of all the music, creativity, and tech, was amazing. Every day pushed me to learn more, try new things, and dive deeper into the world of digital media. It felt like so much. More than just a job. I discovered so much about myself, including a passion I never knew I had. It wasn't just about the tasks or the skills I picked up; it was about realizing that this world of creativity and innovation was where I belonged. The internship reshaped how I saw my future, making me realize this wasn't just something to do—it was something I loved.

When the actual internship wrapped up, leaving L.A. just didn't sit right with me. The city had quickly become a place I wanted to be.

I took a chance and asked the manager I'd been working for if there was any way I could stay on as an intern while attending a Music Technology program at a local college. She'd been more than happy to say yes, which solidified for me the decision to stay in L.A.

The Music Technology program was the launching pad I didn't know I needed. I felt that the program meticulously designed each class and every project to pull me deeper into the fusion of music and digital technology, a field where I increasingly saw my future unfolding. It wasn't just about the skills I was acquiring; it was about finding a community that shared my passion, a place where I felt I truly belonged.

It was during one of our end-of-semester showcases that the unexpected happened. I met Lincoln, a charismatic guitarist with ambitions as high as the L.A. skyline. He was in the early stages of forming a rock band, searching for something unique to distinguish their sound in the crowded scene of the city. We struck up a conversation backstage, sharing our musical influences and aspirations. When I mentioned my background in violin, he listened. But it was my idea of incorporating an electric violin into their rock ensemble that really got his attention.

We decided to work together, just to see what it would sound like. The chemistry was instant. The electric violin, with its haunting, vibrant tones, added an entirely new layer to their rock sound. It was as if we'd unlocked a hidden dimension in their music, and the band's dynamic shifted overnight. We began collaborating, adding violin tracks to their songs, and before we knew it, the music we created together started gaining traction.

But as our collaboration bore fruit and the band began to attract a following, I was faced with a decision. The more attention the band received, the more opportunities there were for shows and eventually, talks of touring began to surface. The band's success thrilled me, and I felt proud of the role I had played in it. Yet, the prospect of touring, of being on the road away from the studio and the tech side of music I loved, didn't excite me in the way I thought it would.

This realization didn't come overnight. It was through countless hours in the studio, laying down tracks, experimenting with sounds, and engaging in deep discussions with Lincoln and the band about our musical visions. It was in these moments that I found myself more intrigued by the process and the people behind it than the end product.

My time with the band reminded me why I love music and made me realize there's more to the industry than just performing. I loved the collaboration and the friendships formed, but I knew my path was meant to go in a different direction. While I hadn't known exactly which direction that would be, it most certainly was not the direction I ended up taking.

38

CASSIDY

The online platform EchoStream provided eventually became the space where I shared my music and media creations after the unexpected disappearance of OurSpace. My uploads were a collection of covers, originals, and experimental pieces where I blended my violin with digital sounds—a fusion that represented my journey through music technology. While my previous posts garnered a steady stream of likes and encouraging comments, nothing had prepared me for the reaction to my latest upload.

It was a song born out of a late-night inspiration, a piece that somehow encapsulated my entire journey in L.A., from the uncertain beginnings to the growing realization of my identity as an artist. I poured everything into it: my hopes, my doubts, and the sound was a throwback to my bluegrass and country roots. When I uploaded the track to EchoStream, tagging it with a brief note about its significance to me, I hoped it might resonate with a few more listeners than usual.

The response was explosive. Within hours, the song had accumulated views and shares far beyond any of my previous uploads. Comments flooded in from EchoStream users raving about the sound and the rawness of the words. It felt surreal, watching the numbers climb, reading the feedback from strangers who felt connected to my music. But it was an e-mail from a producer at a music studio in Nashville, Tennessee who was looking for talent to onboard with the new reality TV show, *Real American Country*, that truly changed everything.

The producer praised the originality of my song and my clear talent as both a musician and a performer. He explained that his studio was searching for unique voices in the country music scene—artists who could bring something new and old to the genre. My latest upload, they believed, demonstrated that I had exactly what they were looking for. They offered me a spot on the show, a chance to compete with other aspiring musicians on a national stage.

The offer was as intimidating as it was exhilarating. *Real American Country* wasn't just any platform; it was potentially global exposure. Accepting the offer meant stepping out of the comfort zone of my online anonymity and into the very real spotlight of a televised competition. It meant sharing my music, my story, and my dreams with an audience far beyond the EchoStream community.

In the days that followed, I wrestled with the decision. Reflecting on my past, performing had always been a complex dance of emotions for me. It was something I'd done under my mother's directive, her vision painting the strokes of my early music career. It wasn't that I didn't like performing; I had liked it. But it was always under her watchful eye, her choices dictating the path I'd walked on. My love of music, entangled with the weight of her expectations, had often left me wondering if the stage was truly where I wanted to be.

But then there had been my time with the bluegrass band. That experience, though marred by my experience with Chase, had sparked a different kind of joy in performing. It was a taste of what being on stage could feel like when the strings weren't being pulled by someone else's hands and I had actually enjoyed it.

Now, considering an opportunity like *Real American Country*, I found myself facing the possibility of choosing the stage on my own terms. Could it be that the stage, this time, would feel different? That the lights, the music, the audience would weave together a new kind of magic? One that was wholly mine to claim and shape? The thought brought a flicker of excitement, a surge of adrenaline at the prospect of discovering what kind of performer I could be when I called the shots.

Deciding to join *Real American Country* felt like it might just be the pinnacle of my journey thus far. Yes, it was a competition. But it would also be a test that might finally answer whether the stage could be a place where I learned even more about who I was and what I wanted.

39

NASH

Taking the lead on the Jam Session track again, this time with Jet lending a hand, turned out to be incredibly fulfilling. Watching Jet transform from a quiet presence to a confident leader was a beautiful thing.

I'd also enjoyed catching glimpses of Cody and Jet's relationship blossoming. They were always sharing looks across the room as though they hadn't just seen each other. Cody's smile any time Jet was in her vicinity made it clear something special was happening between them. It made me happy seeing Cody find someone who shared her excitement for life and seeing Jet open up in ways I hadn't seen before. It awakened something in me—happiness for them, obviously, but also a surprising twinge of jealousy. Not the kind of jealousy that wishes ill, but the sort that made me want something like it for myself.

I'd taken to writing these feelings out in the form of song lyrics, and ended up with a notebook full of potential songs. Which is what inspired this year's big project for the music tracks. We worked on writing lyrics and expressing ourselves through words. It had been a challenge, pushing the kids to explore their creativity and express their thoughts and feelings through music.

Their bravery and the stories they told in their songs inspired me to write a song that reflected on my journey of losses and healing.

Like every summer since my first, the youth center showcase was our grand finale, a night for the kids to share their work with family and friends. Encouraged by their enthusiasm and a fair bit of coaxing on their part, I agreed to perform my song. I was nervous. There was a buzzing feeling in my skin, but when I saw the excited faces in front of me, I knew this was what I needed to do.

Jet, ever the supportive friend, recorded the performance, uploading it to EchoStream without my knowing. It was a simple act, one he thought might bring a few more smiles and perhaps some recognition for the youth center's program. Neither of us could have anticipated what would come next.

40

NASH

nswering the call from *Real American Country* was a moment frozen in time, the kind that splits life into a before and after. It came out of nowhere, the voice on the other end offering me a chance to compete on a reality TV show for up-and-coming country musicians. My heart raced, thoughts swirling in a storm of excitement and disbelief. This was it—the chance I didn't know I'd been waiting for until I hung up the phone.

Phone in hand, I stood there in silence, thinking about how I got to this point. Music had been my way to escape from everything and just to be myself.

Yet, here I was, on the cusp of something that felt like destiny. It made me think about the accident that had sent me spiraling, the one that ultimately brought me back home from school. Losing my scholarship had felt like the end of one dream, but it set the stage for something I hadn't even imagined hoping for.

Everything, it seemed, had fallen into place exactly as it was supposed to, even if I hadn't seen it at the time. The accident, the return home—it all stripped away the life I thought I wanted, revealing what I truly needed. Music. It was meant to be more than just a hobby, and the universe had affirmed my choice.

I knew the first thing I needed to do was sit down with my folks and lay everything out on the table. The future I'd imagined for myself was shifting once again, and this opportunity with *Real American Country* was too significant to just spring on them without the courtesy of a conversation.

I found my parents in the living room, the TV casting flickering shadows across their faces as they watched the evening news before dad set out for the nightly chores. They looked up, surprised to see me pacing the doorway.

"Mom, Dad, can we talk?" I asked, my voice carrying a weight that immediately caught their attention. They muted the TV, and both turned to me, an unspoken understanding passing between us that this was important.

We gathered around the kitchen table, a familiar setting for family discussions, where we often made the most significant decisions of our lives. The words I'd rehearsed in my mind suddenly felt heavy on my tongue.

"I got a call today," I started, "from a show called *Real American Country*. It's a reality TV show competition for country musicians. They want me to be on their show."

The silence that followed was thick. I rushed to fill it, explaining the opportunity, what it could mean for my future, and how it felt like everything I'd experienced had led me to this.

My parents listened, their expressions remaining neutral as I spoke. The farm, the life they knew, it was all rooted in reality, in the tangible. This leap into the unknown, into the world of music and reality TV, was as daunting for them as it was exhilarating for me.

"But what about college?" my mom finally asked, voicing the concern I knew was at the forefront of their minds.

I nodded, having anticipated this question. "I've thought about that. For now I would have to put going back on a more permanent hold, which is something that had been floating around in my mind for a while, anyway. Taking out loans had never felt like the right choice, and without my scholarship..." I trailed off, watching their faces for any indication of reaction. When they didn't say anything, I continued. "But this—this feels right. And I honestly believe it's what I'm supposed to do."

We talked for an hour, laying everything out on the table.

Their reactions ranged from pride to concern. "Nash, we're proud of you, truly," my mom started, her voice steady but her eyes betraying her worry.

Dad nodded, echoing her sentiments. "We just want to make sure you're thinking this through. Running off to Nashville's a big leap. But we're here to help, however we can."

I understood their concerns, I really did. But deep down, I felt this pull, an undeniable direction I was meant to take. "I know it seems like a big risk," I said, "but I feel like everything's been leading up to this. It's like everything that happened was for a reason, you know? And this," I paused, gathering my conviction. "This feels like the direction I'm supposed to go."

The conversation went back and forth, but in the end, they saw the determination in my eyes, and heard the belief in my voice. They gave me their blessing, albeit with a promise to return to my studies if things didn't pan out.

Energized by their support, I wandered out to the barn, lost in thoughts about the future. I found Cody and Jet lost in their own little world, their laughter floating on the breeze.

"Get a room, you two," I teased, breaking into their bubble. Cody's giggle and the blush flooding Jet's cheeks had me smiling right along with them. The affection in their eyes for each other was obvious.

I couldn't keep the news to myself any longer. "So, I got a call today and apparently that video you posted, Jet, got the attention of someone at a network that's making a reality TV show for Country artists. They asked me to be on the show. Looks like I'll be heading to Nashville soon."

The reaction was immediate. Cody squealed, rushing me for a hug, while Jet clapped me on the back, a broad grin spreading across his face. "Man, that's awesome! Nashville, huh? They better watch out, because they won't know what hit 'em," Jet's enthusiasm genuine.

"And who knows? Maybe one day we'll go on tour together or

something," he added, the idea sparking a new round of excitement in his eyes.

Walking back to the house later, the whole day felt surreal. Me, heading to Nashville to be on a reality TV show? It was worlds from where I thought I'd end up, but somehow, it felt exactly right.

I had trouble falling asleep that night because I was excited and maybe a little scared, thinking about what could happen next. My thoughts raced as I imagined all the ways my life could change.

As I tossed and turned, I thought about how far I'd come and how much I'd grown. This was my chance to prove myself, to take a leap of faith, and to see where the journey would lead. I fell asleep with dreams of performing on stage and bright lights shining down on me. I imagined the applause, the excitement of the crowd, but mostly the thrill of doing something I loved.

41

CASSIDY

As I read the message from the Nashville music producer for what was probably the hundredth time, my mind raced. The offer to join *Real American Country* was not just an invitation; it was a pivotal moment where the decision I made could change the entire trajectory of my life.

The following day, I decided to discuss the offer with my manager, Elizabeth Morrow, who also happened to be the CEO of EchoStream. She was a visionary woman and had always been supportive of innovative ideas and talent.

As I approached her office, I took a deep breath, my heart pounding with a mix of excitement and nerves. I knocked on the door, and Elizabeth's calm, confident voice invited me in.

Her office was a shrine to EchoStream's success, adorned with sleek technology and awards that gleamed under the soft gallery lighting. She was sitting behind her desk, smiling as I entered.

"What can I do for you today, Cassidy?" Her voice was calming and eased some of the nerves I'd been feeling.

"So here's the thing. I've been offered an incredible opportunity. A producer reached out and offered me a spot on a new show called *Real American Country*," I began, hesitantly. "It's not something I sought out, but I think I want to take it. That being said, I'm also concerned about how it'll affect my job at EchoStream. I love it here and could see myself working here for a very long time."

Elizabeth listened intently, stare intense. When I finished, she leaned back in her chair, a more thoughtful expression crossing her face. "Cassidy," she finally said, "this could be a fantastic opportunity not just for you, but for EchoStream as well."

I blinked, puzzled. "Really?"

"Imagine the visibility," Elizabeth explained, her voice laced with excitement. "EchoStream sponsoring *Real American Country* would be a groundbreaking collaboration. And you, Cassidy, could be the bridge between our worlds."

The idea was good but ambitious, which gave me concerns. "Wouldn't that be a conflict of interest? Me, competing on a show that my company sponsors?"

Elizabeth waved away my concern with a confident smile. "We can navigate the specifics to avoid any direct conflicts. What's important is the mutual benefit. And Cassidy," she added, her gaze firm yet encouraging, "I've seen your work, your passion. I believe in you, not just as a part of EchoStream, but as an artist."

Her confidence was infectious, yet I felt compelled to propose a safeguard. "If things don't work out with the music, could Echo-Stream consider holding a space for me to return?"

"Consider it done," Elizabeth agreed without hesitation. "But let me be clear, Cassidy—I don't see you coming back because you failed. I see you soaring and we'll all be there, supporting you as you fly."

Leaving Elizabeth's office, I felt a weight lift off my shoulders. I knew what I was going to do. Win or lose, I was ready to take on the stage like I never had before. And that excited me more than anything else.

42

NASH

The sun was just beginning to dip below the horizon as the SUV pulled up to the sprawling mansion in the suburbs of Nashville. It was everything I'd imagined and more—a 12,000-square-foot colonial-style farmhouse sitting on six acres of land, with breathtaking views from every corner. The excitement bubbling inside me was almost too much to contain. This was it, the beginning of a new chapter in my life, and I was determined to make every second count.

As I stepped out of the vehicle, my boots crunching on the gravel of the motor court, the mansion's magnitude was undeniable. I squared my shoulders and marched toward my future with a grin plastered on my face. The moment I entered the two-story foyer, a host of surprised and welcoming faces greeted me. A few contestants who had arrived earlier than I had paused their conversations momentarily as they turned to see the new arrival.

The show had sent us each a huge document that included profiles of each contestant so we wouldn't be walking into a house full of complete strangers. Granted, the profiles were sparse with only names, ages, and a headshot. Of course, I'd taken to memorizing the names and faces if for no other reason than to make myself feel more comfortable.

"We've got another live one, y'all!" Austin Blake called out, his easy charm and quick smile infectious. Laughter filled the air, providing an ease to the tension I'd been fighting since leaving the airport. Christopher Jordan, leaning casually against the staircase railing, raised an eyebrow in amusement, while Willow Gracin, seated on one of the plush sofas, offered a warm, inviting nod and a small wave.

The house itself was alive with activity—crews adjusting lighting, cameras positioned to capture every angle, and the undercurrent of anticipation for the competition that lay ahead. I made my way through the grand foyer, taking in the opulence of the formal living and dining rooms, both boasting massive fireplaces. The two-story great room, with its own fireplace, seemed tailor-made for large gatherings.

As the afternoon wore on, I mingled with the other contestants, matching their energy with my own brand of enthusiasm. Wyatt Turner, my soon-to-be roommate and a man of few words, offered a firm handshake, but what held my attention was the steel behind his eyes that contradicted his easy demeanor.

The arrival of Cassidy Raye Stanton was a moment I couldn't have prepared for if I'd tried. Her entrance was quiet, yet it commanded the room's attention. Our gazes locked, and I felt an instant attraction towards her, as if there was a magnetic pull between us. I'd stared at her profile image, practically studying it far longer than I would ever admit out loud, because I could hardly tear my eyes away. But in person, she was even more. She was breathtaking.

Cassidy, with a grace that seemed effortless, offered me a polite smile and turned her attention to the others. That one look sent a shock through my system, leaving me feeling dazed. There was something about her—a familiarity that I couldn't place. If she'd asked me, I'd have sworn we'd met before. Maybe we shared conversations and dreams in another lifetime, but how would that even be possible?

Cassidy moved with a confidence that wasn't overpowering, but demanded my attention.

As the evening progressed, the mansion buzzed with the energy of new friendships being forged. Cassidy seemed to float just outside of the conversation, an attentive observer. But her presence just drew people in, making them open up. I found myself watching her, intrigued by the way she interacted with everyone. Her laughter was genuine, her smile warm. Yet every time our paths crossed, that sense of familiarity tugged at me.

We'd all found our way to the huge outdoor living area out back where the strings of lights cast shadows on faces. Across from me, Cassidy's platinum curls looked like molten gold under the amber glow. I found myself debating keeping my distance from Cassidy and wanting to be right next to her. Her presence left me feeling unexpectedly unnerved, but I couldn't look away for long.

In an effort to distract myself, I engaged in light-hearted and meaningless flirtations with some of the other contestants. Willow's laughter and Harper Lane's fiery spirit were the perfect distractions. No matter how hard I tried to stay engaged in a conversation, my attention kept drifting back to Cassidy. She had this thing about her that was both exhilarating and intimidating. Watching her from a distance, I couldn't shake this strange, unexplainable connection.

Austin brought out his guitar, breaking the comfortable silence that had settled over us. "I think this calls for some music," he said with an enthusiasm that invited no arguments, just a collective nod of agreement.

As he strummed the first chords, a familiar tune took shape, and one by one, we all joined in. The competition that awaited us suddenly felt like a secondary reason we were all here.

Singing along with the group, Cassidy's voice stood out. It was familiar in a way that sent a shiver down my spine. I couldn't place where I'd heard it before, but it struck a chord and brought back hazy memories.

The night was devoid of any air of competition, a fleeting peace I knew wouldn't last. Yet, in that moment, we were just a group of dreamers, sharing our love for music under the Tennessee sky.

Despite the silence that enveloped the mansion as everyone was tucked away in their rooms, Cassidy's familiar voice continued to haunt the corners of my memory. The day's excitement still buzzed through me, and I couldn't wait for whatever happened next. Though far from home and surrounded by strangers, I felt an undeniable sense of belonging. Nashville felt like the perfect place for me, even if I had no idea what would happen next.

43

CASSIDY

I'd walked into the mansion to a boisterous greeting from Austin Blake. His presence alone was enough to soothe anyone's frayed nerves. However, my nerves were only temporarily eased as I found myself ensnared in the inexplicable force of a thread that was pulling me toward Nash Montgomery.

A curious stir of familiarity bloomed in my chest at the sight of him. Despite never having met before, his eyes hinted at recognition and his smile was full of mischief and charm. And based on the way he laughed and flirted with every girl in the room, I knew Nash Montgomery was dangerous. Good thing my secondary mission to blowing the competition out of the water was to avoid dangerous men.

As we all settled on the back patio where I stayed close enough to the group so as not to look stuck up but I was far enough away to avoid being the center of attention. I made small talk with a couple of the girls, but I mostly watched everyone as the group began to meld into something more cohesive.

Eventually, Austin picked up his guitar, and the atmosphere shifted. Suddenly, it was as if we had all been singing together for years, our voices blending seamlessly. Nash's voice, in particular, stood out, prodding the edges of my memory. I had this strange sensation that we had sung together before in a past that didn't exist.

When the yawns became frequent and more contagious, we called it a night and headed for our rooms. I laid in bed, thinking about the familiarity of Nash's voice and the pull he had on me. Just thinking about it was enticing, but felt risky. I couldn't afford to be distracted by fleeting emotions or get too close to anyone who could easily become a competitor.

This competition was an opportunity of a lifetime, and I needed to remember why I was here. A handsome man with brown eyes that sparkled with mischief as if hiding a million untold stories waiting to be discovered was sure to distract me from doing just that.

44

CASSIDY

The day of our first dress rehearsal finally came, and the house was buzzing with excited voices and a flurry of movement. We'd spent the last couple of days getting acquainted with schedules and voice coaches. There was a tour of the studio and so many instructions, names, and job titles. I was pretty sure if they gave us a quiz on any of it, I'd fail. All I could do was hope "the powers that be" had mercy on us and repeated themselves—often.

Dress rehearsal would be a chance for each contestant to simulate the actual performance. It also gave the crew a chance to capture footage for promos. Hoped it was a cure for the nerves I'd felt growing more and more jittery by the minute since getting out of bed.

The rooms and hallways were alive with the sound of vocal warm-ups echoing off the walls, each contestant finding their own space to mentally and vocally prepare for the day ahead. The common areas transformed into impromptu rehearsal spaces, with performers going over their chosen pieces, fine-tuning guitar chords, and running through scales. Every face I passed was tight with concentration. This wasn't the real thing, but it may as well be as we were all expected to give our best under the rehearsal's simulated pressure.

As we boarded the shuttle to the studio, the energy from the morning's preparations seemed to funnel into a silent hum of focus and anticipation. I found a seat by the window, trying to gather my thoughts and visualize my performance. It wasn't long before Nash made his way on and when our eyes met, his presence broke the bubble of solitude I had cocooned myself in. Before I could make any objection, even the half-hearted one on my tongue, he smiled and slid into the seat next to me.

I stared at him, struck by his handsomeness, and all words evaporated from my brain.

"Mind if I join you?" he asked, settling in the seat next to me. His casual confidence was vastly different from the tension I felt, and it was oddly calming.

"Not at all." I managed to sound far more confident than I actually felt. His proximity caught me off guard, but I also couldn't deny that I liked it.

Nash's striking features caught my attention as he greeted the guys walking by. His dark brown eyes, framed by dark lashes, seemed to be in a constant state of amusement and waiting for mischief. The sandy blonde hair that fell in a seemingly intentional disarray added to his rugged charm, while a shadow of facial hair, somewhere between a five o'clock shadow and a beard, lent to his carefree demeanor. And then there were those dimples. They appeared with his easy smiles and seemed to demand my attention, causing any resolve I'd had to remain detached to begin to crack. Being this close, I could physically feel the pull he had on me. It took conscious effort to not lean toward him but instead to lean toward the window on my other side.

As we rode toward the studio, Nash's sociable nature was on full display, greeting everyone with an easy familiarity that made me feel more at ease. The conversation between us began tentatively, a dance of words and shared glances.

"So, Cassidy, what got you into music?" Nash asked, his tone genuine, inviting me into a conversation.

"Um," I hesitated, but only because words no longer existed in my brain. "It's just something I've always loved." I wanted to crawl under the seat and hide. What kind of answer was that? "What about you? You seem pretty natural being around and in front of people." Maybe if I turned the conversation to him, I'd survive the rest of the ride to the studio.

Nash smiled a full-wattage smile, a sight that made my heart flutter. Get a hold of yourself, Cassidy.

"Always been a part of me, I guess. Music wasn't always something I shared with other people, but it's apparently something I'm pretty good at. Not sure about the cameras and stuff, but I don't think they hate me," he said with a wink, followed by a self-deprecating chuckle.

I couldn't tell if I was mad or relieved that our conversation was suddenly interrupted by one of the crew members standing at the front of the bus, providing us with detailed instructions for the day. Probably a little bit of both.

They outlined everything from where we would find our wardrobe to how the makeup process would work upon arriving at the studio. The thorough rundown of the schedule filled the remainder of our ride, leaving no room for further personal conversation.

As the crew member spoke, an intense silence fell over the contestants. The shared nervousness about the dress rehearsal seemed to unify us in quiet contemplation. The earlier atmosphere of excitement and casual banter was replaced by focused attention on the instructions, each of us lost in thoughts about our upcoming performances and the reality of being so close to the actual competition.

When the bus came to a stop, the reality of the air shifted again, determination scoring the underlying tension. Nash turned to me with a reassuring smile.

"You've got this, Cassidy," he said, his tone earnest, those brown eyes conveying a belief in me I hadn't realized I needed. "I've heard you sing."

His words were simple, but cut through the cloud of my anxieties. With a grateful nod, I suddenly felt more confident. Before I could respond, he was spinning on his heel and following the group.

We were herded through a door on the back of a large metal building and into narrow hallways bustling with people. Guided through the maze of hallways, I found myself standing at the entrance of the wardrobe area, the next stage in today's adventure.

Stepping into a small room, a sea of fabrics and styles that seemed to span the entire spectrum of fashion surrounded me. The crew member assigned to help me with my outfit immediately began pulling out pieces that veered sharply from my personal style, suggesting I try something bold and edgy.

"How about trying something a bit more daring today?" she suggested, holding up a garment that was more sparkle than substance.

I hesitated, my gaze drifting back to the pieces that felt more 'me'—clothes that blended my love for bohemian chic with my country roots. Politely, I navigated to those racks of clothing.

"Thank you, but I'd rather go for something that suits my usual style," I explained, confidently picking out an outfit that felt more natural for me.

Next was the makeup artist's chair, a new experience for me since I'd always been my own "stylist". He was a bundle of energy, praising what he called my "natural beauty" with every brush stroke.

"You're absolutely stunning; there's hardly anything for me to do!" he gushed, applying the lightest touches to enhance my features.

Despite his kindness, sitting there surrounded by professionals fussing over my appearance, I was definitely out of my element.

The second I stepped out of the room, Lanie Tisdale wasted no time in latching onto me, looping her arm through mine and dragging me down the hallway. "Oh, Cassidy, you look... so quaint. It's brave, really, choosing simplicity when the rest of us are aiming to stand out," she said, in a tone that I think was supposed to sound motherly but was only condescending.

As she adjusted her tight-fitting dress that sparkled with rhinestones, I heard her muttering, "It's all about making an impression, after all."

Before I could dismiss her comment, Lanie's focus suddenly shifted to Charles Young. She grabbed my arm, her grip firm, leaving no room for refusal as she dragged me towards him. "Let's go introduce ourselves," she declared, her intentions clear as the gleam in her eye. I rolled my eyes, unseen by her, as we approached.

Charles, a famous country music bad boy that heralded from a line of country music royalty, greeted us with a wide, unsettling smile. His attention overtly focused on Lanie, who basked in the attention. My conscience, on the other hand, was telling me to hightail it out of there. It felt like being part of a covert deal in a dark alley. I studied the hem of my shirt very thoroughly, hoping for an excuse to make an exit.

Fortunately, when a loud voice echoed through a sound system calling Nash Montgomery to the stage, we were reminded to make our way to a holding area. I started walking in that direction amidst the workers dressed in all black hustling through the area until I caught sight of Nash wrapping a guitar strap around himself while chatting with a petite woman who appeared to be beaming up at him. She swiped a makeup brush down his nose with a little flourish before tapping the end of his perfectly shaped nose that sat between what I knew to be two very cute dimples that I could only see one of as he smiled back at the makeup woman who needed to get back to her job.

Oh my gosh, Cassidy. What are you thinking right now? Jealousy, really? Stop it. You don't even know the guy.

Not sure what prompted me to do it, I found a spot between some of the heavy black curtains and tucked myself away until I was basically hidden in the wings. When a deep voice called, "Action!" I edged my way out from behind the curtains to get a view of the stage.

The melody Nash strummed made me smile. It was a song I'd played plenty of times on my violin as though it had been made for the instrument. The longer I watched and listened, a sense of déjà vu crept in. My ears tingled and my spine straightened. I'd heard that voice before and I'd heard it sing this exact song. More than that, I'd played alongside this voice to this song. Granted, the voice was a little deeper now and definitely stronger than it had been three years ago. If it wasn't the same voice, it was a hauntingly similar one that had me getting pulled under by a sea of resurfacing memories.

Shaking myself back to the moment, I told myself it wasn't possible. The likelihood that the one person I'd always wanted to meet but had lost contact with would end up on the same reality televised singing competition I was on had to be infinitesimal. Regardless, I couldn't help the small bubble of hope that it was true.

His last chord echoed through the auditorium. Not wanting to be caught spying, I pushed away from my hiding spot and hurried towards the green room. My heart was a riot of emotions and not just from my own impending performance. But there were only two singers performing before me, so I had to get my head straight, calm down, and concentrate on the music.

The space felt crowded, even with only five or six of us there. I had been trying to work through the song I was supposed to sing for the third time when my name was called over the speaker. It was now or never.

I was practically speed-walking, trying to keep my head down and emotions in check. All the thoughts about Nash and our possible connection from years ago were swirling around, making it hard to focus. Then, just my luck, as I was darting towards the stage, I didn't notice Nash until I practically crashed into him. The impact would've sent me reeling if his arms hadn't shot out to steady me.

"Whoa, careful there," Nash said, a playful glint in his eyes. His voice, so warm and full of concern, made my heart do a little flip. He seemed genuinely pleased to have caught me.

You would have knocked him over if he hadn't reached out. Calm down.

Embarrassed and a bit flustered, I straightened up, muttering a quick, "Thanks," barely meeting his gaze. My heart was doing somersaults—not from the near fall, but from the unexpected closeness to

Nash. I pulled away slightly, eager to put some distance between us. I needed to focus.

Nash just smiled, that easy, charming smile that seemed to say he hadn't minded the collision. And then, as if realizing he was holding onto me a bit longer than necessary, he let go, stepping back but still watching me with an unreadable expression.

As I turned to leave, Nash called out, "Hey, Cassidy? Good luck out there." His words, simple yet sincere, halted me in my tracks. For a fleeting second, I considered the possibility that he knew where this strange pull between us had come from, too.

Turning back to him, I managed a small smile. "Thanks," I said, the tension in my shoulders easing ever so slightly.

Standing on that stage, surrounded by cameras, was nothing like the small-town gigs I was used to. Playing at fairgrounds and community centers, where you could see every face in the crowd and knew half of them by name, felt like a different world. Here, the lights were brighter, and it appeared that when they were in the seats beyond the stage, the audience would be a sea of shadows. It was all the more intense, like stepping up from singing in your backyard to performing in a stadium overnight.

As I left the stage, the adrenaline slowly receded, replaced by a wave of relief and lingering nervous energy. Making my way back through the dimly lit corridors, the sound of voices pulled me towards an unintentional eavesdrop.

Peeking around the corner, my heart lodged firmly in my throat as I watched Lanie Tisdale spell out for Nash many of what she considered my shortcomings.

"No offense, but I think Cassidy really needs to step up her game if she wants to make an impression here," Lanie's voice floated through the air, tinged with false concern. "I mean, her look is just so... plain, you know? And she's nice, but nice doesn't win competitions."

Her words, meant for Nash, cut deeper than I expected. I paused, hidden just out of sight, my heart sinking. Was he agreeing with her? Did he see me as just 'nice' and 'plain'? His expression had been blank, so there was no way for me to gauge what he'd been thinking. The warmth of Nash's earlier encouragement turned cold in my memory.

I wrestled with the urge to confront them or to simply walk away. But pride and a newfound determination steadied me. Lanie's words, though hurtful, wouldn't define me. I'd show them both—show everyone—that I was nice, but I was also a force to be reckoned with.

The hurt from overhearing Lanie was one thing, but the sting of seeing Nash as part of the conversation felt worse. I'd harbored a crush on my anonymous online friend *GuyWithGuitar*, and cherished our friendship above any other I'd ever had. I didn't want to think that Nash and *Guy* could be the same person—not now. In fact, I refused to believe it. The doubts started creeping in. I had to stop it and focus on what I could control. I deserved to be here as much as anyone else. We'd all been hand-picked for this job for a reason. It didn't matter what Nash or what Lanie or what anyone thought about me. What mattered is what I did on stage.

45

NASH

When Cassidy, in a flurry of clear determination and nerves, nearly collided with me, my arms reflexively shot out to catch her, steadying us both.

"Whoa, careful there," I found myself saying, a light-hearted attempt to calm the sudden tension.

Her quick thanks, muffled by embarrassment, had my heart doing a strange little dance. Despite the rush, there was a moment—brief but potent—where something unspoken passed between us. I was there, lingering in the hallway, not for any particular reason other than to soak in the experience of my time on stage. I was suddenly glad I'd taken a detour back to the green room.

As she pulled away, something inside me wanted to hold on, to not let the distance grow between us. "Hey, Cassidy? Good luck out there," I called out, not wanting to let her walk away.

My head was still in the moment with Cassidy when Lanie Tisdale appeared seemingly out of nowhere, her timing less than impeccable as always, pulling me into conversation. As she launched into a monologue mostly about her own rehearsal experiences and aspirations, I found myself nodding along, feigning interest while my thoughts wandered back to Cassidy.

I wished I could be there to see her take the stage, to witness the talent I knew she had. Lanie's voice became background noise as I imagined Cassidy under the lights, her voice filling the room.

My attention snapped back to Lanie as she veered into unexpected territory. "No offense, but I think Cassidy really needs to step up her game if she wants to make an impression here. I mean, her look is just so... plain, you know? And she's nice, but nice doesn't win competitions."

The casual dismissal in her tone and the way she talked about Cassidy irked me.

I held up a hand, interrupting her. "You know what, Lanie? Maybe Cassidy doesn't need to impress anyone here because her talent could carry her to the end. I know you've heard her sing. And maybe nice is exactly what this world needs more of."

I turned to head toward the stage, hoping to catch a glimpse of Cassidy again, but Before I made it too far, a crew member tapped me on the shoulder. "Hey Nash, we need you for a quick promo clip."

My heart sank a little; I knew this was part of the gig, but the timing couldn't have been worse. With a reluctant nod, I followed, casting a last look towards the direction of the stage, silently wishing I'd followed Cassidy after she'd run into me.

I didn't get another chance to talk to Cassidy. She was probably dealing with her own obligations for the production team. By the time we all regrouped at the shuttle, exhaustion was the unanimous sentiment, etching itself on every face.

Climbing aboard, my eyes immediately sought her out, only to find Cassidy already seated, deep in conversation with Christopher Jordan. They were engrossed in a quiet, seemingly private discussion. Wanting to catch her attention without intruding, I hesitated, hoping for a moment of eye contact. When Cassidy briefly glanced my way and just as quickly returned her focus to Christopher, the sharp sting of rejection hit me.

Taking a seat, all I could think about were the missed opportunities of the day and Cassidy's sudden indifference. It had me wondering what, or maybe I should wonder who, happened between the hallway and now.

46

NASH

I still hadn't gotten used to waking up in a different place. It was disorienting to say the least. It wasn't as nearly as disorienting as having people with cameras in your face first thing in the mornings. They told us the cameras would always be around, but that we were supposed to ignore them. That was definitely easier said than done. It was weird enough sharing a massive house with eleven other musicians. Adding in the cameras was not the solution to reducing the anxiety or tension that sometimes made an appearance.

I probably should have expected it, but I never actually considered the fact that twelve different personalities would need to share a space. Fortunately, I was pretty easy-going and could roll with the punches when I needed to. And even though we were really early into the whole process, I didn't foresee too many issues arising. Granted, after my run-in with Lanie and hearing how she talked about Cassidy without any pretense or prompting, I would definitely be keeping my eyes and ears open when she was around.

One morning, they shuttled us to a studio where we faced even more cameras, which accompanied interviews and questions about ourselves and how we ended up on the show. I was so far outside of my element, all I could do was rely on my ability to turn up the charm as high as necessary. I'd make a joke about knowing more about peanuts than I did about being on stage, but it was a nut I was willing to crack. It usually got a chuckle or two.

Wardrobe fittings were a trip—rows and rows of clothes that screamed 'country western star' more than a farm kid from Georgia. Most of the time, I tried to pretend like I knew what I was doing and act like I was having a blast doing it. And truth be told, it was fun. If people were watching, I preened in front of the mirrors, throwing a wink at whoever caught my eye.

Evenings were a different beast. The production team had this idea of "bonding" that translated into group dinners and activities that felt like summer camp on steroids. It was here, amidst the clinking of glasses and the constant buzz of conversation, that I found myself easing into the rhythm of this new life. My laughter was louder, my stories more animated.

I found myself flitting from one conversation to another, leaving a trail of laughs in my wake. I couldn't remember ever feeling this free. It was starting to feel like maybe I'd been hiding the real me all this time. I'd never shied away from attention, but I never sought it out, either.

Flirting with the ladies became part of the nightly entertainment —at least for me. Most of them played along, all of us understanding that it was in good fun. They even flirted back and sometimes their shots were sharper than their nails. But not Cassidy.

Every time I threw a line her way, she'd meet it with an aloof graciousness that left me stumped. There was no playful comeback, no dismissal, just a quiet, pleasant stare that seemed to see right through me. It bugged me, not being able to read her, but it also made every interaction a challenge I was itching to take on. I thought she and I had shared a moment earlier in the week, but now when I even glanced her way, it was like hitting a wall—a pleasant and beautiful wall, but a wall nonetheless. It added an edge to my week, a code I was determined to crack.

Most evenings, a large part of the group would find their way to the back patio. I'd find myself watching Cassidy from across the way.

Someone would share a story or talk about back home, but Cassidy just listened and watched. It was frustrating and intriguing all at the same time.

Knowing the actual competition was starting soon, I knew things were about to get intense. But every time I tried to get my head in the game, my thoughts would drift to Cassidy. I was determined to figure her out, to break through that serene exterior and find out what lay beneath. For now, though, I could only wait and watch, hoping that the upcoming challenges would bring us closer—or at least give me more clues to unravel the mystery that was Cassidy.

47

NASH

The previously high energy and casual confidence that fueled the first few days took a backseat when the first day of competition rolled around. It wasn't just me feeling the shift either, as was evident throughout the mansion. Anticipation filled the air, creating a shared tension that quieted the usual morning activity.

Everyone was dealing with the nerves in their own way. Some retreated into quiet corners with headphones, lost in their music, while others paced the halls, repeating lyrics to ensure every word was secure in their memory. I spent the morning trying to replay the rehearsal in my mind and make mental notes about where and how to make adjustments.

This wasn't just another performance. It was the moment when all of our efforts would be tested. I wanted to make sure I struck the perfect balance between being a performer and just a singer, and I needed to focus. Today was the moment that would draw the line between being a contestant and a contender.

As we all headed to the studio, you could feel the emotions running high through all of us. We were all in our heads, running through our sets, barely swapping the usual pep talks. Even Cassidy seemed a bit on edge, though I could tell she was trying hard not to show it. I'd noticed that when she got lost in her thoughts, her fingers moved in random rhythms as though they were tapping out a beat of some kind. Today they were moving fast. I wasn't sure she would accept it if I offered her any kind of encouragement, so I tried to send them silently across the bus.

The pressure was heavy as we all got shuffled through wardrobe and makeup, a routine made smoother since we picked out our outfits the day before. Then, herded into the green room, it felt like we were on display, with cameras catching every anxious glance and fidget. This room, usually a place to chill before going on, now felt like a stage itself, where every nervous laugh or deep breath was part of the show. It was a strange mix of feeling prepped for battle and yet, under a microscope, as we waited for our turn to prove we deserved a spot on the real stage.

As the anticipation in the green room built up, an assistant came over to me, breaking through the buzz of hushed conversations and last-minute vocal warm-ups. "Nash, you're up next. Time to head to your spot," they said, their voice cutting cleanly through the tension.

I nodded, feeling the heaviness of the moment settle on my shoulders. As I stood, scanning the room for something to anchor me, my eyes caught Cassidy's. She'd been so closed off, but in our brief exchange, there was something. She held my gaze, her eyes full of emotion, before mouthing, "Good Luck."

That simple gesture, coming from her, threw me. I didn't have time to think about it. I clung to it and let it ground me as I headed to the stage.

As quickly as I had taken the stage, I was being guided by the show's host, Gunner Haynes, to the judges' area. "Let's hear what our esteemed judges have to say about Nash's performance tonight," Gunner announced, his voice booming with enthusiasm. Trying to catch my breath as the applause faded, I awaited the judges' feedback.

Charles Young was the first to speak, nodding appreciatively. "Nash, you've got a natural stage presence that's hard to come by, and your voice has a warmth that's just as inviting," he praised, then added, "Just watch your pitch on the higher notes, it tends to waver a bit."

Randy Hunt, with a grin, chimed in, "Boy, you've got the charm and the chops. That song choice was spot on. Just make sure you're connecting with every word you're singing. It's all about believability."

Nicole Alan, the sole female judge, offered a softer, encouraging smile. "Your performance was adorable. There's definitely something about you. But I'd love to see you take even more risks on stage. Push the boundaries of your comfort zone."

With a wink, I thanked them and tipped my chin, acknowledging their advice. The feedback, a combination of compliments and constructive criticism, was a catalyst. As I walked off stage waving to the audience, the judges' words replayed in my head, not as criticism, but as fuel. Time to push harder and show them what I'm really made of. A new level of determination took hold of me.

48

CASSIDY

The atmosphere in the green room was electric, charged with the kind of nervous energy that could both drain and energize you. I couldn't imagine how I would feel when this day was over. Anticipation filled the air as the other contestants awaited their turns, their faces mirroring the excitement and nervousness I was experiencing. Cameras and crew members navigated the cramped space, capturing every moment of our pre-performance rituals, turning our anxiety into part of the show's narrative.

In the corner, my back against the cool wall, I let my mind wander through a field of thoughts and melodies. Without my violin, my fingers danced over invisible strings, moving with practiced finesse to only a tune I could hear.

Across the room, my eyes found Nash as he was making his way to follow the crew member that had come to retrieve him for his performance. He looked around the room as though he needed to find something. As he glanced my way, he stopped searching and stared at me with a look of confusion and maybe relief. It was hard to tell. I offered him a silent message, mouthing, "Good luck." I hoped he could feel the weight with which I said them, because I really did mean them.

Nash had just returned to the green room when I was called to the stage. My heart beat a staccato rhythm, setting the racing tempo of my nervous energy. The walk to the spotlight felt surreal, each step a beat in the countdown to the moment I'd been preparing for. I wasn't a stranger to the stage. It welcomed me like an old friend. I was, however, new to the pressure that came with knowing everything I did from this point forward would determine more than just whether I was a good singer. Out here, I needed to be the best. And that terrified me.

As the opening chords of Terri Clark's *I Wanna Do it All* began, I lost myself in the music, allowing myself to shake free from the nerves that had been holding me hostage. The judges watched with keen interest, their expressions shifting between entertained and scrutiny. Charles Young's eyes lit up, while Randy Hunt couldn't help but drum his fingers and bob his head to the beat on the table. Nicole Alan's smile brightened with enthusiasm.

The lyrics were a blend of playful banter and emotion and flowed effortlessly, inviting everyone in the room to forget about the competition and just enjoy the music. When I changed the lyrics from "watch the Yankees play ball" to "watch the Sounds play ball," a nod to Nashville's minor league team, the audience lost their minds.

As the final note echoed through the auditorium, I allowed myself a moment to bask in the cheers and applause that filled the room. My heart was pounding, not just from the exhilaration of the performance, but from the response from the live audience. Their response was beyond my expectations. It was confirmation that I had not only chosen the right song but delivered it.

The show's host, Gunner Haynes, approached with a wide smile, his presence on stage signaling the transition from performance to feedback. "Ladies and gentlemen, let's hear it once again for Cassidy Raye!" he exclaimed, leading me toward the judges' area. The applause intensified, a tangible wave of support that escorted me across the stage.

As we reached the judges, Gunner continued, "Cassidy, that was an incredible performance. Now, let's see what our judges have to say." He gestured towards the panel, each member prepared to offer their insights.

Charles Young leaned forward, his expression one of genuine admiration. "Cassidy, you've just shown us exactly what this competition is all about. Your song choice, your energy, and that little tweak to the lyrics—brilliant! It's clear you understand your audience and what it means to connect with them. That was a performance full of personality and charisma."

Randy Hunt nodded enthusiastically. "I have to agree with Charles. What a performance! You brought the house down, Cassidy. You're not just singing songs; you're telling a story that we all want to be a part of."

Nicole Alan, her smile warm and encouraging, added, "Cassidy, there's a joy and authenticity in your performance that's truly captivating. You have this ability to draw people in, to make them feel a part of something special. And tonight, you did just that. Keep doing what you're doing, because it's working."

Gunner, turning back to the audience, summed up the judges' sentiments. "Well, there you have it, folks! Cassidy has certainly made her mark tonight. Thank you, judges."

Once I stepped away from the judges, Gunner's voice echoed through the auditorium, and the audience kept clapping as I exited the stage. The kind words and encouragement from the judges, the connection with the audience—it all felt like a dream, one I didn't want to wake up from. I'd never felt anything remotely similar after any other performance.

Back in the green room, the atmosphere was thick with the impact of performances combined with the significance of the judges' critiques. Some of the other contestants offered smiles and nods, silently acknowledging the shared ordeal. My thoughts bounced back and forth from my performance to the judges and to my silent exchange with Nash.

I'd avoided looking in his direction as long as I could. When I finally let myself seek him out, he was already watching me as though he'd been waiting for my eyes to find his. He raised his eyebrows in question as though to ask, "How'd it go?" I offered him a smile and a shrug of my shoulders to wordlessly reply, "I'm happy with how things went." His face cracked wide open with a smile and he nodded. I felt the blush rise up my neck and into my cheeks.

Our silent communication was interrupted when my roommate Harper joined me on the couch and started giving me a play-by-play of her time on stage, wanting to compare notes. She needed a place to process her thoughts, and I was a willing listener, though at the moment I was a distracted listener. I desperately wanted to continue my secret conversation with Nash, but forced myself to stay present with Harper.

It was probably for the best, as I still wasn't sure how I felt about everything where Nash was concerned. Besides, at this point, there was no good reason I could find to let myself become preoccupied with anything other than the competition.

49

NASH

Still riding the high after our debut performances, we awoke for a schedule that started early and lasted all day. We were all bussed to the studio, but this time it wasn't for singing. We met in a conference room where the organizers split us into groups to shoot commercials for Nashville's tourism board. My group? Cassidy, Austin, and Willow.

To say I was excited to be in a group with Cassidy was an understatement. Though I could tell she wasn't going to make it easy for me to get her attention. She was polite and agreeable, which was no surprise. But she stayed close to Willow most of the time.

Working alongside Austin and Willow was a blast; their energy made the whole experience feel less like a job and more like an adventure. Our group dynamic was interesting, to say the least.

The filming process was full of laughter and retakes. When we first arrived, the director outlined our task with a high level of excitement.

"Today, you'll be showcasing the magic of Nashville's Botanical Garden," he began. "Austin and Willow, you two will be a couple in a romantic engagement scene. Nash, Cassidy, you're walking the gardens and attending a concert series as a couple. It's all very romantic and beautiful. Any questions?" Austin and Willow responded with an enthusiastic high five and started talking about how to make their relationship look real.

I smiled, turning to Cassidy. "Well, being paired with you is definitely not a hardship considering I could have been teamed up with Austin," I teased, hoping to lighten the mood.

Cassidy offered a polite smile in return. I thought back to the first night on the patio and the shuttle ride, where it felt like we were starting to connect. How were we supposed to be part of a romantic commercial if she wouldn't even give me a real smile when I made a joke?

The director chose to film Austin and Willow's scene first, trying to capture the image of a couple in love, strolling through the Botanical Garden. They held hands, admired the blooms, and paused on a bridge overlooking the Japanese Gardens. It all looked completely natural and unscripted.

The climax was Austin attempting to present a ring, which would have been amazing except for when he accidentally dropped it into the koi pond below. The long pause followed by Willow's break into uncontrollable giggles transformed the set into a blend of laughter and mild chaos, with crew members scrambling and the director eventually calling for everything to cut action. It took several takes, but eventually the ring landed on Willow's finger and Austin successfully spun his pretend bride-to-be in the celebratory scripted hug, although he was sweating bullets by the time the director called "Cut!".

We all cheered and clapped, still laughing about the series of events leading up to the winning shot. Then it was time for Cassidy and me to take center-stage. Even though it was still early afternoon, the crew utilized special lighting to transform the set we were on, giving it the illusion of a sunset.

Cassidy emerged from the hair and makeup tent, transformed with her platinum blonde hair styled in soft waves and half-pulled back. It highlighted her striking blue eyes, and I was momentarily at a loss for words. Her beauty, accentuated by even a manufactured golden hour light, was breathtaking.

The director instructed us to act like a couple visiting the gardens on a date. That meant feigning conversation and affection.

Our scene unfolded with us walking hand-in-hand through the gardens, an idyllic setting that felt almost too perfect. Holding her hand had me feeling warm all over. It was surprising how natural it felt. We stopped on our marks to admire the scenery. Not wanting to miss an opportunity, I used it to try to get to know my new partner.

"How was your stage time yesterday?" I asked as we moved slowly through our scripted route.

"It was a lot harder than I'd expected it to be," Cassidy responded, her voice even.

Her eyes held mine for several seconds before returning to the path ahead and I almost stopped walking so I could get lost in them. Fortunately, I remembered this wasn't actually a date, and that there were cameras involved.

I hesitated before asking, "Have I done something wrong?" The question came out more desperate sounding than I'd intended.

We stopped on our next mark, where Cassidy's instructions were to turn and face me. Looking up at me, she gave a slight shake of her head as she said, "No, you haven't. I'm just focusing on getting this right," she assured, her tone still guarded but sincere.

I wanted to believe her. Her eyes were searching mine. I had this feeling she wanted to say something, but she didn't.

In a spontaneous moment, I reached out an arm and wrapped it around her, pulling her toward me. Leaning in, I whispered, "Is this OK?"

Her subtle nod and the softness in her eyes gave me the go-ahead. Something shifted between us and I didn't want to let go. I was afraid if I did, everything would shift back to the way it was before. When her hands moved slowly up my arms, I had to stop myself from tightening my hold on her. I didn't know this woman, but this just felt right.

Trying not to get lost in her eyes, I asked quietly, "Do you think we could hang out later? I feel like our conversation on the shuttle got cut short the other day."

Cassidy stood still, like the leaves on the trees surrounding us. Before she answered, the director called, "Cut!"

The director gushed over the improvised affection and encouraged more contact to really play up the romantic experience the Gardens could be. He wasn't wrong. There was plenty of romance to be had if the right people were experiencing it. If only this was real and not scripted, and there were no cameras. When Cassidy was near, my heart was constantly attempting a jailbreak from my chest.

The highlight of our scenes together was attending a staged concert set up to promote the summer concert series. As the music enveloped us, we danced, lost in the rhythm and each other. I was sure I could feel Cassidy's walls coming down.

"Hey, about hanging out later...?" I ventured again, trying to relight the spark we'd found earlier.

She hesitated, her struggle visible. "Nash, I..." she began, her voice trailing off.

"Would you tell me if I'd done something wrong or something to offend you?" I asked.

Cassidy offered me a placating smile that made me mad. "It's not you," she said, her voice soft but firm. "It's just... this whole competition. I need to stay focused, and I don't want to get distracted."

I could sense there was more behind her words. I was only asking to get to know her, but she wasn't ready to do the same. That was OK. I could be patient. It didn't mean I liked it, but I would win her over, eventually. Something inside me told me I had to; and when I did, it would be a game-changer. This was just the beginning.

As soon as the director called cut, she retreated back into her shell, putting the distance back in place, leaving me to wonder if I'd actually be able to get through. This dance, both literal and metaphorical, left me confused. Cassidy's momentary lapse into openness offered a glimpse into what could be, only to be masked again by her polite indifference.

As we headed back, Austin and Willow recounted the day with

Cassidy, filling any silence in the SUV. The three of them laughed and talked, but my mind and eyes were on Cassidy. I couldn't get her laughter out of my head, especially when combined with our semi-private moments of the day, which made me realize how my feelings for her were becoming more complicated.

It was a weird feeling, wanting the attention of the only person who didn't want to give it to me. As we headed back to the mansion, the day's activities weighing on us all, I found myself replaying our interactions, wondering if there was something I could do to convince Cassidy to take the wall down she was putting up between us. What made it harder was watching her laugh with the other contestants, but not me.

That evening, as the twelve of us shared stories of the day's shoots over dinner, there were others who had stories of mishaps similar to Austin's that had everyone rolling. It was a good distraction because the next morning we were slated to film the results show that I had a feeling we were all wishing didn't have to happen.

With my gaze constantly diverting to Cassidy, I noticed she was wordlessly communicating with the guy she'd sat with on the shuttle yesterday, Christopher Jordan. Jealousy twisted inside me, causing me to stand without thinking and head to my room. I was exhausted and confused and all I wanted to do was get a shower and try to stop thinking about blue eyes and sweet smiles and the feel of her hand in mine.

Wyatt was sitting on his bed when I walked into the room. His posture was one of frustration, with his elbows resting on his knees and his hands clasped around a cell phone. He was staring at the floor as his forehead rested on the phone in his hands. Despite his background as a Navy SEAL, a person you'd assume was always in control, in this moment, he appeared anything but. The room was heavy with the unspoken weight of whatever conversation he was either about to have or just ended.

"Hey, man, you OK?" I asked, my concern genuine. It was rare to see Wyatt as anything less than composed.

He looked up, his expression one of resignation, and sighed, a sound that seemed to carry more than just a phone call. "Yeah, all good," he replied, but his tone suggested otherwise. It wasn't my place to pry, especially knowing Wyatt's private nature and his tendency to not talk about personal stuff often.

I nodded, understanding the silent request to leave it be, and grabbed my stuff for a shower, leaving him to his thoughts. The hot water did little to wash away the confusion and disappointment of the day. Cassidy's words and actions replayed on a loop in my mind.

When I emerged from the shower, the room was empty. I wondered briefly where my roommate might have gone, but I didn't care enough to go in search of him. I was actually grateful to have the space to myself for the moment.

Lying in bed, I set my alarm for the next day. As I drifted into sleep, the woman with striking blue eyes and wild blonde curls became more than a dream. She was real, her touch like lightning, her laughter like a symphony's final note, filling my heart with joy. But doubts and fears crept in, reminding me of the walls that separated us in reality. I held on tighter to every stolen moment, to the fleeting happiness that only my dreams could offer.

The first rays of morning light piercing through the curtains brought me back to the real world. The dream had been a momentary escape from the competition and my tangled emotions towards Cassidy. But the new day waited for no one.

Facing another day filled with stages, cameras, and these new ever-present feelings, everything felt heavy. But as I got ready, a newfound determination settled in. I decided once and for all that I was going to pursue Cassidy, even if she didn't know it yet. I would be patient. I could tell I wouldn't be able to win her over with some grand gesture; instead I would show up, be there for her, get to know her, and make sure she knew that she mattered to me.

50

CASSIDY

The first week in Nashville felt like living in fast-forward. Every morning, we had photo shoots and interviews that pushed us to reveal our personal stories. It was strange and uncomfortable being on this side of the questions, as I was used to being the one asking and listening. Suddenly, I was the one sharing, baring parts of myself under bright lights and cameras. The transition from observer to subject was hard for me.

Group dinners and "getting to know you" activities that were supposed to make us feel more united often left me feeling awkward and out of place. Watching Nash effortlessly charm his way through conversations, I felt both admiration and maybe a touch of wariness. His interactions were always light and friendly, but I held back. I was afraid that anything more than a friendly distance would create more complicated feelings down the road as the competition ramped up.

I hadn't had many deep relationships beyond classmates who came and went. Chase and Mia from the bluegrass band were friends, but that changed when I left the group. Lincoln and I still texted occasionally, but our friendship is more professional and centered on his band's stuff. One of my deepest connections had been with my old online friend *GuyWithGuitar*, but circumstances beyond my control ended that one. If I was being honest, the idea of growing close to anyone in these already pressurized circumstances scared me.

Surviving the first round of elimination should have made me relax, as I hadn't fallen into the bottom two. But the fact Nash and Wyatt, two of the stronger performers in my opinion, had been in the bottom two made me realize there was little room for distractions.

Then there was the project for the tourism board that had thrown me directly into the fray with Nash. Working closely with Nash had me in a state of emotional whiplash. I truly enjoyed his company and when we'd been physically close to one another, I had to force myself to stay calm on the outside regardless of the thousands of tiny butterflies that had taken flight inside me. Reminding myself it was all for show had practically become my mantra for the day.

I'd seen him flirt with all the girls, so it seemed pointless and even foolish to let myself get caught up by his repeated requests to hang out. I also hadn't forgotten the exchange I'd overheard between him and Lanie. He didn't strike me as the gossiping type, but he had been there and I didn't hear him correct her.

Being paired with Nash had been both a curse and the most enjoyable time I'd had since being in Nashville. Deep down, I wanted to give him the benefit of the doubt. Even more than that, I wanted him to be *GuyWithGuitar*. But that would mean letting part of me out and into the open that I had never shared with anyone. And there were enough things going on that adding that to the mix might be more than I was ready to handle.

Did the pull towards Nash grow stronger the more I was around him? Yes. Did I need to stay focused on the competition and shut these emerging feelings down so deep they wouldn't know how to find the light of day if they had a map? Also, yes. Did I want to? That was a question I was too afraid to answer. I knew that I wanted to push him away but also know everything about him. I also wanted to get lost in his charm, but hide every time he came into the room. I was all over the place and didn't know what to do except shove all of my feelings into a box, leave them there, and walk away.

We were sitting around the huge dining table swapping stories about our experiences shooting the commercials when I felt someone staring at me. I glanced around, only to find Nash's eyes on me, filled with an emotion I couldn't quite decipher. I might have drowned in his gaze had Lanie's hand not grabbed ahold of my wrist when she started telling the room about how she had changed the script of the commercial she had shot with Christopher Jordan and how the director had loved it.

When my eyebrows had risen as high as they possibly could, I slowly turned to look at Christopher, whom I'd dubbed CJ, much to his chagrin, and his response made me giggle. His eyes closed and I could hear the silent tortured groan as his shoulders sagged and his head fell backwards. We both understood that neither of us were Lanie's biggest fans, though we'd never said it in so many words.

Out of nowhere, Nash stood and made a sudden exit from the table. Lanie's storytelling had been so loud and animated, no one else seemed to notice. But I'd noticed. His abrupt departure surprised me, but because Lanie still had her perfectly manicured talons wrapped around my arm, I was not in any position to chase after him.

When I could finally make an exit, I got ready for bed, feeling all of the day's emotions pressing down on me. This new place, with all its unfamiliar sights and sounds, was really overwhelming. I was surrounded by people who were supposed to be my competitors, but they were surprisingly nice, making it harder to keep my defenses up. Their friendliness seemed real, giving me this confusing mix of hesitation and maybe wanting to make friends.

Then there was Nash. He really threw me off. I was so drawn to him, and it made me uncomfortable. For starters, I didn't want to be attracted to someone I was competing against. I wanted to succeed on my own terms, without any distractions. But every time I saw him or heard his voice, my resolve just wavered just a little.

It was a constant struggle to keep my guard up, to remind myself of my goals and why I was here. I couldn't afford to let my emotions get the best of me, especially not romantic feelings for someone who could mess up my dreams. I decided it was best to continue keeping my guard up.

But as I started to drift off to sleep, I remembered the way Nash's arms had felt around me and the way my hand fit perfectly in his. It made me wonder if the walls I was so determined to keep up were already starting to crumble.

51

NASH

Personal time had become a rare commodity in the house as the attention garnered by the show ramped up over the last three weeks. If we weren't in a coaching session, we were in an interview or other event. So, when I saw Cassidy alone in the kitchen while everyone else was outside, I seized the moment.

I watched her briefly as she waited for water to boil on the stove. Her gaze was distant and thoughtful. The only sound was the soft hiss of the kettle. As I approached her, the coolness of the kitchen contrasted with the warm air from outside, and I felt the familiar mix of anticipation and nervousness that marked all our encounters.

"Got enough for two?" I asked.

Cassidy looked up, clearly pulled from her thoughts. After a moment's hesitation, she nodded, a small smile gracing her lips. "Sure."

She reached into a cabinet and retrieved a second mug, then pulled another tea bag from the basket next to the stove.

As Cassidy poured water for a second cup of tea, the charged silence between us swirled with unspoken thoughts. The soft whistle of the kettle was the only sound. I leaned against the counter, watching her movements, searching for a way to close the distance.

"The elimination last night was a shock, huh?" I ventured, hoping to steer us into safe conversational waters. "Austin going home... I didn't see that coming."

Cassidy paused, the tea bag suspended mid-air. "Yeah, it was unexpected. Austin was a good performer. But I guess this competition isn't just about performance and personality. Willow's taking it pretty hard, too." She carefully placed the tea bag in the mug, her words and actions very deliberate.

"It's getting real, isn't it? We're almost a third of the way through," I added, trying to gauge her reaction. "Makes you think about every note and every movement you make on that stage."

She finally met my gaze, but her response was hesitant. "It does. Every week feels like a new challenge, not just in performing but in staying real amidst all this competition."

The conversation stumbled forward, a dance of words that felt both necessary and awkward. Cassidy maintained a guarded demeanor, reverting back to her usual distance with me instead of the newfound openness I had observed with the other contestants. It was frustrating, this barrier she maintained, but also a puzzle I was increasingly determined to solve.

"Can I ask you something?" I said, breaking a lull in our conversation. "You seem different with me. I mean, you're open and friendly with everyone else, but whenever I get close to you, you put up some kind of wall. Have I done or said something to offend you?"

She was silent for a long moment, her eyes fixed on her hands. When she finally spoke, her voice was low, carrying a weight of reluctance. "It's not something you've done. It's more what I've seen. You're super friendly with everyone, and I've seen you flirt with almost every girl here."

Her voice trailed off, but the implication was clear. I felt a twinge of frustration—not at her, but at the picture of me she clearly had in her mind. Before I could respond, she continued, "And there was that conversation with Lanie. I overheard you two talking about me. I didn't catch it all, but it... it didn't feel great."

Realization dawned on me. Relief, followed by regret, burned through my veins like acid.

So that was it—the root of the distance she'd been maintaining. Cassidy had heard some part of my conversation with Lanie, but obviously not the part that mattered most. She hadn't heard me defend her, hadn't understood that my view of her was worlds apart from Lanie's assessments.

I carefully chose my next words, taking a moment to gather my thoughts. "Cassidy, I wish you'd heard the whole conversation. Lanie. She has her opinions, but I made it clear that I don't share them. I defended you because I believe in your talent, and I think you're an incredible person, competition aside."

Her eyes met mine, searching for the truth in my words. "You did?" There was a hint of vulnerability but mostly relief in her voice, a softness that hadn't been there a moment ago.

"Yes, I did. And not just because it was the right thing to do, but because I meant every word. You are talented, Cassidy, and you bring something unique to this competition. Your 'niceness,' as Lanie put it, is actually one of your strengths. It's just one of the things that sets you apart."

Cassidy's gaze lingered on mine, a dozen emotions flickering across her face. "I... I don't know what to say. I guess I jumped to conclusions about what you thought of me."

"It's OK," I reassured her, my voice soft. "This place, this situation —it can make anyone feel on edge, second-guessing everything. But, you can trust me. What you see with me, what you get from me. It's all real, especially when it comes to you."

There was a noticeable shift in things between us. Everything felt recharged, but with a new understanding, like maybe a tentative bridge had formed between the space that was keeping us apart. Cassidy nodded, a silent acknowledgment of my words. The hope I'd been holding onto suddenly started to grow.

"We're in this together, you know," I added with a wink. "And no matter how this competition turns out, I'm glad to have met you, Cassidy. Truly."

It wasn't big or flashy, but the smile she gave me was real and beautiful. As we resumed our conversation, the topics lighter now, I felt something between us begin to click into place. It was a fragile thing, whatever it was, but it felt real, and it was a start.

As the night wound down, we eventually went our separate ways. I reminded myself there was always tomorrow. And even with its rehearsals, challenges, and the always looming pressure of the competition, tomorrow seemed a little less daunting now.

I was feeling optimistic as I lay in bed, replaying our conversation in my head. Cassidy and I had reached a turning point. Now I just had to tread carefully so as not to scare her because I was ready to go all in on getting to know her. I only hoped she was willing to let her guard down a little more so I could.

52

CASSIDY

I dreamed about *GuyWithGuitar* and *Wildfire*. In the anonymity of the Internet, we had shared our dreams, fears, and music, and I found what I'd always thought was what a best friend would feel like. And over time, I'd eventually harbored a secret crush on *GuyWithGuitar*, his words and melodies embedding themselves on my heart like a tattoo.

It was a connection as real as any I had experienced in the physical world, yet we had never crossed the threshold to reveal our true identities.

The dream was vivid, a replay of one of our late-night chats where the conversation had veered into personal territory. We talked about where we saw ourselves in five years, our aspirations not just as musicians but as people searching for our place in the world. In the dream, *GuyWithGuitar* talked specifically about heading to Nashville and playing his music on the biggest stages.

Also, in the dream, as in our chats, there was a strong desire to ask the one question that could change everything: "Should we tell each other who we are?" But, just as it always had, fear held us back. Fear of breaking the magic, fear of disappointment, fear that reality could never match the connection we'd found in anonymity.

Waking up from the dream, the lines between Nash and *GuyWithGuitar* blurred even more. The warmth of his smile, the timbre of his voice, even the way he strummed his guitar—all seemed to whisper echoes of those conversations. My heart raced with the possibilities churning within me. If Nash was *GuyWithGuitar*, it would imply that the connection I had felt with him, both online and in person, had a deeper root than mere coincidence. But doubts clouded the hopeful light of that realization.

As the day began, I found myself watching Nash more closely, searching for any sign, any hint that he was *GuyWithGuitar*, though I wasn't sure what that would even look like. Maybe he would say something I'd read in our conversations before we lost OurSpace.

The competition continued, a constant schedule of rehearsals, performances, and cameras that left little room for introspection. Nash and I also hadn't had more opportunities for one-on-one inter-action like we'd had before the actual competition started. But I was always watching him.

If Nash was indeed the person behind *GuyWithGuitar*, it meant he had been privy to my deepest thoughts, fears, and aspirations long before we met under the stage lights of Nashville. This realization was comforting, like finding a safe harbor after years of navigating stormy seas alone. It promised a level of understanding and accep-tance that was rare, a shared history that could be the foundation of something truly meaningful.

Yet, the thought of confronting this possibility was equally terrify-ing. The vulnerability that came with exposing that truth. Nash, if he was *GuyWithGuitar*, held pieces of me I had never intended to share with a real person. The thought of how this revelation could alter our current dynamics scared me. What if it changed the way he saw me, or worse, pushed him away? Did *Wildfire* hold the same significance for him as *GuyWithGuitar* did for me, or were my feelings only one-sided and not reciprocated? I'd been there before and wasn't really looking for a repeat. My chest ached with the fear of losing the fragile bond we were nurturing.

Despite these fears, I knew I couldn't let the question go unanswered. The connection I felt to Nash, both in person and potentially, from our online past, was too significant to ignore. I found myself constantly looking for the right moment, the perfect opportunity to try broaching the subject. Every time my mind would race with possible scenarios, each one ending with a different reaction from Nash. And every time I would convince myself that I'd look again, tomorrow.

53

NASH

I tried to brush off the feeling as mere exhaustion. The past month had been a barrage of rehearsals, performances, interviews, and the constant pressure of the competition. "Just tired," I muttered to myself, pushing out of bed with an effort that felt heavier than usual.

At rehearsal, my voice held up, hitting each note with precision, but my energy flagged and my head ached. Each step, every move, felt like it was dragging me deeper into a state of lethargy. I pushed through, attributing the lack of steam to the relentless pace we'd been keeping. "A good night's sleep is all I need," I convinced myself.

But as the day wore on, the symptoms piled up—aches that wormed their way into my muscles, a chill that I couldn't shake despite the warm Nashville sun, and a fatigue that felt like it was trying to crush me. It was clear by evening: I wasn't just tired; I was sick. The team doctor confirmed it- the Flu had taken hold with an unrelenting grip.

Secluding myself in my room seemed the only responsible action. The close quarters of the competition made any illness a communal hazard, and the last thing I wanted was to be the reason someone else's performance might suffer. So, I kept to myself, missing the excitement of group dinners and the usual late-night chats that had become a favorite part of our routine.

My self-imposed isolation was only briefly interrupted when a soft knock echoed against the door of my room. Dragging myself from the bed, I shuffled across the room. Through the door, Cassidy's voice, gentle and laced with concern, broke the silence.

"Nash, it's me. I brought you some dinner. You need to eat something."

Her gesture filled me with a warmth that no fever could match. "Just leave it by the door, please," I managed to say in a hoarse whisper. The thought of her seeing me in such a weakened state was embarrassing, but her kindness overrode my pride.

"There's some medicine if you want it and hot tea. At least drink the tea," she said before I heard the soft clink of the plate and silverware being set down. Her footsteps paused for a moment before retreating. After waiting for a few minutes, ensuring she had returned to the safety of the communal spaces, I cracked open the door. There, on the floor, was a plate covered with a clean kitchen towel, the warmth radiating from what smelled like the roast we were supposed to have for dinner. Next to it was a box of cold and flu medication on top of a mug of hot tea.

After eating, I drifted in and out of restless sleep. During my few moments of consciousness, I considered ways to show my gratitude and let her know she brightened my day. Before I could come up with anything tangible, I was asleep again and my mind was restless with thoughts of a beautiful forest being overtaken by a blazing wildfire.

The next day was performance day, and I was a shell of my usual self. My body felt heavy like lead, and every movement required effort, as I sang each note through a haze of discomfort. Yet, I performed, giving it everything I had left, which wasn't much. I knew it wasn't my best—far from it. The judges' polite smiles and carefully worded critiques only confirmed my fears. I had survived the first three rounds of elimination by the skin of my teeth, but after today's performance, I felt the shadow of elimination looming closer than ever.

I'D BEEN RIGHT. Standing on that stage two nights later, as the results were announced, I pasted on my best smile, the one that hid the disappointment and the physical ache that had lessened but still left me feeling weak. When my name was called as the next contestant to leave, I accepted it with as much grace as I could muster, thanking everyone for the opportunity, for the journey.

As the reality of my departure sank in, amidst the hugs and well-wishes of my fellow contestants, I sought out Cassidy. Her concern was evident in her eyes, a silent question that asked how I was feeling without needing to voice it aloud.

When we finally got back to the mansion after the longest day ever, I went straight to my room to avoid the pitying looks and sympathetic pep talks. Maybe it was the lingering effects of the sickness or the medication, but I was surprisingly okay with the fate I was facing. Was I disappointed in the way things were ending? Yes. I know I could have gone far if not for getting sick. Am I proud of what I did accomplish while I was here? Absolutely. And I was excited about whatever came next.

Pulling clothes from hangers and out of drawers, I was surprised by a knock on the doorframe of the room. My head fell momentarily until I heard the only voice that I didn't mind hearing while I was in this state.

"Hey," Cassidy said before walking into the room.

Unable to stop myself, I smiled as I turned to face her, feeling immediately better just seeing her standing there.

"Hey," I said, blindly tossing the shirt I was folding onto the bed. "Might not want to get too close in case I'm still contagious."

Cassidy stepped inside. She held a small bag in her hands, which she extended towards me. Her voice carried a warmth that seemed to fill the room as she said, "I thought you might need these for the road."

I took the bag, curious, and peeked inside to find an assortment of snacks and a couple of bottles of water. "Thanks," I said, genuinely touched by her thoughtfulness.

She shrugged, a gentle smile playing on her lips. "You've been through a lot this week. I just wanted to make it a little easier, I guess."

Silence filled the space between us, words left unsaid and suspended in the air. I wanted to say more, to express how much her support had meant to me, especially in these last few days. But finding the right words felt surprisingly difficult.

"Cassidy, before I go, there's something I need you to know," I finally said, setting the bag aside. Her eyes grew wide as she looked at me, her expression open and attentive. "These past weeks, getting to know you, it's been one of the highlights of this whole experience for me. And last night, when I was feeling at my worst, knowing you were there, even just outside my door... it helped more than you can imagine."

Her eyes softened, and she took a small step forward. "Nash, you don't have to thank me for being a decent human being. I... I've enjoyed getting to know you, too. More than I thought I would, honestly."

Her admission struck a chord within me. "I just wish we had more time," I said, the regret clear in my voice.

We stared at each other silently for several seconds.

"You know," I drawled, a grin slowly growing on my face, "there's something you could do for me, something that would make leaving a bit easier."

Her brow furrowed slightly, curiosity mixed with concern. "What is it?"

"Give me your number?" I asked, the request wrapped in a hint of playfulness. I gave her my best pouting face and said, "It would be the perfect consolation prize, don't you think?" I batted my eyelashes like a sad puppy.

There was a moment's hesitation, a flicker of surprise, before her lips curved into a smile and a laugh escaped. "I think that can be arranged," she replied.

Exchanging numbers was a small act, but it felt significant. Shoving the rest of my clothes into my suitcase, the knowledge that this wasn't the end lessened the disappointment of my early exit. My journey in Nashville might be over, but new beginnings felt just a phone call away. And in that, there was a glimmer of hope.

54

NASH

It was just after lunchtime when my flight landed at our small municipal airport. It was the last perk of the experience for a while, at least until the *Real American Country* Tour they had planned for the contestants after the finale. I'd texted Jet before I left Nashville asking if he'd meet me there and give me a ride the twenty minutes to the house. When I stepped off the plane, he was leaning on the front of his truck outside the hangar. He had his arms wrapped around a girl I knew well. Catching sight of me, my sister turned and placed a quick kiss on Jet's cheek, then bolted in my direction.

As Cody ran across the tarmac, it felt like a scene from a movie. I could sense her excitement even from a distance. As soon as she wrapped her arms around me, any feelings of disappointment from the competition vanished.

"You're back!" she exclaimed.

Jet came over at a more leisurely pace, a wide grin on his face as he approached. "Welcome back, buddy," he said, shaking my hand before pulling me and giving my back a solid clap.

Cody filled the drive home with endless questions about the show, the other contestants, and my experiences in Nashville. Jet chimed in now and then, but mostly he let Cody lead the interrogation, his glances in the rearview mirror meeting mine with an understanding but also a look that made it clear he found her enthusiasm sweet.

As we turned onto the familiar dirt road to our family's peanut farm, a sense of peace settled over me. The vast fields on either side were a testament to the generations of hard work that had shaped our lives.

My parents were waiting on the front porch. Mom's eyes were misty as she pulled me into a tight hug, while Dad's handshake was firm, his "Welcome home, son," carrying a weight of pride and love.

If I didn't know better, I would have thought I'd been gone a lot longer than a month. Then again, it had felt like an entire lifetime in a lot of ways.

The afternoon passed with laughter and stories, my family hanging on every word as I shared the highs and lows of my adventure. Mom ranted about the unfairness of me having to perform while sick, her protective instincts in full force.

"It's part of the competition, Mom," I assured her, amused by her rallying on my behalf. "It could've happened to anyone."

"But you're not just anyone to us," she countered, her fierceness a reminder of where I got my own determination.

Dad's contribution was less verbose but no less emotional. "Seeing you up there, following your dream... you've made us all proud," he said, his voice thick with emotion.

Cody, ever practical, was already looking ahead. "So, what's next? You've got the tour coming up, but what about after that?"

I smiled at her forward-thinking. "I've got some ideas, some calls to make. But first, I'm just happy to be home, to catch up with you guys, and to enjoy a little bit of normalcy before the next thing."

The competition had been all-consuming, with every minute accounted for. Stepping back into the familiar surroundings of home, I was struck by the contrast between the fast-paced world of the competition and the steady, unchanged rhythm of home.

Time seemed to have both flown by and dragged on. Their eager questions and the way they hung on my every word about Nashville showed how much they had missed me and how closely they had been following my journey. It reminded me of the bubble I had been living in, where days blurred into nights and the competition was all that mattered.

After a full afternoon of catching up, laughter, and shared stories, Mom finally stood, ready to shoo everyone out of the house. "Alright, alright. Let's let Nash get some rest. I'll call when dinner's ready," her voice carrying the gentle authority that had always managed to corral our family, no matter the excitement.

We all dispersed, moving in the comfortable silence that comes with familiar company. I headed upstairs to my room, the same one I'd left only five weeks ago, which now felt both foreign and incredibly comforting.

Alone in my childhood room, I felt the weight of my early departure from the competition. Collapsing onto the bed, I released a deep sigh, not only from the physical fatigue of illness and travel, but also from the emotional strain of a journey cut short, just as it was really getting started.

Pulling out my phone, I hesitated before unlocking it. I had faced the competition with all the grit and determination I possessed, only to be sidelined by something as mundane as the Flu. It was another hard reminder of the unpredictability of life, of how quickly dreams can veer off course by circumstances beyond our control.

Despite everything, as I sat there, a sense of acceptance settled within me. The disappointment was there, a dull ache that accompanied the what-ifs that ran through my mind. But there was also a recognition of the growth I had experienced, of the resilience I had built. I had left for Nashville a hopeful musician; I was returning home with a clearer vision of who I was and what I wanted to achieve, sickness or no.

Of course, it didn't take long for my thoughts to drift towards Cassidy. The competition was still ongoing for her, and I wondered what she was doing.

> Hey Cassidy, I'm back home in Georgia.
> How's Nashville without me?

Her reply came quicker than I expected.

> Hey! It's quieter, that's for sure. We all miss
> your voice around here. How's home?

I could almost hear her voice in the message. I smiled, imagining the slight tilt of her head, the way she'd bite her lip as she thought about her response. We texted back and forth, avoiding any deep topics and sticking to things like her hopes for progress in the competition, my thoughts on being back home. It was comforting, even from far away.

After we said goodbye, I laid back and stared at the ceiling. My mind wandered to my online friendship with *Wildfire*. It had been years since we lost touch, but my easy conversations with Cassidy stirred memories of the connection I once had with *Wildfire*. The realness, the understanding, and a shared love for music made it impossible not to draw parallels between the two. It was weird if I thought about it, how close I felt to someone I'd never met face to face. Even now, I'd consider *Wildfire* to have been one of my closest friends. And now, experiencing a similar bond with Cassidy?

I mulled over the irony of the situation.

With Cassidy, it felt different. There was a tangible connection, a spark that seemed to light up whenever we were together. It was more than just shared interests. There was chemistry. Was it fate or a weird coincidence that I was growing closer to someone I could easily see becoming as important to me as *Wildfire* once was? And would she be unexpectedly taken away, too?

As these thoughts cascaded through my mind, a wave of exhaustion washed over me. My eyelids grew heavy, the comforting and familiar weight of my own bed lulling me into a sleep I hadn't realized I so desperately needed. The last thing I remembered was the afternoon sun peeking through the curtains.

When I woke, the room was dark. The only light was coming

from the dim light of my bedside lamp that I didn't remember turning on. A disoriented moment passed before I remembered where I was: home. I reached for my phone; the screen lighting up to show a series of missed calls and texts from my family, indicating dinner had long passed.

Rubbing the sleep from my eyes, I sat up, surprised to find the lethargy and ache that had been my constant companions over the last week seemed to have mostly dissipated. The remnants of the sickness I'd been battling, the unwanted souvenir from my time in Nashville, felt like it had finally faded, leaving me clearer-headed than I'd felt in days.

Quietly, I made my way downstairs, finding the kitchen dark except for the glow of the stove light. There, on the counter, was a plate covered and left out for me, evidence of my mom's love. I smiled, warmed by the gesture, and realized how much I'd missed home.

After the quick meal, I found myself reflecting on the number of experiences that had brought me back to this point. The competition had its highs and lows, and I made some great friends, especially Cassidy. I reminded myself that every step is all part of a journey I'm still on.

As I headed back to bed, my thoughts lingered on Cassidy and the future. Everything from the competition and now, through our new text conversations, felt like a positive step forward. It was definitely something I was eager to explore, to see where it could lead beyond the confines of reality TV and into actual reality. Maybe she was, too. I should ask her.

Drifting back to sleep, the possibilities of what lay ahead filled my dreams, anticipation for the tour, the excitement of thinking about the future, and the potential of something more with Cassidy. In that space between sleep and wakefulness, I allowed myself to imagine a future where everything fell into place. I liked that place. Maybe Cassidy would like it, too.

55

CASSIDY

Two weeks after Nash's departure, the competition's intensity had notched up significantly. When Stella went home the week after Nash, the field had narrowed to just seven competitors with six weeks left. The mansion, once filled with the constant buzz of hopeful contestants, now echoed with a tense, focused energy.

My roommate Harper, usually a beacon of positivity, had become a bundle of nerves. Landing in the bottom two with Stella the previous week had shaken her confidence. She practiced non-stop; it was a wonder her voice hadn't given out. The threat of elimination she experienced overshadowed her usual bright demeanor. When she suggested she wanted to move into one of the empty rooms but insisted it wasn't because of me, I was more than understanding. And honestly, it was a small reprieve from some of the anxious energy.

All the judges gave consistently and overwhelmingly positive feedback, proving my hard work and passion paid off. Their words should have buoyed me, filled me with confidence. Yet, as each judge took their turn to praise my efforts, a different sort of weight settled on my shoulders. I felt a familiar pressure building that I hadn't felt in years since I'd told my mom I wanted to pursue something other than the stage. When I agreed to do the show, I thought it had been a sign from the universe that I was supposed to get back to music. Now I wasn't so sure I'd read that message correctly.

Nicole Alan's remarks stood out the most. "Cassidy, with performances like these, you're not just competing; you're setting the bar. I truly believe you could take it all the way." Her confidence in me was both exhilarating and daunting. The idea of winning, of being the last one standing, was tempting, but it also brought into sharp focus the fear that success might strip away the joy I found in music. It wasn't about the fear of failing anymore, but about the possibility that achieving my goals could change my relationship with music, turning what I loved into just another competition to win.

This struggle wasn't new. It mirrored the times when Mom pushed me hard, her expectations casting a shadow over my love for music. Back then, every note played or chorus sung felt like it was for her approval, not for the love of the art. Now, standing on the precipice of potentially achieving everything I'd worked towards, I found myself wrestling with similar feelings—this time, not for my mom's approval, but for the judges', the audience's, and maybe even my own. It was starting to exhaust me.

Then there was the absence of Nash, who had become a surprising source of comfort and distraction amidst the stress. His being gone left a void. His encouragement and ability to bring levity had been a counterbalance to the pressure. Without him, the weight of it all felt even heavier.

I thought of our text conversations and couldn't help but smile. Those exchanges, filled with jokes, encouragement, and the occasional deep dive into our personal thoughts, had become a highlight of my days. Even though the competition was a demanding presence, our messages were like a secret escape, a place where the pressure momentarily lifted, and I could just be myself.

The more I dwelled on our interactions, the more convinced I became that Nash was *GuyWithGuitar*. The way he spoke about music, the comfort in our exchanges—it all pointed to the friend I'd once known as *GuyWithGuitar*. Even with everything that was going on, I felt a spark of joy and nostalgia. The problem was, I was having trouble deciding how to bring it up.

What if I mentioned it and Nash had no idea what I was talking about? I mean, I'd probably be embarrassed, but what if revealing my suspicion somehow altered the dynamic between us? Every scenario I imagined ended with a question mark; so many possible outcomes left me paralyzed with indecision.

As much as I wanted to share this revelation with him, to see that spark of recognition in his eyes, I also feared the potential repercussions. The timing also felt less than ideal. But, the more I thought about it, the more the desire to ask, to find out for sure, tugged at me.

I pushed the idea away for now and in the mean time, I prepared for this week's performance. The theme was a tribute to our hometown and that should have been right up my alley. The more I rehearsed, the harder it was to shake off the creeping dread. The stage that once felt like a platform for expression started feeling like a battleground where every note determined my fate.

Backstage, I tried to center myself, to find that place where music was my escape and not a source of anxiety. I reminded myself why I was here—because I love music.

Inhaling deeply, I felt a rush of excitement as I stepped onto the stage. The opening notes of *Take Me Home, Country Roads* filled the space. I forced a practiced smile, the familiar melody wrapping around me like a warm embrace. As I began to sing, any weight of apprehension started to lift. This song, a tribute to my home state of West Virginia, held a special place in my heart. It reminded me of where I came from, grounding me in the midst of the competition's intensity. For those few minutes, the stage transformed into those fairgrounds and community centers back home, where music was a shared joy, not a contest.

The judges' feedback was once again positive. Randy Hunt's comments were particularly poignant.

"Cassidy, that was more than just a performance; it was a heartfelt journey. 'That song wasn't just a song for you. It sounded like you were sharing a piece of your soul. You've brought us all a bit closer to

West Virginia tonight. I have no doubt, if you continue like this, you could win this competition."

His words, intended as encouragement, highlighted the complexity of my feelings towards winning. They were both exhilarating and sobering.

Walking off the stage, the doubts crept back in. Had it been enough? Was I enough? Did I want it to be?

56

NASH

The farm's routines were the same as always, but I had changed. The work was hard and kept me busy, but in the moments between all the chores, under the huge, open skies, my thoughts kept drifting to Nashville, to music, and to Cassidy. It could have been because the sky was as blue as her eyes or the clouds as white as her hair. But, honestly, I think it was because I really liked her. And yet, I realized I barely knew her.

Leaning on the fence, taking a much-needed break, I thought about the path not taken. Had the competition gone differently, where might we have ended up? Would we still be in it together? My phone buzzed in my pocket. As though Fate was smiling down on me, I had a message from Cassidy.

I don't know if I want to do this anymore. The pressure's getting to me, and I'm starting to hate the very thing I loved most about this whole thing.

I knew those feelings well. The competition had been both a dream and a nightmare, testing my passion against pressure. The weight of expectations often felt heavy. And even before going to

Nashville, when the plans others had for me clashed with my own dreams, I'd felt overwhelmed.

I started typing, words that flowed from a place of experience.

> Hey. I get it. The competition is intense, but don't let it change how you feel about music. What's important is that you don't lose sight of what you love. It's OK to step back, to remember why you started. Music is about connecting, joy, and expressing who you are. Don't let the competition take that from you.

While pressing send, memories of a conversation with *Wildfire* from years ago came flooding back. She'd told me the same thing. We'd both learned through experience that the pressure to perform and to succeed can overshadow the pure love of creation, turning passion into obligation; and when that happened, you sometimes needed to find a new perspective.

Cassidy's response came quickly.

> Thank you. I really needed to hear that. Sometimes I forget why I even started this journey.

I smiled and a seed of curiosity planted itself firmly in my brain as I pocketed my phone. The parallels, the irony, the connection of past and present were almost too much. But I'd trusted the journey this far. I wasn't going to stop now. Especially when I think about where it's brought me, and what it's given me. It was almost enough to make me wonder about the mysterious forces that weave in and out of our lives, connecting us in ways we might not immediately understand.

For now, though, there was work to be done.

57

NASH

I was lost in the rhythm of our work, the comfortable silence between Jet and me filled with the clank and hum of machinery, when suddenly, a bolt came loose, and the inverter bar clattered to the ground with a metallic thud.

Jet cursed under his breath, shutting off the engine. We both crouched down to assess the damage. As we worked side by side to fix the digger, Jet turned the conversation to a topic I hadn't anticipated. "So, I've been meaning to tell you something," he began, his tone unusually serious. "I bought a ring for Cody."

The news hit me like a cool breeze on a hot day—unexpected but welcome. "You did? That's awesome, man!"

He smiled, nerves and excitement playing at the edges of his expression. "Yeah, I did. And I've already talked to your dad about it. I would have mentioned it to you sooner, but you've had a lot on your plate."

I was genuinely thrilled for them. Cody and Jet had practically been inseparable for the last three years from what I'd gathered and observed. "I'm really happy for you both. Cody's going to lose her mind."

Jet chuckled, his gaze drifting toward the horizon as if he could already picture the moment. "That's the plan. And there's more—we're moving to Athens next fall when Cody heads to the University of Georgia."

"That's amazing news! Man, things are really coming together for you two," I said, clapping him on the shoulder.

"Yeah, it's all happening," he agreed, his voice carrying a note of disbelief at the rapid changes unfolding in their lives.

Our conversation was cut short by the shrill ring of my phone. I glanced at the screen, not recognizing the Nashville number that flashed across it. "Sorry, I've got to take this," I said, stepping away from the digger.

"Hello?"

"Is this Nash Montgomery?" The strong country twang on the other end was unfamiliar, yet it carried an air of authority.

"Yes, this is Nash."

"This is Mike Howard. I'm the owner and a music producer here at Riverbank Records in Nashville. I caught your performances on *Real American Country*, and I've been meaning to reach out. I'm interested in discussing the possibility of having you sign a recording contract with us. I know you've still got some obligations with the show, but I wanted to get in early and see what we might work out."

The words took a moment to register. A recording contract? This was the call every musician dreamed of, and it still felt surreal. And of all times it was happening now, amidst the dirt and machinery of the farm.

"Think you might be interested?" Mike pressed, breaking through my dazed silence.

"Yes. Yes, I'm definitely interested." I tried not to sound too eager, but I was pretty sure I failed.

"Great," he said with a chuckle. "I'll send over some preliminary information and we can set up a time to meet. I like what I saw on the show and I think you've got a lot of potential, Nash."

"Thank you, Mr. Howard. I look forward to it."

The call ended, and I stood frozen for a moment, the phone still pressed to my ear. This could change everything. My mind raced with the possibilities, the dreams I had temporarily shelved in the wake of being sent home from the competition suddenly springing back to life.

Jet watched me, a knowing smile spreading across his face. "Good news?"

I nodded, still processing. "Yeah, you could say that. A music producer from Nashville wants to talk about a recording contract."

"Man, that's fantastic!" Jet exclaimed, as genuinely excited for me as I was for him and Cody.

"Yeah, it is," I agreed, a broad grin overtaking my face.

The future, for all of us, was bright and packed with potential. When we went back to working on the digger, all set to take on the inverter bar one more time, I had this feeling that this moment was the start of something incredible. For Jet and Cody, a new life together in Athens; for me, a potential path back to Nashville as a musician with a real shot at making my dreams come true. And the first person I wanted to tell was most likely in a voice rehearsal and wouldn't have her phone turned on.

Waiting to tell her felt like holding onto a secret that was too good to keep. I really wanted to tell her face-to-face, to see if her eyes would light up and her smile would widen when I shared the news. But I didn't think I could wait that long. I needed her to be the one I shared my excitement with. I'd tell her as soon as she returned the message I just sent, letting her know I had news.

Since returning home, my evenings had found a new pattern, one that revolved around conversations with Cassidy. We had graduated from texts to actual phone calls, stretching late into the night on the weekends, and not just about the competition, either. We talked about everything—life, dreams, our fears, and the music that ran deep in our veins. Our connection felt both new and incredibly familiar, not different from what I once shared with *Wildfire*.

The thought had crossed my mind more times than I cared to admit that maybe, just maybe, Cassidy could be *Wildfire*. The similarities in their passion for music, the ease with which we talked, the way our conversations flowed, the fact that she was from West

Virginia—it all seemed too aligned to be mere coincidence. But each time the idea surfaced, I pushed it away, labeling it as wishful thinking. The world isn't that small, and life isn't that kind to just bring *Wildfire* back to me in such an unexpected twist of fate. Or so I told myself, trying to temper the hope with a dose of reality.

58

CASSIDY

There were three of us left in the competition. I hadn't actually thought I'd make it this far, but here I was. Backstage, I could feel the nerves, like electricity in my veins. Lanie Tisdale, Christopher Jordan, and I were the last ones standing. CJ and I had grown close over the weeks, a friendship forged in the fires of competition. I was genuinely happy that both of us had made it into the top three. In my heart, I believed he would be the best choice for the winner. His voice, his stage presence—it was all there, and then some. And while I was still not sure I wanted the top spot, I knew deep down I absolutely did not want Lanie Tisdale to have it.

The judges chose the song theme this week as a curveball to push us out of our comfort zones. My assignment? Miranda Lambert's *Gunpowder and Lead*. It was a style I was far less comfortable with. It was loud, and brash, and it was everything I wasn't used to performing. But I was determined to give it my all, to pour every ounce of myself into the performance, despite feeling it probably wouldn't be enough to secure my place in the final.

The moment I stepped off the main stage, with adrenaline still coursing through my veins, the judges hit me with critical but kind feedback. Despite their comments on my effort and bravery for trying something new, I knew that my performance fell short. Disappointment was a bitter pill to swallow, but I also felt a stitch of guilt for feeling relieved that I could be going home.

Trying to keep a smile I didn't feel like having on my face as I walked off something—or rather, someone—cut through the fog of my disappointment. Nash. He was there, in the flesh, standing just beyond the stage lights. I didn't hesitate, not even for a second; I ran to him, and without a thought, jumped into his arms and wrapped myself around him. The relief that washed over me was indescribable. With so many emotions trying to push their way to the front, it was hard to pinpoint just one. It was as though in this single moment, everything that had weighed me down—the pressure, the fear, the uncertainty—just evaporated.

He caught me effortlessly and laughed. After several moments, I realized what I had done. I had practically tackled him and was now trying to fight the embarrassment that was causing me to blush hard. I loosened my grip and attempted to return my feet to the ground.

"Hi," he breathed with a smile that lit up his entire face, not releasing me beyond allowing me to stand on my own.

Still overwhelmed with everything that had just happened, I barely got out, "Hi."

"How are you?" Nash asked after we'd pulled apart, his eyes scanning me for visible signs of distress.

"Relieved," I admitted, the word feeling too small to encompass everything I was feeling, which right now was a lot. "What are you doing here?"

Nash smiled, that reassuring, warm smile that I'd come to miss more than I realized. "Are you kidding? Since I was in town, I wouldn't have missed this for the world," he said.

And I believed him. I should have headed to the green room, but Nash took my hand, distracting me with his touch, and sending a current of calm through the chaos of my emotions.

"Come with me," he said, leading me away from the bustling backstage area to a quieter part of the venue.

We found ourselves in a room that appeared to function as a

dressing room or break room as needed. It was basically empty, except for a few chairs and a sofa that had seen better days, but it was a welcome respite from the sounds coming from the stage. He faced two of the chairs toward one another, and we sat, his knees on either side of mine. He took both of my hands in his and stroked his thumb over the back of one of them.

"Why are you really in town?" I asked, curiosity getting the better of me. Nash, being here now, felt like more than just a coincidence. He hesitated for a moment before his expression grew into one of excitement and nerves.

"I'm here laying down some preliminary tracks at the studio. Mike figured it would be a good time to do it since I had to be in town next week, anyway," he explained, the pride and excitement evident in his voice.

My heart swelled for him, a rush of excitement coursing through me.

I freed my hands and threw my arms around his neck. "That's amazing!" I exclaimed, genuinely thrilled for him.

His dream, the one he'd worked so hard for, was becoming a reality. He thanked me as I sat back down, but then there was a shift in his demeanor. He reclaimed my hands and started to say something, but stopped, then started again. It was unlike him to be hesitant, and my curiosity turned to concern.

"What is it?" I prompted, waiting patiently for him to find the words.

Finally, he looked me straight in the eyes, a seriousness in his tone that I hadn't heard before. "I need to ask you something," he said, and suddenly, I was the one who was nervous.

The combination of his intensity and the weight of his voice worried me.

"Years ago, I used a website called OurSpace. I know this sounds crazy, but I had a friend on there named *Wildfire*. And over the last month... I get this feeling every time I talk to you that you could be *Wildfire*, and *Wildfire* could be you. Like I said, it sounds crazy, but I had to ask. It's been driving me crazy wondering."

My world tilted on its axis, and tears burned my eyes. Excitement, nervousness, disbelief, and hope swirled within me, more intense than any emotion I'd felt on stage. He knew I was *Wildfire*. I was suddenly giddy with the revelation. My face hurt from smiling so much. I'd harbored my suspicions for so long, the pieces of the puzzle slowly coming together with each conversation, every shared laugh, and the quiet moments of understanding. Yet, I'd held back, unsure and afraid to confront the possibility head-on.

"You're still the guy with the guitar, then?" I asked.

Nash's reaction was priceless - his eyes went wide in a moment of realization, and then he couldn't stop grinning.

"It is you. I knew it had to be, but the chances were so small..."

We sat there in the quiet room, the magnitude of the moment sinking in. The world outside—the competition, the judges, the audience—faded into insignificance. It had finally happened. *GuyWith-Guitar* and *Wildfire*, reunited under the most unlikely circumstances. The realization that we'd unknowingly reconnected was overwhelming.

Every feeling I'd had from the instant I laid eyes on him finally made sense. I'd always held a place in my heart for him because it was like I always knew we were meant to find each other again.

59

NASH

We sat there and stared at each other in silence, the discovery hanging between us. The fact that Cassidy, the one person I'd immediately felt drawn to, was also *Wildfire*, left me speechless.

Cassidy broke the silence, her voice full of wonder and vulnerability. "I've wanted to ask you the same thing for so long..."

Her confession caught me off guard. "Really? When did you start suspecting?" I asked, eager to understand her side of the story.

"It was during our first dress rehearsal," she said, her eyes brightening at the memory. "You sang *Wrapped up in You*. I thought I recognized your voice. Hearing it that day... it felt like a sign. But, I was scared to bring it up because how crazy would I have sounded? Except, it apparently wouldn't have been crazy at all."

The memory brought back a lot of feelings.

"That's incredible," I said, still processing. "I had no idea. To think, you've been right here, and all this time..."

"Yeah. I wish I would have said something, sooner." Cassidy said softly, her lips curling into a playful smile. "It's been a wild ride, hasn't it?"

Wild didn't even begin to cover it. From the anonymity of OurSpace to the spotlight of the competition, our paths had intertwined in ways I never could have imagined. And now, sitting in this nondescript room, the noise and chaos of the competition felt worlds away. Here, it was just us, our shared past and an unwritten future.

"I guess it really is a small world after all," I mused. "Or maybe it's just that some connections are too strong to be denied, no matter how unlikely they seem."

Cassidy squeezed my hand, her presence grounding me. "I like the sound of that," she said, her eyes meeting mine with a warmth that made my heart stutter. It was a rush that had me feeling a little dizzy.

The conversation flowed naturally from there, as we shared stories and memories from OurSpace, marveling at how our separate journeys had led us to this shared moment. Each word, each laugh, felt like a piece of a puzzle clicking into place, revealing a picture that had been there all along, waiting for us to see it.

Just as we were getting lost in the moment, a shrill bell rang, jolting us back to reality and signaling the conclusion of the show. We both stood, knowing we had to leave, but there was a hesitation, a reluctance to break the bubble that had enveloped us in this room.

I looked at Cassidy, trying to appear stronger than I felt. "I don't want to let you go," I confessed, the words heavy with an emotion I couldn't fully articulate. "I'm afraid if I do, this will all turn out to be a dream, or something will happen that keeps us apart for years again. I don't want to go through that again—not now that I've actually met you."

Cassidy reached out, her hand finding mine, her touch a reassurance. "It's not a dream. And nothing will keep us apart this time. We've waited too long to let go now. Besides, now I know your real name and you've got my number," she said with a smirk.

Her confidence and snark made me chuckle. This was real, and we had total control of what happened next. The fear of losing her again lingered in the back of my mind. But her hand in mine gave me the same confidence.

"We should probably head out, though. I'm not sure anyone would miss me for a while, but I think it would be creepy getting locked in this place," Cassidy said with a soft laugh, breaking the tension. "But let's make a promise, here and now, that no matter what happens, we won't lose touch again. We've been given a second chance, and I don't want to waste it."

I nodded, the promise cementing something deep within me. "Nothing is going to keep us apart this time," I repeated her words back.

As we left the room and walked into the chaotic aftermath of the show, I felt strangely peaceful. Rounding a corner, the bustling energy of the competition's aftermath enveloped us. Crew members hustled by and the air buzzed with busyness and exhaustion, a contrast to the quiet space we had just left behind.

Trying to avoid the busiest part of the hallway, we tried to stay far to one side where we ran into Christopher Jordan. His attention went straight to my hand around Cassidy's.

His expression softened and with a knowing smirk on his face, he said, "Oh, there you are, Cass. And Nash, hey, man, when did you get here?" His voice cut through the noise, his casual demeanor belying the sharpness in his eyes.

"Just a bit ago," I replied, trying to match his ease but feeling the significance of the moment press down on me. Cassidy squeezed my hand, reminding me she was next to me as I faced the one other person I'd watched her get close to, the one who had been present with her through all the highs and lows of the competition after I left.

His gaze shifting between Cassidy and me, his eyebrows raised, he said, "Well, this looks like it will make for an interesting story."

Cassidy laughed, a light, happy sound that filled the space between us. "Yeah, you could say that," she said, her eyes sparkling. "It's kind of a long story."

"I've got time," he said, leaning against a nearby wall, clearly not planning to go anywhere until he got at least part of the story.

But before Cassidy or I could respond, he raised a hand and stood up straight, his expression one of amusement. "I'm just kidding. Save it for later. Just know I'm happy for you both and I saw it coming from a mile away."

With a tip of the cowboy hat perched on his head, he winked at Cassidy and spun on his heel before walking away.

Cassidy turned and buried her face in my shoulder, her body shaking. At first, I thought she was upset, and I gently asked, "What's wrong?"

She lifted her head, revealing not tears but silent laughter. "Christopher," she managed to say between laughs, "told me probably a week after you left that he was disappointed he wasn't going to get to see just how desperate I could make you. He said you kept ramping up your antics to get my attention, but it kept backfiring and got the other girls' attention instead. I told him he was crazy and that it had just been your personality."

Her words, so unexpected, made me burst into laughter. The idea that Christopher had seen something between us even then, and his jab about desperation, struck me as hilarious. The laughter between us was a release, a moment of euphoria in the craziness and the intensity of our reunion.

As we composed ourselves, still chuckling, I wrapped an arm around Cassidy's shoulders, feeling more than ever that this was right where I was meant to be.

"I know you need to get changed and finish up here. I'm going to head to my hotel. If you feel like it later, give me a call?" I suggested, hoping she'd sense the genuine invitation in my voice.

Cassidy nodded, her smile soft but radiant. "I will," she promised, and there was something in the way she said it with certainty that filled me with expectation.

We lingered for a moment longer, neither of us eager to break the connection. But her need to return to her schedule pulled at us. Finally, with one last squeeze of her hand, I let her go, watching as she turned to head back to the wardrobe department.

Stepping into the cool night air, my mind raced with thoughts. Cassidy's presence, her laughter, the way she looked at me—it all felt like a piece of myself I hadn't known was missing until now.

It was a new beginning, but I knew we had to be careful. We were more than just online friends now, and I was determined not to lose her again, knowing she was worth fighting for. I was also aware that so much of the future was uncertain for both of us. That's what scared me the most.

60

CASSIDY

I settled into the plush chair by the window of my Nashville hotel room, the city lights twinkling below like distant stars. Holding my phone, I waited for the familiar ring that would connect me to my parents halfway across the world in Tokyo. This weekly call had become a lifeline, a moment of normalcy in the whirlwind of my life since coming to Nashville.

After my elimination, competition rules dictated I had to vacate the premises of the mansion the next day. It was a strange feeling, leaving the place that had felt like both a battlefield and a home. But the competition wasn't over for everyone just yet. Next week marked the finale, and the producers expected all the ousted contestants and the two finalists to return for a group performance. We'd also be there to celebrate the journey, to support Lanie and Christopher as they competed for the top spot.

After that, I'd be heading back to L.A. for work, the welcome reality waiting to embrace me until the tour kicked off in a few months. It was a weird case of limbo.

The phone screen lit up, and soon enough, I heard my parents' voices.

"Hey, honey! How are you really holding up?" my mom's voice came through, clear despite the miles between us.

We'd been in touch through messages, but the time difference always made it hard to connect directly. The sound of her voice was a balm to the swirling emotions inside me.

"I'm actually really okay, Mom. I think leaving the competition when I did was the right time for me. I'm relieved, to be honest. I can say I tried and know for certain that a life on stage is not for me."

There was a pause, and then my mom's voice, softer now, filled with understanding, she said, "I'm sorry we can't be there for you, especially with Thanksgiving coming up. It must be hard."

"It's OK, Mom," I found myself saying, my smile widening as I answered. "Actually, I'm going to Georgia with Nash. He invited me to spend Thanksgiving with his family."

The line went quiet for a moment before my mom's laughter filled my ears. "Nash, huh? It sounds like things are getting serious."

I blushed, thankful the room was dim enough my mom couldn't see it. Playing with the hem of my shirt, I couldn't contain my smile when I said, "He's amazing, Mom. Spending time with him feels... right, you know?"

My mom's voice was warm, filled with the comfort that only a mother's voice could bring. "I do know, sweetie. I'm so happy for you. It's been wonderful seeing you open up about your feelings for Nash. And I'm glad he's there."

"Yeah, me, too," I found myself agreeing, my memory drifting to Nash waiting for me backstage after the announcement of my elimination. "I guess I didn't realize how much I needed someone like him in my life until he was there. And to think he'd been part of my life before knowing who he was. Now, I don't really want to imagine it without him."

I'd filled Mom in after Nash and I had discovered the truth, and she'd been shocked then delightfully amused for probably ten minutes as she laughed and asked, "What are the chances?" at least a hundred times.

The conversation shifted, veering into 'girl talk' territory as my mom asked about Nash's family, if I knew what they were like, and if I was nervous about meeting them. Even though I didn't have a ton of answers, I found comfort in my mom's questions.

After hanging up, I couldn't shake this feeling of gratitude for my parents. Their support had gotten me to where I was, even if we had been thousands of miles apart. Thankfully, our weekly calls had kept us close, even if they were few and far between.

Life had changed a lot since going to Nashville, but there were some things I was looking forward to in L.A.. The management at EchoStream had been incredibly supportive, holding my position until I could come back. It was comforting to know I had a job waiting for me. I was looking forward to some normalcy and a routine after an experience that was a far cry from normal.

The idea of sitting at my desk creating content, drafting post strategies, and analyzing engagement metrics felt so distant from the stages and spotlights I'd grown accustomed to. I wondered if my colleagues would look at me differently, knowing I'd chased a dream and would be returning home second runner-up. The transition back to "normal" loomed over me, but I was ready to get back to it.

And then there was Nash and the promise of something blossoming there. The thought of exploring what we had, without computer screens and without the pressure of cameras and competition, was both thrilling and terrifying.

As I packed my bags for the quick trip to Georgia before facing the reality of L.A., I found myself getting excited. The prospect of seeing Nash in his element, away from the chaos, made my pulse quicken. It felt like the start of something beautiful, and I couldn't wait to see where it might lead.

61

NASH

Driving down to Georgia with Cassidy next to me, I couldn't shake the feeling that everything had come full circle. Only this time, instead of just knowing *Wildfire* through the glow of a computer screen, I had her right here, in person. The thought came frequently and had a permanent grin plastered on my face like an idiot, but I didn't care. This was the kind of moment you wanted to hold on to forever.

We decided to rent a car for the trip rather than fly. Obviously we wanted to avoid the insane holiday traffic at the airports, but I was also really excited for the hours we'd get to spend together, just Cassidy and me. There's something about a long drive that invites conversation and there was plenty to be had. There were so many topics we'd only skimmed over the last couple of months due to time constraints and obligations.

Cassidy was definitely nervous, her hands fidgeting in her lap, but I reached over and gently took one in mine. Our relationship had been progressing slowly, sure, but every step forward had felt right. It was as if we were carefully laying down the tracks for something meant to last, and I was all in for the ride.

"We're almost there," I told her, giving her hand a reassuring squeeze.

She smiled, but I could tell she was still a bit anxious. "Are you sure it's okay that I'm coming with you? I could try to get a flight back to L.A.."

"My folks are going to love you," I said confidently. "My mom is thrilled and my little sister, Cody, is going to be over the moon. She was rooting for you to go all the way – well, after I went home, of course," I said, glancing at Cassidy and giving her a wink, causing her to smile and roll her eyes.

As we neared my hometown, the familiar landmarks coming into view, I could sense Cassidy's nervousness returning. I squeezed her hand again, offering her a reassuring smile. "Hey, it's going to be great. Trust me."

She nodded, her smile returning as she looked out the window, taking in the quiet scenery of rural Georgia. It had to be a far cry from the bustling streets of L.A. and the high stakes pressure of Nashville.

Pulling into the driveway, I felt something that was a cross between excitement and relief. The journey here had been long, both in miles and in the steps it took for Cassidy and me to reach this point.

"This is it," I said, gesturing towards the house. "Welcome to my family's home sweet home."

She took a deep breath, steeling herself for the introductions ahead. We approached the front door, hand in hand, but before we could even knock, the door burst open, and there was Cody, practically bouncing with excitement. "Nash!" she exclaimed, launching herself at me first, then turning her wide, eager eyes on Cassidy. "And you are Cassidy! I've heard so much about you besides what we saw on TV!"

Cassidy, taken aback by the enthusiastic welcome, laughed and returned Cody's hug. "It's so nice to finally meet you. Nash has told me a lot about you, too," her initial nervousness melting away under Cody's genuine enthusiasm.

Behind Cody, my mom appeared, a warm, welcoming smile on

her face. "Welcome, Cassidy. We're so glad you could join us for Thanksgiving," she said, stepping forward to envelop Cassidy in a gentle hug. "I'm sorry you couldn't be with your parents but I am so glad you agreed to join us."

I could see Cassidy relax under the warmth of my family's welcome, any lingering nervousness fading away. I knew they would love her and that her initial worries were clearly unfounded. I hoped she could see it, too.

"Come in, come in," my mom urged, leading us into the house. The familiar scents of home filled the air, enveloping us in comfort.

Cody, ever the bundle of energy, grabbed Cassidy's hand and started to pull her toward the living room. I smiled as I watched Cassidy get caught up in my sister's excitement.

This was exactly what I'd hoped for—my two worlds coming together seamlessly. Cassidy was here, in my home, being welcomed with open arms. I knew this Thanksgiving was going to be unforgettable.

Before I could follow Cassidy and my sister into the living room, my mom placed a hand on my arm.

"Give them a minute, Nash. Let's have a moment, you and me," Mom said, her eyes twinkling with mischief and warmth. We stepped into the kitchen, a place of countless memories and heart-to-heart talks.

She leaned against the counter, her gaze soft but probing. "You know, you never brought Riley home for the holidays," she began, a gentle reminder of the past.

A small laugh escaped me as I rubbed the back of my neck.

"Yeah, things with Riley were... different," I admitted, avoiding her gaze as I traced the pattern on the kitchen towel hanging from the oven handle with my eyes.

She nodded, giving me the space to gather my thoughts. "And yet, here you are with Cassidy," she observed, her voice laced with something akin to hope. "She seems to have brought out a light in you, Nash. It's beautiful to see."

Cassidy's arrival in my life, first as *Wildfire* and now in person, had turned a new page for me. She was like a melody that I didn't know the words to yet, but every note was already engraved deep within my soul. It was a feeling so different from anything I'd ever experienced before.

"Not to mention she's beautiful," she mused, watching me closely for my reaction.

I smiled, picturing Cassidy in the next room, probably laughing at something Cody said.

Sighing, I knew the truth, and it was undeniable. "You're right, Mom," I said, finally meeting her eyes. "Cassidy... she's different in ...a good way. She's incredible," I confessed, feeling a rush of affection for the woman who had unexpectedly become so important to me.

Mom's smile widened, satisfied with my admission. "I'm glad, Nash. It's been a long time since I've seen you this happy," she said, reaching out to squeeze my hand. "I just want you to know, your dad and I are happy for you and so proud of you."

I nodded, grateful for her support. "Thanks, Mom. That means a lot."

Just then, laughter echoed from the living room, pulling us out of our conversation. Mom gave me a gentle push. "Go on, I know you're dying to be in there. But, Nash," she called out as I started to leave, "remember, love isn't something you find one time. It's something you build day by day, through the good times and the bad."

Her words stayed with me as I joined Cassidy and Cody. *Love was something you build.* I didn't know that I'd go so far as to say this was love, but with Cassidy, I felt like we were definitely building the foundation for something special.

Later that evening, Cassidy and I found ourselves walking alone in one of the pastures. The sky was a clear canvas of stars, and the world around us was quiet. I unrolled the blanket I'd been carrying onto the grass and we both silently laid back and stared up at the heavens. It felt like the first moment of true quiet I'd had in months. My mind began to tick into motion, thinking about what would happen after this weekend when Cassidy would head back to California. I'd probably be going between home and Tennessee. I knew I'd see her again in February when the tour started, but that seemed too far away.

"So, I know you have to go back to L.A. until the tour starts," I began, breaking the silence between us.

She nodded, her gaze fixed on the night sky. "Yeah, and you'll be in Nashville?"

"Yeah, part of the time," I answered, not wanting to think about the distance that would soon be between us. "But I was thinking, maybe I could visit you in L.A.? See what all the hype is about."

Cassidy laughed, turning to me with a sparkle in her eyes. "I'd like that. You'd be welcome anytime."

"You know, I always had a crush on *Wildfire*," I confessed, trying to see her face in the dim light. "Which was pretty inconvenient, considering she was just a nameless faceless girl from another state."

A soft smile played on her lips. "And here I was, crushing on *GuyWithGuitar*," she said, her voice filled with a warmth that eased the tightness in my chest. "It's funny how things work out, isn't it?"

I chuckled. The absurdity of it all was not lost on me. "I kicked myself regularly after OurSpace was gone. For not going out on a limb, asking for your real name at least. It felt like I missed my chance without even knowing what I was missing."

Her hand found mine in the darkness. "We were both just a couple of kids online, Nash. It's not like we knew where life was going to take us. But, look at us now," she laced her fingers with mine, "right where we're supposed to be."

Her words were reassuring. It was true; back then, neither of us could have predicted where our paths would lead. Yet, here we were, together, the present and our futures suddenly intertwined.

"Yeah, you're right," I agreed, feeling a sense of peace wash over me. "It's just... I really don't want to mess this up, Cassidy. Whatever this is between us, it's important to me."

Cassidy shifted, turning to lie on her side, bringing our hands up between us, resting her chin on them. "We've both come a long way since then. And no, we haven't exactly defined what this is," her grip tightening in mine, "but I feel it too. I know it's special."

Turning, I mirrored her position. "I guess what I'm trying to say is, I don't want to wait until February to see where this goes. I want to take advantage of every moment I can with you, even if it means figuring out long-distance."

Cassidy nodded, her eyes searching mine in the starlight. "I'm all in, Nash. We don't have to put a label on it if you don't want to, but I definitely want to see where this goes."

The relief that flooded through me was like diving headlong into a cool lake on a hot day. "That's all I needed to hear," I said, leaning in.

Our lips met in a kiss that felt like a promise, tender yet intense, filled with unspoken emotions. It was a connection that wrapped around us, a moment where time seemed to stand still, leaving only the warmth and certainty of our closeness. In this moment that would never be long enough, the significance of everything past, present, and future became clearer.

As we pulled apart, the world around us seemed to remain frozen, the stars bearing witness to the beginning of something neither of us fully understood yet, but were both more than ready to explore.

We laid there for a while longer, her hand in mine, our hearts aligned with the possibilities of tomorrow, talking about nothing and everything, especially the future. It was a conversation filled with more questions than answers, and even then, the future seemed not only hopeful, but within reach.

62

CASSIDY

Rolling back into Nashville was like waking up in the middle of a dream left unfinished. The city obviously hadn't changed in a week. It was still buzzing with music and hopes, but something inside of me had definitely shifted.

Tonight, all twelve of us, the season's contestants, reunited for one last performance. *Life is a Highway* by Rascal Flatts was our anthem, a fitting metaphor for the journey we'd each taken to wind up here on this stage. No longer competing against one another, there was something special about this performance. Being on stage together felt like a celebration of our goals and achievements.

As we took our seats in the audience afterward, Nash was right next to me. We watched as memories of the past few months rolled on giant screens. It was a sweet reminder of everything we'd done, like flipping through a visual diary of our journey, each image sparking moments of laughter and tears among all of us.

By the time the last song of the night ended, I had a death grip on Nash's hand. When they announced Christopher Jordan as the winner, I was thrilled. His victory felt like a win for all of us who'd seen his dedication and talent up close. I was the one cheering the loudest, pride swelling in my chest for my friend's well-deserved triumph.

The after-party was a mix of laughter, congratulations, and relief that the competition was finally behind all of us. Nash and I navigated the crowd together, eventually finding Christopher amidst a sea of well-wishers.

"Congrats, CJ!" I exclaimed, wrapping him in a hug. He rolled his eyes at the nickname but hugged me back, grinning.

"Thanks, Cassidy," his smile seemed permanently etched onto his face, the tension of the past months all but dissipated.

Nash clapped him on the back, adding his own, "Well done. You earned it, man."

As the night stretched on, Nash and I carved out quiet moments for ourselves amidst the buzz of the celebration, staying back to observe; our closeness punctuated by stolen touches and kisses.

When I yawned for the third time, signaling the weariness settling in, Nash gently took my hand and said with a soft concern, "Let's get you back to the hotel so you can catch some sleep."

His voice was a gentle reminder of the reality waiting for us with the sunrise. I nodded, reluctantly agreeing, aware of the fleeting moments we had left together. I'd held out as long as I could because come morning, we'd be going our separate ways. But he was right. I had to be at the airport in just a few hours.

Standing outside my hotel room, Nash's voice was soft but firm. "Have breakfast with me. I don't want you to leave without saying goodbye," he said, the earnestness in his eyes mirroring my own feelings.

I reached for his hand, squeezing it gently. "I would never," I promised. Our goodnight kiss sealed the promise.

As Nash's footsteps faded down the hallway, I was left with a heart full of hope and a mind buzzing with possibilities layered with exhaustion.

The competition had brought us back together, but it was our unfinished story that would carry us forward. Tomorrow would bring farewells, but it was just the beginning for us.

63

CASSIDY

Breakfast with Nash at the hotel had been a cozy but quiet affair. We'd found a private corner away from the morning rush, a space where time seemed to slow, allowing us to savor the moments left together. Every longing look and gentle touch was a reminder of what we were about to leave behind, even if only for a little while.

As we stood outside the hotel, waiting for the Uber that would take me to the airport, Nash pulled me into his arms, his embrace a shield from the impending separation.

"Remember, let me know when you land," he whispered, his voice a low hum against my ear, sending shivers down my spine.

"I will," I promised, my words muffled against his chest. Pulling back just enough to look into his eyes, I found the same affection and sorrow I was feeling. It was then that Nash leaned down, capturing my lips with his in a kiss that was both a promise and a plea.

It deepened, fueled by the imminence of goodbye. We clung to each other as if to memorize the feeling. Around us, the world went on, but for those moments, it felt as if we were the only two people in it. Whistles and catcalls from a few passersby finally broke us apart.

Our laughter made puffs of white in the cool morning air, a temporary cure for the misery of goodbye.

The flight back to L.A. gave me some much needed time to think, the sound of the jet engine a backdrop to my riotous thoughts. Flashes of the last few months played out in images of conversations on the patio, stories at the dinner table, and the impromptu concerts that were likely to break out any time two or more contestants were together.

As I gazed out the window at the clouds passing by, a realization settled in with a clarity that surprised me. Performing music, being on stage—it wasn't the life I wanted. The competition had been a rush, but it had been stressful and not the path I'd been searching for. Instead, I realized it was always the people and the moments of shared experience that stayed with me. The question then became, could I make that a career?

Landing in L.A. felt like coming home to a question mark. As I switched my phone back on, a notification popped up—a text from Nash. It was a screenshot from a website showing flights to L.A., accompanied by a simple message: "Counting down the days until I see you again. Just say when." My heart swelled, a smile spreading across my face despite the fatigue of travel and the uncertainty of the future. I already knew he meant more to me than anyone ever had. Nash's excitement about seeing each other again made me realize how much we mean to each other. I'm not sure how I'll survive being so far away from him.

I texted him back.

> Let's make it happen soon. Miss you.

The ride home from the airport felt quick as my mind spun with possibilities and plans. There was a lot to figure out. And I promised myself I'd get started on it right after I made a few phone calls—starting with one to the only person whose voice had me longing to hear it the moment I couldn't.

64

CASSIDY

Walking back into EchoStream felt like stepping into a parallel universe. The office was alive with the comforting sounds of keyboards clacking and creative minds at work. I pleasantly discovered my desk exactly as I had left it, but my coworkers had adorned it with a vibrant bouquet of wild-flowers and several congratulatory sticky notes. It was a warm welcome back, one that made my heart swell with appreciation for this place and these people.

EchoStream had always felt more like a community than a work-place, and coming back only reinforced that feeling. People were eager to hear about my experiences and asked questions about the show, the other contestants, and some of the music. But talking about my experience felt like I was talking about someone else's life. Each story, each memory I shared, felt like it belonged to a version of myself that I couldn't quite reconcile with the person who had returned to L.A.. It was a bizarre sensation, talking about moments that were vivid in my memory yet somehow felt borrowed from another person's story.

A week into my return, I was called to Elizabeth's office. As CEO of EchoStream, she had always been a figure of inspiration for me—driven, insightful, and remarkably approachable.

"Cassidy, come in! Have a seat," Elizabeth greeted me with her trademark bright smile. Her energy was contagious, and I couldn't help but smile back as I took a seat in the chair opposite her desk.

"I just wanted to say personally how proud we all are of you," she began, her eyes reflecting genuine pride. "Your journey on the show was incredible to watch. And I won't beat around the bush. It brought a lot of positive attention to EchoStream."

I felt my face grow warm at her words. "Thank you, Elizabeth. It was a wild ride, but I'm glad to be back."

Elizabeth leaned forward, her expression turning slightly more serious but still warm. "The exposure you've brought to EchoStream has opened some exciting doors for us. We're currently in talks with a satellite radio broadcasting company about a potential partnership. And I have to say, they became interested because of the buzz around you being discovered on our platform."

I felt taken aback, with my mind racing to process her words. "Really? That's... that's amazing, but I'm sure it would've happened eventually, with or without me," I tried to brush it off, uncomfortable with taking too much credit.

Elizabeth's laughter was light, but her eyes were sharp with intelligence. "Perhaps, but it happened now, and a lot of that is thanks to you. Don't underestimate the impact you've had, Cassidy."

Her words settled over me. EchoStream wasn't just where I worked; it was a part of who I was, and now, it seemed, I was a part of its growing story.

"Thank you. That means a lot to me. I just... I want to make sure I can actually contribute, not just ride on the wave of a personal adventure," I said, more to myself than to her.

Elizabeth's smile was reassuring, her confidence in me clear. "You already are contributing, Cassidy. Just by being you. And I have no doubt you'll continue to do so in ways we've yet to imagine."

～

WHEN I'D SENT my final e-mail of the day, I started gathering my things from my desk, replaying my conversation with Elizabeth in my mind. If I was being honest, working at EchoStream was more than a job; it was a place where I'd felt seen, valued, and part of something bigger than myself. But I also felt a little untethered. I liked my job, and it checked off a lot of boxes for me, but if I was being completely honest, I wanted more. I just didn't know what that looked like in the scope of EchoStream.

As I slipped my laptop into my bag and took one more glance around to make sure I had everything, I let my thoughts wander to the weekend that awaited. I rushed towards the exit, eager to see Nash again. We had agreed it had been too long since our last goodbye, even if it had only been a week, and Nash had booked a flight that would be landing a couple of hours after I got home.

As I pushed through the doors and into the fading L.A. sunshine, I mentally mapped out my next two hours—home, a quick change, order dinner. That's when I heard it, a voice that cut through the constant noise of the city and went straight to my heart.

"Excuse me, Miss. Do you have a name, or can I call you mine?" The familiar timbre of Nash's voice had me spinning around, my heart leaping at the sight of him leaning casually against the side of the building, a playful smile on his face. He was here, in L.A., hours earlier than expected.

Laughing, I couldn't contain my surprise and delight, rushing into his open arms. "You're early!"

"A seat opened up on an earlier flight. I couldn't wait another minute to see you," he explained, his eyes shining with affection. His spontaneity, his willingness to bend time just to be with me, filled me with an overwhelming sense of love and acceptance.

Love? The thought blew through my mind, unbidden yet undeniable. It was a surprise, this inner acknowledgment of something I'd felt growing between us, something deeper yet unspoken until this moment.

Standing there, looking up at him, seeing my happiness mirrored in his eyes, made me wonder if this was what love felt like. This ease, this desire to be near each other, to make sacrifices just to share moments together. It was a revelation, finding that love might have been the undercurrent of our connection all along, its presence subtle but steady, growing stronger with every laugh, every conversation, every shared silence. I brushed the thought away, wanting to get lost in the present instead of trying to work through the myriad of things pummeling my heart and mind.

Our reunion was sweet and unhurried. Our kisses were a language of their own, speaking of missed moments and the promise of time together, even if it would be short. I didn't even care who saw us. Right now, this was the only thing that mattered, and I was going to make the most of every second.

When we finally broke apart and I was certain I wasn't dreaming, we walked holding hands the two blocks that led to the parking garage where my car was parked.

"I cannot believe you're here," I told him. "I knew you were coming, and I have been excited all week but now that you're here it doesn't feel real."

Nash squeezed my hand, his smile spreading from ear to ear. "Trust me, I'm here and it's real. And there is nowhere else I want to be."

On the twenty-minute drive to my apartment, Nash entertained me with a story from his trip about the little girl who sat across the aisle from him on the plane. She'd recognized him, which he said had made him feel special and a little weirded out. But then she started offering him up critiques and suggestions she thought would have given him the chance to have remained in the competition longer. One such suggestion had been that he should have, according to her mom, "worn tighter blue jeans like Austin and a cowboy hat like Christopher Jordan."

The mom, who had been sitting next to the little girl, shushed her daughter and offered her a box of colored pencils and a sketchbook, suggesting she leave the nice young man alone. Nash had apparently had to force himself to smile and not laugh while telling the little girl he would take her suggestions under advisement.

I had been listening and smiling as he told the story. Then he said he'd pretended to call CJ and asked loudly if he had an extra cowboy hat lying around that he could loan out, just in case. And when the pretend response had been "Yes", Nash had given the little girl a thumbs up, resulting in a knowing nod and a returned thumbs up. By that point, I was giggling uncontrollably.

Picturing it was as plain as day because it was exactly something Nash would do. It had my heart warming and expanding, like it needed any kind of reminder of who the man was sitting next to me. He was kind, and he was funny, and he went out of his way to make people feel validated. I loved that about him.

And there was that word again. I had to get that reaction under control because it was far too soon to be feeling anything like it. Sure, we had known each other for longer than we'd realized, but that didn't count. Did it? I wasn't sure. He hadn't given me reason to believe he was anyone other than who I'd come to know over the last several months and the way my heart seemed to be feeling, it was as though I'd known him forever.

We pulled into my parking space on the street and we made our way through the gated entrance and across the courtyard to where my apartment sat. Once inside, the familiarity of my space felt more alive with Nash there. I changed clothes, opting for something comfortable, while Nash browsed the takeout menus I'd directed him to. It felt so domestic, so simple. Who am I kidding? I loved it.

When I walked out of my bedroom, Nash was leaned back on my couch reading a takeout menu. His gaze lifted from the menu and fixed on me. He'd seen me in practically every state of being possible and he still had the look of a man in the desert desperate for water, and I was that water. It sent a chill through me, making me shiver even though I was already wearing my favorite cozy, oversized sweater. I felt a blush creep up my cheeks as I struggled to focus on our dinner plans.

Attempting to break the spell he was apparently under, I motioned toward the stack of menus and asked, "So, what are we having for dinner?" I asked, trying to focus on the task at hand.

He shook his head as though dislodging his thoughts and randomly handed me a menu from the collection.

"Oh, yes! Enrique's Tacos is the best," I told him. "They have the best fish tacos and their churros are to die for."

Nash nodded enthusiastically. "Sounds perfect. Enrique's Tacos it is," he declared, a smile playing on his lips.

I picked up my phone and scrolled through my contacts to find the number. "What do you feel like trying?" I asked.

"Definitely those fish tacos you mentioned. And let's not forget the churros. You had me at 'to die for,'" he replied with a chuckle. I don't think he had even read the menu he'd handed me.

"Got it. Fish tacos and churros," I confirmed with a smile, dialing the number. As I placed our order, Nash watched me, an amused and appreciative look in his eyes. It felt good to share this piece of my life with him, to introduce him to the little things that made up my world here in L.A.

Once the order was placed, I put the phone down and turned to Nash. "Food will be here in about forty-five minutes," I informed him.

"That gives us some time to catch up," he said, pulling me into his lap and placing a quick, gentle kiss to my lips.

"Perfect," I sighed, leaning into his embrace. The prospect of spending a quiet evening in with Nash, enjoying good food and each other's company, was exactly what I needed. It was a simple pleasure, but in that simplicity, there was a depth that I knew would only grow deeper and more complex if given time.

A knock at the door came almost exactly forty-five minutes after we'd placed our order.

I hopped off Nash's lap, feeling a flutter of excitement for the night ahead.

"I'll get it," I said, making my way to the door.

Opening it, I was greeted by the delivery person holding a bag. After exchanging quick pleasantries and handing over a tip, I took the bag and closed the door behind me, the enticing smell wafting through my apartment immediately.

Nash had moved to grab the drinks and utensils from the kitchen and moved them to the two person table in the small eating area. "Smells amazing," he commented as I placed the bag on the table and began unpacking our dinner.

"Wait until you taste it," I replied with a grin, excited to share one of my favorite meals with him.

As we settled into our seats, the conversation flowed naturally between us. I told him about the offer Elizabeth had made.

Nash listened as I recounted the meeting, his focus solely on me. "She was really impressed with how the show brought attention to EchoStream. Apparently, it even opened up talks for a partnership with a satellite radio company," I explained, still a bit in awe of the whole situation.

His eyes widened, and he looked impressed. "That's incredible, Cassidy. It sounds like you've had quite the influence."

I shrugged, feeling a tad uncomfortable with the praise. "Maybe, but I think it would have happened, eventually. It just happened to coincide with the show."

Smiling with a look of pride and admiration, Nash shook his head. "Don't downplay this. It's a big deal, and you should be proud. It's not everyday someone manages to shine so brightly they spark interest in a partnership like that."

I wasn't sure why, but it felt like I was getting too much credit for something I didn't really have any say in. But his encouragement was sweet and not unappreciated.

"Thanks," I said, hoping he knew how much his words really meant, even if they weren't what I wanted to hear.

Nash must have sensed my unease as he nudged my foot under the table with his. "What is it?" he asked.

I stabbed my fork into the rice in front of me several times before putting the fork down and sighing.

"When I got the call from the show, Elizabeth was super excited and talked about all of the opportunities it could open up for the company. And while she didn't say it was the case, I never want to feel like I have to keep performing to keep my place at EchoStream. But, because I did well on the show and it led to a boon for EchoStream,

I'm afraid that I'll be asked to give more than I want to give. Does that even make sense? I don't know. I do know that I love music and there is something great and exciting about performing, but I don't want it to be something I just do for the rest of my life. I want it to be something I love doing, whatever that ends up being."

He reached across the small table, his palm upturned and waiting. I rested my hand on top of it. His hand holding mine grounded me.

"Hey," he said softly, his gaze earnest, "you should never feel like you owe them more than you're willing to give because you don't owe them anything. What you did was incredible, Cassidy, but it doesn't mean you're obligated to keep performing or be something you're not."

I let out a slow, heavy breath, his words slicing through the fog of my doubts. "I know, it's just... hard not to wonder, you know? If now there's this expectation for me to be more," I confessed.

He nodded in understanding. "I get it. But remember, you're valued for who you are, not just for what you did on the show. Echo-Stream, Elizabeth, they all saw something in you before all this. Your success on *Real American Country* just highlighted what was already there."

His reassurance put an ease to my worries and was a reminder of my worth beyond the spotlight. "You're right," I said, managing a small smile. "I guess I just need to find a balance, figure out how to go after what I want without feeling like I might lose myself in the process."

Nash squeezed my hand gently. "You'll find it, Cassidy. And I'll be here, cheering you on every step of the way."

With tears burning my eyes, it was at that table sitting across from him that I realized I was indeed falling head over heels in love with Nash Montgomery.

65

NASH

When I arrived in L.A., the lack of Christmas decorations in her apartment was the first thing I noticed. "We definitely need to fix that," I'd said, and she'd smiled, agreeing that it would be our Saturday project.

That morning, with a light breeze whispering through the city, we set out with a single mission: to bring Christmas to Cassidy's apartment. Our first stop was a small Christmas tree lot we'd found online, nestled between towering buildings, an oasis of green in the concrete jungle. The scent of pine filled the air as we wandered through the tight rows of trees, Cassidy's laughter mingling with the sounds of the city. We settled on a modest fir that seemed to stand out, promising to be the perfect fit.

With the tree secured to the top of her car, we headed to The Grove. Cassidy had talked about how it transformed into a Christmas wonderland each year, and she wasn't exaggerating. The place was a spectacle of lights even in the daytime, with an enormous Christmas tree that made ours look like a twig in comparison.

We joined in the festivities, sipping on hot chocolate even though it was almost sixty-five degrees, as we strolled through the market, picking out ornaments and decorations. Each choice sparked a new conversation, or became part of a shared joke, or a story of a memory, cinching our lives more tightly together with every passing second.

The day faded into evening as we returned to her place, arms laden with bags. Decorating the tree became an exercise in creativity and laughter, with Cassidy insisting on a theme of "whimsical chaos." Christmas music playing in the background, we worked together, stringing lights, singing to and with one another, and hanging ornaments, the tree coming to life before our eyes. Every so often, she'd stand back, tilting her head, assessing our work with a seriousness that made me laugh. "It's perfect," I'd say, and she'd roll her eyes and pull me in for a kiss, the kind that said without words how right this felt.

As Sunday morning dawned, the conversation I needed to have with Cassidy pressed heavily on my mind. The offer from Riverbank Records was an incredible opportunity, one that could shape my career, but it meant staying in Nashville and on the road for likely another year after the RAC Tour. I knew Cassidy loved her job at EchoStream and loved L.A., and I wouldn't ask her to give that up, not when she was just beginning to explore what her future could hold. Not to mention, I wasn't going to be in any one place for long.

As we sat on the couch with our coffee, the tree cast a soft glow around the room. I blew out a breath and set my mug on the end table, ready to share my news with Cassidy. "So, as you know Riverbank offered me a pretty incredible deal," I began, watching her reaction closely.

Cassidy's eyes lit up, her smile spreading wide as she nodded.

I explained the details. The excitement in my voice tempered with the knowledge of what this meant for us. "They want me to do a festival circuit, which means after the tour, I'd be on the road or in Nashville for close to a year."

She turned and placed her coffee on her end table before her hand grabbed mine, her touch reassuring. "I'm so proud of you. This is what you wanted, right?"

"Yeah, but I can't help thinking about what this means for us," I admitted, the uncertainty clear in my voice.

Cassidy squeezed my hand, her gaze steady and full of warmth. "We'll make it work, Nash. If the universe could bring us back together after the fall of OurSpace, I think we can make a little long distance work."

I chuckled softly, the tension easing from my shoulders. "I guess we're practically pros at this long-distance thing."

She laughed, the sound like music to my ears. "Exactly."

I nodded, her optimism infectious. "You're right. I just... I hate the thought of being away from you for so long. I'm scared you'll get tired of me calling you non-stop," I teased, trying to lighten my mood.

Cassidy stood, moving to sit in my lap, her arms wrapping around my neck. "I promise to not get tired of your calls if you promise to always call."

I hugged her tight, the rightness of her words sinking in. "I promise," I echoed, the word heavy in my heart with a commitment that went far beyond just making phone calls.

Cassidy's support and enthusiasm for my opportunity with Riverbank Records, despite the implications for us, amplified everything I felt for her. Her excitement at my success knowing it meant facing the challenges of distance—it became crystal clear and something inside me stirred to life. It wasn't subtle either, but a profound acknowledgment, an admission to myself that I was irrevocably in love with her.

Cassidy's voice, light and carefree, pulled me back from my introspection. "What are you thinking about?" she asked, her gaze curious and warm.

For a moment, I considered sharing my newfound realization to tell her of the love that flooded my heart for her. But I held back, choosing instead to save those words for a moment when I could give them the weight and presence they deserved. Hours before I was leaving her for who knew how long was not that moment.

"Just thinking about how lucky I am," I said, offering her a smile that held more than I could articulate. "To have found you again."

Her smile in response was everything—affirming, understanding, and promising all at once. "We're both lucky," she said, and in her words, I heard the echo of my own feelings.

The rest of our day together was bittersweet as we continued our morning, wrapped up in the comfort of each other's company. I felt a sense of peace amidst the uncertainty of our future. Yes, challenges awaited us, but in admitting my love for Cassidy, even just to myself, I found a strength I hadn't known I'd possessed before.

And as I boarded the plane back to Nashville the next morning, a piece of my heart stayed behind in L.A.. The promise of our next reunion, of the next chapter in our story, was the only thing that made leaving bearable. Because for Cassidy and me, it was never really goodbye. It was just a pause, a breath between the moments that made up who we were meant to be — us.

66

CASSIDY

Landing in Nashville, the February chill was vastly different from Los Angeles' eternal sunshine. The thought of reuniting with Nash sent a shot of heat right through me and the chill was all but forgotten. Around us, the airport bustled with activity, but the moment our eyes met, the world around us stood still.

I scheduled a quick weekend visit to Georgia in January when Nash was planning to be home. It had been a fast visit, full of happiness and laughter. Being with Nash's family made me feel like I was one of them. While Thanksgiving had been my first introduction, this visit felt even more like coming home. I cherished the way they included me, sharing stories and moments as if I'd always been a part of them. It made me miss my parents.

Cody, Nash's younger sister, had been especially excited to share her news with me — her engagement to Jet, her best friend, had been a highlight of their Christmas. The joy in her eyes as she recounted the proposal was infectious, and I found myself genuinely thrilled for her. It was these small, intimate moments with Nash's family that deepened my affection for him and his world. The love and affection they shared so freely made me dream of a future of my own where such warmth and closeness were a constant.

When a path cleared, I wasted no time rushing towards the man whose presence was a beacon, drawing me in with a pull stronger than gravity. He stood there, a wide grin lighting up his face, as if he knew just how much I needed to see him. Our embrace was a silent conversation of missed moments and renewed silent promises.

"I've missed you more than words," I murmured into his shoulder, the vibration of his chuckle against my cheek causing my heart to beat faster.

"I think we should make up for lost time," Nash whispered back, his voice a soothing melody that played on every string of my heart as his lips consumed mine.

I'd made every effort to get the earliest flight possible so Nash and I could have almost an entire day together before the real reason for my return to Nashville was set to begin.

Both exhilarating and nerve-wracking. The *Real American Country Tour* was set to kick off in just a week, and rehearsals were starting tomorrow. It was an opportunity to once again share the stage with Nash, this time as teammates and not competitors, and I was excited. Spending three months in the same place as Nash, even if ten other people shared most of our days, was better than being two thousand miles apart—I could, however, do without the three months of tour busses and hotels.

After a quick stop at the hotel to drop my luggage off in the room, which I'd be sharing with Harper, my roommate from the competition, I was ready to explore Nashville with my favorite person.

"So, what's the plan for today?" I asked, curious about how we'd spend our precious hours together.

Nash's response was a grin, his eyes twinkling with a plan. "Thought we'd dive into the heart of Nashville—see the sights, taste the food, maybe even cause a little trouble," he teased, his excitement contagious.

Our first stop was the iconic Grand Ole Opry, where Nash playfully narrated its history with exaggerated enthusiasm, making me laugh. We posed for pictures by the giant guitars embracing the kitsch and charm of it all. We wandered through Madame Tussauds where I learned wax figures creep me out and Nash thought it would be akin to winning a Country Music Award and added it to his list of dreams and aspirations. Despite the corniness, I found joy in every moment, seeing the city through Nash's eyes.

Lunch was at a quirky diner that seemed to capture the essence of Nashville's vibrant music scene, followed by a visit to the Country Music Hall of Fame. Nash's commentary, filled with more fabrication than facts, made the experience uniquely memorable.

As the day unfolded, Nash's surprise was a visit to the studio he'd been recording for the last couple of months.

"Thought you'd like to see where the magic happens," he said, his casual tone belying the excitement in his eyes.

Nash led the way, his warm hand wrapped around mine, as we navigated through a maze of corridors. The walls, lined with framed gold and platinum records and black-and-white photos of music legends, whispered stories of dreams and songs that had touched millions. Stepping into the booth, the world outside seemed to fade away, leaving just Nash, me, and the music that awaited.

Mike Howard, with his easy Southern charm, suggested *Baby Don't Go* by Dwight Yoakam and Sheryl Crow. Nash's eyes lit up, a playful challenge in his gaze. He took the lead, his voice wrapping around the lyrics with a familiarity and warmth that filled the small space. I followed, my voice finding its place beside his, the two of us weaving through the melody like dancers in a well-rehearsed duet. The song was a musical tug-of-war that had us both fighting smiles as we sang.

Watching Nash embrace the role of a man begging his girl to stay inspired my own performance. I sang dramatically from the perspective of the woman who had to leave town but might come back someday. Singing alongside Nash felt like a dream come true, our voices blending harmoniously in the studio that had birthed countless melodies. I was so caught up in the song that I forgot anyone else was there until Mike's voice came through the headphones.

"Now, Cassidy, I know you've got your own thing going on in L.A., but if you think for a minute I'm not gonna ask you to head back this way and join us here, you need to think again."

Laughing, I removed the headphones and handed them to Nash. He was beaming as he hung them on the hooks in the wall. We exited the booth and met Mike in the tech room.

Mike reiterated his words from moments before. "I'm serious. There's a place for you here if you want it."

"Thank you, Mike. That means a lot, but I think I'll stick to the occasional duet with Nash here. This is his world," I said, gesturing to the room. "I'm just visiting."

With an outstretched hand, Mike said, "Well, if you change your mind, you know where to find us."

Shaking his hand, I smiled and thanked him again.

He turned to Nash. "I guess we'll see you back here in a few months to get the big ball rollin'."

"Yes, sir," he said, still smiling.

As we left the studio, the conversation shifted towards the upcoming tour. "Three months of this, huh?" Nash mused, a note of wonder in his voice. "Seeing each other every day, on stage, off stage..." Nash began. "You may not have gotten tired of my calls, but you definitely might get tired of seeing me every day."

The idea was thrilling. The tour busses, the hotels, the constant travel—I could already feel the stress of all of it building. Yet, looking over at Nash, his profile softened by the twilight, I knew every moment would be worth it.

"I love the idea of being with you every day," I admitted, my heart full. "I will say, though, the thought of tour busses, hotels, and performing almost every night is going to be a lot."

His touch reassuring, Nash took my hand. "We'll get through it together," he promised. "The good, the bad, and the tour busses. What matters is we'll be together."

Our walk back to the hotel was reflective. Despite the challenges ahead, the thought of facing them with Nash by my side made every-thing seem possible.

We reached the hotel, the day's adventures leaving us both exhilarated and exhausted. Having Nash by my side every day made me feel whole. It did not, however, prepare me for the long days ahead.

THE AIR CRACKLED with excitement as I stepped into the rehearsal space, a marked difference from the quiet anticipation of the early morning. The room was a hive of activity, with the arrival of the other former contestants exchanging hugs and laughter-filled greetings. It had been months since we last saw each other, but nothing seemed to have changed in the interim.

Around us, technicians and crew members navigated through clusters of reunited friends, setting up for what promised to be an intensive day of rehearsals. The sense of community was obvious, a shared journey that had brought us all here.

Our attention was soon drawn to the whiteboard at the front of the hall, where the set list for the tour was prominently displayed. It was a roadmap of the weeks to come, a blend of ensemble pieces and individual showcases.

Glancing at the list, my eyes locked on one line. My name alongside Nash's was written next to "Song: *Wrapped Up in You*". It brought back a flood of memories, of sharing this song across screens, miles apart, with Nash before we'd even met in person. Seeing our names next to that song, our accidental anthem, now felt like a full-circle moment. Here we were, about to perform it live together. A weird sense of nostalgia worked its way through me. Revisiting this song brought back a flood of emotions and transported me to a different time and place.

Kicking off the rehearsal with a group medley, the stage echoed with late '90s and early 2000s country classics, and it felt electric. Here we were, voices and instruments mingling, creating something almost magical. Just weeks ago, we were all sizing each other up as competitors, and now we were a team, a single unit pouring our hearts into every note. It's funny how things change. We'd gone from competing to collaborating, and that shift felt as powerful as the music we were making.

A few run throughs later, we took five before watching Savannah, Harper, and Willow flawlessly tackle *Wide Open Spaces*. Nash and I were up next, so we stood in the wings, waiting. As my hand tapped against my leg to the music, Nash leaned in and whispered next to my ear, "You know, if I'm being honest, I think I'd rather be wrapped up in you instead of this rehearsal."

As I turned to face him, his eyes sparkled and my heart skipped a beat. "The feeling's mutual," I replied, stifling my laughter at his corny play on words. I decided I really liked having a secret moment hidden away from the others. "Let's get this rehearsal out of the way and see what happens next."

When it came time for Nash and me to take the stage for our duet, the room's anticipation shifted subtly. Nash picked up his guitar, and with a nod to me, the opening chords floated through the air. I lifted my fiddle to my shoulder, letting the bow glide across the strings, the notes intertwining with Nash's melody in a dance that felt as natural as breathing. Our performance was playful, our glances and smiles weaving a story of flirtation and fondness that needed no words. The chemistry between us was plain as day, sparking laughter and applause from our fellow contestants.

The day progressed with individual and smaller group rehearsals, each performance promising the upcoming tour would be far from boring. There was a constant flow of supportive comments and jokes filling the space between sets, making the time go by even more quickly.

As the week of rehearsals wrapped up, each day running headfirst into the next under the bright stage lights and the echo of constant music, I was exhausted and running on adrenaline. It was a strange cocktail of feelings, like being too tired to sleep but too wired to rest. Looking around at the faces of my fellow contestants, now friends, I saw my own weariness mirrored back at me. We were all running on the same high-octane blend of adrenaline, caffeine, and determination.

The thought of the next three months—cramped in those tiny tour busses, living out of suitcases, and performing night after night —loomed large. It was daunting, the idea of such close quarters and non-stop movement. But if I were to be completely honest, I was pretty excited about the upcoming adventure. This tour was not just a series of performances; it was a journey we were all embarking on together, proof of how far we'd come and how much further we could go. Even if being on stage wasn't part of my future plans, I had no intention of wasting the opportunity to enjoy it in the present.

Standing beside Nash as we packed up our instruments, I felt a wave of gratitude wash over me. Whenever the schedule felt overwhelming or the fatigue too heavy, a quiet moment with him seemed to reset everything back into balance.

Reflecting on the week, I could see how much I'd grown—not just as a performer, but as a person. Everything we'd been through had transformed all of us from strangers into a cohesive group, each of us pushing one another to be better, to shine brighter. And now, as we stood on the brink of this tour, I felt that transformation more acutely than ever. The nervousness was there, a fluttering in my stomach at the thought of the unknowns that lay ahead. But it was matched, maybe even overshadowed, by a deep-seated excitement for the experiences to come, for the stories we'd have to tell, and for the music we'd share with every crowd.

Sure, the road would be long and the quarters close, but the music—the reason we were all here—promised to make every cramped bus ride and every night we spent in a borrowed bed worth it. And with Nash along for the ride, I felt ready to face whatever challenges came our way. But first, I needed a really good night's sleep in a real bed at least once more before sacrificing some of the creature comforts I should really learn to appreciate more.

67

CASSIDY

month into the tour, and life on the road had settled into a rhythm as familiar as the songs we played night after night. The days began early, sometimes with the hum of the bus engine carrying us to our next destination, or, if we were lucky, a slower start with sound checks in the city we'd called home for the night. Each city brought its own flavor, its own energy that infused our performances with something unique, something memorable.

Promotional activities filled our afternoons. Radio station visits were unexpectedly fun, with hosts eager to explore the stories behind the songs and the dynamics of our tour family. Meet and greets were the highlight, though. There was something magical about the encounters made in each of those brief events, the way fans' eyes lit up as we shared our favorite moments, conversations, and our thanks.

Evenings were the culmination of our day's efforts, the stage a place where all worries faded into the background, leaving only the music. And after the final note had echoed into silence, while the crew packed up the maze of cables and instruments, we'd linger, engaging with fans who'd stayed behind, their support a visible reminder of why we were on this journey.

I found myself more relaxed around the other musicians. The initial barriers I'd erected months ago at the beginning of the competition now completely dissolved. Nash and I grew closer to each other, but also to Christopher Jordan, Wyatt, and his girlfriend, Kensi, who happened to be the tour manager.

Kensi, with her calm efficiency and warm smile, managed the chaos of tour life with an ease that fascinated us all. Wyatt, once Nash's quiet and reserved roommate during the competition, had transformed. His newfound sociableness was as surprising as the smile Kensi always brought to his face. Nash and I often mused that Kensi's presence was the key to this change; she brought out a side of Wyatt we'd never seen.

Their relationship was a sweet mystery, the depth of their connection evident in the way Wyatt's eyes followed Kensi, protective yet filled with an unmistakable adoration. It was clear to everyone that Kensi's influence was a force of good. Her sweetness and obvious love for Wyatt drew him out of his shell, revealing the personality he'd kept hidden. Despite appearing stoic and broody, his dry sense of humor catches you off guard and guarantees a laugh for the next ten minutes.

As Nash and I navigated the complexities of tour life together, our own relationship deepened, steeled by shared glances, stolen kisses, and inside jokes that created a quiet space for us amid the noise. It was already hard to imagine not seeing Nash every day now that it had already become part of my routine. Although I constantly told myself this was just a temporary situation, the comforting embrace of his arms and the feel of his hand in mine easily brushed aside my thoughts. He had become embedded in my heart and it was crazy, unthinkable even, that I would not live in the here and now, soaking up every second of this time we did have together.

IT WAS a rare moment that brought us all together for something other than sound checks or strategy meetings. Kensi, always the bearer of news and schedules, gathered us with an unusual sparkle in her eye, signaling this wasn't just another meeting.

"American Heartland, the network that's been our sponsor and cheerleader through this, just struck a deal with a leading cell phone service provider," Kensi began, her voice brimming with excitement. "They've decided to gift each of you the latest phone model—state of the art camera, impressive storage, the works. They believe artists on the move should have the best tools at their fingertips."

The room erupted into cheers and disbelieving laughs, the energy shifting from curiosity to outright excitement in seconds. Boxes were distributed, and the air filled with the sound of packaging being eagerly torn open. Nash and I, caught up in the excitement, were among the first to power on our new gadgets. The camera—a feature touted as groundbreaking for its time—was immediately put to the test. We snapped photos of each other and together, capturing the moment, our smiles wide and genuine. Those pictures becoming digital keepsakes of our days together.

That night, nestled in the dimly lit corner of the bus with Harper, my former roommate and someone I would consider a best friend, I decided to document a part of tour life. The phone, propped up against a stack of pillows, recorded our laughter-filled conversation.

"So, Harper, for the folks at home, give us the scoop. Where's this incredible talent from?" I teased, mimicking the tone of a seasoned interviewer and holding a hairbrush as a microphone and gesturing at her as though I were a game show model showing off a prize.

"Born and raised in Austin, Texas, the live music capital of the world," Harper replied with a proud grin. "Guess you could say I was steeped in music before I could walk."

"And influences? If you had to pick three artists who've shaped you, who would they be?" I continued, genuinely curious about her answers.

Without missing a beat, Harper listed, "Dolly Parton, for her storytelling; Shania Twain, for that cross-genre appeal; and Johnny Cash, for the raw honesty."

Our casual interview peeled back layers of Harper's personality, while showcasing her roots and musical inspirations.

After watching the recording back with her, I turned to her and said, "That was awesome. Would you mind if I uploaded it to Echo-Stream? Maybe see if people are interested in getting a peek behind the curtain?"

Harper gasped, "Seriously? Yes! I think that would be so fun."

We shared a few more laughs, musing about what our families back home would think about everything we were doing, then called it a night, the drone of the tires against the road lulling us into a deep sleep.

Waking up to the repeating buzz of notifications was a new experience for me. Bleary-eyed and still half in the dream world, I grabbed the phone from my nightstand, expecting the usual texts from my mom, or maybe a reminder from Kensi about the day's schedule. Instead, I found myself staring at notifications that I had thousands of comments and views on the video interview with Harper. It seemed that while we were sleeping, our little behind-the-scenes video had captured the attention of more than just our families and friends.

"Harper, wake up," I whispered, nudging her gently from across the aisle of the bus. "You're not going to believe this."

Rubbing her eyes, she sat up, squinting at the screen I held out to her. "What...is that real? Thousands of people watched it?" Her voice going higher on every work.

"Tens of thousands, and they're asking for more. They want to see everyone, to get to know the whole crew," I said, scrolling through comments that ranged from enthusiastic support to heartfelt requests for more interviews.

"Are you gonna do it?" Harper asked, all drowsiness erased from her features.

With hesitation, I locked my eyes on the screen, feeling a shock of exhilaration course through me.

"Cassidy, this could be a big deal. Look at how many followers you gained overnight," Harper said as she retrieved her own phone from under her pillow. After a few seconds of her own scrolling, she turned her phone screen toward me. "And my following tripled overnight. Come on. Let's get Willow up and see if she'll do it."

Before I could say anything, Harper was out of her bunk and was poking Willow, who had been sleeping in the bunk above Harper's.

"Willow," Harper whisper-shouted.

Willow blinked awake with a confused, "What's going on?"

"Cassidy's famous," Harper announced, unable to keep the excitement from her voice.

Despite feeling nervous about being unexpectedly thrust into the spotlight, her exaggeration and enthusiasm were so contagious that I couldn't hold back my laughter. "What she meant was, people really liked the interview I did with Harper. They're asking for more. Do you want to be next?" I asked Willow, who was now fully awake and sitting cross-legged in her bunk, looking intrigued.

"Really? Like, a behind-the-scenes tour diary?" Willow's eyes sparkled with the idea, her creative mind clearly already turning. "Count me in. This could be fun—and good exposure."

The decision felt like stepping into an uncharted territory full of unknown challenges and hidden obstacles, but with Harper's encouragement and Willow's quick agreement, it seemed like this was becoming something that could be more than just a one-off video.

As the bus rumbled on to our next city, we all did the best we could to get ready for the day when there were six people constantly bumping into one another in the small space.

In the back corner of the bus, which had been transformed into an impromptu film studio, Harper held the phone steady while the bus carried on. The small space was brimming with excitement and the familiar noises of the road below.

Willow and I were positioned across from the camera where we talked about her musical journey from small-town bars to the show. Wanting to shine a light on Willow's fun side, I transitioned our conversation.

"Let's lighten the mood a bit. There was this commercial shoot you and Austin did—something about an engagement scene at the botanical garden?"

Willow's face lit up, a chuckle escaping her before she even began. "Oh, that was a disaster in the best possible way," she said, her smile widening at the memory. "We were supposed to be this madly in love couple, right in the middle of this picturesque scene with flowers everywhere, getting engaged."

She paused for effect, her eyes dancing with mirth. "Austin, bless him, he's cute but apparently not the most... coordinated guy. So, he's down on one knee, and the director's like, 'Action!' He reaches into his pocket to get the ring, and it's stuck. Like, really stuck because... well, we've all seen his bluejeans."

The bus echoed with giggles. Having witnessed this story first hand, I was replaying the scene in my mind and it was just as funny as it had been then. Harper, hovering just out of frame, was trying—and failing—to stifle her laughter.

"We have," I said, trying to keep a straight face. "So, then what happened?" I prompted.

As she swiped a tear from her eye, her shoulders shook with laughter, and she managed to say, "Then, when he finally gets it out, he's so flustered that he fumbles and—sploosh!—right into the koi pond. The ring, not Austin," she added, in a fit of giggles.

The bus erupted into peals of laughter, the kind that leaves your sides aching but your heart light. Willow's storytelling had transformed a cramped space on a moving bus into a theater of joy, her recounting as vivid as if we'd been there to witness it ourselves.

"The look on his face," Willow continued, wiping away tears of laughter, "was this mix of horror and disbelief. And me? I'm trying to stay in character, looking lovingly into his eyes while internally I'm screaming, 'Did that just really happen?' Just before I lost it."

Harper, through her laughter, managed to say, "I would've paid to see that!"

Willow nodded, still chuckling. "The crew had to fish it out, and we did another take, but nothing beats the genuine shock of that first shot. Needless to say, that take didn't make the final cut, but it's one of my favorite memories."

Wiping tears from my eyes, I said, "It's one of mine, too. Even though I was there to witness it firsthand, I can vouch that hearing the story will never get old."

The camera was turned off, and the bus erupted in another round of laughter and chatter about that week of the competition when we'd made commercials and other promotional material. We'd all still been strangers vying for the top spot in the competition then. But now, we were friends. Well, most of us. Lanie had opted to occupy a space at the other end of the bus, which had been her action of choice any time the group was together on the bus. Off the bus, if we weren't expected on stage, she would disappear and reappear when the schedule required it of her.

When the bus pulled in at the restaurant for breakfast, the general mood of the group was upbeat and excited. There were days when a few of the girls would be moody or cranky and we'd passed a head cold around two weeks ago. These kinds of days, though, made the struggles far more bearable.

As he always did, Nash had gotten off the guys' bus fast enough to be waiting for me. Out of habit, I automatically turned to the right and practically landed in his arms.

"Good morning," I murmured with my face squished against his chest, breathing him in.

"Morning," Nash replied, his voice a warm hum that resonated through me. He pulled back slightly, a playful curiosity lighting his eyes. "So, how's my budding filmmaker this morning?"

I laughed, the sound muffled against his shirt. "Did you see it? The interview with Harper has exploded overnight. People loved it." I stepped back, fishing the phone from my pocket to show him the burgeoning view count and the flood of positive comments.

Nash whistled, impressed. "What's next? Going to turn this into a series?"

"Maybe. Think you're ready for your close-up, Mr. *GuyWith-Guitar*?" I teased him, wiggling my phone in his face.

"With you behind the camera? Always," Nash replied, his grin wide and genuine, making my heart flutter.

We followed everyone else into the restaurant. News about Harper's video had already circulated among the crew, and it didn't take long for Austin and Levi to seek me out and volunteer to join the interview train. I told them I'd let them know how we'd work it out.

After breakfast, with the day's schedule not kicking in for a couple of hours, I took the opportunity to capture some candid behind-the-scenes moments. The tour, with all its orchestrated chaos, offered an abundant supply of unscripted moments that watchers would never know existed otherwise.

Slipping the phone out of my pocket, I started recording. First up was Nash, lost in a moment with his guitar, fingers dancing over the strings. The melody was soft, introspective—so different from the fast-paced performances on stage. It was Nash in his element, a side of him that few got to see, and I captured it all, the focus and passion in his eyes telling a story all their own.

Later that day, after lunch, I caught Willow, Stella, and Harper in a burst of laughter, their heads thrown back in unison. The sound was infectious, and even without knowing the punchline, I found myself smiling along. These little moments of happiness were like glue, holding our days together and reminding us of the amazing friendships we formed on tour.

Austin and Levi, ever the dynamic duo, were my next targets. They were engaged in an impromptu juggling contest with oranges pilfered from each of the busses. The concentration on their faces, mixed with the outcome of fruit scattering in every direction, was comedy gold. I zoomed in just as Levi made a particularly ambitious toss, the orange arcing beautifully before landing squarely on Austin's head, prompting roars of laughter from all of us watching.

Even Lanie, often a solitary figure, offered a candid moment as she sat by a window, sunlight framing her in a contemplative silhouette. She was lost deep in thought, scribbling in a notebook.

Content with the memories captured in the morning, I slipped my phone into my pocket and started imagining how I would edit all of these clips together. It would be a montage of laughter, music, and quiet reflection, a behind-the-scenes look at the people behind the performances.

"Got some good stuff?" Nash asked, sidling up to me as we prepared to leave.

I nodded, a conspiratorial glint in my eye. "Just wait until you see it."

I made a plan that would allow me to sit down with each member of the group that wanted to, letting the lens reveal the people behind the personas. It would be a series of intimate portraits, set against the backdrop of life on the road—early mornings, late nights, the spaces in between shows where real life happened.

This project, initially born from a simple interview with Harper, had grown into something much larger than what I'd had in mind, and it happened literally overnight. Now it looked like a documentary-style series that promised to offer fans a backstage pass to the heart and soul of the tour. It became a way to showcase not just the talent that graced the stage night after night, but the real and personal moments that happened when the lights went down.

With each new video, the anticipation grew, not just among our fans, but within our makeshift family. Sharing our stories, our laughs, and sometimes our tears, we were no longer just performers on a tour. We were storytellers, each with our own tale to tell, brought together by the music that pulsed through our veins.

These documented experiences with familiar faces would be more than just interviews. They would serve as evidence of our incredible journey and how magical it can be when diverse voices come together. This wasn't just my project anymore; it was our story. I was just the one lucky enough to tell it.

68

CASSIDY

As I navigated the weeks, interviewing each contestant, the lens of my phone camera became a window into the hearts and souls of my fellow travelers.

The interview that caught everyone's attention, however, was the one I had with Nash. We hadn't intended it to be a multi-part series, but as we started talking, the depth of our conversation and the ease between us demanded more than just one upload. We delved into everything from our earliest musical memories to the dreams that fueled our journey. With each question, Nash opened up. His answers were thoughtful reflections infused with the warm humor I'd come to adore.

Watching the footage back, it was impossible to miss the way his eyes softened when he looked at me, or the way my laughter seemed to come so easily around him. The comments section quickly filled with observations and comments like, "that boy is in love" and "she's smitten". My favorite part was the birth of "Cashidy," a moniker given to us that fit perfectly and started following us everywhere we went.

The people we were around every day already knew Nash and I were together and had been for months, but we still tried to maintain privacy and had agreed we wouldn't deny anything that was true, but we wouldn't offer up details to just anyone, either. Our inner circle was relatively small, and we both liked it that way.

Our decision not to broadcast our relationship wasn't about secrecy; it was about appreciating the authenticity and simplicity of what we had. We chose subtlety, a path that felt true to us, allowing our actions to speak volumes more than words ever could. Yet, as our EchoStream interviews went live, the candid moments captured on camera peeled back the curtain on our relationship to an extent, revealing to anyone watching there was most likely more going on than what met the eye.

So rather than leaning into the reality of Cashidy, we left it up in the air for viewers and subscribers to figure out for themselves. We uploaded clips of us singing together but also clips of us having strong disagreements on things like the validity of auto-tune being used in music. The buzz around "Cashidy" was fun.

But as our story gained traction, another narrative was unfolding —one that would unexpectedly shift the dynamics of the entire tour.

The sudden absence of Lanie Tisdale from the lineup caught everyone off guard. Rumors swirled, the most persistent linking her departure to an ill-advised entanglement with one of the judges from the show, Charles Young. The official statement cited mental exhaustion, but whispers of scandal made their way to all the members on the tour, while igniting a frenzy of speculation among the media.

While the tour buzzed with gossip, Nash and I found ourselves unexpectedly grateful for the diversion from our own story. It wasn't that we desired scrutiny or misfortune upon Lanie; quite the opposite. We were genuinely sorry for whatever the circumstances were that led to her early exit and hoped for her well-being. Yet, the shift in focus allowed us to breathe, to enjoy our relationship without the intense heat of the spotlight.

With about four weeks left on the road before we landed in Nashville for the finale, we sought out moments away from the cameras and the gossip as often as possible. In those instances, I discovered myself falling even more in love with Nash Montgomery.

Every shared glance, every whispered conversation under the

concealment of night, felt like a precious secret we were lucky to hold on to. Because as much as neither of us wanted to acknowledge it, once we were back in Nashville, everything would change. Nash would stay in Nashville, then begin the music festival circuit, and I would go back to my job in L.A.

69

NASH

The tour had been a sprint through city after city, each night ending with the echo of our final song. Cassidy and I, we were like two comets caught in each other's orbit, burning brighter together than we ever did apart. As the tour wrapped up, returning us to Nashville, where it all began for us in person, an inevitable conversation loomed, casting a shadow over our final days together.

It was the day after the grand finale and the morning sunlight filtered through the windows of our favorite Nashville brunch spot where we tucked away near the back of the small room. We found ourselves enclosed by comforting walls of familiarity, with the gentle murmur of other patrons and the clinking of coffee cups and silverware surrounding us.

Cassidy and I sat next to each other at a small table in an attempt to eliminate any distance between us. Our hands found each other's, fingers intertwining, clinging to what had grown between us. The air carried the aroma of coffee and sweet pastries, enveloping us like a warm blanket that somehow made the conversation we needed to have seem a little less disheartening.

Cassidy shifted slightly, turning to face me more directly. Her eyes, a deep well of emotions, met mine, searching, questioning. "Feels like we've come full circle again, doesn't it?" she mused, her voice a delicate blend of sadness and wonder, the corners of her mouth twitching in a hesitant smile.

I held her gaze, nodding slowly. "Yeah, it does. It's funny how much can happen in just a few months." I paused, my breath catching slightly as I braced myself for the heart of our conversation that was about to unfold. Our eyes remained locked, a silent exchange of fears and hopes passing between us.

The silence stretched, a moment suspended in time, until Cassidy broke it, her voice a whisper that seemed too fragile for the room. "I don't want this to end." Her eyes, shining with unshed tears, held mine, a plea written in their depths.

In response, my hand squeezed hers, seeking to offer comfort through touch, a physical affirmation of my words. "I know. Me, neither," I confessed, the admission feeling like a heavy stone in my heart. Despite the certainty of our separation, my voice was steady, imbued with a quiet resolve. "But we knew this part was coming, didn't we?"

Cassidy's nod was slow, her gaze never wavering from mine. It was a mirror to the turmoil roiling within me. "It's just, seeing you every day, making all those memories together, it's been a dream. Going back to reality, being apart, it feels like waking up from the best dream to the darkest day."

Our hands remained clasped, a lifeline in the uncertainty of our future. "We can make it work, Cassidy," I said, my voice low but firm, trying to infuse the words with hope. "I know it's not ideal, but I'm not ready to give up on us because of a little—OK, a lot of distance."

Cassidy sighed softly. "Neither am I. But we have to be realistic, Nash. We're both at the beginning of our careers, thousands of miles apart. It's not going to be easy."

The honesty in her voice was a sharp knife, cutting through the last threads of my denial. "I know," I said, the words heavy on my tongue. "But I also know that what I feel for you, Cassidy, it's worth fighting for. It's worth every mile that'll be between us."

The following silence said it all - we were both scared and wanted something more. It was Cassidy who broke it, her voice soft but determined.

"I love you, Nash. That's my truth. No matter where we are, that won't change."

Hearing her say those words, feeling the truth of them resonate deep within me, was both exhilarating and terrifying. "I love you too, Cassidy." It was the first time I'd said it aloud, and the words felt like a promise that could somehow close the distance between us.

"We'll figure it out," she said, leaning her head against my shoulder. "We have to."

I knew that no matter how difficult the path ahead might be, we had something worth fighting for. Love, as we would discover, wasn't just about the moments spent together; it was about the commitment to hold on, even when miles apart.

As we slowly picked at the food in front of us trying to make conversation through the haze of lingering fatigue and the looming distance, I made a silent vow under the watchful eyes of the universe —to love, to wait, and to make sure we could always find our way back to each other, no matter the distance.

AFTER BRUNCH, we lingered at the restaurant, neither of us eager to face the next step. The warmth and comfort of the place was a welcome distraction from the cold farewell that awaited us. Eventually, time, relentless in its forward motion, forced us to leave. We headed back to the hotel, silence enveloping us, filled with words we couldn't yet bring ourselves to say.

At the hotel, retrieving Cassidy's luggage from the concierge felt like the final act in a play neither of us wanted to end. Our parting was now just steps away, evident in the heavy suitcase, and our hearts filled with memories that we wished we could freeze in time.

I called an Uber to take us to the airport. I rode with her in an effort to draw out our last moments together. Walking her inside, holding her hand, I tried to memorize the feel of her fingers laced with mine. This walk through the airport was the complete opposite to the last time we were here three months ago; every step was measured, every glance laden with heartache.

Getting as far as I could go with her, I stopped. We'd reached the final barrier between us and the goodbye we'd been dreading. "I'll call as often as I can," I promised, keeping my tone even despite the turmoil inside. "And I'll send you my schedule as soon as I have it. We'll figure out visits, make this work."

Cassidy nodded, her eyes glistening with tears not different from my own. "I know we will. I love you, Nash."

"I love you too, Cassidy. More than I thought possible," I replied, pulling her into a final, lingering embrace. It was a promise sealed with a kiss that had to last us until the next time we could be together.

Watching her walk through security, I felt a part of me leave with her. I stood there until she was out of sight, holding onto the hope that buoyed us both. Then, calling another Uber to take me back to my hotel, I was alone with my thoughts, the silence a painful reminder of her absence.

The ride back was rough. I was devastated by the idea of being so far separated from her, but full of gratitude for what we shared. I was clinging to our promises and plans to reduce the distance between us. Cassidy and I had something rare and beautiful, and though the road ahead was uncertain, I knew our commitment to each other was fixed, unshakeable. And I was ready to fight for us, no matter the miles apart.

70

CASSIDY

Finding a note on my office door upon my return to work was the last thing I expected. It was a simple message, urging me to see Elizabeth in her office as soon as possible. The handwriting was Elizabeth's, which conveyed its urgency with no need for a reason.

The walk to Elizabeth's office was a short one filled with anxiety and speculation. What could be so important that it warranted an immediate meeting? My time on the road, while away from Echo-Stream, had been a period of personal and professional growth, documented and shared on my own channel, not directly related to my work here. Yet, the note suggested that something significant had happened during my absence that couldn't wait.

As soon as I tapped on her open door, Elizabeth's voice greeted me with, "Cassidy, come in! Have a seat." Her tone, bright and inviting, pulled me from my thoughts. I took the offered seat, still unsure of why I'd been called to her office.

I closed my eyes and took a deep breath, trying to ready myself mentally for the conversation ahead. Elizabeth, seated behind her desk, looked up with a smile that was both welcoming and enigmatic.

Her ability to maintain an air of calm assurance in every situation I'd ever seen her in was something I'd always admired.

"Thank you for coming so quickly, Cassidy," she began, her voice carrying the familiar tone of leadership mingled with genuine warmth. The energy in the room was palpable, a strange prelude to whatever revelation awaited me.

"I want to start by saying how proud we are of you," Elizabeth began, her eyes alight with genuine admiration. "Your performances on the tour, the interviews... they've all brought a new level of attention to EchoStream."

I felt a blush color my cheeks. "Thank you," I managed, the words feeling inadequate to express the clamor of emotions that her acknowledgment stirred in me.

Elizabeth leaned forward and lowered her voice. "Your success has opened an unexpected door for us," she continued, her gaze locked on mine. "The merger with StarWave—it went through. And they were particularly impressed with your viral interviews and behind the scenes content."

I blinked, processing her words. StarWave, the satellite streaming giant, was a behemoth in the industry. Being noticed by them felt surreal.

"They've proposed something...unique," Elizabeth said, a smile playing at the corners of her lips. "They want you, Cassidy, to consider hosting your own radio talk show. Interviewing artists, exploring their lives and music. It's an incredible opportunity."

The room seemed to tilt slightly as her words sank in. My own show? It was so different, so much more than anything I'd considered. Connecting with artists on a personal level, sharing their stories with the world? It sounded perfect for me. Yet, as my heart soared with the possibility, a jolt of realization grounded me. This would mean staying in L.A. permanently.

"I...wow, Elizabeth. This is...it's amazing," I stammered, my mind racing. "Can I have some time to think about it?"

"Of course," Elizabeth nodded, understanding flashing in her eyes. "Take all the time you need. But Cassidy, know this—whatever you decide, it's going to be fantastic. But you're a natural, and if it's what you want, we'll support you every step of the way."

With Elizabeth's words echoing in my mind, I retreated to my office, closing the door behind me to mull over the proposal in solitude. Hosting a show was not anything I would have ever dared to envision, yet here it was, being laid out before me. The excitement of the possibility was overwhelming, but so was the realization of what it meant for my relationship with Nash. Staying in L.A. would cement my career path but at the cost of the possibility of ever being close to Nash for any length of time.

Sitting behind my desk, staring out the small window, I allowed myself to truly weigh my options. The silence, usually a space for focus and productivity, now served as a backdrop for the internal debate raging within me. Could I embrace this opportunity and still hold on to the one thing, the man who had become my anchor? The decision was mine to make, yet it felt impossible without sharing it with Nash.

Picking up the phone, I dialed, seeking the comfort of Nash's voice, craving the clarity his perspective always brought me. As soon as I heard his voice on the other end of the phone, a wave of relief washed over me and tears threatened to fall. "Nash, you won't believe what just happened," I began, my voice trembling with excitement and nervous energy.

"What's going on, Cass?" His voice was steady, though laced with concern.

After a long exhale, I launched into the details of the offer from StarWave, trying to explain both the incredible opportunity it represented and the melt down I was on the verge of having. "They want me to host my own show, Nash. Interviewing artists, exploring their music and lives on a satellite radio channel. It's... it's everything I didn't even know I wanted."

I wished I could see his expression, but apparently I didn't need to because I could hear it in his response. "That's amazing!" His voice was full of genuine excitement for me. There was a long pause before he asked, "You're worried about us, aren't you?"

His understanding cut right to the heart of my fears. "Yes, I mean, staying in L.A. for this... it feels like we'd be deciding to permanently live worlds apart."

Nash's response came after a moment, thoughtful and deliberate. "Sweetheart, listen to me. This is a huge opportunity for you, and I couldn't be prouder. Yes, it will be a challenge, but hasn't everything worked out this far? We'll figure it out, just like we always do."

His words were like a lighthouse in the fog of my doubts. "But the distance... it scares me. Until now it felt less permanent, like it could change."

"I know, Cass. It scares me too. But think about it—this doesn't change how we feel about each other. Love isn't about proximity. It's about choosing each other, every day, no matter what. And we're good at that," he said. His tone was firm, eliminating any room for doubt.

I let out a breath, releasing with it every ounce of stress that had been building inside me. "You're right. We can figure out the logistics. Visits, calls... we'll make it work."

"Love finds a way, right? You take this opportunity if you want it, and we'll tackle the rest together. I'm here rooting for you, always."

"Thank you. For believing in us, for believing in me. I love you."

"I love you too, Sweetheart. Always will. Now, if it's what you want, go tell Elizabeth you'll take the gig."

71

NASH

I t had been eight months of non-stop travel, and I had seen Cassidy in person for a total of six days on random weekends when we could make the timing work. The break-neck pace of the music festival circuit took me from coast to coast, playing under the open skies of sprawling fields, on beaches, under the bright lights of city parks, and in the intimate setups of local, smaller venues. Each festival had its own rhythm, a unique heartbeat that pulsed with the energy of countless fans coming together for the love of music.

The schedule was grueling. Mornings often started before dawn, with sound checks and rehearsals that stretched into the early hours. The afternoons were a flurry of meet-and-greets, last-minute tweaks to the set list, and the adrenaline-fueled anticipation of stepping onto the stage. Nights were usually when the magic happened, when the air electrified with the first chords strummed and the crowd's response fueled a high I imagined no substance could match. But after the last note faded, the exhaustion set in, a constant companion in the lonely quiet of hotel rooms.

Being part of the festival scene was a dream becoming fully realized. It was a world where music was the universal language, uniting strangers in a shared experience that eclipsed the ordinary. Yet, amid the exhilaration, there was a solitude that clung to the fringes, a reminder of what was missing. Cassidy's absence was a pall that darkened the brightest moments, a void that the roar of the crowds couldn't fill.

The thrill of playing live, of seeing my music affect people, was incomparable. Yet, each city melted into the next, and the faces in the audience, while always appreciative, never held the gaze I searched for among them. The nights were the hardest, when the adrenaline wore off and the silence became a freeway for my thoughts. That was when I wondered if the price of this dream was too high.

Two days after my last concert, I was back in Nashville, where I found myself sitting across from Mike Howard in his office.

"Nash, you've been killing it out there," Mike began, his tone proud and earnest. "But between your call and now looking at you, well, it looks like you're carrying a ten ton weight. Talk to me."

I hesitated, the words caught in the tightness of my throat. Admitting my struggle felt like acknowledging a weakness I couldn't afford. Yet, the truth spilled out; the words painted a picture of my internal battle, the longing to be with Cassidy clashing with the momentum of my just starting career.

Mike listened attentively and when I finished, he leaned back, his response thoughtful and deliberate. "Nash, L.A. has recording studios too, you know. And with the trajectory you're on, as long as you're willing to travel, you could be based anywhere."

The simplicity and clarity of his suggestion slammed into me, causing me to sit up straight in my chair. It was a solution that had hovered at the edge of my consciousness as a question that I'd been too afraid to ask. The idea of moving to L.A. to be with Cassidy, to join our lives without sacrificing the momentum of my career or hers, suddenly seemed not just possible but necessary.

The decision to relocate would involve numerous discussions, planning sessions, and logistical considerations. But the seed Mike had planted immediately grew into a decision that felt as right as any song I'd ever written. I couldn't wait to make my next very important phone call.

The walk back to my hotel was spent rolling through thought after thought, questions, doubts. It was all swirling in my mind like it was in a blender. When Mike laid it out plain and simple–L.A. had studios, and my music could travel–it was like he flipped a switch. Sure, the idea of packing up, leaving Nashville and being even farther from my family in Georgia, it sparked a moment of panic. What if L.A. changed things? What if grounding myself meant losing the thrill I got from the road? But then, the what-ifs about Cassidy started to weigh heavier. What if it meant our relationship could be about more than stolen moments and quick visits?

All the nights I'd spent on the road, tossing and turning, I realized my fear of change was nothing compared to the fear of losing what Cassidy and I had. It came down to this–I could make music anywhere, but I couldn't find another Cassidy no matter where I went. That settled it. Deciding to move to L.A. wasn't giving up on my dream; it was about chasing a bigger one, one that included both the music and the girl. I just hoped she was on the same page.

ALONE IN MY HOTEL ROOM, I was a jittery bundle of nerves and excitement after talking to Mike. The room felt too large, too empty, a lot like the distance currently between Cassidy and me-a distance I wanted to close more than anything. Glancing at the clock, I calculated the time difference, realizing she still had hours left at work. It gave me too much time to think, to doubt, but also to dream.

Needing something to take my mind off the ticking clock, I reached for my guitar. It'd always been a kind of anchor for me, something tangible when my thoughts went haywire. There was a tune I'd been messing around with for weeks, something that started taking shape every time I thought about Cassidy. It came flooding back as I let the melody overtake me.

I lost track of time, the song slowly coming together under my fingers. It was about us, me and Cassidy, and everything we were trying to be despite the miles. The sun had started to set by the time I put the guitar down; the room growing dim around me. It felt like the right moment to call her, like maybe working through the song had been a way to get me here, ready to say what needed to be said.

Picking up the phone felt heavier than usual. The anticipation of hearing her voice, of telling her everything, made my heart beat faster. When she answered, that familiar sparkle in her voice was everything I needed. "Hey, Sweetheart," I said, my voice catching in my throat. Those two words carried the weight of every emotion I'd been holding back.

"Hey yourself," she replied, her voice warm, wrapping itself around my heart.

I pictured her on her couch, a leg tucked under her, and immediately wanted nothing more than to be stretched out behind her with my arms wrapped around her.

Unable to help myself and knowing it would make her laugh, I dropped my voice low and asked, "What are you wearing?"

"Your hoodie and my favorite pajama pants," she confessed, and I couldn't help the groan that escaped me, picturing her in my mind's eye. The sound of her giggling filled the room, a sound that made everything seem right in the world.

Immediately, I pressed the video call button.

"I miss you, Nash," she whined as soon as we were connected, her voice playful yet sincere. "I miss you so much."

Her words hit me hard. Taking a slow, deep breath, I braced myself for whatever came after my next question. "What if I told you I could change that?" I ventured, trying to maintain a calm tone despite the grip of uncertainty on my insides.

"Are you coming to visit?" The excitement in her eyes and hopeful note in her voice were almost my undoing.

I paused, gathering my thoughts. "I spoke with Mike today," I began, hesitantly. "He mentioned something about L.A. having recording studios. About how, with my current trajectory, I could be based anywhere."

A hand flew to her mouth as she stared into the camera. The silence that followed was deafening. My heart thudded in my chest, each second stretching out interminably. Had I misjudged? Did she not want this as much as I did?

But then Cassidy spoke, her voice barely above a whisper. "Nash, what are you saying? Are you saying you'd move here, to L.A.?"

The vulnerability in her question was palpable, and I rushed to reassure her. "Yeah, Sweetheart, that's exactly what I'm saying. I want to be where you are. I don't want us to be apart anymore."

Another pause, and then with tears in her eyes she said, "I want that more than anything," Cassidy finally said, her voice thick with emotion. "I just... I was afraid to hope."

When she said those words, feeling the gravity of what this decision meant for both of us, I knew we were on the brink of something incredible. "Then let's make it happen," I said, a promise that spanned the miles between us. "Let's close the distance, for good."

72

CASSIDY

"Let's close the distance, for good."

Nash's words lingered long after the call ended, echoing through the quiet of my apartment like a promise forged from both hope and commitment. I sat there, phone still in hand, stunned into silence. This wasn't just words and dreams; it was the turning point we'd both silently wished for but never dared to voice until now.

The prospect of Nash moving to L.A., of us finally sharing more than fleeting weekends and late-night calls, filled me with an overwhelming mix of emotions. Excitement, certainly, at the thought of not always counting down the days until we could be together again. But also a flicker of apprehension at the level of this change. Our long-distance relationship, with all its challenges, had become a familiar rhythm, a test of patience and commitment we navigated with a combination of love and stubborn resolve.

The apprehension stemmed not only from logistical hurdles but also from a deeper, more personal concern. Our relationship was strong, even though distance had largely defined it. Seeing each other practically every day, sharing the ordinary alongside the extraordinary, presented a new set of challenges. Would the intensity of our weekend visits translate into the day-to-day of a shared life? These unvoiced questions added layers of complexity to what should have been an unquestionable decision.

As the initial shock ebbed away, replaced by cautious optimism, I replayed our conversation. With a confident yet emotional tone, he described his plan to join me at this location. It was a bold decision, showing not only his dedication to his music but also to our relationship. I was ecstatic, but in the back of my mind, I couldn't help but think about the sacrifices he would have to make for us to be together here.

Moving to L.A. meant leaving Nashville and the small community he'd built there, stepping into a new chapter that was as uncertain as it was exciting. I paced the length of my apartment, thoughts racing as I tried to envision our life together in L.A. There were logistics to consider. Would we stay in this apartment? How would we split the bills?

Beyond the practicalities, however, there was the deeper reality of finally building something lasting, something together.

I knew closing the distance was about more than just geography. It was about making a deliberate choice to join our futures, to prioritize 'us' in a way that went beyond mere words. It was definitely a leap of faith.

Forcing myself to stop pacing, I took a deep breath and told myself to stop overthinking everything. There would be challenges, undoubtedly, and adjustments to be made. But the thought of waking up to Nash's face every morning, of sharing not just moments but a life together, made every potential obstacle seem surmountable.

"Let's close the distance, for good," he'd said. The logistics, the fears, none of it mattered. We'd work through all of it together. What mattered was that I was finally going to have the man I loved here with me, not two thousand miles away. "For good" couldn't get here soon enough.

73

NASH

This was a mistake. That's what I thought, as I was trapped in the snarl of L.A. traffic that seemed to epitomize all my doubts and frustrations. The relentless sea of cars was far from the easily navigated sidewalks and quick rideshares available in Nashville, and was a daily reminder of the trade-offs that came with my decision to move here. Two months in, and the city's charm was waning in the light of reality.

My mood didn't improve as I thought about the previous night when Cassidy and I encountered one of our toughest conversations yet. An opportunity had come up for me to open for Christopher Jordan, a career milestone by any measure. It was not something unexpected, but the thought of hitting the road again, of reintroducing distance into our relationship so soon, felt like a step backward. Watching Cassidy process the news, her struggle to balance disappointment with support, had been heart-wrenching. She tried to mask her feelings with excitement for me, but the effort it took was obvious, a thin veneer over the sadness we both felt.

Sitting in the barely moving line of cars, my thoughts drifted to a darker place, one I'd been avoiding ever since I decided to move to L.A. for Cassidy. Our story, as unconventional as it was, had always felt like something out of a fairy tale. But fairy tales don't tell you about the toll of long-distance relationships or the strain of conflicting careers. They take you straight to the "happily ever after" as soon as the prince kisses the princess awake or returns her show.

The reality was, Cassidy and I had spent more time apart than together. Cassidy and I built our relationship on stolen and hurried moments, from phone calls and text messages to those brief, shining days together on tour. And now, just when we were starting to try and lay down roots in the same city, my career was pulling me away again.

The question that gnawed at me, growing louder with each passing moment stuck in this traffic, was whether it was fair to keep doing this to Cassidy. Was it selfish to hold on to her when my life was so unpredictable? I wondered if the kindest thing, the most loving act, would be to let her go, to free her from the cycle of reunions and farewells that had come to define us.

I thought about our history, the way we had found and lost each other before. There was a painful irony in the fact that, even after uncovering our true identities and overcoming the odds to be together, we were still at the mercy of circumstances. The anonymity that had once allowed us to connect so deeply at one time seemed like it would be a luxury now, a simpler time before the strain of real-world decisions bore down on us.

The more I dwelled on it, the more the idea of cutting ties for her sake took hold. Not that my love for Cassidy had waned—far from it. It was that love that made the thought of holding her back or constantly hurting her unbearable. We had both entered the relationship fully aware of the challenges, but the reality of living them was so much harder than I ever expected.

When I finally parked and turned off the engine in the studio's parking lot, a memory surfaced. It was a moment from one of those rare weekends together, a simple, quiet morning where the world outside seemed to pause just for us. Cassidy had made coffee, the aroma filling the small space of her apartment. As we sat side by side on her patio overlooking her apartment's courtyard, we talked about everything and nothing, laughter mingling with the soft notes of the city waking up. It moments like these, the small pockets of time we carved out for ourselves, that I felt the strength of what we'd built together.

These memories, these moments of pure contentment, clashed with the doubts clouding my mind. They reminded me of the happiness we found together, the countless shared smiles and whispered dreams in the dead of night. This happiness is what made moving to L.A. to be with Cassidy feel like the right call.

We had fought hard for every moment together. I'd be an idiot to toss that aside so freely. Even as I took my guitar and entered the studio, the unrest remained. Our relationship had never been easy, but maybe it was the challenges that made it so meaningful.

I wanted desperately to hold on to that glimmer of hope. But there was a lingering blade of doubt wedging itself between my ribs and directly into my heart. Picturing the look on her face as she forced herself to smile for my benefit had nearly shattered me. What if what was best for Cassidy was for me to let her go so she could find someone who would give her the stability she deserved?

74

CASSIDY

Nash left this morning with only a kiss to my forehead, a gesture so gentle but taxed with an unspoken heaviness that seemed to hang in the air long after he'd gone. I had felt the shift in his mood last night, and it clearly hadn't lifted. The silence of his departure was louder than any words we had shared the night before.

As I moved around our apartment, getting ready for work, I whispered quiet wishes for an easy commute, hoping the notorious L.A. traffic would spare him today. It'd been a challenge for him, adapting to the relentless pace of the city, and I knew it was wearing on him.

The memory of our conversation from the night before lingered, casting a cloud over the brightness of the morning. My heart ached, not because Nash was leaving again—that was a part of his journey I'd come to accept and, in my own way, embrace. It's his dream unfolding, and I'd always wanted to be there, supporting him, cheering for every success. No, my sadness wasn't because he was leaving but because I was missing out on an opportunity that I had been so excited about.

StarWave's offer to host my own radio show had come as a surprise, one I was eager to embark on. Even more exciting was their suggestion to have Nash as my first guest. The prospect of sharing that moment with him, to couple our dreams in such a public, meaningful way, had filled me with an indescribable excitement. But with his upcoming tour, that dream would remain just that—a possibility unfulfilled. I hadn't mentioned it to him, not wanting to add to the weight he already carried. The disappointment of what could have been—a shared milestone, a joint celebration of our successes—was a hard pill to swallow. But it wasn't earth-shattering.

Pulling on my blazer, I glanced at the empty space where Nash had stood this morning. Once he'd left, the apartment was too quiet, too still. As I grabbed my keys and headed for the door, I couldn't shake the dark cloud trying to form over me. The excitement for the day ahead was usually bubbling just beneath the surface, but the left-over tension from what had been an unfinished conversation and Nash's upcoming goodbye dampened my mood.

The chaotic streets of Los Angeles failed to distract me from the inner turmoil I was experiencing while driving to work. Every red light seemed to hold me back, not just from my destination but from finding a solution to keep the emotional distance that I was feeling between Nash and me from growing.

Arriving at StarWave's offices, I tried to ready myself for the day ahead. The new role as a radio show host was a dream come true, a chance to carve out my own path in the industry and share the stories and music that mattered most to me. Settling into my new workspace, I pulled out my phone to send him a text just to let him know I'd made it to the office and ask if he'd meet me for lunch.

> I made it to the office. I hope you have a
> great morning. Free for lunch? I love you.

> Morning's busy here. Got some meetings
> lined up over lunch, won't be able to make it.

I blinked several times while staring at his message, disappointment sitting heavily in my chest.

> No worries! I'll miss seeing you, but understand. How about I pick up something for dinner on my way home? Any cravings?

> Anything you want is fine.

The shortness of his responses was out of character. I tried not to read anything into it, but something was very wrong.

> Alright. I'll surprise us then. Can't wait to hear about your day later. Love you.

I kept my eyes fixed on my phone even after our conversation ended, waiting for a response from him. A knock at my door startled me, pulling me out of the hurt and confusion that was building within me.

My spiraling thoughts were thankfully interrupted by a knock at my office door. "Come in," I called, tucking away my phone and the remnants of my sadness with it. The door opened to reveal Stan, the station manager, wearing an easy smile that belied the briskness of his entrance.

"Morning, Cassidy. Settling in okay?" he asked, glancing around my still sparse office.

"Yes, sir. I'm getting there. What can I do for you?" I asked, grateful for the distraction from my earlier conversation with Nash.

Stan took a seat, his demeanor shifting to business. "As you know, we're gearing up for the soft launch of your show. I love the name you came up with - 'Strings Attached: The Artist's Voice'. Very catchy. The marketing team is eager to start pushing out material and sound bytes. How's everything coming along on your end?"

A flicker of excitement sparked within me as I nodded, momentarily dispelling the cloud of my worries. "It's coming together. I've been working closely with the producers, and we've got some great ideas for the show."

"That's what I like to hear." Stan's smile widened. "And how about Nash Montgomery? Any chance we secured that interview?"

A lump formed in my throat at the mention of Nash.

"Actually, Nash will be on the road by then," I said, trying to hide the disappointment that I felt inside.

Stan's expression faltered for a moment, but he quickly recovered. "That's a shame. I was really hoping to get to know a little more about 'Cashidy', maybe get an inside scoop," he said with a wink. "But I understand. His career's on the move, and that's a good thing. We'll work around it. There are plenty of artists who'd jump at the chance to be the first featured on your show."

His use of 'Cashidy' made me chuckle, and I appreciated Stan's attempt to lighten the mood. "Thanks, Stan. I've got a few other names in mind. I'll make sure the first show is a hit. Don't you worry about that."

Stan stood and headed for the door. He stopped and turned to look at me as he said, "I have every confidence in you, Cassidy. This show's going to be great. Let me know if you need anything from my end."

As the door clicked shut behind Stan, I was left alone with his parting words of confidence echoing in the space. Despite the undercurrent of disappointment from not having Nash on "Strings Attached," Stan's belief in my abilities lifted my spirits. I settled back in my chair, taking a quick moment to enjoy the peace of my new office before getting down to business.

Pulling up the list of potential guests for "Strings Attached," I had a rush of exhilaration. This show was my blank canvas, a platform to delve deep into the stories behind the music, offering listeners a glimpse into the souls of their favorite artists.

The day unfolded in a rush of productivity and planning. Each meeting with the producers and marketing team sparked fresh ideas, from thematic episodes that traced the roots of country music to interactive segments designed to engage our audience directly. The show already had so much potential; I was excited and ready to take on the responsibility.

Yet, even as I immersed myself in the work, my mind occasionally drifted to Nash. I wondered how his day was going, if the studio session was proving fruitful, or if he, too, was feeling the strain of whatever was happening between us. The knowledge that he wasn't leaving for another two weeks was a small comfort. Just thinking about his absence made me sad again.

My stomach growled, causing me to glance at the clock and note it was just after lunchtime. Tapping my pen repeatedly against my desk, I felt an idea forming in my mind. I didn't have any more meetings on my calendar, so I emailed everyone of importance to say I would be out of the office for the remainder of the day.

Rushing out of the office with a plan taking shape in my mind, I made a beeline for the nearest store. My heart fluttered with nerves and I was giddy at the prospect of what this evening could be. I picked up ingredients for Nash's favorite meal, ensuring everything was perfect. The store's aisles became a race track as I quickly gathered everything I needed, my thoughts solely on creating a special evening that might give us a redo on last night.

I wasted no time once I got home, immediately setting to work to create a romantic haven out of our apartment, complete with dimmed lights and a cozy ambiance. Tea light candles were strategically placed around the living room, casting a warm, inviting glow. I filled a vase with fresh flowers, their fragrance subtly perfuming the air, and queued up the romantic playlist I had created, each song a chapter in the story of us.

As the food finished in the oven, I drew myself a bath, allowing the warmth to soothe the day's tensions away. Wrapped in the comfort of our home, I chose an outfit for the evening, knowing it was one of Nash's favorites, and did my hair and makeup a little bolder than usual.

The table was set with care, plates and silverware arranged, a bottle of wine chilling in the refrigerator. Everything was perfect, or as perfect as it could be without Nash there.

And then I waited.

And I waited.

The sky outside darkened, transitioning from the soft hues of twilight to the deep, inky black of night. One by one, the tea light candles flickered out, their warm glow replaced by the cool, distant light of the moon through the blinds on the sliding glass door. The playlist, once a backdrop of anticipation, now seemed to mock my solitude with its romantic melodies. The food had long grown cold on the stove. I'd swapped out my dress for my sweats, washed my face, and pulled my hair up on top of my head.

Nash hadn't called or answered my calls, and each passing moment stretched longer than the last. My excitement waned, replaced by a growing sense of loneliness and worry.

It was late when the key finally turned in the lock, Nash's silhouette appearing in the doorway, but the relief at seeing him safe was quickly overshadowed by a surge of anger. Why hadn't he called? His phone had been off, leaving me to imagine the worst, oscillating between worry for his safety and distress over our last conversation.

"Welcome home," I quipped, my voice dull and quiet.

He looked sad. "Cass, I'm so sorry," he started, his voice low and filled with remorse.

The sight of him, weary and standing amidst the remnants of a night that had gone so differently in my head, momentarily dulled my anger. Most of the candles had burned out, some of their wax spilled over like tears, and the playlist had long since ended, leaving only silence between us.

I waited for him to continue, to offer some explanation that could make sense of why I spent the evening alone, bathing in anxiety and disappointment. But as we stood there, the gap between us felt more like a void, filled with unspoken words and unresolved feelings.

75

NASH

As I entered the apartment, it was clear that I had made a grave error. The faint light only outlined the set table, left completely untouched, and the remnants of mostly extinguished candles. It was a physical reflection of the turmoil I had been struggling with all day in my heart and mind. Witnessing how my jumbled emotions had destroyed what could have been a perfect evening left me feeling gutted.

Cassidy's voice sliced through the dimness emanating from a shadowed corner of the couch. "Welcome home." The words, sharp, laced with worry and anger, stopped me in my tracks.

I stood there, the door still ajar behind me, as her words—and the implications of my absence—settled over me. Gently pushing the door closed, I took a hesitant step into the room.

"Cass, I'm so sorry," I began, my voice cracking on the last word. I knew a simple apology couldn't fully convey the extent of my failures this evening; it was feeble and lacking.

I never meant to shut her out. My doubts about our future, however, about being the partner she deserved, had consumed me. Standing amidst the once beautiful, now silent scene Cassidy had created, I couldn't ignore what my indecision had cost us both.

The stillness of the apartment, broken only by the sound of our breathing, felt oppressive. I could sense Cassidy's disappointment, her pain at being left in the dark, both literally and metaphorically. The darkness seemed to amplify my guilt, making each step toward her feel like wading through a thick fog of regret.

"I... I needed some time," I admitted, though the words sounded hollow even to my own ears. "To think, to clear my head. But I lost track of everything." The confession was painful, a raw acknowledgment of how deeply I knew I'd let her down.

Cassidy remained silent, her presence a question mark in the shadows. I wished I could see her face, gauge her reaction, but maybe the darkness was a mercy, sparing me from the full impact of her sorrow. The silence felt like a physical barrier, a divide that my hours of introspection had only widened. I realized then that my attempt to spare her from the turbulence of my thoughts had only inflicted a different kind of pain—the pain of feeling forgotten, left waiting alone in a moment meant for two people.

"The truth is," I started, but had to stop to try to pull myself together before I broke down. Just thinking the next words were was a knife to my heart. But she needed to know what I had been wrestling with.

"I've been questioning whether it's fair to you, all of this—my career, the uncertainty it brings into our lives." I paused, the torment of my next words clawing at me from inside my chest. "I wondered if letting you go was the kindest thing I could do. To free you from the cycle of waiting and goodbyes that seems to come with being in a relationship with me."

It was the heart of my anxiety laid bare, the fear that my presence in Cassidy's life brought more shadows than light. Yet, saying it aloud, after seeing what I'd missed, the special evening she'd planned for us, it felt like exposing a wound to the air—though not to deepen it, but in hope of healing.

I could barely make out Cassidy's form as she shifted in the darkness, the quiet rustle of fabric the only hint of her movement. She was standing in front of me, but was still too far away. My heart ached for the light, to see her face, to read in her eyes the impact of my words.

Tension filled the air, a calm before the storm that was her response. Her voice, when it came, was steady but carried an edge that made me realize I had entered into a space that was far more volatile than I had anticipated.

"You thought about letting me go?" Her words were measured and angry, each one a blade landing with precision directly into my heart.

I couldn't breathe. The darkness of the room seemed to close in around me, Cassidy's quiet anger more intimidating than any outburst could have been. It was the calm, the control behind her words that intensified the gravity of my mistake.

When she spoke again, each word was said through gritted teeth as though she were fighting for control of her emotions.

"I love you, Nash. And not despite the uncertainty and the good-byes, but including them. They're part of who you are, part of what I signed up for when I chose to be with you." Her voice possessed a lethal seriousness. "To think you'd consider 'freeing' me without so much as a conversation... It's insulting, Nash."

I stood frozen, the further realization of my error cutting deeper with her every word. Cassidy's anger wasn't just about the missed evening; it was about my failure to recognize her agency in our rela-tionship.

"You're right," I admitted weakly, feeling the inadequacy of my apology. "I was wrong to think I could make such a decision alone. I let my fears—my insecurities—cloud my judgment."

Cassidy's silence was a weighted blanket in the darkness, her dismay a hovering around us. I understood then that my contempla-tion of letting her go, however well-intentioned, had been a betrayal of the trust and partnership we had built.

"This evening," I gestured futilely toward the remnants of her efforts, "you created something beautiful, something I failed to honor by being here, with you. I let my fears of letting you down, of having to say goodbye and leave over and over dictate my actions, and I am so, so sorry for that."

As the silence hung between us, a sharp reminder of the distance my actions had created, I knew mere words wouldn't suffice to bridge the gap. But I had to try; I had to make her understand the depth of my regret.

"I know I got it all wrong, Cass," I said, the dim light casting shadows that mirrored the restlessness inside me. "Every moment I stayed away from you, every decision made in isolation—it was all wrong. Not because I doubt us, but because I feared... I feared not being enough, of ever being the reason for sadness in your eyes."

Taking a hesitant step forward, I needed to close the physical distance between us, my heart pounding with the need to salvage what I'd so carelessly jeopardized. "But tonight, seeing what you put together for us, feeling the weight of your sadness... seeing you sitting there, it almost killed me. I spent a lot of time thinking today and I need you to know what I concluded. No distance, no career uncertainty, can diminish what I feel for you. You are my home, Cassidy. Coming back to you, to us, is what keeps me going."

A few straggling candles fought against the encroaching darkness. I dropped to one knee, an action that was as significant as the words I was about to speak. I reached into my pocket. The ring I'd spent the afternoon searching for, a symbol of my forever commitment, felt heavy with promise as I held it out to her.

"Cassidy, I love you. I love you more than music, more than any dream I've chased on or off the road. I don't want to come home to anyone but you, ever. If you'll have me, if you'll forgive my foolishness, I want to make this permanent. I am wholly committed to you. Marry me, Cassidy. Let's face every tour, every challenge, together. Because without you, none of it means a thing."

My voice broke with the intensity of my emotions, each word a pledge of my unwavering love and dedication. My heart heavy, tears spilled from my eyes as I silently begged her to say yes. In the quiet that followed, with the ring shimmering faintly in the limited light, I waited for Cassidy's answer, for the words that would either mend the fractures of the evening or confirm my deepest fears that I'd failed her.

Cassidy's gasp was a soft sound that cut through the tension, a single breath that conveyed her surprise, disbelief, and a thousand unspoken emotions. As her figure shifted in the shadows, the faint light caught the moisture in her eyes, transforming them into pools of reflected hope and vulnerability.

For a moment, she was silent. Then, in a voice laced with tenderness, she whispered, "Nash..." My name on her lips, weighted by the gravity of the moment.

Slowly, Cassidy moved closer, her presence a beacon in the darkness. The distance that had felt insurmountable just moments ago began to close, not just by the physical space she traversed, but by the emotional bridges being rebuilt with each hesitant step. Her hand shook slightly as it reached out. She didn't try to take the ring, but instead her fingers gently grazed my cheek, causing my breath to hitch, sending a shiver down my spine.

"Cassidy," I said again, my voice soft but sure, emboldened by her nearness and the warmth of her skin against mine. "I understand that my actions today, my absence, have caused you pain. But please believe me when I say that you are the reason I strive to be better, to be the man you deserve. Marrying you, building a life with you, spending forever with you is what I want. I promise, no matter where my music takes me, I'll always find my way back to you. You are my true north, my constant in a life of variables."

The silence that came after my request was filled with the gentle sound of Cassidy's breathing, reminding me of the life we had together and the life I was asking her to embrace completely, even with the unknowns my career could bring.

Finally, Cassidy lowered to her knees, putting us face-to-face. When she spoke, her voice was a whisper charged with echoes of her emotions.

"Nash, you are my whole heart. The idea of being without you hurts more than any goodbye or any distance ever could. Hearing you question whether you should let me go, as if our love could be so easily undone, it scared me. It scared me because it made me realize the depth of your doubts, the battles you've been fighting alone in your mind."

She paused, and I could almost feel her gathering her thoughts.

"Your music, your journey — it's only part of why I love you. But Nash, love isn't just about sharing the easy moments. It's about facing the hard ones, together. It's about choosing each other, again and again, even when the path isn't clear. My love for you is not something so fragile that the threat of distance or the challenges of your career could break it. Yes, the goodbyes are hard, and yes, the waiting can be agonizing, but they're also a testament to the strength of what we share. Every reunion, every moment we steal back from our separate lives, is a victory. "

Her voice softened, but the underlying strength was unmistakable. "I want all of it, Nash. The tours, the late nights, the goodbyes, and the reunions. Because they all lead back to you. They're part of our story, and I wouldn't have it any other way."

The room, with its flickering candle remnants, seemed to hold its breath as Cassidy shuffled closer, her presence a ballast in the soft darkness. "So, ask me again, knowing that I'm not just saying yes to a ring or a promise of forever. I'm saying yes to the uncertainty, the challenges, and the countless adventures that lie ahead. Because, Nash, there's no one else I'd rather face them with."

Cassidy's words left me breathless, overwhelmed by the depth of her understanding, forgiveness, and unwavering commitment. As she spoke, the room's darkness seemed to recede, her words bringing clarity to my doubts and fears. The emotions swirling within me settled into a single, unshakable conviction.

Gathering every ounce of my love for her, every promise I intended to keep, I asked again, from the depth of my soul as tears streamed down my face.

"Cassidy Raye Stanton, I love you," I said, each word wrapped in all the emotions that swelled within me—the love, the fear, the hope. "With everything I am, and everything I have, I love you. You've been my light in the darkness, my calm in the storm. Marrying you means committing to a lifelong partnership filled with love, trust, and companionship. It means creating a home together and building a life that reflects our shared dreams. And if you will let me, I am ready to walk hand in hand with you, embracing all the ups and downs, and creating a future filled with love and happiness. Will you marry me?"

76

CASSIDY

"Yes," I managed to say, my voice steady despite the torrent of emotions warring within. "Yes, I will marry you. Because there is no one else I can imagine sharing this life with, no one else who makes me feel so deeply understood, so cherished, and so loved. You are my heart, my compass, and my anchor; and I choose you, in every moment, every day, for the rest of our lives."

Nash took my hand in his, the cool metal of the ring gliding smoothly over my finger. A perfect fit. As it settled into place, I felt a surge of emotion so powerful it left me breathless. The simplicity of the act, the profound depth of its meaning, anchored me to the moment, to him, to us. Nash stood, bringing me with him, closing the distance between us in a single, purposeful step. As he wrapped his arms around me, I nestled into his embrace, my head finding its familiar place against his chest. I could hear the steady beat of his heart, a rhythm that had become my favorite song, the melody of home and belonging.

In his embrace, everything else melted away—the doubts, the fears, the uncertainties of our past and future—leaving only the warmth of his love enveloping me.

In the silence that followed my acceptance, a small, almost comical sound broke through the solemnity of the moment—my stomach let out a soft, unmistakable growl, revealing that in the crush of emotions and the wait for Nash, I had neglected to eat dinner.

Nash's embrace tightened momentarily, and then he pulled back just enough to look at me, concern etched across his features. "You haven't eaten?" he asked, his voice laced with guilt and worry.

"It's OK," I assured him, my voice warm with not just forgiveness but an immense love for this man who, even now, was thinking of my needs.

His hands gently holding my face, he said, "It's not OK."

I couldn't stop myself from smiling at how sincere he was, even though my stomach was growling, adding a humorous soundtrack to our special moment. "Nash, really, it's fine. Tonight turned out to be so much more than I'd hoped for," I said, wanting to ease the worry creasing his brow.

But Nash was resolute, his concern for my well-being shining through, making him all the more endearing. "No, it's not fine. You went to all this effort to make tonight special, and I..." He paused, his guilt evident. "I got lost in my own head. Let me take care of you now, like you always take care of me."

His words, so full of love and determination, melted any lingering disappointment. Here was the man I loved, not just willing but eager to put me first, even after a day fraught with emotional turmoil. "OK," I conceded, the warmth in my heart eclipsing any hunger I felt. "But we do it together."

An amused sigh escaped him, a sound that filled the room with its brightness, dispelling the last shadows of the day's earlier tensions. "Deal," he agreed.

Before we could take a step towards the kitchen, Nash drew me closer, his gaze locking onto mine with an intensity that made my heart skip a beat. In one seamless movement, he leaned closer, his lips softly pressing against mine, a kiss that spoke volumes of love, regret, and a pledge to never waver.

As he pulled back, our foreheads rested against each other, a silent exchange of understanding passing between us. "I love you," he whispered, his breath warm against my skin.

And with that simple declaration, any residual doubt melted away, replaced by a profound sense of belonging. Then, without warning, he grabbed my hand and dragged me to the kitchen.

77

NASH

As the final days of the tour approached, relief and anticipation filled me. Relief at the thought of no longer living out of a suitcase, and anticipation for the time off I'd lined up before heading out on another stint as a special guest on a different tour. But first, there was a surprise I had in store—a surprise not even Cassidy knew about.

Landing in L.A., the city that had become as much a home to me as any place could, I had a rush of adrenaline. The taxi ride to Star-Wave was a blur. I concentrated all my thoughts on the moment I would walk through those doors, the moment I would see Cassidy's face light up with surprise.

The studio buzzed with activity, but a nod from her station manager assured me that everything was set. I waited in the wings as Cassidy's voice filled the airwaves, as warm and inviting as always.

"Coming up we have a surprise guest that isn't just a surprise to you, but also to me. In the meantime, let's take it back a couple of decades with the number one song from January 28, 1989, Deeper Than the Holler by country music legend Randy Travis. With over 30 awards and even more nominations to his name, Travis is credited as one of the leaders in the neotraditional country movement, taking country music back to some of its roots and traditions."

I watched as she pressed a few buttons, stood from her seat, removed her headphones, and mouthed "Taking five," as she raised a hand to the man behind the glass wall to her left.

Her gaze met mine as she entered the hallway, and I could read the surprise and disbelief in her expression. For a moment, she stood frozen, as if unsure whether I was real or a figment of her imagination. Then, with a cry that was part laughter, part sob, Cassidy launched herself into my arms. The force of her embrace nearly knocked me back, but I held firm, wrapping my arms around her, grounding us both in the reality of the moment.

"Hey, Sweetheart," I murmured into her hair, the scent of her shampoo familiar and comforting.

Her response, muffled against my chest, had her words lost in the fabric of my shirt, but the sentiment was unmistakable. We stood there, in the middle of the bustling studio, our reunion an island of stillness amid the commotion.

Pulling back slightly, Cassidy's eyes searched mine, a million questions reflected in their depths. "How? Why are you here early?" she asked, confusion and elation playing out across her features. Then the realization hit her. "You're the surprise guest."

"Surprise," I said, grinning.

Her smile, radiant even through her tears, broke through. "This is the best surprise," she said, her voice steadying as the initial shock faded. "But how did you manage it?"

With a chuckle, I nodded towards the studio's entrance where her station manager stood, an accomplice to the surprise. "Let's just say I had a little help."

The moment was broken by the sound of the studio door opening, a producer's voice calling out, "Cassidy, we're back in two."

Wiping away the last of her tears, Cassidy took my hand, her grip firm. "Come on," she said, determination lacing her voice. "Let's give them a show they won't forget."

Sitting down beside her, the headphones felt surprisingly natural.

Cassidy's introduction was flawless, her voice steady and confident as she welcomed me to the show. We shared stories from our time on the reality TV show, laughed at the behind-the-scenes moments from our time on *Real American Country*, and talked about some of our plans for the future.

As we delved into the conversation, Cassidy's ability to steer our discussion with ease and grace reminded me why she was so perfect for this role. Her questions were thoughtful, touching on moments of the tour that highlighted not just the music but the journey behind it.

"Tell me, Nash," Cassidy said, her tone shifting to one of playful curiosity, "what was one of your favorite moments from your most recent tour?"

I paused, sifting through the countless memories, each one a testament to the adventure it had been. "Honestly? It was a night in Nashville," I began, recalling a performance that had felt like coming full circle. "Standing on that stage, looking out at the crowd, I felt this overwhelming sense of gratitude. For the music, for the journey, and for the people who've supported me through it all." I glanced at Cassidy, my gaze holding hers. "And knowing that at the end of it all, I'd be coming back to you made every mile, every show, worth it."

Cassidy's smile in response was soft, her eyes shining with unspoken emotion. "And what about the music itself? Any new inspirations you're bringing back with you?"

"The road always has a way of opening your eyes, of changing how you see the world," I replied. "There's a couple of songs in the works, actually. Stories I've picked up along the way, melodies that came to me in the rare calm in the middle of the chaos. I can't wait to share them with you... with everyone."

As the show neared its end, Cassidy leaned closer, her voice lowering, as though she was asking a conspiratorial question. "And now, with the tour behind you, what's next for Nash Montgomery?"

"A little break, first and foremost," I admitted with a chuckle. "But beyond that, there's so much I want to do. More music, of course, but also taking the time to appreciate the life I have, the people in it.

Starting with planning a wedding with the most amazing woman I know."

Cassidy's laughter rang out, light and joyful. "Well, I think that sounds like a perfect plan."

WITH THE SHOW wrapped and Cassidy's schedule cleared, we stepped out of the studio. The reality of being back in L.A., back with Cassidy, began to truly sink in. I could finally shift my focus to the future, to the wedding, and the life we were building together.

Cassidy's excitement about the wedding, about starting this new chapter with me, was infectious. She talked about potential venues, guest lists, and even band options, each detail sparking new ideas and possibilities as though we had to figure it all out immediately.

The visit from her parents, too, was something we both looked forward to. It would be an opportunity to celebrate our engagement with her family. Cassidy's excitement at being able to include them only added to my own happiness. I was also looking forward to heading to Georgia to see my folks. Cody and Cassidy had become close through texts and phone calls and, of course, they each had plenty of wedding things to talk about.

As the evening wound down, and we found ourselves back in the apartment we shared, the full weight of my return hit me. This wasn't just a visit, a temporary stop before the next tour. I was home with Cassidy, where every moment held the promise of a shared future. My decision to make L.A. my home had been the right one, as everything fell into place.

In the quiet of our home, with Cassidy by my side, I felt a peace I hadn't known in months. The challenges of the tour, the variability of a musician's life, they were all part of the dream. But they paled in comparison to the certainty I felt about us, about the life we were choosing to build together.

CASSIDY

May had graced us with perfect weather, warm but not too hot, with a gentle breeze that carried the scent of blooming flowers and freshly cut grass in the backyard of my childhood home in West Virginia. The soft light filtering through the old oak trees made it feel like a dream, setting the stage for the happiest day of my life.

The backyard, a place of countless childhood memories, became a magical venue for our wedding after we transformed it with neatly arranged white chairs on either side of a flower-lined aisle. The aisle led to a beautifully decorated arch where Nash and I would exchange our vows.

My heart fluttered with excitement and a touch of nerves as I stood at the back, my dad by my side, ready to walk me down the aisle. The music started, a gentle, acoustic melody that filled the air, signaling the beginning of the ceremony.

One by one, the bridesmaids and groomsmen paired off and made their way down the aisle, setting the stage for our moment. Jet accompanied Cody while Wyatt escorted Willow. Harper, as my maid of honor, walked alone, radiating confidence and joy. At the aisle's end, Nash stood waiting, his dad by his side as his best man, both a vision of pride and elegance.

As my dad and I started our walk, every step felt surreal. The faces of family and friends blurred into a sea of smiles and tears, as my focus was on the man standing at the end, waiting for me. Nash, looking handsome in his suit, his eyes locked on mine, filled with love and anticipation.

I experienced a rush of emotions as my dad placed my hand in Nash's, a tender passing of trust and love. Nash's touch was grounding, His quiet "I love you" a whisper meant only for me.

The officiant welcomed everyone, and the ceremony began bringing about some laughter and some tears as he reminded us why we were there, to bind together two hearts and two families. My heart was racing and my hands trembling as he asked us to recite the vows we'd written to one another.

Nash, his eyes never leaving mine, spoke his vows with sincerity and conviction that took my breath away.

"Cassidy, from this day forward, I promise to be your partner in all of life's adventures. I will cherish our moments together, support your dreams, and stand by you through every challenge and joy. There is no distance on earth that will keep me from loving you. You are my home, my heart, my everything. And I will be yours until death keeps us apart."

Uncertain I would be able to speak, I took several breaths and had to swallow the lump in my throat. With a long, unladylike sniffle that drew chuckles from the guests, I breathed out a laugh and finally spoke.

"Nash, I vow to be your steadfast companion, your confidant, and your greatest supporter. I will laugh with you in times of joy and comfort you in times of sorrow. No matter where life takes us, my love for you will remain constant and unwavering. You are my light, my love, and my life. Together, we will build a future filled with love, laughter, and music. I am yours, always and forever."

The ceremony was beautiful and overflowed with love and promises. When we were finally pronounced husband and wife, and

Nash kissed me, cheers and applause erupted around us. It was a moment filled with the purest joy.

The reception that followed was a celebration of love, with dancing, toasts, and stories shared under the stars.

One of the most unforgettable moments was Nash's rendition of the garter toss. Unlike the usual toss, Nash turned it into a full-blown spectacle, mixing drama with his unique brand of humor. Deciding to retrieve the garter blindfolded, it became a theatrical performance, eliciting cheers and chuckles from everyone gathered, claiming it was the only way to ensure "fate's fair hand" in choosing the catcher. With his eyes covered, he exaggeratedly stumbled around, playfully teasing as he pretended to search for me, his hands initially landing practically everywhere on me except where they were supposed to.

His antics had the guests in stitches. When he finally 'found' the garter, his exaggerated surprise and triumphant flourish as he tossed it, still blindfolded, made the moment even more memorable. His over-the-top antics, pretending to fumble and aim in the wrong direction, had everyone in bowled over. When he finally let the garter fly, it landed, of all places, directly into my cousin Tyler's hands. The look on his face was priceless, a mix of shock and amusement that sent a wave of laughter through the guests. And when Harper caught the bouquet with an equally surprised expression, the moment felt like it had been plucked directly from a romantic comedy. The two had been flirting with each other the entire night, making it even more like poetic justice.

Our first dance was to a song that Nash had written for me. As Nash and I moved across the dance floor, it felt like time had frozen and everything else around us became nonexistent.

As the evening's laughter and music filled the air, a hush fell over the crowd when Nash's dad stepped up to the microphone for his toast. In his voice, there was a depth of emotion that immediately captured everyone's attention. He began by recounting the early days of Nash and my relationship, the challenges we had overcome, and the strength of our relationship that had only grown over time.

"With every step Nash and Cassidy have taken together, they've proved that true love can withstand the most complicated of circumstances," he said in a voice that was strong yet laden with emotion. "And how do I know it's true love? It's in the way they look at each other, the way they support each other's dreams, and how they face life's storms side by side. I know because it's the way I look at Nash's mother every single day." This resulted in a room full of 'awws' and sniffles, my own included.

He spoke of the importance of love and resilience, reminding us all that while the path of true love never runs perfectly smooth, it's the journey that forges the strongest bonds. "These two," he continued, gesturing towards us, "have shown us what it means to be resilient, to build a relationship on the foundation of mutual respect, understanding, and an unfailing commitment to one another regardless of time and distance between them."

Laughter bubbled up among the guests as he shared a few lighthearted stories about Nash's younger days, painting a picture of a man who was always destined to find his perfect match in me. "I've watched Nash grow into the man he is today, and I've seen how Cassidy's love has made him even better. Together, they are unstoppable."

His toast concluded on a note of wisdom and warmth, a reflection of the conversations and moments of advice he'd shared with us through our relationship. "To Nash and Cassidy," he raised his glass, "may your love continue to be a light, guiding you through whatever life throws your way. Here's to love, laughter, and a lifetime of happiness."

As glasses clinked in agreement, and a chorus of "To Nash and Cassidy" echoed through the backyard, I felt an overwhelming sense of gratitude.

After Nash's dad concluded his speech, the microphone was passed to Harper. Standing beside me, Harper cleared her throat, her eyes sparkling with emotion and mischief. "For those of you who don't know, I had the privilege of meeting Nash and Cassidy under the most unusual circumstances—a reality TV competition, of all places. And let me tell you, we all knew 'Cashidy' was the real deal long before the rest of the world caught on."

Her words drew laughter and nods from the crowd, especially from those who had shared that unique journey with us. "I've had the honor of witnessing their love story unfold," Harper continued, her voice softening. "Their journey has been nothing short of a dream come true."

She paused, her gaze sweeping over us with affection. "But here's the thing about dreams—they don't always tell you about the trials, the sacrifices, or the sheer determination it takes to make love last. What makes Nash and Cassidy's story so special isn't just the magic of how they met, but the reality of how they've chosen each other, every single day since."

Raising her glass high, Harper's voice grew stronger. "To Nash and Cassidy—'Cashidy'—may your love continue to inspire those around you, proving that true love isn't just found in dreams. It's real, it's powerful, and it's worth fighting for. Here's to the next chapter of your incredible story, and to a love that grows stronger with each passing day."

When the last of the guests departed, Nash and I stood, looking out across the backyard that had hosted the beginning of our forever. The lights strung through the trees still twinkled, but the music had faded, leaving behind a quiet, contented peace.

"Today was beautiful," I murmured, my head resting against Nash's shoulder, his arm around my waist.

"Everything about today was perfect," Nash replied, his voice low, reverberating with emotion. "Mrs. Montgomery," he whispered, a thrill running through me at the sound of my new name on his lips.

I tilted my head up to look at him, a playful smile dancing on my lips. "I could get used to that," I admitted, savoring the sound of my new title, a beautiful symbol of our newly minted union.

Nash's eyes, faintly lit by the few remaining candles, searched mine. "I meant every word, Cassidy. Being here with you, marrying you... it's everything I've ever wanted."

"Me, too," I responded, my heart swelling with an indescribable love for this man who had become my everything. "But tell me, Mr. Montgomery, what are you most looking forward to now that we're officially husband and wife?"

He considered the question, his gaze drifting to the sky above, where the first stars of the evening had begun to emerge. "Everything."

The End

EPILOGUE

Cassidy

Life with Nash had settled into a rhythm of work, music, and the inevitable goodbyes that came with his career. But our love, strengthened by distance and time, only grew deeper. We celebrated our first wedding anniversary with a few stolen days in the heart of Las Vegas. We laughed, we danced, and we reveled in the joy of simply being together, a quick break in the madness of his touring schedule.

Six weeks after our Vegas trip, I noticed subtle changes, hints of something new on the horizon. Excitement and joy bubbled within me as the truth settled in—I was pregnant.

Nash was still on the road, his return weeks away, but I couldn't contain my excitement. Inspired, I turned to music, the language that had always connected us.

The night Nash returned, the mood between us was intense and desperate, heightened by the longing that always accompanied his homecomings. Each glance, every touch, charged with an unspoken desire, as if the time apart had only magnified our need for each other. The air was thick with need, and every moment was a reminder of the passion that always pulsed between us.

But the secret I was hoping to keep for just a little while longer was relentless. It consumed my thoughts, turning every shared moment into a struggle to maintain my composure. My heart raced not just with the thrill of his touch, but with the weight of what I was dying to reveal.

Each second stretched into an eternity, my mind swirling with the anticipation of how he would react. His every whispered word and lingering gaze made it hard to focus on anything else. But it wasn't enough.

Finally, I couldn't hold it in any longer. The excitement was too overwhelming, interrupting the moment we were sharing. "Nash, wait," I blurted out, my voice trembling with nerves and excitement. "I've been working on something." I paused, trying to steady my breathing. "I wanted your professional opinion, especially since it's been a while since I've recorded anything."

He looked at me, amusement and confusion on his face. "Now?" he asked, his eyebrows twitched as a half-smile played on his lips. He was clearly caught off guard by the sudden shift.

"Yes, now," I insisted, righting myself and grabbing his hand, pulling him towards our in-home studio. He followed, still bemused, as I led him down the hall. The excitement inside me was making it hard to not just blurt everything out right then.

Once inside, I sat him down and quickly set up the track I had been working on. As the lullaby played, the words and melody were like a gentle embrace in the quiet room. I watched Nash's face, saw the emotions flicker across his features. His eyes widened, and his breath seemed to catch in his throat. The song ended, a soft echo in the silence that followed.

He turned to me, a mix of awe and pride shining in his eyes. "You did this?" he asked softly, his voice filled with genuine admiration.

"What do you think?" I asked, my voice barely above a whisper, the moment suspended between us. My hands were trembling, a host of emotions coursing through me.

"It's beautiful," he said, his voice thick with emotion. "What inspired you to write a lullaby?"

I saw the moment of realization dawn in his eyes, the understanding of why, of what the song truly meant. I could see his jaw twitching, his eyes filled with a mix of disbelief and happiness as he stared directly into mine.

"Nash," I began, trying to steady my voice, "we're going to be parents."

For a moment, time stood still. Then, as if breaking free from a spell, Nash's face lit up with a joy brighter than I'd ever seen. "We're... we're going to be parents?" he repeated, his voice trembling. He reached out, pulling me into a tight embrace. Tears welled up in his eyes, spilling over as he buried his face in my shoulder.

"My heart won't stop racing!" he chuckled, his voice muffled.

I held him tightly, feeling his body trembling with emotion. Tears of my own streamed down my cheeks as I whispered, "We're going to have a baby."

Resting his forehead on mine, Nash spoke quietly. "Together." His voice was reverent and full of love. "We're going to do this together."

"Always," I replied, my heart swelling with even more love for the man who would soon be the father of our child.

We stood there, wrapped in each other's arms, both of us laughing and crying as the reality of our new future settled over us. Everything was just as it should be, with a beautiful new beginning on the horizon.

Cassidy's Lullaby

Under the moon's gentle glow, in night's soft embrace,
I hum this lullaby, in our quiet space.
A melody for dreams, where love only grows,
A song for you, my child, as peaceful slumber flows.

Sleep my darling and remember this truth
Wherever you are I'll always love you.

In this cradle of stars, where night turns to day,
I promise I'll hold you close, in my arms gently sway.
With every heartbeat grows my love for you,
Dream your dreams so sweet, let your sorrows be few,

Sleep my darling and remember this truth
Through all our days, I'll always love you.

Will you dream of seas, or castles up high,
Of untold adventures, beneath the vast open sky?
Will you dance in the rain, will you chase the sun's light?
Let my love give you wings, and lift your heart in flight.

Sleep my darling and remember this truth
In the seasons of change, I'll always love you.

So rest now, my love, let peace fill your night
Wrapped in my arms, everything is alright.
As you drift into sleep, hold fast to this truth
In every moment, I'll always love you.

ACKNOWLEDGMENTS

I can't do ANY of this apart from the grace of God. Psalm 145:1

Rob, you are my favorite. I love you. Being 'wrapped up in you' is my favorite thing, ever.

Ashley, you made it happen. Thank you.

Stanley 🐻 , the way you tackled this bear-handed is extraordinary.

YOU, the reader, without you my words would never make it beyond the page. Thank you for taking the chance on this book and (hopefully) enjoying Nash and Cassidy's love story.

Independent authors NEED reviews in order for their work to be discovered. If you have the time, please consider leaving your honest review on any platform for others to find.

ABOUT THE AUTHOR

Having always enjoyed books, writing, and daydreaming, Jennifer wanted to know what it would feel like to combine the three and write a book. Once she started writing, everything changed. Within a matter of months, she had multiple projects started and found a love for writing in a way she never knew was possible.

Married to her childhood best friend and the mom of a creative daughter, Jennifer enjoys the quiet life on their farm in Alabama drinking coffee and reading romance novels.

You can connect with Jennifer on Social Media (@jcarrwrites) or her website www.jcarrwrites.com

ALSO BY JENNIFER CARR

Real American Country Series

Fall When You're Ready, Jordan & Rachel (Book 1)

Wrapped Up in You, Nash & Cassidy (Book 2)

No Matter What Series

No Matter What

The Lost and Found

Available on Amazon, Kindle, Kindle Unlimited

Signed copies can be found at jcarrwrites.com